Atlantean Secrets

Volume 1

Sleeper Awaken!

Samuel Sagan

Clairvision™

PO Box 33, Roseville NSW 2069, Australia
www.clairvision.org
info@clairvision.org

By the same author:

* Atlantean Secrets, Volume 2 – Forever Love, White Eagle
* Atlantean Secrets, Volume 3 – The Gods are Wise
* Atlantean Secrets, Volume 4 – The Return of the Flying Dragon
* Bleeding Sun – Discover the Future of Virtual Reality
* Awakening the Third Eye
* Entities, Parasites of the Body of Energy
   (published in the US as Entity Possession)
* Regression, Past Life Therapy for Here and Now Freedom
* Planetary Forces, Alchemy and Healing
* Clairvision Astrology Manual
* Clairvision Knowledge Tracks, correspondence courses in meditation and esoteric knowledge including audio-cassettes, videos, printed material and electronic texts.

Visit the Clairvision Website for book excerpts, free books, Atlantean Secrets music, and a full concordance of the *Atlantean Secrets* saga:

www.clairvision.org

Book cover by Michael Smith

Copyright © 1996, 1999 by Clairvision School Foundation
Published in Sydney, Australia, by Clairvision
PO Box 33, Roseville NSW 2069, Australia
E-mail: info@clairvision.org
Website: www.clairvision.org

Apart from any fair dealing for the purpose of review or research as permitted under the Copyright Act, no part of this book may be reproduced by any process without written permission.

ISBN 0-9586700-7-2

Clairvision is a registered trademark of Clairvision School Ltd.

Atlantean Secrets
The Tetralogy

Volume 1 – Sleeper Awaken!
1 – The Book of the Beginnings
2 – The Book of the Blissful Sleepers
3 – The Book of the Call of Destiny
4 – The Book of the Salmon Robe
5 – The Book of the Mysteries of Eisraim
6 – The Book of the Great Dragon of the Deep
7 – The Book of the Nephilim Spice

Volume 2 – Forever Love, White Eagle
8 – The Book of the White Eagle
9 – The Book of Elyani
10 – The Book of the Naga King
11 – The Book of the Princely Suite

Volume 3 – The Gods are Wise
12 – The Book of the Flying Dragons
13 – The Book of the Encounters with Evil
14 – The Book of the Ascension Ritual
15 – The Book of the World of the Gods

Volume 4 – The Return of the Flying Dragon
16 – The Book of the Nephilim Giants
17 – The Book of Paradoxes in Highness
18 – The Book of Death Terrible
19 – The Book of the Fields of Peace
20 – The Book of the Last Days
21 – The Book of the Valley of the Necromancer
22 – The Book of Virginia and Hiram

ACKNOWLEDGEMENTS

First and foremost to Lord Gana, whose flow of inspiration was the driving force to begin, carry on, and complete this epic novel.

Then to the people who edited, proofed and illustrated *Atlantean Secrets*: Avril Carruthers, Catherine Ross, Debianne Gosper, Eva Pascoe, Gilda Ogawa, Michael Smith, Oonagh Sherrard, Orna Lankry, Philip Joseph, Ros Watson, Rosa Droescher, Ruth Camden, Tobi Langmo and Wilhelmina von Buellen.

Last, but certainly not least, to Gervin extraordinaire, friend and master in Thunder. Without him, none of this would ever have happened. *All glory to the teacher!*

A note on the use of italics

Italics have been used to indicate the following:
1) Quotes from the Law of Melchisedek, for example:

One of the most misunderstood of all verses of the Law was *"One Law, one way. Praise the Lord Melchisedek!"*

2) Discourses of gods, angels, and Flying Dragons:

The White Eagle responded,
"Soul of Highness,
Child of eternity,
Angel of the human hierarchy,
I have waited for you since earlier than time.
And here you come, shining,
Punctual for the cosmic appointment,
Making the Mother of the Light proud of her seed."

3) Discourses engaged in by human beings while raised to the level of consciousness of gods, angels, and Flying Dragons (therefore including communications through the power of the Point). For example,

"Gervin!" I Point-called. *"Please do something! Quick!"*

4) At times, italics have been used to emphasize a particular word in a sentence, for example:

"Gervin," Teyani said, "if it wasn't coming from you, I would *never* believe this story!"

From Volume 3 onwards, however, due to the marked increase in conversations with angels, gods and Flying Dragons (categories 2 and 3), common expression from the Law of Melchisedek have been left unitalicised.

Foreword

The twenty-two books which constitute the four volumes of *Atlantean Secrets* follow a carefully arranged sequence, designed to take you through a succession of spaces of consciousness and realisations. To enjoy the effects woven behind the lines, it is therefore essential to start from the beginning of Volume 1, *Sleeper Awaken!*

At the end of Volume 2, you will find a large map of the temple of Eisraim. For a map of the counties surrounding Eisraim, see p. 4. For a diagrammatic representation of the different worlds where this story will take you, see the cosmological ladder p. 374.

A glossary of the main names and terms used in *Atlantean Secrets* can be found at the end of *Sleeper Awaken!* For a more comprehensive study, see the saga's concordance, *From Eisraim to Philadelphia*, which can be obtained from the Clairvision School's Internet site.

Like Flying Dragons, the *Atlantean Secrets* epic is musical in essence. Characters, gods, angels and worlds each have their themes, and a number of scenes are accompanied by musical scores. This music, which forms an important part of the epic, can be heard in full at the Clairvision site:

www.clairvision.org

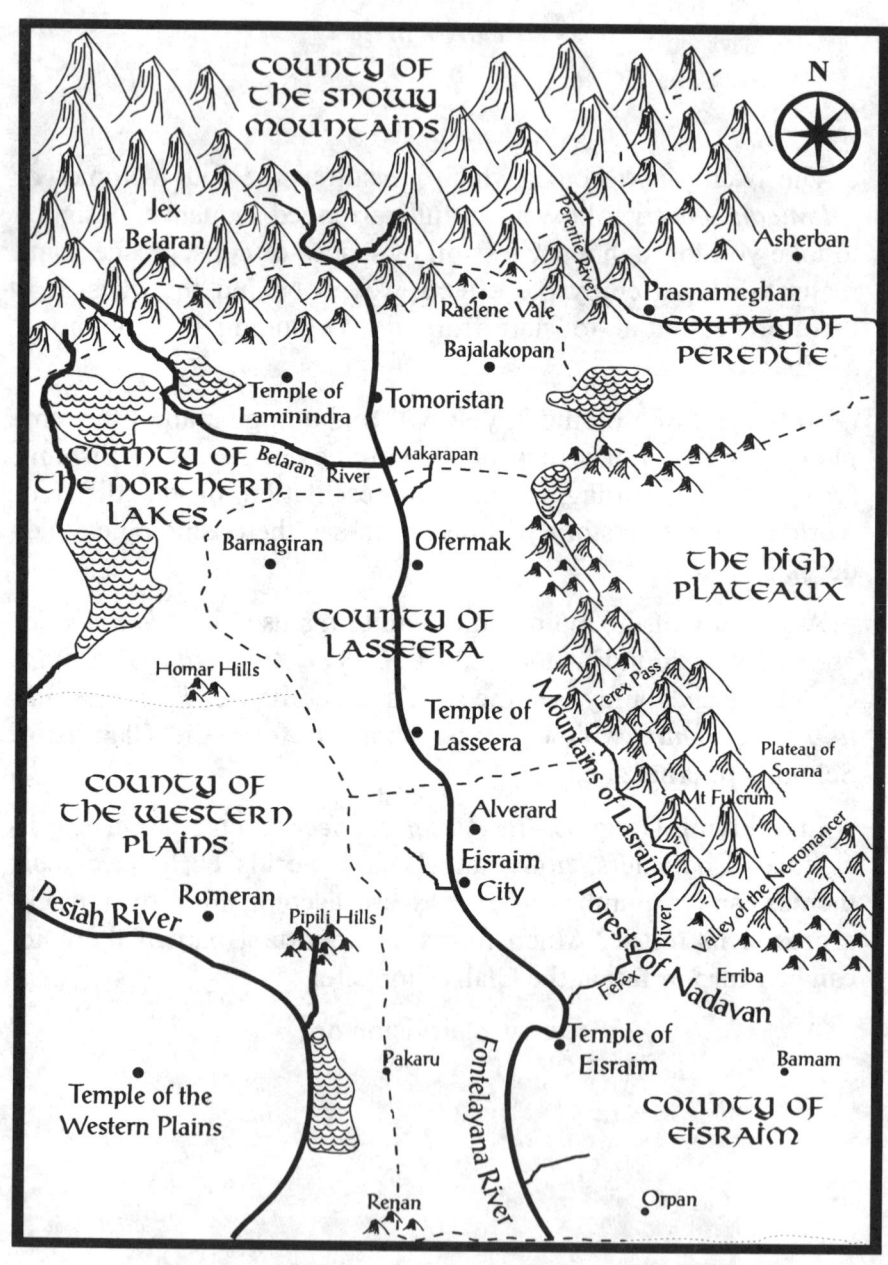

The Counties of the Centre North

Volume 1

Contents

Atlantean Secrets, the Tetralogy	1
A note on the use of italics	2
Foreword	3
Map of Eisraim and the Counties of the Centre North	4
Elyani's courtyard	6
1 – The Book of the Beginnings	7
2 – The Book of the Blissful Sleepers	43
3 – The Book of the Call of Destiny	58
4 – The Book of the Salmon Robe	78
5 – The Book of the Mysteries of Eisraim	96
6 – The Book of the Great Dragon of the Deep	216
7 – The Book of the Nephilim Spice	303
Glossary	366
The Cosmological Ladder	374

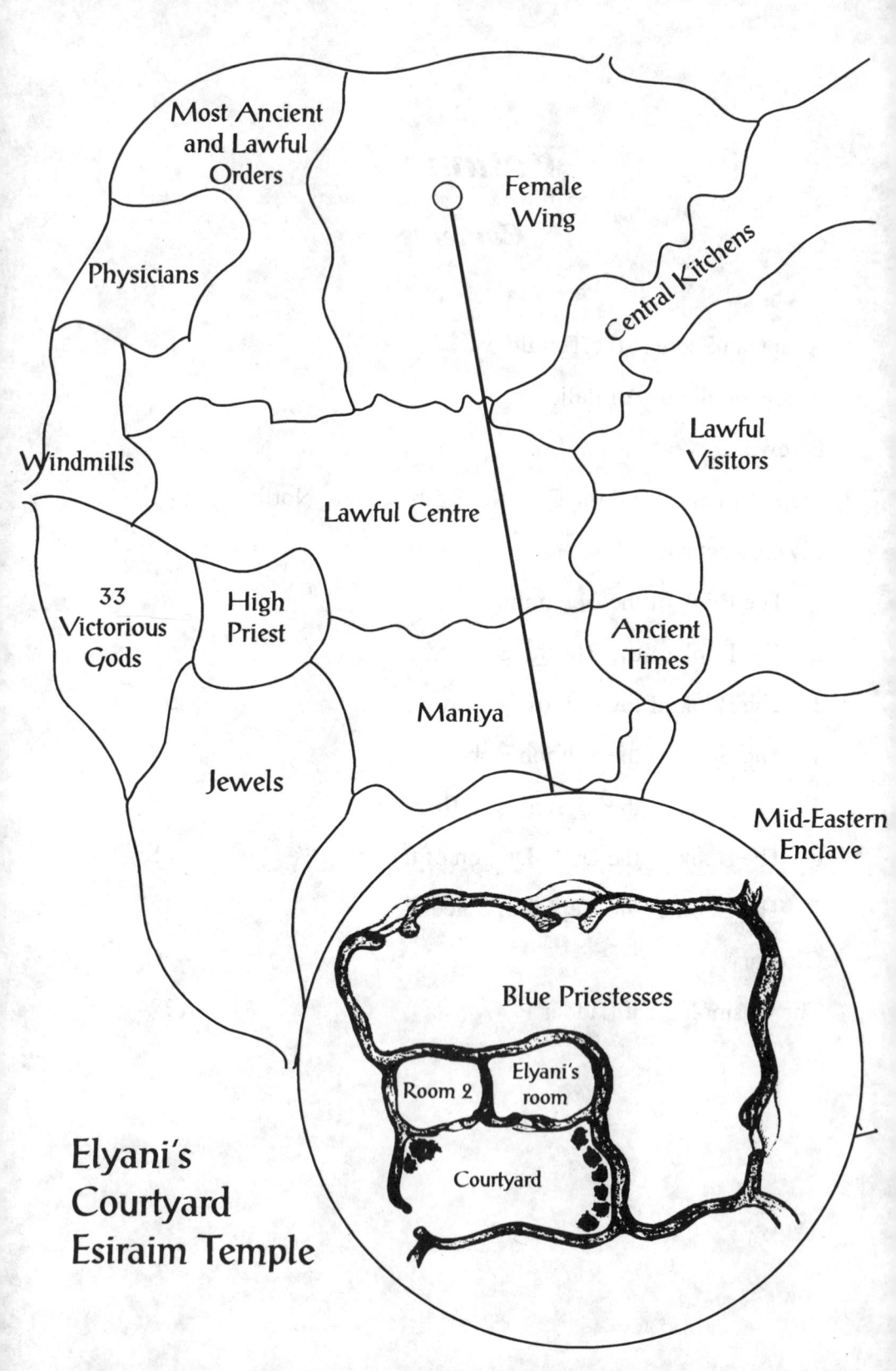

1
The Book of the Beginnings

1.1 The Forever Love Legend

Blue.
Gigantic.
Totally ancient. Totally unknown.
An awesome cloud, coming from remoteness.
Born to travel, it moved fast and with great ease.
It illuminated the spheres with a majestic dark-blue glow as no one had ever seen. Not even the gods. Not even the Nagas who know all the secrets of the Underworlds.

The gods of Amaravati were standing in one long row on the shore of the Molten Sea, watching the cloud drawing near.

Among them, Kartendranath. Fingering his triaxe, the god shivered, "If this thing attacks us, then the Lord Melchisedek have mercy on us!"

The cloud's hugeness was what confounded him. He had seen Flying Dragons before, but never so close. Finding himself face to face with one, he was shocked by the sheer magnitude of the being. And the music...

The music was beyond anything his Point could comprehend.

As the Flying Dragon was approaching, inexplicable harmonies filled the spheres. Music multidimensional. Enigmatic vastness.

The Song of Creation.

Trillions of Voices answering each other's calls.

Aeons of strangeness. Dreaming from before the Cosmic Night. Long, long before the gods were born.

When it reached the edge of the spheres of Melchisedek, the cloud stopped.

The music went on. Unfathomable weirdness made sound.

It reflected in the Molten waters – fire at the bottom of the sea, mirroring the flames of astonishing blueness in the heavens.

No one moved.

Silent, the gods contemplated the festival of light.

The language of the gods has a thousand names for blue. Not one of them fitted the aurora that illuminated their sky.

"It wants something!" Kartendranath intuited. "It is waiting for us to do something." He turned to the god on his left, "Gana?"

Eyes fixed on the horizon, the god of the golden helmet responded, "The Web of Love is what has brought it here. As it wants, so it will receive."

The Web of Love, which shines the Light of the Lord Melchisedek.

All of a sudden, the White Eagle of the gods took its flight. From the edge of the Molten Sea it darted skywards.

There was a pause in the music.

The gods held their breath.

The silence after the sound of the Flying Dragons is packed with mysteries. Endlessly profound like a Cosmic Night.

Shaped as a White beam, the Eagle travelled towards the foreign cloud.

A frail beam of light, compared to the cloud's immensity.

In the silence, infinity was held.

As it reached the blue blaze, the beam faded.

The White Eagle of the gods vanished.

Evaporated into nothingness? Engulfed by the cloud?

It was hard to tell, even for the gods.

Until the music was heard again.

A different music. Extraordinarily melodious. It was still multifarious and untraceable like the Dawn of Creation, but its strangeness had softened. Its mathematical fire was enthused with solar fortitude. It carried the White Eagle's unbounded heartness.

The Flying Dragon had comprehended the secrets of the Web of Love.

A legend was born.

On the shore of the Molten Sea, Lord Gana began to dance.

And for an entire night, the gods celebrated the mysteries of remoteness. Through the eye of the White Eagle, they beheld the cloud's glory. The Flying Dragon had come from beyond the Abyss of the Deep and the Fault of Eternity. It had lived through many a cosmic cycle, travelled through many a thousand spheres from the Blue Lagoon to the Great Ant, and from the bottom of the Fault of Eternity where the Mother of the Light can be seen smiling to the Black Night of Remoteness where all secrets of the creation are concealed. Beyond time, space and infinity, beyond pralayas and cosmic births, there are mysteries that elude the gods themselves.

The White Eagle invited the Flying Dragon to stay.

This was not part of the order of the universe. A traveller through eternity, the Flying Dragon had to resume its course.

At dawn the White Eagle reappeared, emerging from the blue fire in the heavens. The spheres were vibrant with music, the gods intoxicated with elixir of infinity. The blazing cloud started moving – slowly, at first, so the White Eagle could fly in its trail.

1 – The Book of the Beginnings

The Eagle followed it to the edge of the spheres of Melchisedek, where the Web of Love ends and the spheres of remoteness begin. This was where the legendary farewell was exchanged,

"Forever love, Flying Dragon!"

"Forever love, White Eagle of the gods!"

The Flying Dragon disappeared in the immensity of remoteness. Echoes of its music kept resonating through the spheres for a thousand years.

Ever since, whoever cognises the Eagle can contemplate not only its infinite Spirit of Whiteness, but also a tinge of this multidimensional blueness from beyond the Abyss of the Deep and the Fault of Eternity. And whoever crosses the Great Abyss can hear the song of the Flying Dragon –

With all my mind, with all my heart,

I am with you, even when I am far away.

1.2 Seventy-five thousand years later, Atlantis, the temple of Eisraim

When Gervin[1] first came back to his senses, Marka was standing by his side. "*Praise the Great Apollo,* Gervin of Thunder, ambassador of our Lord Melchisedek," she whispered into his ear.

A thunderous presence filled the room. Loud, hissing sounds, like furious snakes, shook the serenity of the night. They shattered the soft cocoon of shimmering starlight which patient Marka had woven around the sleeping body. From far away, a mysterious, foreign voice whispered, "*Space Matrix time reconnection completed.*" It was but an elusive breath, an improbable thread of meaning in a cosmos riddled with nebulous enigmas, but pregnant with ancient forces of incomprehensible magnitude. When she heard it, Marka shivered. And in a nearby chapel, the principal space controller of Eisraim also heard the wondrous murmur. He was amazed, and he knew – led by Space Matrix, Gervin of the Brown Robe had returned from the remote spheres of the Flying Dragons. He was now re-entering his body, which had been hibernating for thirty-two weeks under the expert supervision and tender care of Marka, the young priestess of Malchasek.

Completely disregarding the lawful necessity for slow transitions, cautious reconnections, and gradual reawakenings, Gervin smiled.

Marka was not in the least surprised. She had learnt the art of travelling from Gervin, she knew what the man was capable of. Despite being less than thirty years of age, Gervin, disciple of Orest, had conquered all the powers of the Masters of Thunder. Softly she chanted an ancient ritual lullaby which invoked her angel of Highness, "*O great Malchasek, wings*

---

[1] Pronounced Djervin.

of infinity, silent fullness which moves the world, protect this newborn child."

Using her voice as a thread, Gervin pulled himself back into his body all at once, and opened his eyes.

Marka was a short, dark-haired woman from the counties of the south. She was not beautiful, but what made her special among all the priestesses of Eisraim were her eyes. Looking into Marka's eyes was like catching a glimpse of a primordial glory that had long disappeared from the kingdom – an enchanting, irrational feast of light to celebrate the extravaganza that ran through the world shortly after it had been delivered.

Young Gervin, who wore the long brown gown of the Masters of Thunder, looked into the eyes of the priestess clad in the orange dress of the order of Malchasek. Light met light, and there was fullness.

"Welcome, friend! You are shining with the wonders of remoteness," Marka's smile was glowing. "What extraordinary things you must have seen!"

Gervin kept smiling, silently rediscovering the magic of her eyes after his lengthy odyssey. To him, the journey had lasted not seven months but seven aeons. For in the spheres of remoteness, time can be stretched, curved back, then concentrated all in one point, made to explode in lines that run in every direction and again can be stretched, and curved into an infinity of temporal paradoxes.

Gervin did not use his physical voice. After hibernating for so long, the rule was that no body part be moved for at least three and, preferably, seven days. He spoke to Marka's consciousness through a voice channel of space. "Marka, *wise woman in the Law*, what a joy to see you again!"

"I have waited for this moment with such impatience, *my friend in the Law*!" Marka used her normal voice.

"My body is teeming with wonderful energies. Much clearer than when I left. What a feat you have accomplished, Marka! I have none of the dull inertia that usually afflicts travellers when they re-enter their body. How can I thank you for your tender care?"

"Do not thank me, Gervin, thank Malchasek the great angel. It is his light that I have projected into your body. Tell me, friend, how does it feel to be in a human body after having been spread in the infinity of space for so long?"

"Like being squeezed into a tiny dot. The consciousness of the Flying Dragons is incommensurable, Marka. Far beyond anything the human mind can conceive."

"The visions you sent me were staggering."

"So you received them!" the voyager rejoiced.

"Every day, every night – every hour! The images were so beautiful they often made me cry with joy. I was especially moved by those you sent on your way back."

1 – The Book of the Beginnings

˲ Fault of Eternity?" Gervin asked, wondering how Marka's eyes ⁄hen she cried.

d the Abyss of the Deep, where the Mother of the Light can be seen smiling. This was the most beautiful of all."

"Mm..." Agreeing, Gervin brought the subject around, "Marka, the Flying Dragons made me promise that the first thing I would do upon returning to the kingdom would be to inquire about the order of the White Eagle. Unfortunately I had never heard of this order. Can you tell me anything about it?"

"It's a female order. Extremely ancient."

"Do we have any of them in our temple?"

"I know there used to be a chapel of the White Eagle in the female wing of the temple. But it would have been at least hundreds of lawful years ago. I believe the order of the White Eagle has more or less disappeared from the kingdom."

"Well, Marka, this is going to change. I have engaged the Word of Thunder – I will find the White Eagles and make a nest for them in Eisraim."

"Engaged the Word of Thunder?" Marka laughed with wonder. "But this is extreme, Gervin!"

"The Flying Dragons have declared themselves the allies of the Masters of Thunder."

"You negotiated an alliance between the Brown Robe and the Flying Dragons?" Marka marvelled.

"The Flying Dragons have bestowed a shower of gifts on my order, Marka. They have given us full access to their Universal Knowledge Banks. And they have given the Masters of Thunder permission to use Space Matrix, the phenomenal guidance system which they use when travelling through the spheres. But on one condition: that the Brown Robe will give its total and unconditional support to the White Eagles, and even share with them some of its most precious secrets. Had I not accepted immediately, the Flying Dragons would have thrown me out of their spheres."

Marka was in awe, the glory of ancient worlds ablaze in her eyes, "This is quite a story!"

"Poetry in remoteness. It started aeons ago. And the Flying Dragons believe that one day the children of the White Eagle will fly to their spheres, and that an illumination of Love will follow. They call it the Flight of the Eagles."

"And how are you going to find these White Eagles?"

"The Flying Dragons told me that Barkhan Seer, the mighty Master of Thunder, knows one of the White Eagles and will direct her to me."

"Barkhan Seer! But doesn't the legend say it has been more than six hundred years since he last incarnated in the kingdom?"

"He now lives in Highness, but this is not an obstacle for the Flying Dragons. They have already contacted him and arranged everything."

"Gervin, you know what the wise people of Eisraim say about your teacher Orest? That he is not always easy to follow, but one *never* gets bored in his company. Well, this has become so true of you, my friend. Life with you is always eventful!"

Gervin's eyes flared. Was this the right moment? Crossing the Fault of Eternity on his way back to the spheres of Melchisedek, he had promised himself that the first movement of his physical body would be to take Marka's hand – an Atlantean way of asking her to marry him.

Gervin decided it was too early. He cared about Marka, the delicate soul, and did not want to be abrupt with her in any way, not even with the sweet abruptness of an untimely declaration of his love for her.

"Tell me, Marka, what has been happening in the kingdom since I left?"

"Not only good news, Gervin."

Still smiling, Gervin replied with one of the sayings of Thunder, "Let us start with the worst!"

"Bobros, the giant who lives in the Valley of the Necromancer, has been terrorising the people who live in the forests of Nadavan. And he has destroyed all the crops and the cattle in the north of the county, killing many peasants."

"Bobros, son of Bobros... The Nephilim giant has caused all this havoc?"

"But there is much worse. He has used the magic of the Valley of the Necromancer to manifest ancient dark forces and spread them like a plague in the forests of Nadavan. Thousands of trees have died, Gervin. The elves and the fairies who escaped Bobros' black clouds have all fled from the county. If it continues like this, there will be nothing left of Nadavan. The entire area is becoming a desolate wasteland of dead wood and barren rocky ground. And two months ago, a plague broke out in Eisraim city, killing hundreds of people. It has created panic in all the cities of the neighbouring counties. It strikes people suddenly and causes violent fits of convulsions. And it kills them after a few hours of shivering in terror."

"Has there been any outbreak of this pestilence in our temple?"

"No, not yet. But in the northern part of the county, around Eisraim city, it is spreading very fast."

"What does Orest of the Brown Robe say?"

"Three weeks ago, the prince of Eisraim came to the temple in person for a meeting with Orest. The day after, Orest left for the forest of Nadavan, taking Ran Gereset, Esrevin and Melchard with him."

"This sounds very serious! Have you heard from Orest since then?"

"Five days ago, he sent me a message saying he wanted you to join him as soon as possible. He is waiting for you with Esrevin and Ran Gereset at the ford of Erriba, in the northern part of Nadavan."

"As soon as possible?" Gervin paused.

1 – The Book of the Beginnings

"Within reasonable limits, Gervin!" Marka quickly added. She knew what irresistible fire drove Gervin when it came to serving his master.

Reasonable limits and Thunder had never gone together well.

Gervin now knew for sure this was not the right moment to take Marka's hand. "And what about you, my good Marka?" he inquired. "What has been happening to you in the last months?"

Marka's eyes shone with the inspired Light of her angel. "Gervin, Gervin... something wonderful has happened. I have applied for the high priesthood of my order and received a favourable response from the oracle!"

"Are you going to become a high priestess of Malchasek?" Gervin's eyes opened wider.

"Yes, Gervin!" she answered joyfully. "The first of the three vows has already been spoken."

This meant she would never be married.

Gervin turned his head and bit his lip, thus breaking the promise he had made to himself with the Fault of Eternity as his witness.

Sensing his immense disappointment, Marka exclaimed, "Gervin, but... Do you mean..." In a second she understood. She was shattered.

Marka was a person of great humility. She looked up to Gervin as a shining warrior of the Spirit, destined for the highest functions in Eisraim. Despite his young age, he was already a famous healer, doctor of the Law, and a teacher of several occult arts. Three times, the prince of Eisraim had asked him to become one of his ministers. Each time Gervin had declined, preferring to serve his teacher Orest, the kingdom-famous Grand Master of Thunder whose rare public appearances attracted crowds of pilgrims. Never had Marka suspected that a man like Gervin, Orest's heart disciple and close friend, could have wanted her. He was the most beautiful man she had ever met.

She looked at the fine, curly blond hair that had grown down to his shoulders while he was asleep, the noble beard she had trimmed a few days earlier, the high forehead of a man of the north, and the shining grey-green eyes which she had remembered every day of the last thirty-two weeks. Suddenly, his body was no longer that of a child under her care.

The beautiful light in her eyes dimmed, and she cried.

Devastated, Gervin didn't know what to say. Marka had been his friend and confidant for more than four years. She had not only been a constant support but also a source of inspiration for him, and he had come to admire her so much that he had elected to give up his passion for celibacy, judging that her company would make him a better man. One hundred times in the last year he had nearly taken her hand. But he had wanted to be wise, and avoid rushing like a *young fool in the Law*, and choose the best possible moment. Now that he had lost her, he found it difficult to believe he could have been so stupid.

Marka was shocked by the cruel reality. "Would you have wanted me, Gervin?" she asked in an uncertain voice.

Gervin shrugged his shoulders. Her first vow had been spoken. It could not be withdrawn.

But certain things in life are too important to remain unspoken. Marka needed to hear it from him. "Gervin, please, answer me. Would you have wanted me?"

Drawing from the high fountain of Thunder, Gervin brought down an infinite softness into the room. "Marka, wise woman, let me tell you something that Orest taught me a few years ago, when he announced that he would initiate me as a Master of Thunder. He warned that during the nine months which separated me from the initiation, many alluring offers would be made to me, and a number of circumstances would concur to try and pull me away from my destiny in the Brown Robe. 'Make no mistake,' Orest said, 'these are temptations coming from the Prince of Darkness.' One week later I was approached by a representative of His Supreme Majesty the King of Atlantis, offering me a high office at the royal palace. This was only the beginning. At one stage the Prince of Darkness even sent one of his emissaries, Aphelion, to put a mind-boggling proposition to me," Gervin paused, remembering the dreadful episode that had nearly cost him his life. "Marka, perhaps this is happening to you at the moment. I would hate to be the one sent to you by the Prince of Darkness to take you away from Malchasek."

"Gervin, I promise I will never mention this again if you do not want me to. But, please! I need to hear this from you. Would you..." Marka hesitated.

"Of course I want you. I love you, Marka. I can't imagine a better husband for you than Malchasek. But if it hadn't been him, I would have been proud to take your hand."

1.3 The man who granted a personal favour to Barkhan Seer

"Nadavan, what has happened to you?" Gervin cried.

Erriba, like the rest of the forest, had been ravaged. Gervin could hardly believe his eyes. The friendly woods where he had often come to seek inspiration, to listen to spirits of wise trees and chat with the frivolous pixies, had turned into a landscape of death. Every single stream had dried up. The lakes had vanished, as if sucked from below by some insatiable creature of hell. The leafless trees stood in shock, erect and with all their branches, not having yet realised they were dead. Gnomes, undines, elves, fairies, pixies, spirits of precious herbs, all had taken off, leaving behind them a parched ground devoid of any grasses. New crevasses were

1 – The Book of the Beginnings

appearing by the hour, releasing noxious fumes that smelled like the filth of the Underworld and thickened the mists with dark, ominous hues.

When Gervin arrived at the ford of Erriba, he saw from a distance a silhouette clad in the hooded, dark-brown gown of the Masters of Thunder.

He hurried, wondering which of his companions was waiting for him. But as he came closer, he realised that the man was too tall to be either Ran Gereset or Esrevin, or even Orest.

Gervin was surprised. There were less than ten Masters of Thunder in the entire kingdom, whom he all knew well, and none as tall as this stranger. Yet the man wore the characteristic brown gown, and his energy was sealed with the unmistakable symbols of Thunder. His light was shining bright – a warm aura of pure, liquid gold that contrasted with the black desolation of the forest.

As Gervin approached, the broad-shouldered man pushed his hood back revealing a square face, short black hair and a short curly beard. *"Praise the Great Apollo*, Gervin, Master of Thunder!" his greeting was delivered in a deep, melodious voice.

"Who are you, *man of the Law*?"

"My name is Barkhan Seer, young man. Your master, Orest, sent me to meet you and take you where he is waiting for you in the company of Esrevin, Ran Gereset, and several of our brothers."

"Barkhan Seer!" Gervin laughed with amazement, for his teacher had taught him the superior value of laughing when one is surprised, or happy, or disappointed, or appointed by destiny. "But I thought you lived in the spheres of Highness!"

"I do. But today I reveal myself to you."

Twinging his beard – thank God, Marka hadn't cut it too short! – Gervin took a closer look at the apparition from Highness. Barkhan Seer looked like a man, but his features were incredibly finely wrought, and he shone with a light that felt strangely familiar.

"This light which is with you..." Gervin exclaimed thoughtfully, "it has come to visit me many times before, hasn't it?"

"Many times, yes."

"*All glory to the teacher!*" Gervin joined his hands in front of his heart, remembering in a flash some of the difficult situations when the light had supported him. One of the most spectacular had taken place six years earlier, in the mountains of the county of Perentie, when Gervin had been caught in an avalanche. Barkhan Seer's light had pushed him violently into a small crevasse, saving him from being crushed by a huge boulder that was rolling down the hill. But Barkhan Seer's interventions had not all been so dramatic. In many simple situations of daily life, his beautiful light had inspired Gervin and warmed his Spirit.

"What gives me the immense privilege of your presence today, Master Barkhan Seer?" Gervin asked with sincere reverence.

"I have come to take part in an important ceremony which is to take place in the coming hours. And I need to speak to you, Gervin."

"An important ceremony?" From his knowingness of Thunder, Gervin immediately hated the sound of this announcement. "What ceremony?"

"We are going to put an end to the obscene black magic of Bobros, son of Bobros. Let us go." Barkhan Seer took Gervin's arm, and he started walking on what used to be a lovely path in the wood, now a track of jagged pebbles surrounded by terrorised rocks and skeletons of trees. Gervin walked by his side, remembering the splendour that was Nadavan, and sending loving, pacifying thoughts to the rocks.

"I believe the Flying Dragons have spoken to you about the White Eagle, Gervin."

"I hope I didn't make a blunder by engaging the Word of Thunder and promising to protect this order without knowing a thing about it."

"Not at all!" Barkhan Seer replied with the unique sweetness of those who are mighty among the mighty. "Had you said no, I would have had to materialise myself in the spheres of remoteness instantly and explain to our Flying Dragon friends that their nebulas of supermental light had stupefied your judgement, and that what you meant to say was yes. Plain yes, and yes, thank you."

"So is this what it takes to obtain the privilege of your divine intervention, Barkhan Seer: a cosmic blunder?" Gervin smiled. "No wonder I have felt your presence around me so many times in the past!"

"Not a good direction to pursue!" Barkhan Seer laughed, gently slapping Gervin's shoulder.

"Will you tell me about the White Eagle you will direct to me?" Gervin asked.

"A great saint, she is. And a knower of the powerful magic of the Ancient Days of the Earth. You will learn a lot from her, but first you will have to train her."

"What is her name?"

"Teyani." Barkhan Seer pronounced the name affectionately, and with a touch of deference.

"Lady Teyani of the White Eagle. In which temple does she live?"

"Well, this is part of our problem, son. Little Teyani, who lives far away in the western shores of the kingdom, is only nine years old. She is not yet part of a temple, and she has never heard of the White Eagle – apart from dreams, of course, for the Eagle visits her every night."

"Would you like me to go and find the child, Barkhan Seer? Shall I bring her to Eisraim?"

"No, this is not what the gods have decided. She will have to find the order of the White Eagle first, and join a temple where she will receive her preliminary initiations. This will probably take some years. Then she will have to find you by herself. Of course, I will help her a lawful little bit. But the gods have insisted that she should first undergo certain trials that will

1 – The Book of the Beginnings

fortify her soul and help recover the unique strength of character that was hers in former lives."

"So what am I to do?"

"Let her come to you. As I have said, I will help, as much as the gods permit. Then you must teach her. Give her as much knowledge and power as you possibly can. And let her create a beautiful nest for herself and her Eagles in the temple of Eisraim."

Barkhan Seer stopped walking. Pointing to Gervin's heart with the index finger of his large hand, he plunged his fiery black eyes into him and added, "And more than anything else, Gervin, be her friend!" The tall man paused, then gently hammered, "Her teacher, her father, and her friend! Gervin, I am asking this from you as a personal favour: not just because of the Flying Dragons, but for me, will you please take care of Teyani?"

Surprised by the solemn tone of the request, Gervin closed his eyes for a second. Then his thunderous gaze met Barkhan Seer's, "My Word of Thunder. I will take care of Teyani."

"Thank you, friend," Barkhan Seer answered softly, as if from high in the spheres.

The two men started walking again. For a long time they remained silent, enjoying the deep space of compassion which Barkhan Seer had created by not speaking an order but by humbly requesting a favour, and the friendship that Gervin had started by giving his word with total sincerity.

As they were passing a small pond which the beast of the Underworld had forgotten to suck dry, Barkhan Seer declared in a joyful voice, "By the way, Gervin, I will send you a present with Teyani!"

"A present?" Gervin smiled with curiosity. No doubt a present from Barkhan Seer would be special.

"A little boy."

Gervin frowned, slightly worried at the idea of all these children who were on their way to him.

Reading his thoughts, Barkhan Seer burst out laughing. "And the Flying Dragons will send you another one, but later."

"Another present, or another little boy?" Gervin asked with a touch of concern, as he suddenly saw his family swelling out of all proportion.

"Both!" Barkhan Seer teased him, laughing.

"What a beautiful mother Marka would have been for these children," Gervin thought to himself as they passed the remnants of a huge fig tree. Breaking under their own weight, all the main branches had collapsed, leaving a shaven totem pointing to heaven like a finger in reproach.

Barkhan Seer felt Gervin's grief. "Are you drinking bitter herbs, friend?"

"I guess I am." Gervin did not try to hide the wave of sorrow that was welling in his chest.

"Will you tell me more?"

Gervin shrugged his shoulders. "For years, I have heard Orest repeat this principle of Thunder, 'Truth can't wait!' and I thought I did my best to live up to it. But in one set of circumstances, I forgot to apply the holy principle." He sighed deeply, "And now that I have lost a treasure, I can't blame anyone but myself, can I?"

"There is not much that can be done about this, friend. The past cannot be changed. Better think about building the future."

Gervin thought of asking Barkhan Seer a question, but decided it was futile and kept silent, contemplating the carcass of a deer rotting by the side of the path. Bobros' black art had done so well that no birds of prey were left to clean up the dead meat. Directing his gaze to the other side of the path, Gervin saw more carcasses. One of them still stood on its four legs, so sudden had been the pounding of death. Looking up, Gervin smelled the stench that hung in the mists. As he realised the question would not let go of him, he turned to his friend, "Barkhan Seer, knower of past, present and future events, would you do me a great favour?"

"What?"

"Answer a question for me. Was it bound to be, and planned by the Lords of Destiny, and wanted by the gods, that Marka should become a high priestess of Malchasek rather than Gervin's wife?"

"No, it was not," the omniscient sage replied, matter-of-fact. "Had you asked her in time, Marka would have become your wife."

Gervin pushed his lips forward and nodded. What Barkhan Seer had said, he already knew very well. But for some strange reason he felt better after hearing it. "How could I be such a sleeper?" he blamed himself. But in the desperate dryness of the forest, he found it impossible to cry.

Barkhan Seer's presence of liquid gold came towards him. It did not erase the sorrow, but it added a depth of Spirit to it.

"Will you tell me what bitter herbs are waiting for me at this ceremony you are taking me to?"

"No bitter herbs, Gervin. Only the unavoidable changes that accompany the passing of time."

Barkhan Seer had spoken with so much softness that Gervin immediately guessed. He stopped, closed his eyes and took his head in his hands, "Oh, no! You are not going to tell me that Orest is about to leave his body?"

Barkhan Seer put his hand on Gervin's shoulder, shining the infinite compassion of the Mother of the Light into him. He waited a few seconds and said, "Only a Great Sacrifice will stop the tidal wave of dark forces that Bobros the giant has unleashed from the Valley of the Necromancer. Orest must now give his life, that a massive clearing be performed and the evil magic sent back into the abyss."

In the fields of stars, on his way back from the Flying Dragons, Gervin had sung a hymn to the Great Mother for having given him a teacher like Orest and a friend like Marka. As he sang, the Great Mother had smiled, for she could feel how strong his love for them was.

Having lost one, Gervin was now about to lose the other. For one second, his consciousness was back in the infinity of space, and he looked

1 – The Book of the Beginnings

down to the kingdom, wondering if he wanted to be part of a world where Orest would be no longer, and Marka would be locked in a cell of the tower of Malchasek.

"Gervin," Barkhan Seer called him back, "this is not all. As Orest, Grand Master of Thunder, departs for the Fields of Peace, he must be replaced by a new Thunderbolt Bearer. You are the one, Gervin."

Heard from the fields of stars, where gigantic clouds of light and colourful nebulae drifted mindlessly under the watchful eye of Space Matrix, the news sounded innocuous enough. But when he found himself back in his body and heard it a second time, Gervin was appalled. Until then, he had often thought that the high office of Grand Master of Thunder was wondrous, like a vast sacred crypt with doors open to all the mysteries of the creation. But now he realised the solitude that awaited him in the crypt.

The mists had thickened around the two men. Because of Nature's grief, twilight brought no reddish hues, only darkness.

"Is there no chance I could depart with Master Orest, and follow him into the Fields of Peace?" Gervin asked tentatively.

"We need you here, Gervin. A monumental task awaits you, a work with far-reaching consequences. Dramatic changes are about to take place in the kingdom, so much so that our lineage will have to withdraw into the Fields of Peace. You will be the last of the Thunderbolt Bearers in the kingdom for a long, long time. You are the one we have chosen to secure the transition, and the transfer to the Fields of Peace of an immense archive where the Atlantean lore will be kept."

Gervin nodded, contemplating the still, thickening mists.

1.4 The Great Sacrifice of the Thunderbolt Bearer

Barkhan Seer and Gervin arrived at the plain of Erriba with the first light of dawn. There, an extraordinary vision was waiting for them.

A great fire had been lit. Behind it, Orest was sitting in meditation, his eyes closed, his head covered with the hood of his brown gown. Gervin immediately recognised him by his long, curly, silvery-grey beard and the special light in his aura. Ran Gereset, his son, was meditating on his right, Esrevin and young Melchard, two other brother-disciples of Gervin, were on his left.

Orest, Grand Master of Thunder, had engaged all his power. Chanting ancient hymns of the Law, he had awakened a huge column of light which started in the pyre and ascended high in the sky, where it disappeared into the grey mists. The majestic obelisk of light stood erect like a gigantic lightning rod, ready to convey Orest's offering to the sky of the gods.

Atlantean Secrets

But the most incredible part of the scene was the assembly of one hundred Masters of Thunder who had descended from the spheres to take part in the sacrifice and the installation ceremony of the new Thunderbolt Bearer. Never in the kingdom had Gervin contemplated so much power. Dressed in their long brown robes, they stood still, and silent, forming two rows which delineated a broad alley starting from the pyre. They faced each other. The space between them turned into a corridor of mind-boggling shimmers and fast-moving lights of all colours.

"Oh, my God!" Gervin shed tears of awe.

"These are some of the Thunderbolt Bearers who preceded you, Gervin. Each of them was a Grand Master of Thunder." Barkhan Seer slowly led Gervin to the entrance of the illuminated alley. "They have come to communicate their powers to you."

The plain of Erriba was a large, flat empty space with no trees. Where it had been green and lush, now it was grey and barren. In this unreal landscape rendered even more eerie by the complete silence and the uncertain glimmers of dawn, Gervin found himself at the entrance of a temple of light. At the other end of the alley stood the shining obelisk rooted in the fire, with Orest behind it.

Now that he had taken his position for the ritual, Gervin could no longer see Orest. But Orest enveloped him with his presence and his love, and he spoke to him through the space, "Gervin, my child in Thunder and dear friend, the great day has arrived."

"*All glory to the teacher!*" Gervin gave his thanks as he always did when he met his master. But this time he did not say the words joyfully. Not yet adjusted to the unexpected turn of destiny, his heart was heavy. "I wish I could be stronger, Orest. There is not one thing in the world I could want more than to be capable of conducting this sacrifice instead of you, that my life might be given to negate the magic of Bobros, and your precious life not wasted. This kingdom is going to be so sad and empty without you. And so dull."

"Gervin, shining soul, you could very well have performed this sacrifice instead of me, and reduced Bobros to ashes of oblivion by your own Great Sacrifice. But by leaving my body today, I will take advantage of these unfortunate circumstances to achieve a massive transfer of forces into you. The evil elemental slime that Bobros has spread across our county will be my offering to the sky of the gods, feeding the greatest fire ritual I have ever conducted. Aided by these one hundred Thunderbolt Bearers, I am going to shake the sky of the gods, Gervin. Let me tell you, the gods will remember this! And by tonight, so much power will have been concentrated into your thunderwand that nothing in the kingdom will be able to stand in your way. And you will need this power, Gervin! At the end of the great task which the Masters of Thunder have prepared for you, you will have to perform a ritual of even greater significance and magnitude than this one: the Archive transfer."

1 – The Book of the Beginnings

"Who better than you could perform a ritual as important as this, Orest?"

"Gervin, your time has come. Now it is up to you, Ran Gereset, Esrevin and the others to carry out the task. And that task will be enormous. Preparing the fields for the Archive transfer will take you at least twenty years. I am not leaving you an easy legacy, my friend. But I trust you will succeed. You have what it takes. And from the Fields of Peace, I will be with you all the way through. Besides this, you will be the most invested Thunderbolt Bearer ever.

Look in front of you, Gervin! At sunset, when you walk the corridor of light, all these great sages will ignite your thunderwand with their powers, and by the time you reach the pyre, I will be lucky if there is still one thing I can give you that you will not have already received."

The light in the corridor had become brighter. Against a background of moonlight-silver, pink-quartz and dark-sapphire hues, white-blue lightning-like shafts zapped wildly from one Master of Thunder to the other. The glow seemed so solid, and the shimmering waves so tempestuous that Gervin wondered if he would have to fight his way through the light.

"Gervin, there are many things I would have liked to tell you, but the time is coming. After the ritual, Barkhan Seer will give you all the instructions you need. *Farewell, my friend in the Law*, and thank you for being who you are. You have given me great joy."

"*All glory to the teacher!*"

"*Glory to the God who was in the beginning, who is, and who shall be!* We shall meet again in the Fields of Peace."

"You stay still and do nothing," Barkhan Seer whispered into Gervin's ear. "Your role begins at sunset."

Orest was the first one to chant. He intoned a slow, low-pitched recitation of one of the most ancient hymns of the Law, which praised the Mother of the Light for having initiated the creation. Concurrently, he threw ashes into the fire, and drew with his consciousness a whisk of the dark energies that Bobros had spread through Nadavan and beyond. The little black cloud moved up into the obelisk of light and vanished.

One of the greatest clearing rituals of all times had begun.

Two days' walk from there, in the gloomy heart of the Valley of the Necromancer, Bobros the giant, whose vision was great, sensed that a fire ritual was under way. He shrugged one huge shoulder in contempt. Considering the tidal wave of black sludge that he had made the valley vomit onto the county, this clearing was no great threat to his evil plans. At their present pace, the brown piglets – as he called the Masters of Thunder whose gathering he was observing in his third eye – would need more than a year to clear just the plain of Erriba.

At the second hymn, Ran Gereset, Esrevin and Melchard joined voices with Orest. The four men pulled small clouds of Bobros' dark influence into the column of light.

Atlantean Secrets

But at the third hymn, everything changed. Following Barkhan Seer, the one hundred Thunderbolt Bearers started projecting the Voice. An awesome sound was released as expansive waves of incandescent energies poured from their mouths.

The glow in the corridor went from bright to blinding. The obelisk of light tripled in width, and ugly clouds of black smoke were drawn into it by the power of the hymns.

Down in the Valley of the Necromancer, Bobros frowned. He dropped the piece of raw meat he was eating for breakfast and watched with curiosity to see what would happen to the strange column of light, once attacked by his black smoke. To Bobros' dismay, it soon appeared that instead of being dimmed, the obelisk was becoming brighter by the minute.

On the plain of Erriba, the deluge of Voice resounded unabated. The chanted hymns, rendered alive by the power of the Voice, seemed insatiable. They swallowed larger and larger clouds of black energy and consumed them in the fire of the obelisk, sending them up as an offering to the sky of the gods. Soon the column of light became so wide that Orest and his disciples were engulfed by it, and it kept growing until it encompassed the entire alley and the one hundred Thunderbolt Bearers, Barkhan Seer and Gervin with them.

United in the light, they projected the Voice relentlessly.

It was not yet eight in the morning.

Bobros, worried, withdrew into his cave and started preparing his defence.

In the temple of Eisraim, Marka had been the first to sense the seismic waves of light coming from the clearing in Erriba. In her small cell in the tower of Malchasek, the air was thick with sorrow, for she had been crying all night, and the day before, and the night before that. But as soon as the Thunderbolt Bearers started projecting the Voice, the room shone with white light, and she felt Gervin's presence with her. Through the space, she tried to call him. In response, the light became brighter, and Gervin's presence became stronger. No words were exchanged. But the force was so intense, and the imprint in the space so clear, that not once in the coming thirty-four years that Marka spent meditating and praying in that room, did Gervin's presence disappear. It remained with her and constantly supported her, not just in the first years, when she fought against herself not to run away and throw herself in the arms of the man she could not forget, but also in the last years, when the deterioration of the energy fields in Atlantis became such that Malchasek's light could hardly be felt any longer, and his high priestesses started dying one after the other from despair and from boredom.

That morning, a few chapels away from the tower of Malchasek, Mouridji the prophetess caught the vision of the obelisk of light, and she heard the Voice of the Thunderbolt Bearers. *"Oh my Lord Melchisedek! Luciana!"* she called her young friend, "Luciana! Go and tell them, quick!"

1 – The Book of the Beginnings

"Hey?" Luciana of the Green Robe had fallen asleep in her meditation. She rubbed her eyes. "Tell who, Mouridji?"

"Everyone, Luciana, tell everyone! And tell them to send a message to the temple of Lasseera immediately. But tell them to keep it very quiet. It's probably a secret ceremony."

"But tell them what?"

"Orest of the Brown Robe is transmitting his power to Gervin! All his power! Everything! It might even end up in a Great Sacrifice." And from her prophetic vision the little priestess added, "And then Gervin will have to go and challenge Bobros the giant, and one of them will die!"

Mouridji of the Purple Robe, whose gossip was a central part of the communication system in Eisraim, sent messages through the space to all her friends, who in turn warned their friends, and in a matter of minutes all the priests and priestesses of Eisraim knew. The cooks dropped their saucepans, the gardeners their bags of seeds, and the masons left their construction sites. All converged to the chapels and sat still and silent. And those priests whose normal function was to sit still in their chapel sat stiller and more silently. The cows, who were always extremely sensitive to the spiritual vibrations of the temple, refrained from mooing. In the small lake outside the first hall of Melchisedek, the swans became still too, and the fishes swam cautiously. In this cosmic hush they all tuned into the gigantic clearing from a distance, and they received the light.

By the end of the morning, so much of Bobros' evil slime had been offered to the sky of the gods that in Eisraim city, the heavy atmosphere of fear and despair which the pestilence had created began to clear. Some of those who had fallen ill the night before stopped convulsing and they woke up, stunned at still being alive. Many of them even wondered if perhaps they were dead, after all, and when they returned to their normal activities they looked at each other suspiciously, unsure whether they were surrounded by ghosts, but not daring to ask, in case they themselves were the ghosts among the living.

When noon came, the forests of Nadavan had been entirely cleared. The first birds had returned. In some areas it had even started to rain again.

Bobros, furious to see the clearing ritual so successful, launched a massive counteroffensive. He did not waste any time with lower forms of magic. He went straight to the Abysmal Crevasse, which lay close to the marshes outside his cave. There, long ago, when the kingdom was still young, Harmag the Necromancer, a son of Azazel the Watcher, had called on the ominous powers which had made the valley turn dark, and the nature spirits evil, and the mists thick and menacing, and the landscape atrociously gloomy and full of shadows and visions of hell – after which the valley had been known as the Valley of the Necromancer.

Bobros, who believed he was the descendant of Harmag the Necromancer through a long line of Nephilim giants, raised defiant hands towards heaven and turned his head down to the abyss. Using the Voice, he mumbled a mysterious invocation which he had not learnt from Bobros his father but from Bobros his great-grandfather, and which former giants of the Bobros lineage had passed on from generation to generation, perhaps ever since the time of Harmag himself. The dark vibrations of death began pouring out of his mouth, evoking an instant response. The crevasse vomited a flood of slime, and the valley instantly turned darker. Furious winds swept the marshes, to the jubilant delight of the evil nature spirits who, ever since the time of Harmag, had been completely out of their minds and rejoiced only when they smelled a disaster on its way. Soon an ominous umbra overtook the entire area of Nadavan, frightening away the birds that had ventured back, and drying out the first rains.

High above, the denizens of the worlds of the gods looked down to the kingdom and watched with interest, but also with some degree of alarm. The forces that Bobros the giant was releasing were so powerful that they could easily get out of control, flooding the entire kingdom with pitch-black sludge and upsetting the balance of the spheres.

Down in the kingdom, in the citadel which the Nephilim giants had built for themselves on top of steep cliffs at the extreme end of the Eastern Peninsula, so as to proudly receive the first sunrays that swept the kingdom every day, the word soon spread that Bobros the Necromancer was enraged, and about to engage in a duel of magic. The giants, tuning into the powerful fields of energy which allowed them to spy on just about anything in the kingdom, held their breath and watched, wondering who would emerge victorious out of this titanic confrontation.

Neither above nor below, but from the nowhereness where he forever dwells, Ahriman, the Prince of Darkness, also watched with interest, ready to strike like a beast of prey hidden in the night. Like the gods, he knew well that Bobros could lose control over the forces he had unleashed. Were this to happen, he would be washed away, and the aphotic tidal-wave of black slime would present a perfect opportunity for Ahriman to launch a devastating attack on the kingdom, spreading plagues, wars and chaos.

In the plain of Erriba, the column of light had become so wide that it not only comprehended the alley and the one hundred Masters of Thunder, but the entire plain itself, and some of the surrounding forests. When they heard the abyss resounding with the evil clamour and when they saw the horrendous filth erupting out of the depths, the Thunderbolt Bearers raised their Voices. Together, they projected the Word of Thunder, which is the Voice of the Earth and the highest power of the sky of the gods.

It was awesome, unthinkable. Trembling from her own Will, the Earth shook, again and again. And from higher up than the gods, lightning struck the obelisk which by now had become a gigantic flame of light, visible from all the spheres. And the hymns of the Law, rendered ever more hungry by so much fire, started swallowing the darkness that was covering Nadavan.

1 – The Book of the Beginnings

Bobros too raised his Voice, and from the abyss he called on the dregs at the end of time, and on the endless darkness that is to engulf all things at the end, when everything is accomplished, or much earlier, if the dark side can win.

Above the clouds, the gods frowned, wondering if they had been careless in letting things go so far.

Far in the east of the kingdom, the Nephilim giants shouted cheers of encouragement which Bobros never heard, so loud was his own shouting while he drew sludge from the abyss.

Ahriman, cold, impassive, precise, kept observing.

The Abysmal Crevasse which Bobros had invoked was turning into a volcano of doom, spilling darkness instead of lava. Proud of his works, Bobros laughed, convinced not one power in the creation could resist him.

But the insatiable hymns of the Law swallowed the darkness as soon as it came out of the volcano, converting it into an offering of light which ascended through the obelisk.

Bobros, pulling with all the strength of his kidney and calling on all the necromancers of his lineage for help, drew yet more darkness from the abyss. But the more soot he manifested, the hungrier the hymns of the Thunderbolt Bearers became, and the more darkness was converted into light.

Bobros saw that the light was gaining the edge, slowly but surely, and in terror he realised that Orest's clearing could result not only in stopping the plague he had caused, but also in cleaning up the entire Valley of the Necromancer. In a glimpse, he saw himself becoming the shame of his lineage, the destroyer of the beauty of black arts that Harmag had created, and which had lasted ever since then.

Seeing that time was working against him, and knowing from his prophetic sight that Orest had vowed to leave his body at sunset, Bobros sought recourse to an ancient device of magic. It was a trick that his ancestors had used in the distant past, when many more things used to be possible on Earth, and time was nowhere near as rigid as it had become with time. Bobros, son of Bobros, tried to speed up the course of the Sun, to make twilight arrive early.

This was his fatal mistake.

The magic charms which, long ago, could control time, had long ceased to have the predictable effects they had had in the time of Harmag. The truth was, time, the destroyer of all things, had long since destroyed its own magic. Bobros had hardly spoken his dangerous formula when a tremulousness of all things made itself felt in the Valley of the Necromancer.

The gods held their breath.

The Nephilim giants of the Eastern Peninsula became pale.

Ahriman smiled.

The Abysmal Crevasse became hesitant, as if taken by self-doubts. The soot it vomited not only dropped in volume, but it too seemed to be unsure as to whether it really existed. The evil enthusiasm of the valley and the orgasmic frenzy that animated the perverted nature spirits looked at each other in disbelief. The ghastly winds wavered, uncertain in which direction to blow. Bobros, rendered incredulous by his own spell, wondered whether all this was really happening.

But in a flash he realised that a complete disaster was imminent. He caught sight of a wave of destruction that respected nothing, not even itself, and therefore threatened everything with extinction, including himself.

Drawing on all his power and might, he howled with the Voice to seal the crevasse and to stop everything before the unstoppable was unleashed.

For a minute or two, the entire Valley of the Necromancer wobbled, while groaning bubbles plopped from the marshes.

Then the spell vanished, and an uncannily peaceful silence followed. For one second the valley recovered its former self, when it was lush and joyful, and when happy cattle used to graze on its rolling slopes.

"Oh, shit!" Bobros exclaimed.

In a desperate attempt to restore darkness, he turned towards the Abysmal Crevasse, "Harmag! Harmag! I call onto your venom!" and he held the spirits of his valley, repelling the light with every fibre of his being.

"Harmag! Harmag!"

He plunged his consciousness into the chasm, resolute to reach the bottom of the pit – that mysterious domain where darkness and light are one, all powers are comprehended, and all things are possible.

Tightening every muscle of his huge body and squeezing his kidneys for strength, he furiously invoked, "Harmag! Harmag!"

From the depths of the abyss, a hungry hissing breath of infinite darkness responded, enveloping him, inviting him into the pit.

So great was the pull, so irresistible the charm, that Bobros threw himself into the arms of his beloved evil night.

He jumped into the Abysmal Crevasse.

He sacrificed himself, releasing into the valley the fruits of his life-long necromantic passion for the dark side. The mists were thickened with his venom, the spirits of nature were fed with his wrath.

The furtive glimpse of light vanished. Doom and gloom were back.

The Valley of the Necromancer lived.

Meanwhile, the formidable power of the Thunderbolt Bearers went on consuming the evil sludge, the tension rising so high that in less than three minutes, all the darkness that Bobros had spread was neutralised. Nadavan was completely cleared, the plague of Eisraim destroyed, and all traces of Bobros' evil influence had disappeared from the county.

When Orest saw that the power of the hymns was about to attack the darkness of the Valley of the Necromancer, he raised his hand and stopped

1 – The Book of the Beginnings

the ritual, for he was wise and knew that all things have their place in the world. The valley was the keeper of ancient forces, and deserved respect for the uniqueness of its energy. Victory was total, in any case. There was nothing left of the foul vibrations with which Bobros had thought he could poison Eisraim and its neighbouring counties.

The Thunderbolt Bearers became silent.

In the heavens the celestial beings applauded and sung astonishing hymns, ready to receive Orest like a hero among gods and men.

In the Eastern Peninsula, the giants, enraged at seeing one of their champions defeated, roared their fury and swore revenge.

Nowhere, Ahriman shrugged his shoulders, unconcerned, and resumed his tasks of endless darkness.

"We won, Luciana! A triumph!" Mouridji the prophetess hurrahed.

Luciana, unsure of what exactly had been won, but taken by an irresistible feeling of victory, stood up and clapped her hands, and all the priestesses in the chapel followed her. They laughed loudly, and congratulated each other.

Thanks to Mouridji, the word soon reached all the other chapels of the temple of Eisraim, and everyone acclaimed Orest of the Brown Robe for what was to be remembered as 'the Clearing of Erriba'.

1.5 The creation myth of the Thunderbolt Bearers

Sunset had finally arrived.

The incandescent obelisk had regained its original size, but the entire plain of Erriba was still inundated with white light.

The one hundred Thunderbolt Bearers stood silent and motionless like pillars of light, their auras ablaze with the unfathomable energy unleashed by the Word of Thunder.

Gervin, Barkhan Seer by his side, stood at the entrance of the corridor of light, with the fire and the obelisk at the other end, and Orest meditating behind the fire.

"Now!" Barkhan Seer gave the signal, touching Gervin's shoulder.

Gervin turned his head towards him briefly, saying farewell with his eyes. Truly, he was bidding farewell to himself. He knew that as soon as he entered the corridor, he would never be the same again.

Three steps separated Gervin from the corridor of light and the mysteries of the Thunderbolt Bearers.

He took the first step, whispering the verse of the Law, *"One Law, one way! He who never sleeps, never dies!"*

Then the second step.

Atlantean Secrets

From the tower of Malchasek, Marka heard the farewell. She surrendered to the High Light of her angel and whispered back, "Farewell, beautiful man!"

Far away in the north, close to the great lake of the county of Perentie, an old, wrinkled woman remembered the son who had left her long ago, and she cried. She called her husband, "Arvin of the Law! Gervin is dying! Our son is dying, we'll never see him again." Old Arvin bit his lip – a habit he had caught from his father and cultivated through a long life of disappointments – and he prayed the good Lord Melchisedek had mercy on his son. He had been such a good boy, and smart, when he was little. "Why the Underworld did he want to travel and follow that damn brown monk?" Arvin puzzled once more. "Such a waste! He could have been so happy as a ferryman, with me and his uncle." And he sighed, his eyes fixed on the smoky fire at the centre of the one-room shack of mud bricks, pondering on the wonderful opportunities missed, and the good life Gervin could have had if only he had listened to the wisdom of his father.

In a chapel of the female wing of the temple of Eisraim, Mouridji of the Purple Robe was shocked out of her meditation by one of the brightest visions she had ever received. "Luciana!" she whispered in her prophetic voice, her eyes half closed, astonished by what she was seeing. "Go and tell them!"

"What, Mouridji?"

"They're going to throw Gervin into the fire!"

"Who?" Luciana froze in terror. "The Nephilim giants?"

"No, Orest and his friends. Oh, my God! If Gervin survives that, then... then... Oh, my God!" Mouridji was interrupted by another vision, coming from the world of the gods. "And tell them that the gods..." she started saying, but a celestial providence shut her up.

Far above, in the sky of the gods, the Sons of Apollo stopped their flight and directed their blazing gaze to the plain of Erriba.

Much, much further away, beyond the fields of stars and the mysterious Fault of Eternity, spread in an infinity of superimposed spaces and lateral realities, a Flying Dragon heard Gervin's farewell. *"Welcome to eternity, friend of the human hierarchy,"* went the whisper.

And the Mother of the Light smiled.

Gervin took the third step.

As he entered the corridor, all light disappeared, and the obelisk of fire, and the one hundred Thunderbolt Bearers.

He saw but darkness, surrounded by darkness,
As it was before the beginning,
When the creation had not yet begun,
And time had not yet started its course.
There was neither left nor right, neither top nor bottom,
Neither death nor immortality.

1 – The Book of the Beginnings

In an uncontained voidness,
A fluid breath of nothingness swept a naught-dimensional space,
A womb-ness of times to come,
Where all possible futures were contained as seeds.
In this Noble Chaos, which was both nowhere and everywhere,
A symphony of Voices rose,
Which revealed Life out of darkness,
And prepared for the birth of the light.
The Voices were chanting the Dawn of Creation.
It was the first breath, the first wind.
And there was a centre, and a periphery,
And limits were born, so that infinity could breathe.
And Up looked down, and Down smiled back.
The One had become two,
Ready to desire each other,
But not yet fully aware of how far they would have to go,
And how long it would take
Before they could become One again.
By then, time was already born.
A cosmos of immense complexity had begun:
Myriads of expanding spaces,
Worlds running in all directions,
Spheres revolving around spheres,
And creatures born in all the worlds.

The asuras came first, and they were formidable.
Standing on top of the creation, their primordial powers unchallenged,
They shouted loud, amazed at their own glory,
Intoxicated with their own might.
And they became proud and arrogant.
They proclaimed themselves the One God,
Forgetting that their shining lights were but reflections
Of the One Glorious Source to whom they owed their birth.
Thus the asura of life became the asura of death,
The asura of might became the lord of war.
Great angelic lighthouses turned into principles of darkness,
And after them, the blazing light-bearer fell into Lucifer.
And the Ancient of Ancients cursed them,
And shattered their worlds,
And caused a second creation of gods.
Born from the Mother of the Light, the gods woke up in the Molten Sea,
And they sacrificed to the One God,
And the strength of the One God was their strength.
And there were wars in the heavens,
Awesome clashes in which the spheres were set ablaze,

Atlantean Secrets

And entire planets shattered into asteroidic pebbles.
Light fought against darkness, gods against asuras,
Angels against titans, Spirits of Truth against fallen angels.
The gods triumphed at the summit of the spheres.
They conquered the nectar of immortality, and its archetypal powers,
Mastered the mathematical magic of the uppermost sky,
And with genius and boldness, repelled their enemies into lower regions.
A safe heaven they made for themselves,
A glorious world of light and fire, the top of a high pyramid of worlds,
Towering upon innumerable other spheres of lesser fire, lesser clarity,
Lesser joy, lesser fun, and marred with mirages, illusion, boredom.
Such was the victory of the gods and it was great and absolute,
But only at the top of the pyramid of the worlds.
Elsewhere, an uncertain and precarious balance remained,
A cosmos of compromise and half-truths which were but flagrant lies,
And where light and darkness kept fighting wars,
But only by proxy, and often in disguise,
And none ever gaining the decisive edge,
Dilly-dallying seemingly endlessly, delaying
The deadly apocalyptic toll of a final, total confrontation.

In this established order of clear blurriness,
Human beings were still fast asleep,
Having not yet noticed the cosmic night had ended.
They lay blissfully in the bosom of the gods
And basked in the gods' glorious light,
Which they could not distinguish from the Primordial Darkness.
Spread in a bottomless chasm of forever One-ness, they slept.
They slept a dreamless sleep, a beatific embrace with God,
A soporized ecstasy of transcendental magnitude.
To help them awaken, the gods fashioned a world for them.
A young, fresh, juicy maiden Earth,
An all-fluid virgin, teeming with unbridled life force,
And youthful folly, and strange gigantic beasts, and volcanic wonders.
These were the Ancient Days of the Earth, the early land of Mu,
When every atom was vibrant with magic,
And the breath of the One God breathed through every wind,
And the wet air's warmth was enthused with Cosmic Fire,
And the pregnant ocean remembered the secrets of the Primordial Night.
Few, very few, were those who awoke in the first hour.
They became the great magicians of the Ancient Days,
They commanded over the awesome forces of the young world.
Nature was their enslaved lover, never refusing them a thing,
And they penetrated all her mysteries,
And they stamped her bosom with their spells.

1 – The Book of the Beginnings

But these magician-conquerors of Nature were but scarce exceptions
In a world where all other human beings were still fast asleep,
Drifting blobs, monotonously fulfilled and hopelessly peaceful,
With no desires, and good food in plenty,
Their needs satisfied before they could even feel them,
Painlessly they dropped blobettes behind them to populate the new world.
And it lasted a long, long time, but they did not wake up.
When the gods sent the call and resounded the trumpets of destiny,
The magician-conquerors heard, and they understood,
And guided by the gods, they left.
But the blobs heard nothing, for they were fast asleep.
And the Earth was shaken, continents rose and others disappeared.
The stupefied Adam-Eve blob became Adam and Eve, naked,
Already desiring each other, but why did it have to hurt so much?
And how far would they have to go, and how long would it take
Before they could find each other again?
The Moon, which by then had just arrived, completely unnoticed,
Knew the secret, and kept it for a distant future.

Seeing this rapidly deteriorating world,
In which the winds of God would soon run out of breath,
And sleep had become the antidote to the agonising pain
Of being separated from him, from her, from the Light and from God,
The Lord Melchisedek had mercy.
With his great angels, he manifested a Law,
And the Law was revealed to Manu, and Manu revealed it to men.
The kingdom of Atlantis was born, safely enclosed in womb-like mists.
Set into motion by the Law, the blobs became cobblers, builders,
Fishermen, fathers and mothers, priests and priestesses.
Everyone had a place, a name, a caste, a role, and a destiny.
A language, alive with many powers of the gods, was given to them,
For them to chant the magic hymns of the Law and sacrifice to the gods,
And thus bring kind weather onto themselves, and rains in plenty,
Gorgeous orchards, abundant crops, and healthy offspring.
Through the power of the hymns, the gods were with them,
And the Spirit of the One God breathed in their blood,
That they might slowly awaken, and stop being sleepers.
Tens of thousands of years passed. A glorious civilisation grew,
A large, majestic tree, rooted in the revelation of the Law –
Arts, and lores, and a masterful know-how of all things of Nature,
Phenomenal mastery of etheric forces and plants' growth,
And fields of energy which accomplished all manner of miraculous feats,
And oracles and temples in plenty to celebrate the mysteries.
And tens of thousands of years passed.
But when the Lord Melchisedek looked down to the kingdom,

Atlantean Secrets

He saw that the children of His Law had not yet awakened.
Now they were sleeping with their eyes open,
Having turned His wonderful revelation into lengthy codes of rules
Which they repeated like parrots,
While fixed in habits and customs they comfortably slumbered,
A perfection rendered smothering and sterile by so much zeal and faith.
The bold knowledge which He had given them to break new ground,
To step out of the blob stage, and to awaken to the infinity of creation,
They had made a prison, with His high priests the jailers.
The Lord Melchisedek saw the cosmic tragedy and judged
That the time was coming. The prison would have to be shattered,
So a new kingdom could be born.
And moved by compassion for the children of His Law,
He prepared the chaos, and the plagues,
And the deluge that was to destroy the kingdom of Atlantis.

Gervin had arrived in front of the fire and the obelisk of light. In one glimpse he realised the unavoidable fate which awaited the kingdom. He saw cities in flames, ransacked temples, large-scale pillage, famines, and epidemics. More frightening even was the collective insanity which accompanied this tragedy, and which only the final flood would wash away from the surface of the Earth. There followed barbaric times – a world of darkness and desolation, emptied of the presence of the gods, and in which the Law and all the knowledge of the temples were lost.

On the other side of the fire, Orest now stood up, and raised his arms.

Responding to his signal, Barkhan Seer and the one hundred Thunderbolt Bearers once more projected the Word of Thunder.

The obelisk of light exploded, and the plain of Erriba was flooded with white light.

Through the fire, Gervin saw the eyes of Orest.

From the uppermost reaches of the sky of the gods, a shaft of lightning struck.

The flash brought a revelation to Gervin's consciousness: the master plan of the Brown Robe. In the Fields of Peace, the temple of light stood ready to receive the entire knowledge of Eisraim and Lasseera in the form of a phenomenal Archive.

"*All glory to the teacher!*" he projected with the Word of Thunder, and walked into the fire.

Orest, looking straight into his eyes, joined him in the fire, and a massive transfer of forces was sparked.

Gervin screamed.

And from the uppermost sky, the ultimate summit of the worlds of the gods, he saw the Primordial Night, and the chant of the Dawn of Creation, the superb asuras, the birth of the gods, the wars in heaven, the magicians of the Ancient Days, the Moon leaving the Earth and the blobettes torn

1 – The Book of the Beginnings

asunder, and the Lord Melchisedek, and his Law, and the deluge at the end of the kingdom, and the kingdom of the rainbows after it, and the kingdoms which followed, the true and the false messiahs, the War of All against All, the Knights of the Apocalypse fighting in space, the triumph of the Light, and those left behind, and the maturity of the human hierarchy, when Eve finally found Adam (the Moon had known all along), the spreading in multi-dimensional enlightenment, and the end of time, and the Cosmic Night – all in one second, all in one point.

And he saw the Web of Love which the Lord Melchisedek had woven in His spheres, and it shone far in remoteness.

From beyond the Abyss of the Deep, the Flying Dragon smiled at Gervin and repeated his welcome message, using universal language, "1472839234713408972415734634068734596024356284584158394953022092043583243564957085639572649670189174769403858709..."

Mouridji saw, and she remained silent.

1.6 The Archive and the temple in the Fields of Peace

It was late at night. Melchard – Melchard the pure, as Orest used to call him – was sitting on a log at the edge of the plain of Erriba, wondering what would happen to him now that his master had left the kingdom. At the age of nineteen, he was the youngest of the Brown Robe, having been initiated by Orest only nine months earlier. At the time he had thought the initiation ceremony the most incredible of all the rituals performed in the kingdom. Now, he looked back and smiled.

Ran Gereset, his elder by fifteen years, came to sit by his side. He put his hand on his shoulder, "Feeling a bit low?"

"Perhaps."

"After such a high, it's more than normal. Did Barkhan Seer speak to you?" Ran Gereset asked.

Melchard shook his head.

Esrevin was walking towards them, carrying a bundle of dry branches. "Barkhan Seer is coming," he announced. "Let's light a fire. Now the Thunderbolt Bearers have left, it feels much colder down here."

Melchard and Ran Gereset gathered a few more branches, and the fire was soon lit.

"Praise the Great Apollo, Master Barkhan Seer!" Melchard exclaimed with a touch of wonder when he saw the great sage approaching. Barkhan Seer's legend made even the most accomplished of the Masters of Thunder raise their eyebrows in amazement. As foretold in many prophesies, each time he appeared to the kingdom he deeply influenced the fate of the Brown Robe.

"Here are the Masters of Thunder! *Praise the Great Apollo, my brothers!*" Barkhan Seer saluted the three men in his warm voice. "Let us sit together, if not *in* the fire as your brethren do when they meet in high spheres, at least *around* this beautiful fire." He turned to Melchard, "How is the Mother of the Light treating you, young man?"

"Well, Master Barkhan Seer," Melchard smiled. Being addressed by Barkhan Seer was like receiving a high wind of Spirit that illuminated your energy and filled you with enthusiasm.

"You must not blame destiny for taking Orest away from the kingdom," Barkhan Seer's voice carried the balm of the waters. "If we have chosen Gervin to be the Thunderbolt Bearer at the time of the Archive transfer, it is because he is an extraordinarily gifted man, who will be remembered as one of the greatest masters of our lineage. You are privileged, really, to have the opportunity of learning from him and serving Thunder under his guidance, especially during these critical times when so much will depend on you."

"*Praise the Great Apollo!*" Esrevin voiced his enthusiasm. "When shall we begin the great task?"

Barkhan Seer replied with one of the sayings of Thunder, "Right now!" And the three men laughed and rejoiced.

"Esrevin will direct the operations in the temple of Lasseera," Barkhan Seer went on. "The Archive will gather the spiritual forces and the knowledge from both temples, Lasseera and Eisraim. Gervin and Melchard will hold Eisraim while Esrevin holds Lasseera."

"What about Ran Gereset?" Melchard asked.

"My mission is to go north, brother," Ran Gereset said with great softness, for he knew that Melchard would not like the news.

"North? Where?" Melchard asked anxiously.

Ran Gereset took a long breath. "Far. Beyond the seas of the northern shores of the kingdom, in a desert land where there is nothing but ice."

Melchard had tears in his eyes. "Does this mean you are not coming back?"

"I'm afraid so, brother."

"Ran Gereset is needed in the lands of the far north, at the extreme limit of the world," Barkhan Seer explained. "From there, he will conduct a long ritual. Indispensable for the Archive transfer."

Melchard's sadness was deep. During the difficult years of his apprenticeship in the Brown Robe, Ran Gereset had not only been a marvellous teacher but also a real brother to him. Having to lose him, just after losing Orest, was a devastating blow.

"Friends, you shall meet again, and sooner than you think," Barkhan Seer said, his voice comforting like the Sun. "In a matter of months, Gervin will initiate you into the art of being parallel."

"Living in two worlds at the same time!" Esrevin slapped Melchard's shoulder, bringing a glow of wonder in the young man's eyes.

1 – The Book of the Beginnings

"Exactly. This art is central to the higher echelons of the initiation in the Brown Robe. Gervin himself became a parallel at the very moment of his installation as the new Thunderbolt Bearer. He now lives in the Fields of Peace as well as in the kingdom."

This sounded so extraordinary that for one moment Melchard forgot his sadness. The Fields of Peace were the pure world, the World to Come – the perfection which the physical world aspired to achieve, but which already existed beyond the physical world. "The Fields of Peace are the future of humanity," Orest often taught his disciples, "the immaculate dwelling human beings will inhabit when all is accomplished."

"Soon, you will join Gervin in the Fields of Peace," Barkhan Seer was warm. "There you will find a team of extremely powerful Masters of Thunder waiting for you: Alambar Seer and Firen Seer, who were two of my disciples, Matsyendranath, Olembinah (who has lived with the Flying Dragons for more than two hundred years), and Amitabhadass, the shining one. Together with them you will form the Archive council, which will be supervising the progress of the Archive in the kingdom and liaising with the builders of the temple."

"And what about you, Master Barkhan Seer, will you be with us?" Ran Gereset asked.

"Later. First I will return to the Absolute White Light of Highness. When the time for the Archive transfer approaches, I will descend again and work with you in the Fields of Peace."

"Will you tell us more about this temple in the Fields of Peace, Master Barkhan Seer?" Melchard asked tentatively. "How will it be different from the Archive?"

"The Archive will be kept in the temple. But in reality the temple and the Archive will be one, for the Archive will contain much more than just knowledge. Spiritual forces and seeds of initiation – this is what the Archive is all about. The end of the kingdom, which has now become unavoidable, will be accompanied by massive destruction and chaos. The knowledge of all temples will be lost. And when a new kingdom is born, human beings will find themselves in a spiritual desert, with no oracles, no temples, no lineages of initiates and teachers, no priestly orders. Even the Law will have been lost.

Our mission is to prepare for the future. In our Archive we will preserve the flame of all or nearly all the spiritual orders in the temples of Eisraim and Lasseera. We will keep the spirit alive, that men and women of the future may light their torches from our flame."

Melchard's eyes were glowing. "So is this what will happen at the time of the Archive transfer – the traditions which have been kept in our temples since time immemorial will be lifted up into the Fields of Peace?"

"Yes," Barkhan Seer answered joyfully, seeing he had rekindled the young man's enthusiasm. "And all of us will be there with you in the Fields of Peace. Not just the one hundred Thunderbolt Bearers who took part in the clearing ritual, but *all of us*! Our Voices will combine, and it will be the greatest ritual that the Masters of Thunder will ever have performed."

"So, will Ran Gereset, Esrevin, Gervin and I be performing the ritual both from the kingdom and from the Fields of Peace?" Melchard asked.

"No. If everything goes according to plan, only Ran Gereset will be in both places at the same time. His position will allow him to hold the energy in a way that will make it unnecessary for you to be in the kingdom. By then, you will have gathered a large team in Eisraim and Lasseera: great Field Wizards and stone makers, and of course your own apprentices in Thunder. This will be one of your greatest joys, as it has been for the masters of the Brown Robe who came before you: train apprentices, watch them grow in Thunder, slowly, and be with them when they make mistakes, help them stand up again each time they trip along the way, and finally see them reach the summits of power that their elders have conquered before them. By the time of the Archive transfer, your apprentices will have become accomplished Masters of Thunder, and it will be up to them to take care of all operations in the kingdom."

There followed a long silence. The three disciples of Orest drank Barkhan Seer's presence, pondering on the new world which was opening before them.

Melchard, who always sat with his back very straight, was shining. Barkhan Seer plunged his fiery eyes into him and took his hand.

Far above, in the world of the gods, Lord Gana was sitting in front of the silvery waves of the Molten Sea. Between his hands he held a fantastic musical instrument made of thousands of rays of light. His eyes fixed on the horizon, he smiled.

Barkhan Seer smiled.

Melchard smiled with him, and a great opening took place.

1.7 Gervin's second meeting with the emissary of Ahriman

In the deepest of the night, Gervin felt an ominous presence following him. It did not take him long to recognise Aphelion, the former Master of Thunder who had been Orest's teacher, and who had shocked the temple of Eisraim by deciding to defect and serve Ahriman, the Prince of Darkness, thereby cutting all his ties with the Brown Robe.

It was difficult to conceive that a man of such knowledge and integrity could have let himself be tempted by the dark side. At first no one had believed the news because Aphelion, or rather Perihelion (as his name had been before he followed Ahriman) had often surprised his friends with his incredible sense of humour, so people thought it must be one of his pranks. But when it became clear that Perihelion would not come back, and that he had become one of the powerful generals of Ahriman, the consternation

1 – The Book of the Beginnings

that struck the temple was beyond words. Perihelion had been a champion of Truth, a blazing star in the constellation of the Masters of Thunder. He had conquered the arch-mysterious powers of the Deep Underworlds, accomplished mind-blowing miracles, and taught and initiated eight Masters of Thunder to the highest degree, Orest among them. And he had been a humble man, who often healed people of lower castes. He had refused the showers of honours that the prince of Eisraim wanted to bestow on him for having saved his wife, whom the kingdom's best physicians had declared paralysed beyond hope after she fell from the balcony of her royal apartment, but who, nine weeks after Perihelion's good treatment, was seen trotting around like a filosterops.

How could a man like Perihelion be captured by the dark side? This was a question Orest's disciples asked themselves over and over again with undisguised anxiety. For if Perihelion, the teacher of their teacher, could be tempted, then *anyone* could be tempted, especially younger and less accomplished Masters of Thunder like themselves. The wise Orest never tried to reassure them with kind, soothing words. Rather, he exhorted them to *pray to the Mother of the Light, hold onto the Fire, and be ready!* Sooner or later, Ahriman would knock at their door and tempt them with an offer that would probably take them completely by surprise. "The devil," Orest often said, "is no idiot. Wicked he is, but nonetheless abominably intelligent."

As Gervin felt Aphelion approaching (Aphelion was well-known for walking faster than champion runners), he recalled the first time he had got to see for himself what an encounter with the dark side could do to a man. It was when his brother-disciple Esrevin was found half-dead in the woods of Nadavan, only a few hours' walk from the plain of Erriba – a place not actually far from where he was now, though it was too dark to say for sure. Two months before Esrevin had been due to receive his final initiation as a Master of Thunder, he had been visited by Aphelion, whom Ahriman had sent to tempt him.

Esrevin, two years younger than Gervin, had been with Orest since the age of twelve. Gervin, who had met Orest only when he was twenty, regarded him as one of the strongest souls he had ever met. His enthusiasm seemed inexhaustible, and his aura always shone with the light of the uppermost sky, from which he derived his brilliant intelligence and sound judgment. But when they found him, after six weeks spent in the company of Aphelion, he was lying prostrate with a vague look in his eyes. For six months thereafter he could not say a word or move from his bed. He refused food and only survived thanks to Orest's miraculous healing powers.

Gervin was recalling that dreadfully emptied-out and extinguished look of a man whose foundations had been shattered and hopes long forgotten, when Aphelion called out, *"Praise the Lord Melchisedek, Gervin of Thunder!"*

The voice had not changed. It brought back memories of Gervin's encounter with Aphelion five years earlier – so dreadful that he did not even want to remember them.

"Praise the Lord Melchisedek, Gervin of Thunder!" Aphelion called out again.

Gervin did not stop walking.

It was two days before the end of the Moon cycle, and so despite the late hour in the night the Moon had not yet risen. In the total darkness, Gervin saw Aphelion's aura. It was but a black hole in the purple space. The shining emblems of the Masters of Thunder had been eclipsed. The pitch-black doom of darkness of those who serve Ahriman was all that remained.

"Congratulations on that magnificent ritual, Gervin!" Aphelion's deep and marvellously melodious voice rang out – the voice of a great master of the Word. "I watched it carefully, and enjoyed every second of it."

"Aphelion, you are wasting your time," Gervin kept striding forwards. "Whatever you have come to tell me, the answer is no."

Aphelion walked on his left side. "Gervin, this time I haven't come to try to entice you into my camp," he stood on his dignity. "My king has sent me to offer you a truce."

"No."

"An official treatise of mutual non-aggression, Gervin, nothing more. This is what my king is offering: he will not try to tempt any of your disciples, and he will guarantee the safety of your temple in the troubled times which are ahead. This will save the lives of many of your friends, Gervin. And all he is asking in return..."

"No."

"Gervin, I hate to see you walking in the dark. Could I transport you where you wish to go?"

"No."

"I see," Aphelion said thoughtfully. "The new Thunderbolt Bearer is even more stubborn than the former one."

"No."

"Gervin, you are angry at me for the way I treated you when I first visited you. I agree, I was rough. But make no mistake, my friend, it was only because of the high opinion my king has of you. In any case, I offer you my apologies."

"No."

"Gervin, Gervin... as a result of your stubbornness, a lot of innocent people will be harmed, starting with those you love."

Right in front of them, Aphelion conjured up an image of Marka. She was no longer young and fresh, but wrinkled and exhausted. She was meditating in her small cell, in the tower of Malchasek, but the light of her angel was not with her. She looked defeated and empty, and desperately sad, as if she had just spent twenty years crying.

If one image could have hit Gervin, this was the one.

1 – The Book of the Beginnings

"Poor Marka," Aphelion said in a compassionate tone, "her life is about to be wasted. Malchasek has decided to withdraw his light from the kingdom, as you know. And so her high priesthood will not be the illumination she had hoped for, but a long and painful agony. Year after year, the light of Malchasek will dwindle, until it finally dies out. Please, Gervin, let me make her a present. Let me use my influence over the Lords of Destiny. It would only take minimal influence for Marka's first vow to be declared invalid by an official oracle. Then she could run into your arms, and be yours, which is exactly what she wants. For you know how desperate she is at the moment, don't you? See how beautiful she would be if she were your wife!"

The old woman was replaced by a blossoming Marka, whose eyes shone the feast of light of the Ancient Days of the Earth. She not only looked happy and fulfilled, but also wise, and inspired.

"No," Gervin repeated in a neutral voice.

"Gervin, don't be a fool!" Aphelion insisted. "This is a free present I am offering you. You don't have to make any pact, or do anything in return."

"No."

Seeing that Gervin was putting so much will into saying no, the emissary of Ahriman looked for questions that would allow him to keep saying no and yet agree with him.

He manifested images of the temple of Eisraim – scenes of utter devastation. Terrifying hordes of Nephilim giants were charging through the temple's main portal. They slaughtered the guards, and armed with huge maces, destroyed all the statues in the alleys of the temple. Swearing and screaming like madmen, they desecrated the chapels, pillaged the sacred relics and demolished all the buildings.

"None of these images are new to you, are they?" Aphelion sneered.

"No."

"And you know very well that all this could happen during your lifetime. *For the time is coming, and the days are numbered.* Gervin, do you believe these future events are so fixed and pre-determined that not one force in the creation could stop them?"

"No."

"So you would not want to miss an opportunity that allowed you to preserve the temple of Eisraim, while still accomplishing the glorious mission that the Masters of Thunder have assigned to you, would you?"

Gervin did not answer. Any form of alliance or pact with the Prince of Darkness was totally out of the question. He kept walking.

"Gervin, you are not a man of poor judgment, and you do not lack compassion. The pact of non-aggression that my king is offering you is a golden opportunity. You cannot afford to let it slip out of your hands."

Gervin's lips remained sealed.

Aphelion slightly modified his tactic. He raised his voice, "Do you believe yourself as powerful as Ahriman, Gervin?"

"No."

Aphelion rushed forwards and barred Gervin's way. In a threatening tone, he declared, "Gervin, your blunt refusal of my offer could have disastrous consequences for your Archive project. You would not want to take the risk of losing everything by starting an all-out war against the armies of Ahriman just to avoid one treaty, would you?"

"Yes, I would!" Gervin answered at near-Voice threshold, stopping where he was and standing up very straight, ready to engage the full power of his lineage by recalling the obelisk of Thunder.

Startled at this sudden change, Aphelion remained silent, seeking inspiration for his next move.

"Come on, Aphelion, where are your armies?" Gervin challenged him, shouting with the Voice. "Bring them down, now – or stop this nonsense!" He went on in his normal voice, "Anyhow, all this is ridiculous. You and I know very well that Ahriman will not engage any final confrontation with the forces of light until the War of All against All. And that will not be before thousands of years have passed. Now, let us stop this stupid conversation." He started walking again, "Follow me, Aphelion, I need to speak to you about serious matters."

Aphelion, who could see in the dark, looked at Gervin in disbelief. Something inside him secretly rejoiced at seeing the Thunderbolt Bearer so bright and unstoppable. But only briefly, and so deep inside that he himself barely noticed it.

He followed Gervin, not just because he still hoped to sway his mind, but also out of curiosity.

"It must be hard for a man with your sense of humour to work with Ahriman," Gervin dropped, in a conversational tone.

"What?"

"Ahriman totally lacks any sense of humour, doesn't he?"

Aphelion burst out laughing derisively.

"Have you ever seen Ahriman make a joke, Aphelion?" Gervin persisted.

"My king has a wonderful sense of the irony in all things, and often demonstrates it through his acts."

"Mm..." Gervin replied, "you see exactly what I mean, don't you?"

Aphelion, grinding his teeth, made himself cold. "Say what you have to say, Gervin of the Brown Robe!"

"Of course. But first, tell me Aphelion, why do you still wear the brown gown of the Masters of Thunder?"

"Because one day the whole of the lineage of Thunder will rally behind me, and serve my king with me," Aphelion answered with certitude.

"Aphelion!" Gervin exclaimed compassionately, "Do you really believe this?"

"I have the full power of Ahriman behind me, Gervin," Aphelion was cool and measured. "The king of the world is unstoppable."

1 – The Book of the Beginnings

"You don't believe a word you say!" Gervin kept smiling. "It's not just that it goes against common sense – at least four hundred of our brethren live in the spheres of Highness. And you haven't been capable of tempting even one of the seven young apprentices in Thunder you have so far visited. Deep inside you, you simply don't believe that Thunder will rally with Ahriman, even though Ahriman has said so."

"Thank you for your opinion, Gervin," Aphelion maintained a glacial facade. "But the future, as you know, holds many surprises. Now, what did you want to tell me?"

Gervin stopped walking and faced the pitch-black aura. He drew a long breath and spoke with infinite softness. "What I have to say is very simple, Aphelion. The Masters of Thunder have decided that one day, one of them will be sent to rescue you from the dark side. I will be the one."

Aphelion burst out laughing so loudly that at first it was impossible to say whether he was sarcastic or flabbergasted.

But his laughter lasted just a little too long.

Gervin kept smiling, sensing the impact of his words on the emissary of Ahriman. He immediately went on, "Aphelion, why not come with me right now? You only have to say one word, and three hundred Thunderbolt Bearers will be with me to clear the darkness out of you. By dawn, we could all be laughing together. We still remember your sense of humour, you know."

"My boy, what are you saying? You are not serious, are you?" Aphelion was so taken aback that for a moment he almost seemed to be hesitating.

"Very serious, my dear enemy. Follow me! Let us put an end to the nonsense!"

Aphelion burst out laughing again, but not as loudly this time. He was thinking deeply. "Gervin..."

"Aphelion," Gervin interrupted him, "you have just seen what one hundred Thunderbolt Bearers can do. One word from you, and there will be three times as many to help me perform your clearing ritual."

"But..." something in Aphelion's resoluteness was almost softening.

"When we clear we are unstoppable," the fierce Thunderbolt Bearer was matter-of-fact. "You only have to say one word, Aphelion, and you are free!"

After an interminable second of hesitation, Aphelion replied in the icy-cold tones of his Ahrimanic voice, "No! You are completely wasting your time."

"I haven't wasted my time, Aphelion. Something inside you was moved."

"No!" insisted the emissary of the Prince of Darkness. "You are wasting your time. I am the servant of the king of the world. It was my choice, and the choice was made in full free will, and with total understanding of what it involved. It is irrevocable."

Atlantean Secrets

"All right, then," Gervin was serene. With a touch of irony, he threw the words with which Aphelion had concluded their last meeting, "But I want you to remember one thing: my offer remains, you can come to me any time, whether in this life or another."

Recognising his own words, Aphelion burst out laughing again, this time unambiguously sardonic. And he turned his back and walked away.

"We shall meet again, Aphelion," Gervin whispered. "One way... or another!"

– Thus ends the Book of the Beginnings –

2

The Book of the Blissful Sleepers

2.1 Thirty years later, on the south-eastern shores of the kingdom of Atlantis

Praise the Lord Melchisedek!
One afternoon, when I was seven years old, my father called me and told me it was time to start school. The next day I was to be sent to a place which sounded very far away.

There was a vague anxiety at the prospect of being separated from my loving stepmother (my mother had died when I was two years old), and losing the security of our home. But according to the Law – the Law of Melchisedek – a little boy belonging to the caste of the Beige Public Servants of the Prince of Sheringa, the caste of my father, was to begin school at seven, as all little boys of the same caste had done since time immemorial. In any case there was no conceivable alternative, and therefore no doubt or fear. As the Law said, *"One Law, one way! Praise the Lord Melchisedek!"* and, *"The Law is my shelter. The Law is my peace."* And, *"For he who follows the Law of our Lord Melchisedek, how could there be fear?"* How could I, or my father, have wanted anything else but to follow the Law?

There was, however, a touch of emotion in my father's voice. At the time I hardly noticed it. Only several years later, reviewing my memories, did I realise that my father was very ill, and knew it was the last time he would see me.

The Law said, *"Fear not, man of noble caste on the way to the Great Journey. If thou canst not raise thy children, the Law will."* Yet my father had tears in his eyes. He took me in his arms and looked at me for quite a long while, caressing my thin blond hair and the prominent birthmark on my left cheek. "Orlon, my son..." he started saying. Then he whispered something extremely strange into my ear. It was a rarely-used and little-known verse of the Law, not a normal thing to say to a young boy: *"We shall meet again in the Fields of Peace."*

Who was he to speak like this? And what exactly did he know of the unusual destiny awaiting his son? This, as the Law said, was *lost in the mists of time, in the forgetfulness of that which is beyond the gods.*

When the meeting with my father ended, I went out to look for my best friend.

"Lakshman, son of Lakshman, my friend in the Law, where in the mists are you?" I lawfully called as I ran through the neighbourhood. That day, the mists were quite thick. I could hardly see a few meters ahead of me.

Soon I heard his voice, *"Orlon, son of Orlon, my friend in the Law, I am here in the mists!"*

Lakshman was playing with three little boys of his caste, the Recorders of the Law, with whom it was also lawful for me to play.

As soon as I saw them, I uttered the relevant verse of the Law. Of course, I did not understand its meaning, but I knew it was the right thing to say. *"Farewell, my friends. The Law has brought us together, now it takes us apart. All glory to the Lord Melchisedek!"*

As soon as he heard my words, Lakshman lawfully answered, *"Farewell, my friend. The Law has brought us together, now it takes us apart. All glory to the Lord Melchisedek!"* And each of the three little boys repeated the same verse after him. This was the lawful way of responding to the farewell. Since time immemorial, the denizens of the kingdom had farewelled each other in this precisely codified way.

My friends spoke in a contained and mildly sad voice – the lawfully prescribed intonation for that particular verse. Like all verses, it was accompanied by codified body language: my friends kept their lips slightly pursed, their backs bent forward imperceptibly, their hands resting on their thighs. The expression on their faces was grave, with a feeling of surrender to the higher wisdom of the Lord Melchisedek – a very natural feeling, since separations, as well as all other important things, could only be brought about by the Will of our Lord. The lawfully wonderful thing was, we did not have to think in order to say these things. It all came to us automatically. Since our most tender years, we had heard our parents speak the verses of the Law. We had watched the facial expressions of our elders, and felt the emotions that accompanied each verse. As the Law said, *"Model thy parents, as thy parents modelled their parents. Thus spins the wheel of the Law."*

My little friends remained silent for a few seconds, this being the thing to do after reciting that verse.

I shared their silence, copying the expression on their faces.

Then Lakshman followed the course of the codified conversation, *"Orlon, my friend in the Law, where are you going?"*

All I had to do was to repeat the words which my father had spoken earlier, *"The time has come for me to undergo schooling, just as my father*

2 – The Book of the Blissful Sleepers

Orlon, son of Orlon, did before me, and his father Orlon, son of Orlon, did before him."

The four little boys nodded with a serious, understanding expression, as was lawfully expected of them after hearing my explanation. Needless to say, they would have nodded in exactly the same fashion had I told them I was going to hell.

A few minutes of silence went by, in which we stood motionless, our minds blank.

Then Perches (son of Perches), a little boy whom everyone believed would grow up to become a powerful village leader, resumed the nursery rhyme which my friends had been chanting before I arrived.

"What does a madman do when his first son is born?
He dances. He dances."

We all followed his lead.

"What does a madman do when his second son is born?
He dances. He dances.
What does a madman do when his third son is born?
He dances. He dances."

Standing still, our eyes fixed on the mists, we chanted this most enjoyable tune for a few hours, until our parents called us for dinner.

2.2 Atlantean schooling, early years

The Law said, *"A man shall follow the path of his father, as his father followed the path of his father. Thus spins the wheel of the Law."* But not all children went to school.

My friend Grobes, son of Grobes, for instance, never did. His father was a cobbler, from the caste of the Lawfully Shrewd Cobblers of the South-Eastern District of the County of Sheringa. Like the little boys of all castes of craftsmen, he accompanied his father and his uncles to work every day, and he watched them, learning by example. When he came back in the evening, one hour before sunset (the lawful time at which the Lawfully Shrewd Cobblers of the South-Eastern District of the County of Sheringa stopped work every day of the year), he always had fascinating verses of the Law to tell, such as, *"The Lord Melchisedek made me a cobbler, that I may celebrate his glory,"* or *"Mind your fingers when the nail is sharp!"* He showed me all the cobblers' gestures that he had observed in the shop that day. Mesmerised, I watched him repeat the same hand movements, day after day.

Unfortunately, this enlightening friendship came to an abrupt end when Grobes turned eight, the age at which little boys of cobbler castes started accompanying their father during the lawful leisure time prescribed for them: a slow stroll in the marketplace in the company of their peers while chatting with the members of the caste of the Most Lawfully Lawful Cobblers of the South-Eastern and Eastern Districts of the County of Sheringa.

I wished I too could have gone to work with my father, like Grobes. But the Law of my caste said, "*A servant of the prince of Sheringa shall go to school, that he may serve the prince well.*"

The first years of my education took place in nature. The children of my class were led through the forests that covered most counties of the kingdom. During the day, we played simple games and learned to repeat verses of the Law. At night, we slept in wonderfully cosy tree houses.

Tree houses were made of living branches, the growth of which was guided by particular fields of energy. I often had the opportunity to witness how they were built. On certain auspicious days of the calendar, groups of villagers would gather near a large tree, or sometimes two or three trees close together. They first worshipped the trees with offerings of flowers, fruits and grains. After this village priests arrived and conducted a ritual, chanting powerful mantras and hymns of the Law. And that was all that had to be done! Once the energy field had been stamped onto the trees, new branches appeared, gradually grouping themselves into walls, either at ground level or higher up in the air, depending on the blueprint. Time was all that was required before the roof appeared and its branches matted together so tightly that the construction became waterproof. Every few months the village priests came back and reinforced the energy field through maintenance rituals, but essentially, the tree took care of itself.

Despite the fact that the field speeded up the growth of branches, it took at least five to ten years for a small tree house to be built (and up to fifty years for a tree palace). Yet these natural dwellings were found in plenty, for the Law prescribed the construction of a number of them to be started every month. For the villagers, these were happy ceremonies dedicated to the Lord Melchisedek himself. *In the tree houses, the Lord Melchisedek takes care of his children*, said the Law, and *tree houses are havens for* all *the children of the Law* (meaning the people of the kingdom). Thanks to the trees no one, not even the poorest people or passing travellers, was ever left without a roof. When you walked through a forest, it was usually not long before you came across an empty tree house ready to receive you.

Once built, a tree house would remain available for generations, and would mature with time. As the Law said, *unlike men, trees grow in wisdom with age*. A one-hundred-year-old tree house was regarded as a sacred place where those who needed comfort could go and find not only lawful rest but also lawful inspiration.

Tree houses were not the only buildings that grew. Other lawful habitations were made of an organic material that breathed and glowed: the lawful plass. During the day the floor, the ceiling and the inner walls of a plass house gave enough *misty light* for people to carry out their lawful activities. At night, the plass gave a dim glow which made sleep

2 – The Book of the Blissful Sleepers

comfortable and safe. Thus the Law said, *in the house of the Lord the children of the Law are never in darkness.*

The *living walls* of a house required maintenance rituals, some of which were performed by the inhabitants of the house, others by members of the castes of lawful masons and village priests. Hymns were chanted and food offerings were made to the *living walls*. Small piles of food – plass food – were left on the floor by the side of the walls. Over a few days the piles would gradually disappear, absorbed by the floor and the walls. One must not eat food offerings made to *living walls*, as they made you sick with *unlawful indigestion* and monsoon-like diarrhoea.

After a hundred years, or much less if the walls were not fed through proper rituals, the plass would die. The walls of the house would turn thinner and thinner, until they became transparent and finally faded, leaving a ghost-like imprint that could be seen on Full Moon nights. The plass of chapels and temples, however, didn't die after a hundred years. Like the Law, it lived forever – which is why temples were eternal.

As I grew up, more of my education took place in village schools, and less in nature. Learning the verses of the Law remained the main occupation. Why study anything else? Didn't the Law say, *the Law contains all knowledge, and the essence of Knowledge is the essence of the Law,* and *what greater joy can there be than repeating the verses of the Law?* The hymns were made of spellbinding mantras charged with vibrant occult forces. Chanted over long periods of time, they induced expanded states of consciousness, and they imparted a certain depth of feeling in the heart which we intuitively recognised and warmed to. From an early age this special feeling was awakened in us, and it created a sense of wonder and awe for the Law.

Spiritual reasons aside, we just *liked* repeating verses! Take poetry, for instance. A central notion of poetic art was formulated in the Law thus: *any verse repeated long enough turns into the sweetest poem.* Hence our poetry classes were enthrallingly simple. One particular verse of the Law was spoken by the teacher. Then we would repeat the verse together, often for hours at a time. The more we repeated it, the more we liked it. It became alive in the very depths of our life force. Needless to say, the idea of composing a new verse would never have occurred to us. Why would anyone want to invent a new verse, when all poetic perfection was already contained in the Law?

Similarly, we were given art classes in which one model was presented to us – usually a clay statue representing a god, or some other traditional symbolic form taken from the Law. All students were to reproduce the model. The more accurate the reproduction, the greater the artist. For the Law said, *"What more sublime achievement can there be in the life of a sculptor than to execute one perfect replica of each statue of the eighty-four main gods?"*

Each art, and more generally every discipline, had its canon, the rules of which had been established long, long ago, not by human beings but by the divine revelation of the Law. The highest accomplishment human beings could aspire to was to reproduce the perfection of lawfully codified models. By so doing, they not only reached the summit of beauty; more importantly, they came to understand the essence of the Law, in which all wisdom was to be found.

In the wonderfully safe cocoon of the Law I grew up without fear. There was never any doubt or hesitation – only safe paths to follow. For each question, there was a pre-formulated answer. For each situation, there was a precisely codified response. For each human being, there was an already-traced destiny. And thanks to the system of the castes, everyone knew exactly how to play their role in the kingdom. There was no change, and no need for change. Thousands of years earlier, the kingdom had begun with the divine revelation of the Law of our Lord Melchisedek, and no greater joy could be conceived than the perpetuation of the canons of the Law.

Years passed, and I slowly assimilated the part of the Law that the members of my caste were supposed to know. My father being a public servant meant my education was to continue until my late teens or perhaps even longer, if I could pass the difficult examinations that led to the higher echelons of the kingdom's administration. The tests leading to these examinations began when I was thirteen and included, of course, the recitation of long passages of the Law. These presented no great challenge to me or my fellow students, who had the phenomenal memory common to all Atlantean people. We only had to a hear two-hundred-verse poem once and we could regurgitate it effortlessly. Without one mistake. Whether we understood the meaning of the verses was, of course, completely irrelevant. What mattered was that the verses remained engraved in our memory, so we could repeat them at any time. Relatively educated people knew tens of thousands of verses of the Law by heart, and doctors of the Law knew up to hundreds of thousands! But no one could possibly know the entirety of the Law, an oral tradition of millions of verses, which had been transmitted from generation to generation since the creation of the kingdom.

Becoming a public servant was an extremely difficult task because it required learning how to face a great variety of situations. For each situation one had to find the appropriate verse of the Law, so the lawful course of action might be taken. That required superior intelligence. Faced with a situation for which no lawful response had been taught, people commonly became blank. They stood motionless with their eyes open, disconnected from reality.

As part of the selection process that led to higher education, there were tests that confronted us with new situations or problems. Those who tried to tackle the problem instead of standing still with an absent gaze were considered exceptionally gifted. To pass, they did not even have to solve the problem. This would have required divine inspiration of a level that could not be expected from schoolchildren. All they had to do was demonstrate that they did not become blank, perhaps by frowning in perplexity, or scratching their head, or even just looking around them.

Thank the Lord Melchisedek, I passed. So I was duly taken to a different school. I was to be prepared for a much more difficult exam: the grand competition which recruited the high public servants of the King's administration. This grand competition took place once a year, and was to be undergone at the age of seventeen or eighteen, after four years of intense preparation.

In this new school, the students – and the teachers! – were much sharper, and the classes covered a more varied range of topics. They included: history of the Law (an easy discipline that explained why and how the Law had never changed); the Law of the castes; mantric poetry and other lawful arts; knowledge of the gods and of the main rituals of the Law (but no practice of the rituals, which only priests performed); lawful rhetoric, and even, in the last year, a few lessons of politics.

2.3 How music disappeared from my life

Of all subjects, the one I enjoyed the most was music. As I belonged to a caste of public servants, becoming a musician was not even an option. But had I been more gifted, I would have loved to have taken on music as a recreational occupation – a lawful thing for a public servant to do. But despite all my efforts, I had only limited success in reproducing the rhythms and melodies my teachers played to me.

My musical ambitions came to an abrupt end when I was fifteen. I was receiving a lesson from a compassionate teacher who, seeing my genuine aspiration to master a musical instrument, had decided to give me some much-needed private tuition.

We were standing in a garden outside the main building of the school. The old man was playing wooden sticks, which were one of the traditional instruments of Atlantean music. Standing in front of me, he was beating the sticks slowly.

"This is called mono-tony," he explained. "It is one of the most profound musical styles *we have received from the Lord Melchisedek through the Law*."

Fascinated, I let the rhythm sink deep into me.

As he played, he kept on explaining, "The Law says, *the beauty of music does not lie in that which the ears can hear, but in that which the soul can perceive*, and *superior musical pieces are those which induce the perception of the harmony of the spheres*."

After playing in front of me for some time, the old teacher handed the sticks to me, and invited me to imitate him.

Click... Click...

"No," he said, "Try again!"

Click... Click...

"No! Try again," he repeated.

Click... Click...

"No! Try again," he kept saying, and the lawful lesson went on and on. There was no such thing as boredom.

Unfortunately, after a lengthy series of attempts, the old teacher decided there was no point continuing – not out of impatience, but from sound judgment.

"Perhaps, after all, you would be more successful if we tried a more sophisticated musical instrument," he decided. "*Lawfully wait* here for me," he said, and went inside.

Lawfully waiting was never a problem. I looked up and contemplated the mists, letting my mind become blank.

When he came back, he was carrying the most incredibly beautiful instrument I had ever seen. "This one is called saucepan and spoon," he said with reverence. "It is highly praised by the Law."

Then he stood in front of me and started playing a magical melody, "Bang-ting-ting, bang-ting-ting, bang-ting-ting, bang-ting-ting, bang-ting-ting, bang-ting-ting..."

Never had I heard anything like it. This man was a great artist! Spellbound by his musical harmonies, I was transported so high that I completely lost touch with my physical environment.

A vision came to me, but it was elusive, like a mist of faint light among the clouds. It bore some resemblance to a recurrent dream of mine, which I could never quite remember.

The music teacher brought me back to reality by pulling my arm. "Would you like to try, Orlon?"

Filled with awe, I took the large, heavy saucepan in one hand, and the long spoon in the other.

"No," he said, "the spoon must be held with your right hand."

After hesitating a moment, I put the large saucepan on the floor, then took the spoon in my right hand, then took the saucepan in my left hand, and then, keeping the 'bang-ting-ting' tune in my mind, I struck the instrument.

Clang... Clang...

"No, try again," the old man said.

Clang... Clang...

There were many attempts. Each time he repeated, "No, try again."

After a long period of effort, a miracle took place, "Bung... clang-clang... bung-twang... clang."

"Nearly! Try again." The old man's eyes lit up with hope.

The sound was so magnificent that once more, I was transported high in the light, and I lost touch with my body.

2 – The Book of the Blissful Sleepers

One moment later, however, I was suddenly pulled back into the kingdom by a loud scream of pain coming from my teacher.

"*Orlon son of Orlon! You idiot in the Law!*" the old man shouted at me with the corresponding lawful attitude on his face.

Looking down, I realised that I had inadvertently dropped the heavy saucepan onto his foot.

I scratched my head, looking for an appropriate verse of the Law, but could not find any.

After this unfortunate episode, I was no longer allowed to study musical instruments – only singing. But the school's choir masters soon decided that my voice lacked the qualities required to sing the glory of the Lord Melchisedek, and that *for the sake of the Law*, it would be preferable if I focused on the recitation of the hymns.

2.4 Growing in the Law

Years passed. I grew up in the Law. It was a gradual blossoming accompanied by a broadening of my horizons. The Law of Melchisedek was not based on restriction. There were no long lists of 'thou shalt not...' linked to punishments for transgressors. It was exactly the opposite. As one verse said, "*By the Law, a cobbler can be a cobbler, a shepherd can be a shepherd.*" The Law showed which things were to be done, and when and how to do them. Every action was precisely codified. The more verses one knew, the more one could do. Conversely, those savages who lived on distant shores and knew not of the Law were no better than blobs. They spent their days vegetating on the sand, hardly capable of feeding themselves.

A topic I particularly enjoyed at school was the Law of the castes. It taught which caste wore which colour. Each caste wore only one type of clothing. *Thank the Lord Melchisedek*, this saved them from the nightmare of having to decide what to wear every morning. Thus a learned person could immediately know which caste someone belonged to, just by seeing how they were dressed. Knowing their caste, one could greet them in the appropriate way.

The words to salute someone were, "*Praise the Lord Melchisedek!*" to which the other person was to answer, "*All glory to the Lord Melchisedek!*" But the intonation varied totally depending on which caste one belonged to. Thus, for example, the Lawfully Shrewd Cobblers of the South-Eastern District of the County of Sheringa praised the Lord Melchisedek with a descending quarter tone in the fourth syllable and an ascending half tone in the seventh syllable, while the Most Lawfully Lawful Cobblers of the South-Eastern and Eastern Districts of the County of Sheringa did exactly the opposite, except when they addressed a member of their own caste, in which case the rule was to use ascending quarter tones on all unaccented syllables, but not when addressing an elder, for whom all ascending inflexions were to be accentuated. That was simple. The members of higher castes had much more sophisticated rules, with one particular way of saluting *each* other caste, and different ways of saluting the members of their own caste depending on the day of the week and the season. There were hundreds of main castes and thousands of sub-castes – this was why the Law of the castes was such a fascinating topic of study. Of course, it took years of effort. But what a reward in the end! Whenever interacting with someone, there was such profound satisfaction in knowing one could speak to them in *exactly* the lawful way prescribed by the Lord Melchisedek at the beginning of the kingdom.

This privilege, needless to say, was reserved for the members of higher castes. Less educated people only knew a few dozen ways of praising the Lord Melchisedek. To judge someone's level of education, all one had to do was salute them and listen to the way they answered, "*All glory to the Lord Melchisedek!*" It said everything about their origins.

In our later years of schooling, greater and greater emphasis was placed on not becoming blank when faced with a new situation. This goal was to be achieved by gaining a wide perspective on the Law, studying many facets rather than just the precepts of one caste, and also through osmosis. In the years of preparation for the grand competition, the teachers were men of a very different calibre from those who took care of young children. They spoke slightly faster, for a start, and a certain light shone in their eyes. They asked many questions, even disconcerting questions for which the students had not yet learnt the answers by heart. And at times they showed a certain sense of humour (a quality almost totally absent from the majority of Atlantean people).

To me, the most disconcerting of all topics was politics. It was introduced only in the last year, and was not taken very far. Real political studies began at a later stage and only for those who had succeeded in the grand competition. Thus I never really learnt much of this weird art. But the little bit I had to endure always remained a topic of wonder to me.

The art of politics turned the most fundamental lawful concepts upside down. Normally, when faced with a difficult situation a learned person would turn towards the wisdom of the Law to decide on a course of action. Not so with political counsellors! Strange as it may sound, their task was exactly the opposite. A prince or high dignitary would approach them with an already-made decision. The counsellor's task then was to find the verses of the Law that best justified that decision.

I will always remember my total stupefaction when, during one of my first lectures in politics, a teacher asked me, "The prince of the county of the Western Plains has decided to get rid of his wife, who has given him eight daughters and no sons. Find the reasons in the Law which demonstrate that he is right."

2 – The Book of the Blissful Sleepers

"*Oh my Lord Melchisedek!*" I exclaimed, "But that is terrible! This woman is going to be..."

"Orlon, son of Orlon!" the teacher interrupted in an aggravated tone of voice. "These remarks are totally irrelevant! We are here to discuss the Law, *for the Lord Melchisedek's sake!*"

I sighed and went fishing for a verse from my relatively wide lawful repertoire. "*A man must fulfil the Law of his fathers,*" I suggested after a moment.

"Mm..." the teacher did not seem to be impressed.

"*A prince commands, and takes orders from no one,*" another student suggested.

"Yes!" the teacher nodded, "this verse I like much better."

"*The highest duty of a prince is to secure lasting peace in his county. Thus, for the benefit of his subjects, he must have a son, that his son may succeed him on the throne,*" another student said.

"*Lawfully excellent!*" the teacher raised his index finger. "This is exactly what a wise counsellor would say. It clearly demonstrates that the prince has no lawful choice but to get rid of his wife." Then he turned towards me, "Now, Orlon, suppose you are advising the prince's wife. How could you demonstrate that the Law commands the prince should stay with her?"

This time, I was left blank. A major blow had been delivered to my absolute faith in the Law. Never before had I suspected that people could play with its sacred truths and manipulate them for personal advantage. This was so contrary to everything I had been taught that all I could do was gaze into the mists and become blank.

There was even worse. In some difficult cases, it was not possible to find verses of the Law that justified the monarch's decisions. The political advisers then used a mind-boggling technique: they cut parts of lawful verses and recombined them in such a manner that they fitted the monarch's needs perfectly. And they justified themselves by quoting fundamental verses such as, "*That which comes from the Law is lawful,*" or "*The Law is true, therefore, all parts of the Law are true.*"

Thank the Lord Melchisedek, politics was only one of the many subjects we had to study. The lore of rituals was much more appealing to me. The village priests impressed me enormously. I was always mesmerised by the chanting of the hymns and the recitations of the mantras of the Law. Their vibrant spirit moved me and filled me with wonder.

I often followed the village priests when they went to perform rituals designed to maintain the smooth functioning of the forces of nature. These practices were aimed at calling down the rain, fostering the fertility of the land, ensuring the seasons arrived on time, and taking care of the climate in general. As I was not from a priestly caste, I never took part in the chanting, I just sat and watched the rituals. The priests, who in this village wore saffron robes, sat around a small fire, which they lit in a precisely codified manner. Then, chanting their mantras, they poured oblations into the fire. This created sparks of energy in the aura of the flame, which transported me into wonderful, expanded states of consciousness and made me completely lose touch with time.

Another caste with which I enjoyed mixing – within the limits imposed by the Law, of course – was that of the space controllers.

My first encounter with one of them took place after a tragic incident. One morning in my dormitory, a boy was found dead in his bed. He was my best friend, because he slept in the bed next to mine and the Law said, "*Let thy neighbour be thy friend.*" I spent the day mourning, lawfully praying for his soul and crying, as prescribed by the verse, "*When thy friend dies, pray for his soul and cry for one day, then surrender to the higher wisdom of our Lord Melchisedek.*" In the afternoon, the village priests were called, and after examining his body they declared his death was not due to some sickness. The boy had simply lost his way during the night. As we were told, this was not an unusual event.

In the days that followed, our class was visited by Eterne, one of the space controllers in charge of our area. Space controllers were a special caste, whose functions were even more mysterious than those of the priests. They were sometimes called the night shepherds, because they spent their nights travelling through darkness visible, the astral layer closest to the physical world. Their role was to rescue many people who unconsciously wandered too far into astral spaces during their sleep. In a number of cases, without someone to escort them these stray sheep would have been unable to return into their body, and in the morning they would have been found dead in their bed. The controllers brought them home and sent an impulse to make them wake up.

After the death of my school friend, Eterne took special care of the boys in my class. Waking up in the morning, I often remembered having met him during the night. He always thought I was going too far, and when he found me he would tell me off. He thought I was purposely trying to go and explore distant regions of darkness visible – an idea that would have never occurred to me. With time, I learnt from him how to spend my nights in the astral neighbourhood, rather than drifting far away. To thank him, I sometimes visited his house during the day and took him flowers.

Space controllers were not only loved and appreciated for their service, they also enjoyed great prestige. Many stories circulated about their secret powers, and the strange encounters they sometimes had while travelling in remote astral spaces. When I visited Eterne I used to sit, absorbed for hours, while he talked about his work. He told me about the amazing places he had explored in darkness visible and the many sleepers he had rescued from certain death. And he spoke of the souls of the dead which he sometimes met on their way to spiritual worlds – worlds so lofty they could not be seen even from the highest levels of darkness visible. He also told me fantastic stories of high priests and priestesses who had travelled even

2 – The Book of the Blissful Sleepers

further than him, and explored incredibly distant spheres, at least two or three levels above darkness visible.

As he spoke, I sat with my eyes wide open, filled with admiration and awe.

Little did I know that I would end up being trained by some of the most powerful space controllers in the kingdom – the White Eagles, women of phenomenal travelling abilities, for whom darkness visible was but a rather dim and uneventful area located at the bottom of the ladder of the spheres.

2.5 The grand competition

One of the topics which presented me with great difficulty was physical education. I hated running. The Law said that men of my caste were supposed to be able to run *so they may serve their sovereign in cases of great emergency*, and so I patiently submitted to the classes. But physical exercise, not just running, was deeply against my nature. Perhaps it had to do with the fact that, even though tall, I was extremely thin and particularly vulnerable to all forms of colds and pestilences.

Once, in the middle of a sports class which consisted of climbing up and down a stairway, the physical education teacher came over to me.

I was sitting on the bottom step, catching my breath, and remembering a painful episode a few months earlier when I had been chased by a cow across an entire field.

The man stood in front of me and looked at me for a moment with a strange expression on his face. "You are lucky, Orlon! In our county, public servants never have to take part in war operations. Can you imagine what would happen if you had to fight against the Nephilim giants?"

I scratched my head, searching for an appropriate verse. *"Fight with Spirit, man of the Law!"*

"Yes, but *Spirit comes to the strong,* Orlon," he retorted.

I nodded, pondering on the depth of that verse.

Then he put his hand on my shoulder and said, *"He who does well in the grand competition will get a beautiful wife."*

I frowned, wondering what he meant.

"You had better do well, Orlon, son of Orlon," he smiled. "Otherwise I wonder what fool of a public servant would want to give you his daughter for a wife!"

"A wife?" I looked up in the mists and became blank.

When I came back to myself, the physical education teacher had already gone. After this he never spoke to me again.

Most other teachers were much friendlier. In this last year of preparation, they were all trying to awaken a spirit of competition in their students. This was no easy task, especially as far as I was concerned. Once, after a test in history of the Law in which I had done quite well, a teacher told me, "*Lawfully excellent*, Orlon! If you perform like this at the grand competition, you may end up serving the prince of the county of Sheringa himself!"

I nodded. According to lawful rhetoric, the intonation of his sentence indicated that I did not have to look for an answer, just smile politely.

"Wouldn't you like to be an important man from whom the royal family itself seeks lawful advice, Orlon?" the teacher asked.

I became thoughtful, wondering if I would like that.

"You would be rich. You would have a beautiful wife and a large house with servants, and everyone in your native village would respect you," the teacher continued.

I remained silent. I hadn't visited my native village for years. I did not even know if my parents were still alive.

"Isn't there a position in the high administration of the county of Sheringa you would like to occupy?" he questioned.

"Yes," I nodded, "I would like to represent the prince in another county."

"Mm..." the teacher had a dubious expression on his face. "Would you really like to travel?"

I nodded. Travelling was one of the things Atlantean people usually hated the most. It not only implied leaving the comfort of their home, but also adapting to a new climate, and sometimes even to a different lifestyle. Still, for some strange reason it appealed to me.

"Well in that case, Orlon, you *must* do well in the grand competition," the teacher tried to impress on me. "The prince does not appoint many ambassadors."

I put on a decided face, as lawful rhetoric dictated I should after receiving an injunction of this kind. But the need to reach a high score at the grand competition was not as obvious to me as it was to some other students, who seemed to be anxious to join the high ranks of the royal administration.

In the months that preceded the grand competition, many of my fellow students started showing signs of excitement. It all remained lawfully moderate but still, there was no doubt that the prospect of undergoing the critical tests was having an impact on them. They started discussing topics that would never have come to their mind beforehand, such as which positions they wished to reach, and what sort of lawful spouse they would like. When talking, they tended to use fewer stock phrases, and they chose their verses of the Law with more wit. Some of them, whose ambition seemed staggering to me, even studied after classes or engaged in debates, polishing their rhetoric for the examinations.

Finally, the great event arrived.

The competition was to take place in Sheringa city, the capital of the county, where hundreds of students coming from all corners of the county

2 – The Book of the Blissful Sleepers

flocked every year. A few days before leaving the boarding school, a large ceremony took place, during which the students lawfully expressed their gratitude for what they had received from their teachers. A team of priests came and sang hymns for a few hours. Then the teachers all stood in a row, and each student, one after the other, came and thanked each teacher by repeating the same appropriate verses of the Law, which were pronounced in a reserved but moderately sad tone. Needless to say, the Lord Melchisedek was copiously praised before, during and after this lawfully moving exchange. The students also thanked the energies of the land and the trees for their nurturing support. Finally they thanked each other, and the ceremony finished with a lawful banquet during which all were invited to rejoice about the beautiful years ahead of them. Repeating the model of their elders *for the greatest glory of our Lord Melchisedek* – what more enviable destiny could they have dreamt of?

Blissful sleepers!

Little did they suspect their world was about to collapse.

– Thus ends the Book of the Blissful Sleepers –

3
The Book of the Call of Destiny

3.1 The call of destiny

The grand competition consisted of four parts. In the first part, candidates had to undergo various examinations. They were to demonstrate their knowledge of the Law and engage in long recitations of hymns, none of which presented much difficulty for those who had been properly prepared. Then the candidates were submitted to a fire of questions relating to practical situations likely to be encountered by public servants, and to the application of various rules and pieces of legislation. Each time, the challenge was to find a verse of the Law that shed light on the problem and suggested a course of action.

Quite unexpectedly, I found myself enjoying the whole exercise – much more than the months of preparation that had led to it. Unlike some of my fellow students, I had little motivation to become part of the high administration of my county. I wanted to make sure I would never have to run, and keep away at all costs from anything that had to do with cattle. Apart from this, I did not really care whether I ended up being a Grand Intendant of Lawfully Pending Administrative Implementations, a Lower Attaché of Lawful Princely Representation, or a Lawful whatever else. Not preoccupied with achieving a high score, my mood was serene. I surrendered to *the higher wisdom of our Lord Melchisedek*, placing my destiny in his hands. But as the days passed, I enjoyed the vibrant atmosphere of the examination rooms more and more. The examiners were sharp-witted and they conveyed a certain alertness that not only helped me think clearly, but also made me feel more alive than ever before.

So at the conclusion of the first week, when I learned that I was not one of the twelve hundred candidates who had been eliminated, I was genuinely happy. I was curious – lawfully mildly curious – to see what would happen during the rest of the competition.

3 – The Book of the Call of Destiny

The second part was not only supposed to be the most difficult, but also the most crucial of the whole selection process. Of the six hundred remaining candidates, only one hundred would qualify for the third stage of the competition.

The trial took place in a neighbouring forest. It was to last all day. The candidates were separated into small groups, the goal being to reach a certain place hidden in the woods. To find our way, we had to go through a number of checkpoints where we were asked questions, and given directions according to the accuracy of our answers. The race started at dawn and finished at midnight. We had been warned that many candidates would not make it to the final rendezvous. Furthermore, some of us might well lose our life when we encountered the fierce guardians that kept the small bridges spanning many water streams that ran through the forest. Thus my young friends regarded this race as the trial of their life, the single major event which would seal their destiny.

Lawfully anxious, I began the race at dawn. I was part of a group which included five of my school friends. We were but one of a hundred such groups, made up of students from several schools in the county, and of others who had come to compete, trying to secure a bright future for themselves.

We began our trail on the edge of the forest and went looking for the first of the checkpoints.

We had only been walking for half an hour when a voice called us, "Hey! Yes, I'm calling your lawful selves! Come and help me!"

We stopped. The man who had called us was kneeling by a tree, close to a woman and a little girl. The woman was lying on the ground, unconscious. The little girl was standing by her side. Both of them wore grey dresses, indicating they were members of a lower caste with which we were not supposed to mix, *unless lawfully required to do so*. The man wore a brown gown of a kind that was unknown in the county of Sheringa.

"Come quick!" the man called. "I need your help to rescue this woman."

My friends kept moving.

For some reason, I hesitated. It was not out of compassion. If this woman was sick, wasn't it the will of the Lord Melchisedek? But there was something in the man's voice that reached deep into me. I walked a few steps towards him, contemplating the long brown gown. He was probably a monk, although his order was unknown to me. I could not see his face, it was hidden under a hood.

"Orlon!" one of my friends called. *"Don't be a fool in the Law!* There is no time to waste."

The man uncovered his head and looked at me. He was in his late fifties and his attitude bore great dignity, with his piercing grey-green eyes and his grey hair and beard. "Lawfully quick! Come here!" he called again. "Help me rest her body against a tree."

My friends disappeared into the mists.

Had I followed them, I would have missed my destiny.

I kept walking towards the man.

It was *totally illawgical*. Wasting time during the major trial of the grand competition was *an unlawfully foolish thing to do*. According to the instructions which had been drummed into me for months, I should have run off without taking further notice. But the man's eyes had something so familiar, yet so completely different from anything I had seen before, that I felt compelled to answer his call.

"Help me lift her," he beckoned.

I frowned with surprise. This man looked educated. Did he not know that a man of my caste was not supposed to touch a woman of her caste, *unless required by some lawfully exceptional circumstance*?

"Quick!" he commanded with the distinct intonation of someone of a higher caste giving an order to a youth – just the *exceptional circumstance* I needed to be lawfully entitled to touch the woman.

We carried her body to the tree and leant her back against it. But I hardly looked at her, so captivated was I by the man.

He twinged his beard thoughtfully for a few seconds, carefully observing the woman. Then he took her wrists and held them in his hands with his eyes closed, performing some kind of healing.

Close by, the little girl watched silently, her big brown eyes fixed on the woman. She was perhaps seven years old. As her dress was the same colour as that of the woman, I lawfully deduced she was her daughter.

After a moment, I told the man, "Sir, I must go."

"Wait!" he said in a gentle voice. "I have not finished with this woman."

I kept looking at him, wondering what it was about him that resonated so deeply inside me. He was not as tall as I was, and of average build. He looked sharp, like the people who conducted the examinations in the grand competition. But rather than his appearance, it was his presence that touched me – a soft, gentle presence *flowing like a lawful river*.

After resisting the pull to move for one or two more minutes, I finally had to tell him, "Sir, I really *must* go!"

"All right, then, go," the man answered in a neutral voice, his eyes fixed on the woman who was still unconscious.

"Farewell, man of the Law!" I lawfully saluted him.

He did not answer. He was busy taking care of the woman.

I stood up and started walking away.

"Wait, son!" the man called. "You forgot something."

Surprised, I turned towards him. I could not see anything of mine lying on the ground.

He looked into my eyes and smiled. "Come!"

Puzzled, I walked towards him.

As I came close to him, he stood up. Then he took my wrists in his hands and plunged his gaze deep into me. "Take this with you," he said. "You will need it for what you have to do."

3 – The Book of the Call of Destiny

What was he doing? My whole body started buzzing. Strange vibrations came into my head, transporting me into a different space. It was just a few seconds, but whatever was happening was extraordinarily intense.

Then the man let go of my wrists. "Go, now."

I was so stunned that it took a few seconds before I could move. Then I turned around and started to walk off.

This time he did not call me back.

After a few steps, I stopped. Hesitating, I turned my head towards him.

"Go!" he repeated. "You must hurry."

Off I went, resuming the race.

But then something extremely odd happened. Carried by an unusually high spirit, I started running.

Genuinely worried, I immediately stopped. What had this man done to me? But there was no time to ponder on the strange encounter. I had reached a checkpoint, and two examiners started asking me questions.

Again something bizarre took place. My mind started operating faster than ever before. I answered the men's questions with a speed that surprised me even more than it surprised them. And when they said, "Pass!" I started running again.

I soon arrived at a low bridge crossing a small water stream. In the middle of the bridge stood a huge man who held a long wooden beam in his hands. My friends had just arrived. They walked towards him slowly and cautiously. Then, to their complete stupefaction, the man suddenly rushed at them and, using the beam, toppled them into the water.

Normally, I would have cautiously stopped where I was and taken sufficient time to seek inspiration from my repertory of lawful verses. Moved by the powerful forces which the monk had insufflated into me, I walked onto the bridge and established eye contact with the man.

Impassive, he waited for me to come near.

Without actually looking to his left, I pretended to get ready to run in that direction, as if trying to trick him.

The man immediately sensed the impulse and prepared himself, slightly moving towards his left.

I kept walking, looking straight into his eyes.

Then I started running, as if I was going to make a dash to his left, where he expected me to go. But as soon as he started swinging the wooden beam, I leapt to his right and ran past him.

Carried by the beam's momentum, the man did not have the time to change direction. When he saw me escaping, he burst out laughing, and resting the beam on his forearms, clapped his hands in applause.

I was so amazed at what I had done that I did not even worry about the fact I was running. I just kept moving to the next checkpoint.

A powerful force was with me. I could not understand what it was, nor how it operated. But each time a question was asked of me, I could immediately *see* the answer. It was more than just a voice speaking through my mouth, it was a broad vision through which I perceived the reasons why the questions were asked, and the general lawful background in which they were to be understood. This led me to say incredible things. A few times, after passing a checkpoint I had to ask myself, *"Oh my Lord Melchisedek, did I say that?"* Somehow, I could sense the personality of the examiners and gear my answers accordingly. A few times I even managed to make them laugh, as if I was endowed with a sense of humour.

Exhilarated, I flew from checkpoint to checkpoint, thoroughly enjoying the exalted consciousness that moved me. Around midday, when I reached yet another checkpoint, I was received by a group of dignitaries who looked at me with curiosity. There were at least twelve of them, and at their head was a tall man in a crimson robe embroidered with golden symbols, signs of extremely high status in the administration of the King of Atlantis.

I walked slowly towards the group of dignitaries and *praised the Lord Melchisedek* with all the respect due to their rank. Then I stood in front of them and gathered my spirits, ready to face a barrage of questions.

When he saw the glow in my eyes and the decided look on my face, the tall man in the crimson robe smiled. *"Peace, my friend in the Law!"* he said in the lawful intonation of someone threatened by a weapon.

The dignitaries burst out laughing.

I smiled politely, as lawful convention commended I should do in such a situation.

"What is your name, *my friend in the Law?*" the crimson-robed man asked.

"Orlon, son of Orlon, Sir."

"Well, Orlon son of Orlon, you have completed the trials of the day. You can go and rest, now. We will meet you tomorrow night, at the celebration that concludes the second part of the grand competition."

I stood motionless, looking at him in disbelief. It was hardly midday, and I had been told the trial was likely to go on until late in the night. Was this a trap?

"You can go!" the man said in a friendly voice.

As I did not budge, the dignitaries burst out laughing again.

The crimson-robed man frowned. Instantly, the dignitaries stopped laughing. "You can go!" the man repeated, this time in a sharp tone used only by those in the service of His Supreme Majesty the King of Atlantis.

I bent my head politely, and duly saluting him, I left.

3.2 Unlawfully far away

When I returned to the boarding house where my school friends and I had been staying, it was early in the afternoon. I decided that I needed *some*

3 – The Book of the Call of Destiny

lawful rest. I went straight to the dormitory, which was empty, and lay on my bed.

I could not take the monk out my thoughts. Who was he? And what had he done to me? Would I ever see him again? These questions kept running through my mind. But despite the excitement of the day, I soon fell asleep.

When I woke, in the late afternoon, the first thing that came to my mind was that I *had* to find the monk and speak to him. I couldn't tell why, but the certitude was absolute.

It was just before sunset and the dormitory was still empty. None of my friends had returned from the trial. It made me thoughtful. What if I had *really* scored well? Was I going to be offered a high position in the service of the prince? Would I know how to choose wisely?

Rather than worrying, I decided to wait for the results of the competition. They were to be proclaimed the following morning.

A profound impulse moved me.

I got up and went to search for the monk.

I had no idea where he was staying, or even if he was still in Sheringa. So I decided to look for the woman. Sheringa was a lawful town organised in neighbourhoods where castes were strictly segregated, so it was easy to find her. Knowing she was dressed in grey, I inquired after her neighbourhood, and it was not long before I reached a small marketplace full of people dressed just like her.

After walking around for a few minutes, I recognised the little girl. She was playing with her friends near a fruit stall. She led me to her house, and from there a young boy took me for a short walk to the neighbourhood where the monk was staying.

It was a small house at the end of an empty lane. Before knocking at the door, I hesitated. What was I going to tell this man?

Before I could put my thoughts together, the monk opened the door and greeted me, "*Praise the Lord Melchisedek, friend in the Law!*"

"*All glory to the Lord Melchisedek, wise man in the Law*," I answered with due respect for his age and noble bearing.

This time, his head was uncovered. He looked at me for a moment, then he smiled, "*What is your name, my friend in the Law?*"

Again, something in his eyes and in his presence struck a chord inside me. I was both deeply moved and perplexed. I went blank and forgot to answer him.

The man broadened his smile, "My name is Gervin of the Brown Robe," he said. "Come in, *my friend in the Law*."

"My name is Orlon, son of Orlon," I muttered, and followed him along a short corridor into an empty room lit with a whitish blue glow from the *living plass walls*.

"How old are you, Orlon?"

"*I have known seventeen springs and seventeen autumns*," I answered in lawful fashion.

After inviting me to sit with him, the man asked a number of questions about my family, my caste, my activities at school, and the examinations I had just passed. Then for a long while we looked at each other and said nothing.

Again I felt bizarre vibrations in my head, and other sensations I could not explain. My whole body was buzzing. I recognised inside him the exalted force that had supported me during the competition.

Then, out of the blue mists, the man said, *"Orlon, would you like to follow me and become part of my temple?"*

Dazed and amazed, I was speechless.

These lawful words were those used by great spiritual masters when they lawfully invited someone to become their disciple. No doubt, Master Gervin was a powerful monk. The force that had carried me during the competition was clear proof of his spiritual dimension. But even though I had heard several stories of masters coming from other counties and lawfully abducting new disciples, I had never suspected that such a thing could happen to me.

When he saw the stupefied expression on my face, Master Gervin burst out laughing.

"But..." I finally managed to articulate. "But I am from a caste of public servants. I cannot live in a temple."

"Mm..." he nodded with a grave expression on his face. Then he smiled and took me by surprise again by saying, *"Farewell, man of the Law!"* And he stood up, indicating that our meeting was finished.

Stunned, I stood up mechanically and followed him to the entrance of the house.

When we reached the doorway, he smiled again and casually repeated, *"Farewell, man of the Law!"*

"*Farewell...*" I started saying, but the words choked in my throat. As he was closing the door, I blurted out, *"Wait, Master Gervin!"*

He reopened the door and looked at me with a neutral expression on his face.

"Will you still be here tomorrow morning?" I asked.

"Perhaps. Or perhaps not," he said, looking up at a nearby tree.

"And where is your temple?"

"In the county of Eisraim," he kept contemplating the tree.

"Eisraim? But that is unlawfully far!" I exclaimed. Whenever I had dreamt of travelling, it was to lawfully nearby counties. Sheringa was on the eastern shores. To reach Eisraim from there, one had to go west and cross nearly half the Atlantean continent. Boats made me sick, even on rivers.

"Quite far, yes," he said, looking deep into my eyes; and the vibration in my head started again.

We kept eye contact for a moment, then he gave me a final, *"Farewell, man of the Law!"* and with a broad smile on his face, he closed the door.

3 – The Book of the Call of Destiny

3.3 Night of fever

It was well past midnight. For the first time in my life, I could not sleep.

I sat up, and contemplated the dim glow on the *living wall* in front of me.

The dormitory was still empty. What was I to make of that? Of course, my forty-nine school friends were not the only ones who had taken part in the race. People had come from all over the county to compete. Still, it made me wonder. What kind of score had I achieved?

But this was not what kept me awake. The truth was, I could not take the monk's image out of my mind. This man had something... something which I had never felt in anyone else, something more meaningful to me than anything I had ever encountered.

But what was it?

Should I go and speak to him again? And what if it was too late? What if he had already left town? Would I ever see him again? Did the prince of Sheringa appoint ambassadors to the county of Eisraim? Would I have to wait for the present ambassador to *render the lawful ghost* before I could travel over there? But who said my score would ever allow me to reach such a high function as an ambassador? And *for the Lord Melchisedek's sake*, was this rumbling in my head ever going to stop?

I lay down again, turned on my side, closed my eyes and whispered to myself, *"Have a good night in the Law!"*

And what if he had *really* left town? What if I never found him again? Would I regret it all my life? Should I have accepted his invitation?

But being a public servant, I could not live in a temple!

Except, of course, if I became part of an order of priests which recruited members from other castes.

Were there such castes of priests in the temple of Eisraim?

Me, a priest? I really could not see that happening. And I knew nothing about the temple of Eisraim. And what if they kept cattle over there?

Anyhow it took weeks for a boat to reach Eisraim. I could never survive this.

I turned onto the other side.

And what if I went to speak to him right now?

Unless there was a special reason, knocking at someone's door in the middle of the night was not a lawful thing to do. Except of course if his caste had special rules. And what was this Brown Robe caste, by the way?

I turned onto the other side, then sat up again and decided it would definitely not be a good idea to go and visit him in the middle of the night.

Three minutes later, I was walking along the empty streets of Sheringa city, heading towards his house. It was a *balmy Atlantean night*, the light of the Moon filtering through the mists and creating a silvery atmosphere.

Of course I was not going to knock at his door. That would have been against the principles of the Law. I decided when I got there I would stand in front of the house and wait for the first light of dawn, which was not so far away. This way I could not miss him, should he decide to leave in the early hours of the morning. But why was this storm going on in my head? Never before had I felt such unlawful angst and agitation. I was so worried I would miss the Brown Robe priest that I almost felt like running.

When I reached the place, I felt immensely relieved. But not for long. What if the house had a back door to another lane?

Was this a sufficiently lawful reason to knock at the door in the middle of the night?

I stood in front of the door, wondering what a doctor of the Law would do in such a situation.

To my surprise, the door opened. I found myself face to face with the man in the brown gown.

He smiled at me. *"Praise the Lord Melchisedek, Orlon!* Come in," he said in his gentle voice.

Instantly, the storm in my head calmed down. I felt serene and clear.

He took me to the same empty room where he had received me earlier, and invited me to sit with him amidst the pale blue glow exuding from the *living walls*.

I did not feel like talking. I just wanted to drink his presence, which I found even warmer than when I had met him earlier. He did not talk either. He just looked into my eyes and smiled, shining his friendly warmth into me.

What was so different about him? The sharpness and the intensity in his eyes, perhaps. When he directed his majestic gaze towards me, he seemed to be seeing myriads of things that eluded me completely. Or was it the warmth that radiated from his heart? It felt so unusual, and so familiar at the same time. Being in his company I felt like a completely different person. But my inner world was too vague to understand exactly what was happening.

The communion went on for a long time. Then just before dawn, when the *living walls* started to glow more brightly, Gervin twinged his beard thoughtfully and asked, "Are you going to follow me, Orlon?"

After sitting with him for nearly two hours, I felt more lucid than ever before. I was towering over my normal self. From this heightened state, it was clear to me that I wanted to follow him.

This was nothing short of a revelation. For the first time in my life, I really wanted something!

But I could not see how it would be lawfully feasible. "Master Gervin, what would happen if I were to follow you?" I asked, anxiously hoping he would suggest some lawful arrangement whereby a public servant could dwell in a temple.

The answer was not at all what I had expected. He stroked his beard and smiled, "Lots of surprises, and an awful lot of change inside yourself!"

3 – The Book of the Call of Destiny

The words 'change' and 'awful' went together unlawfully well. *Like all normal Atlanteans*, I abhorred surprises.

I swallowed hard. "Being a public servant, what function could I take in your temple? I probably could not live within the temple's walls."

Master Gervin burst out laughing, and for a moment I feared he was going to throw me out of his house as he had done before. But he just placed his hand on my shoulder and looked deep into my eyes. "Orlon, you can be anything. You can do anything!"

I had no idea what he meant.

"Would you like to be a priest?" he asked.

"Only very high orders of priests accept members from other castes," I started thinking. From what I had been taught on the Law of the castes, I knew that in temples, not all priests and priestesses were celibate. But those who were, necessarily had to recruit their members from other castes. As the Law said, *Celibacy cannot be passed down from father to son*. Most priesthood orders, however, recruited their members from specific groups and communities. But the highest priestly castes made exceptions to this rule. Their members could come from *any of the higher castes of the Atlantean society*.

"Would you like to join the Salmon Robe?" Gervin asked.

"The Salmon Robe?" I was astonished. The Salmon Robes were well known. They were powerful ritualists – masters of the Law who handled awesome forces of nature. Compared to them, the village priests I admired so much were but children.

"You can be anything. You can do anything," Gervin repeated with a grave expression on his face.

I still didn't understand what he meant, but I was deeply impressed by the power conveyed by his words.

"Would the Salmon Robe ever consider enrolling a simple public servant like me?" I asked.

Twinging his beard, Gervin pushed his lips forward. "Who knows? By the end of the grand competition, Orlon son of Orlon may be offered a high position in the service of His Majesty the Prince of Sheringa."

"But then, what if I refused it?" I asked anxiously. "Do you think the prince could take offence and throw me in jail, Master Gervin?"

For some reason, Master Gervin did not seem to be the least worried by this eventuality. "*My friend in the Law*, I will take care of this. But before you decide whether you will follow me or not, I want you to go and listen to the proclamation of the results of yesterday's competition."

Together we held a long meditative silence. Then, standing up, Gervin indicated our meeting was over.

3.4 The hour of God when the Lord Melchisedek is calling

When I returned to Gervin's house it was early in the afternoon. The proclamation had lasted for hours.

Just as I was about to knock, he opened the door. Was it each time a coincidence? I wondered. But there were urgent matters to discuss. After a lawful salute, I immediately began, "Master Gervin..."

"You seem to be out of breath, son," he commented.

"I ran nearly all the way here. Master Gervin, something... something... something has happened."

"What has happened?"

"I have been nominated one of the highly eligible twelve!"

"Come in," he smiled. And he took me into the small empty room, where we sat together again. "Do you understand what this means?" he asked.

"It means I do not have to compete in the third part of the contest. I can go straight to the fourth part."

"Which is no competition but a meeting with the prince's ministers to decide which function will be given to you."

There was a long silence.

Gervin once more asked, "Do you still want to follow me, Orlon?"

"Yes!" I nodded assuredly. There was no doubt in my mind, it was the only thing I wanted. "But what am I going to tell the prince's ministers?" I asked anxiously. "If I reject their offer, they might throw me in jail!"

"Is *this* what worries you?" Gervin smiled. "But this is not at all what is supposed to happen at the moment."

I wondered what was supposed to happen.

"At the moment you should be carefully considering your future." The expression on his face was serious. "There is a brilliant career waiting for you in the county of Sheringa. You could become rich and powerful, and enjoy all the pleasures of your rank. Are you sure you want to give up the fruits of your victory to follow me?"

I did not know what to say. Clearly, if there was victory it was all his. Without the forces he had insufflated into me, I would never have achieved such a high score.

Master Gervin expected an answer, I could see it on his face. Thus I went searching in my lawful repertory for an appropriate verse to convey what I felt.

After a long while I finally spoke. "*All glory to the teacher!*"

Gervin responded with the most magnificent smile I had ever seen. It illuminated the entire room. I felt pure bliss.

But Gervin's face became grave again. "It will not be easy to follow me, Orlon," he warned.

This I could already see. What was I going to tell the prince's ministers? At least I had ten days to prepare myself for the meeting. But that very eve-

3 – The Book of the Call of Destiny

ning there was to be a celebration in which those who had succeeded in the second part of the competition were to be greeted by a representative of the King of Atlantis. What to do? Was I to pretend that nothing had happened to me, or take the risk of insulting the high-ranking dignitaries by telling them I did not want their honours?

Gervin slowly shook his head, as if he could read my thoughts. "In the future, there will be much more difficult trials than these, Orlon."

I nodded gravely, as the principles of rhetoric commanded I should do in such a situation, but without the faintest idea of what he meant.

For a long while, Gervin looked deep into my eyes. He seemed to be reading my soul, but I had no perception of what he was seeing. Then he took my hands and again his smile illuminated the room, brightening the bluish glow of the *living walls.*

Deep inside, I knew that he had accepted me.

From there, it all moved fast, as if in a dream. To my immense relief I learned that Gervin had been invited to the ceremony that was to take place that evening. Thus we could go together, and he would tell me what to say and how to behave when my name was called.

But Gervin also instructed me not to return to the boarding house. He explained this by quoting a verse of the Law, "*Having made the step, stride forwards and never turn back, or face perils worse than death.*"

"Does this mean that I will never see my friends again?" I asked, suddenly realising that momentous changes were about to take place in my life.

"*Rejoice, man of the Law! For this is the hour of God when the Lord Melchisedek is calling, and the bell of destiny is tolling. And you have heard the call!*" Gervin answered. But when he saw that my eyes were filled with tears he took on a soft, gentle voice, "Listen, you and I are going to become really good friends. And I promise you that in the temple of Eisraim, you will have friends like you never dreamed you could have – exceptional people who are waiting for you, and who will care for you and love you as people in the kingdom rarely do."

I drank his words.

To cheer me up, Gervin described the many wonders of his temple, where the lawful plass was tens of thousands of years old and the chapels' *living walls* held the awesome presence of the gods. There were magnificent gardens full of statues of all the gods, underground crypts in which fire rituals had been conducted uninterruptedly for hundreds of years, and more than eleven hundred priests and priestesses of a great variety of orders.

Moreover, I learned that hardly any cattle were kept within the perimeter of the temple.

3.5 Gervin plays a trick on the King's representative

That evening Gervin and I walked together to the ceremony. It was held in large gardens belonging to the prince's estate.

Seated in front of a stage was a crowd of a few hundred. This was by far the largest ceremony I had ever attended. Apart from the one hundred candidates who had succeeded in the second part of the competition, there were many high-ranking dignitaries from the county of Sheringa, as well as representatives of other counties. There were even a few members of the King's administration – people of extremely high status, for the many counties of the kingdom were each governed by a prince who submitted to the central authority of the King. The audience was also comprised of eminent members of the community and people of higher castes, a number of whom had brought their eligible daughters, hoping to find lawfully promising husbands for them.

Master Gervin had been invited to sit in the first rows – a great privilege, showing he was held in high esteem by the administration of Sheringa. Rather than letting me sit with my friends, he took me with him.

We waited the customary two or three hours, as in all lawful celebrations – the Law said, *let no beginning be rushed*. Then the crimson-robed man whom I had briefly met at the end of the trial arrived, leading a short procession of top-level public servants. As they were taking position on the stage, Gervin whispered in my ear, "Do you know who this man is?"

"Someone sent by the King?"

"Exactly! His name is Lord Proston. Tonight we are going to play a little trick on him." Gervin winked at me.

I gulped in horror. "Play a trick on an emissary of His Supreme Majesty the King of Atlantis?" I could already see myself being thrown into the darkest dungeon of Sheringa city's jail.

"Don't worry, nothing to do with you," Gervin said. "It is strictly between him and me. When your name is called, just say what I told you and everything will be *fine in the Law!*"

Not at all reassured, I watched the beginning of the ceremony. High priests from the prince's court chanted hymns of the Law, after which Lord Proston lawfully congratulated a number of officials on behalf of His Supreme Majesty the King of Atlantis. Various other lawful formalities ensued until, one by one, the successful candidates were called up to the stage.

The rumbling of ceremonial drums accompanied their slow walk towards the platform. As their names were announced they climbed up the steps, walked towards Lord Proston and humbly saluted him. Lord Proston lawfully congratulated them and decorated them with a beige ribbon. The crowd applauded loudly. The laureates did not return to their place, but climbed down from the stage and took position on the side.

3 – The Book of the Call of Destiny

The more time passed, the more terrified I became. What was going to happen when I refused the ribbon? Could anyone play a trick on a Most Venerable Lord and not end up in jail? Had it not been for the supportive presence of Master Gervin, I would have probably fainted – not such a hard thing to do, considering how loosely people's consciousness was bound to their physical body.

Finally, my name was called.

I stood up and started walking towards the stage. *"Oh my Lord Melchisedek,"* I thought in terror, "these people are all looking at me!"

Indeed, they were. And the drums were rumbling. And the dignitaries were waiting. I held onto my sphincters.

An aeon later, when I arrived on the stage and the drums became silent, Lord Proston immediately recognised me. "Here is our young friend whose thirst for questions is unquenchable," he smiled, referring to our last meeting. The disbelief I had shown had bordered on a breach of protocol.

"Oh no! Why is this happening to me?" I thought, swallowing hard and getting ready to repeat what Master Gervin had told me to say, carefully watching the expression on Lord Proston's face. The broad-shouldered forty-year-old man lawfully congratulated me as he had done with all the candidates before me. Speaking with great dignity and ease, he accompanied his words with eloquent hand gestures. Then an official handed a ribbon to him. A black ribbon, not a beige one.

"Let me place this distinction on your chest, that it may remind you of the grace of our Lord Melchisedek, by which you raised yourself to the highest degree of your caste and gained the privilege of serving His Majesty the Prince of the County of Sheringa," Lord Proston lawfully proclaimed, and moved towards me.

I immediately replied, "Many thanks, Most Venerable Lord, but I will decline this honour. Instead, I will follow Master Gervin of the Brown Robe and become part of his temple in the county of Eisraim."

Lord Proston opened his eyes wide, then frowned. All the dignitaries on the stage frowned after him.

Whispers of astonishment rippled through the crowd.

"Jail! Guaranteed by the Law!" I thought, anxiously watching his face.

Lord Proston looked down to the front rows of the audience, searching for Master Gervin. But to my great surprise, when he located him he just smiled in a strange way.

Following him like puppets, the dignitaries on the stage all started smiling.

For a few seconds, the King's representative and Gervin held each other's gaze. Clearly, they had met before. Even though Proston remained silent, it was as if he was talking with Gervin in a way that no one else could hear.

Then, still with his strange smile, Lord Proston turned towards me. *"May the will of our Lord Melchisedek be done!"* he pronounced in the ceremonial voice of a high-ranking member of the King's administration. Then he placed his large hand on my shoulder, "Go back to your master, my son."

I lawfully saluted him by bending my head slightly, and turned away.

The crowd hesitated, wondering whether to applaud or not.

Looking straight into Gervin's eyes, Lord Proston clapped his hands slowly.

As I walked down the stage steps, back to Gervin, the crowd applauded, following Lord Proston's slow rhythm. When I came back to my place, Gervin and Lord Proston were still looking into each other's eyes. Gervin too had a strange smile on his face.

Perplexed and exhausted, I sat down next to Master Gervin. Inside myself I praised the Lord Melchisedek and I rejoiced to see the end of my trials (or so I thought).

3.6 The death of Orlon, son of Orlon

By the time we returned to the place where Gervin was staying, I was totally worn out. Gervin gave me a mattress. I collapsed on it and slept for sixteen hours.

The next day when Gervin came to wake me up, he instructed me to get ready for a visit to a nearby tirtha.[1] I lawfully rejoiced. Everyone loved these places of pilgrimage. Was this one located by a lake, a waterfall, a river or a mountain top? Probably some beautiful place, even though, as the Law said, *what makes a tirtha a tirtha is not the beauty of the landscape, but a special quality of land energy*. I started preparing myself, for the Law ordained, *in a tirtha thou shalt feel elevated and inspired, and if sick, thou shalt make thyself ready to be healed.*

Walking opens the way to the wisdom of a tirtha. So, Gervin and I walked in an attitude of opening, reaching a small lake about an hour south of Sheringa city. When we arrived, we lawfully paid our respects to the water by chanting a few verses. Then we sat on a pontoon and tuned into the energy of the site.

Everything was tirtha-still. We let the wisdom of the place embrace us.

Gervin turned towards me, a mysterious glow in his eyes, "This is the beginning of a long adventure."

I had no idea what he meant, but I nodded gravely.

"There are some great challenges ahead of you," he said. "The greatest of all, especially in the early phases of your training, will be to change category and realise that you can be anything, and you can do anything."

This still did not mean much to me. I nodded gravely.

"*Anything!*" Gervin repeated in a deep voice.

---

[1] Pronounced teerta.

3 – The Book of the Call of Destiny

Following the principles of lawful rhetoric, I nodded gravely again.

Gervin shook his head in disapproval, "Son, puppets' rhetoric is not what will get you to enlightenment." Then he suddenly projected the power of his Voice at me, "Jump into the water!"

I had several times witnessed people of authority projecting an order with a particular force that compelled all those around to obey, but never anything like this. It was totally beyond my will. Before I realised what was happening, I was in the lake.

When my head emerged out of the water, I looked at Gervin with complete astonishment.

"Can you swim?" he asked.

"Hm... yes."

"Doesn't matter," he joked. Then he became solemn. "Listen, son," he pointed his finger at me. "There will come a time when forces of awesome magnitude turn against you to destroy you. By then, if you haven't become a mighty warrior of the Spirit, it isn't just you that will die – all those you love will be killed, and all the things that matter to you will be destroyed. This is why you are going to have to undergo a very difficult training."

He extended his hand towards me. Lifting me up onto the pontoon, he went on, "After I train you, when people project the Voice at you you will just smile. No more jumping into the water."

"Take off your clothes and throw them into the lake," he ordered. "You won't need them any more."

In any normal situation an instruction like this would have left me blank, or made me faint. But the words Gervin had hammered into me while I was in the water had stirred me to the depths. In this state of heightened awareness the water looked clearer, the mists were luminous, and the master's words made perfect sense to my soul.

I took off my beige clothes and threw them into the water.

From a small bag which he carried on his shoulder, Gervin took a white gown and handed it to me, "This is what the novitiates of the Salmon Robe wear."

I could hardly believe my ears. Was I being accepted into this prestigious order?

Amazed, I extended my hands towards the precious white gown.

Gervin promptly took the robe back, "Orlon son of Orlon will never become part of the Salmon Robe!"

He smiled at me and pointed his finger at the water. "Orlon son of Orlon is dead! We threw him into the lake."

It was a magical moment. A cumbersome part of myself had been shed like an old garment. I felt *light as a bird in the world of the gods*.

"From now on, your name is Szar!" Gervin said, handing me the white gown. And as I put it on, he chanted ritual mantras.

When the chanting was finished, he took me to the edge of the pontoon. "Come on, look at yourself!" he said.

Seeing myself clad in the white robe was strange and powerful. Every single day of my life, I had worn beige clothes, *as my father before me, and his father before him*. All of a sudden the beige had been peeled off my skin and my aura. I *did* look like a different person.

"This is not Orlon, son of Orlon the public servant!" Gervin was emphatic. "This is Szar, Szar the fiery, Szar the traveller, the one who will fulfil several of Gervin's prophecies."

I turned to him.

Orlon would have nodded gravely. I didn't.

Instead, I smiled.

Gervin understood. He smiled with me, and a great opening took place.

We sat on the edge of the pontoon, and he pulled two beautiful *pears of the Law* out of his bag. He gave me one, and bit into the other.

We ate the pears, silently contemplating the water and the mists.

3.7 The reception in Sheringa city's lawful town hall

The following day, Gervin had been invited to a reception held in the lawful town hall of Sheringa city. He invited me to go with him.

When we arrived, the hall was packed with important people dressed in complicated garments indicative of their high castes. They were chatting in small groups. Gervin went straight to a party gathered around Lord Proston.

To my amazement I realised that among the dozen dignified-looking men who were standing close to Lord Proston, two were wearing the richly decorated robe of the ministers of the prince of Sheringa.

When he saw us, Lord Proston interrupted his conversation. *"Praise the Lord Melchisedek, Master Gervin of the Brown Robe, and welcome to you!"* he said in lawfully ceremonial intonations. All in one voice, the dignitaries around him copied his words and tonal sequence.

"All glory to the Lord Melchisedek, Most Venerable Lord Proston of the Crimson Robe, Grand Superintendent of the Warp of Fields for the Counties of the South-East, in the Service of His Supreme Majesty the King of Atlantis!" Gervin answered in the lawfully appropriate tone of reverence.

Following Gervin's instructions, I remained silent.

"So you are depriving His Supreme Majesty the King of another precious asset," Lord Proston smiled at Gervin.

Despite the fact they had no idea what it meant, the twelve dignitaries imitated the mysterious smile on Lord Proston's face.

"What belongs to the King of Kings can only belong to the King of Kings," Gervin answered with a no-less-mysterious smile, patting my shoulder.

3 – The Book of the Call of Destiny

I missed the meaning, but Proston didn't. He burst out laughing. So did the dignitaries. Following protocol, I laughed with them. But Gervin did not.

One of the ministers turned towards him, "Sir Gervin of the Brown Robe, we were just discussing the alarming news we have been receiving from various parts of the kingdom. It seems the famous predictions you made more than twenty years ago are now coming true, one by one. Remind us of the words, Ferrate."

The man on his left recited, "When the keepers of the fields report changes in the red glow of the windmills of the Law, great disturbances in the climate will be observed. Crops will be destroyed by pests. Rituals will fail to bring down the rain. Entire counties will be devastated by drought, and others by floods. Many precious herbs will disappear, and so will rare birds dear to the gods. These signs will occur, and yet no one will listen. *Tremble, man of the Law!* Even greater perils are at hand. When the..."

"Thank you, Ferrate," the minister interrupted.

There was a heavy silence.

Lord Proston looked grim, "His Supreme Majesty the King of Atlantis is particularly concerned about the drought in the counties of the south-west."

The man who stood to his right commented, "These reports of catastrophes have astounded us, Gervin. I must confess that when the news first arrived, I myself did not even know the meaning of the word 'drought'. For thousands of years, thanks to the windmills of the Law, such things have been completely unheard of."

"Do you really think these natural disasters are caused by some sickness of the fields?" the other minister asked.

"Without any possible doubt," Gervin answered sharply.

"But how can you be so sure?" the minister went on. "Could it not be..."

Lord Proston interrupted him, "The fact that the drought began in the months following the alarming reports sent by the keepers of the fields certainly adds weight to your argument, Gervin."

"As you will remember, I am not the only one who has made predictions of this kind," Gervin pointed out.

"I can assure you that His Supreme Majesty the King knows about these predictions, Gervin," Proston was firm. "I have personally made sure that all of them were reported to him."

Someone else added, "The present events are so incredible, Master Gervin, that we cannot blame anyone for not having believed you when you prophesied them."

Gervin became stern. "And now that the facts are in front of you, will you still refuse to listen?"

There was another heavy silence. The minister asked, "But Gervin, do you *really* believe the kingdom could come to an end?"

Gervin closed his eyes for a few seconds. Then he reopened them and declared, "When the blue corn, precious to the gods, is attacked by an unknown insect, and when filosterops let themselves die for no reason, then *tremble, man of the Law*! Terrifying evils will befall the kingdom. Villages will be struck by madness. Neighbours will slaughter each other for no reason. Mothers will be seen slaying their own children. Entire counties will be ravaged by unknown pestilences against which the hymns of the Law will be powerless. Then... *the Lord Melchisedek have mercy on us*! Nothing in the seven spheres will be able to save the kingdom."

A priest shouted in outrage, "Master Gervin, are you implying that the hymns of the Law could be powerless and the..."

Lord Proston silenced him with a quick gesture. "When do you foresee the blue corn could start disappearing?"

Gervin let out a long sigh. "I used to think it could take up to a few generations. Now, after the recent developments in the warp of fields, I have changed my mind. A few decades at the most. We might not even last that long."

"Master Gervin, do you realise the enormity of what you are suggesting?" the minister looked unlawfully upset. "Are you seriously implying that the kingdom is about to end?"

"This is ridiculous!" the priest exclaimed with contempt. "Why should we listen to this unlawful nonsense?"

"Prophets come and go; the kingdom stays," someone else pondered.

"Thank you for your enlightened comments, wise men in the Law!" Lord Proston responded, smiling at the dignitaries in a way that indicated they could lawfully leave.

After saluting him with a reverent nod, they stepped back and left. Gervin held my arm to make sure I stayed by him.

Proston waited a few seconds. When they had all gone, he came close to Gervin and grinned, "Brown Robe or no Brown Robe, if you say things like that in public you are going to get into trouble, *my friend in the Law*!"

"I have been saying things like this for over twenty years," Gervin was composed.

"Oh, this I know only too well!" Lord Proston raised his hands, feigning exasperation.

Gervin laughed.

Then the most venerable lord became grave again, "Listen, other superintendents of the fields have passed on horrendous news to me in the last weeks. Other areas may soon be drought-stricken. The Western Plains, in particular. Tell me about this team of great Field Wizards you have gathered around you in Eisraim. Are they finding any workable solutions?"

"Our position is simple," Gervin said, "the only chance of saving the kingdom would be to disengage all energy fields. But who would ever listen to such advice? If we were to interrupt the fields, too many people would lose their power. Anyhow, at this stage... even that may not be enough to avoid the disaster. It is too late. The situation with the fields has

3 – The Book of the Call of Destiny

become so tangled that *any* modification could precipitate a collapse of the warp."

"Have you tried to adapt the rituals that tap energy from the fields?" Proston asked.

Gervin shook his head slowly. "Too late. Our assessment of the situation is very grim, Proston." After a pause, he asked, "What is happening at the palace of the King?"

"We are like you, and everybody else. We see the disaster coming, and we have no idea how it could be avoided," Proston's look was severe. "And what about this great enterprise of yours? Are you advancing?"

Gervin smiled but did not answer. For a moment, he and Proston looked at each other silently, as if they were talking to each other.

Then Proston nodded. "And how is my friend Lady Teyani of the White Eagle?" he asked with a broad smile.

"Stronger than ever!" Gervin's voice was soft.

"Good, good!" Proston said. "Will you send her my warm lawful regards?"

"Warmly lawfully certainly!"

Before taking leave, Proston turned towards me and took my arm, "Congratulations on your nomination to the *Most Ancient and Lawful Order* of the Salmon Robe, *my young friend in the Law*!"

I nodded politely.

With a teasing smile, Proston asked Gervin, "Is this boy to take part in the unfoldment of your prophecies?"

Solid as rock, Gervin nodded.

"Then," Proston pointed his index finger at my nose, "you have no idea, *my friend in the Law*," he said, looking straight into my eyes. "You have no idea!"

He and Gervin laughed.

I swallowed hard.

Later on in the evening, when Gervin and I were walking to the house where he was staying, I asked him, "Master Gervin, what did Lord Proston mean when he said I had no idea?"

"Mm..." Gervin answered thoughtfully. "Expect surprises, son! Expect surprises."

– Thus ends the Book of the Call of Destiny –

4

The Book of the Salmon Robe

4.1 First days in the temple of Eisraim

My first surprise on arriving at the temple of Eisraim, was to discover how big the place was. I found amazing its hundreds of chapels and meeting halls, all of them extremely holy because extremely ancient.

The outside walls of the chapels didn't look different from those of normal buildings. They just glowed faintly during the day and went dark at night. But inside the chapels, the *living walls* were made of a plass I had never seen before. It shone with a discrete but extraordinarily pure light, vibrant with the presence of the gods. In the halls of Melchisedek the plass seemed to be pure gold, radiant with the presence of the Law. Other chapels were bathed in a silvery glow, in the auburn hues of orichalc, or in breath-taking whiteness. And in the enclave of the jewels, where Master Gervin lived, the plass of the *living walls* was infused with the spirit of precious stones. There the rooms were like huge crystal geodes of emerald, topaz, sapphire, amethyst or aquamarine gems.

Whichever direction you looked, there was a lawful marvel to contemplate. And with its edifices of all sizes and shapes, its huge gardens full of imposing statues of the gods, its holy grounds and mausoleums that housed the relics of great saints, its catacombs and underground crypts, its large warehouses and large but reassuringly near-empty cow-sheds, the temple of Eisraim was the size of a small city. It would have taken half a day to walk around its full perimeter, especially for someone who, like me, enjoyed slow and peaceful walking.

The temple was surrounded by a thick high wall of stone-solid plass. In several places there were large archways through which people came in and out as they pleased. "We got rid of the gates thousands of years ago," Gervin explained as he showed me around. "There is so much power in Eisraim, no one would even consider attacking us."

4 – The Book of the Salmon Robe

Walking the alleys of the temple, I was fascinated by the multitude of colours worn by the priests and priestesses. "Nearly all the most important orders of the kingdom are represented here," Gervin commented as we strolled by the side of a small lake. This meant that Eisraim was a phenomenal repository of knowledge. For in the kingdom, all knowledge was deemed sacred, and no clear distinction was drawn between sacred lore, science, religion and spirituality, all these being gathered under the banner of the Law and given into the custody of priests and priestesses.

As we walked, nearly everyone greeted my teacher with a warm *"Praise the Lord Melchisedek, Master Gervin!"* to which he answered each time with a friendly smile, *"All glory to the Lord Melchisedek!"* If we met the same person again, the same greetings were exchanged, always with exquisite courtesy. This tended to slow us down considerably, but I didn't mind, especially in this serene and holy atmosphere.

I noticed some people did not salute Gervin. This was because they belonged to orders whose rule imposed total silence. On one occasion, Gervin saluted someone who did not answer but just walked past us as if we did not exist. "Take no offence," Gervin told me, "this often happens in our temple. These people don't mean to be rude. It is just that they are in the middle of such high spiritual concentration they can't even see us."

I marvelled that no one ended up in the lakes.

"Throughout the temple, there are energy fields that help them find their way," Gervin explained. "Thanks to these fields, our great mystics don't even have to open their eyes. They are being guided from inside, so they hardly need to be in their body. The priestesses of some female congregations, such as the order of the Dawn of Creation, live in extremely high spheres of consciousness and are only remotely connected to their physical body."

Gervin pointed to a high building in the distance. "See that tower? Some people will tell you it is where the priestesses of the order of Malchasek live. Nothing is less true!" he smiled. "In reality, these enlightened priestesses dwell in lofty spheres of Highness, in the company of Malchasek the great angel. And when they look down to the kingdom, they see this tower with their body in it. This is why a high priest of Eisraim, thousands of years ago, had such a tall tower built for them. So that when the priestesses looked down to the temple from Highness, they would easily see the tower, and then locate their physical body."

"Praise the Lord Melchisedek, Master Gervin of the Brown Robe!"

Gervin stopped to answer the greeting of an old priestess clad in a purple gown, *"All glory to the Lord Melchisedek, Mouridji the prophetess!"*

"So you have brought us a new recruit. From the county of Sheringa, I am told," the old lady said, examining me from head to toe. "Is he going to become one of the Brown Robe?" she asked.

"Szar is joining the Salmon Robe," Gervin answered.

Mouridji sighed, visibly disappointed. "My good Gervin, there are not many of your kind, are there?"

"True, Mouridji!" Gervin sighed with her.

"And how is little Lehrmon of the Brown Robe?"

"*Shining like a fig tree of life!*" Gervin smiled. "But he is no longer little, Mouridji. He has just turned twenty-six!"

"I know, I know... time passes so fast. But he was such a lovely little boy when you brought him to the temple. He was so sweet when he slept in Teyani's arms, wasn't he? How old was he then? Six, if I remember."

"Yes, Mouridji."

"Such lovely curly hair! In the last months he has been in the temple of Lasseera helping Master Esrevin, hasn't he?" the old priestess asked with conversational nonchalance.

"Yes, Mouridji."

"Esrevin is so busy over there, he can do with some help! And what about Melchard of the Brown Robe? He has just returned from his journey to the palace of the King of Atlantis, hasn't he? Must have been lawfully amazing!"

"Yes, Mouridji."

The conversation went on, and in the space of a few minutes Mouridji had sketched the comings and goings of a great number of people. After she left, Gervin commented, "Mouridji is a woman of sight and sharp insights. And she knows everyone in the temple. As a matter of fact, she probably already knows many things about you that you do not even know about yourself!"

As we skirted around a large building in the lawful centre of the temple, Gervin described, "This is where our space controllers operate. You know what controllers are, don't you?"

"The people who rescue astral travellers who have lost their way."

"Correct. But in Eisraim we have special space controllers, because our priests and priestesses astral travel so far away. Normal controllers would be incapable of following them, let alone rescuing them. So it has always been part of the tradition of our temple to train priests and priestesses to guide travellers and perform rescue operations even in the most remote spheres. Presently, our team of controllers is led by the White Eagles. Have you heard of them?"

I shook my head. As far as I knew, there was no order of the White Eagle in the county of Sheringa.

"It is one of the strongest orders in Eisraim," Gervin explained. "The White Eagles are led by Lady Teyani, who is also the grand master of the female wing of our temple. If I can, I will try to have one of her disciples take care of your initiation into travelling."

I had always regarded space controllers as heroes. The idea of being trained by people who could travel even further than space controllers filled me with awe.

4 – The Book of the Salmon Robe

Later, we arrived in a large courtyard at the heart of the enclave of the *Most Ancient and Lawful Orders*. A short, middle-aged man wearing a light-pink gown came to greet us. *"Praise the Lord Melchisedek, Master Gervin!"*

"All glory to the Lord Melchisedek, Prates of the Salmon Robe!"

The priest saluted me, and I lawfully returned his greeting.

"Is this young man the novice you have brought us?" Prates asked with a big smile.

"He sure is, Prates," Gervin answered, placing his arm around my shoulders. *"I bring him to you so he can grow in the Law, and learn the many wonders of your prestigious caste."* Turning towards me, Gervin added, "Prates is a great doctor of the Law, and the head of the Salmon Robe in Eisraim. His knowledge of rituals is immense. By the time you complete your training with him, you too will be a great doctor of the Law."

"Sixteen years is what it takes to complete the training of a Salmon Robe priest," Prates said with the smile that never left his face.

To a seventeen-year-old youth, sixteen years of studies sounded like a very long time indeed.

"This training will be your joy, Szar," Gervin said in a tone of encouragement. "You will find it illuminating. And we will see each other quite often. Tomorrow I will send someone to fetch you, and we will have a long talk."

Gervin left me with Prates, who took me to the large dormitory of the apprentices of the Salmon Robe. It was empty. All the other young men were in the middle of a ritual. I was given one of the low beds with a thin mattress and a few lawful utensils, and was left to rest.

In lawful Atlantean fashion I sat on the bed and looked straight in front of me, watching the yellowish glow of the plass wall and letting my mind become blank.

4.2 Training of the Salmon Robe priests

Gervin was right, the training of the Salmon Robe priests was an illumination.

First and foremost, there was the spellbinding magic of the Atlantean language. Through the power of the hymns of the Law, an entirely new world opened to me. The ritual way of chanting turned each verse into a powerful mantra, vibrant with life and ancient forces. *So* ancient! *So* holy! I spent entire days chanting and reciting hymns, fascinated by their beauty and their depth. I could never get enough. The more I repeated a verse, the more intoxicating it became. I had no mental framework to rationalise the experiences, yet my heart could appreciate their profound mystical dimension.

Then there was the knowledge. As stipulated by the Law of the kingdom, the priests were the keepers of all the ancient lore. Amongst them were many rituals used for healing. The Law said, "*To sing is to heal. There can be no better medicine than the hymns of the Law. He who knows the power of the hymns is the master physician.*" And there were rituals for all situations in life: sacraments to ensure children grew up harmoniously, funeral rites to help the dead find their way, clearings of negative energies from people and from the land. The rituals that secured rainfall and the perfect balance of the climate were not part of the functions of the Salmon Robe, as they were so simple that any village priest could perform them. But there were hundreds of other much more complicated rituals to learn. They not only involved the recitation of lengthy hymns but also the use of fruits, flowers, roots, gems, metals, minerals, animal substances, and ritual utensils – vases, cups, basins, flame holders, and so on. All these had to be placed, oriented, purified and consecrated in precisely codified ways so as to activate the laws and powers of nature. The rituals were so many, so long, and so technical, that I quickly understood why sixteen years would barely be long enough to know them all.

And as Master Gervin had predicted, I soon made fantastic friends. My class was comprised of twenty-nine apprentices, aged between twelve and twenty-five. It did not take long before the one who slept next to me became my friend – the best friend I had ever had. His name was Artold. Like me, *he had known seventeen springs and seventeen autumns*. He was such *a joy in the Law*. His eyes were *sweet like the mists in autumn*. He spoke a bit more slowly than other people (*very* slowly compared to Master Gervin) but he had such a lawful heart! In his company, I could totally relax. In most cases we hardly needed to speak, the understanding between us was intuitive. We just walked together in the alleys of the temple, or we sat silently in front of each other.

Every morning, we lawfully greeted each other, "*Praise the Lord Melchisedek, Artold! How are you, my friend in the Law?*"

"*All Glory to the Lord Melchisedek! Szar, my friend in the Law, I am well indeed. And you?*"

"*I am well indeed, Artold, thanks to the Good Lord Melchisedek! And how are your parents?*"

"*They are well, thanks to the grace of our Lord Melchisedek! And how are your parents, my friend in the Law?*"

"*I trust they are well, Artold, my friend in the Law, even though I have not heard from them for some time.*"

"*I trust this will be a beautiful morning of the Law, Szar, my friend in the Law...*"

And after such a friendly exchange, it was bound to be a lawfully good day.

Every few days, or less often when he had to travel, Master Gervin would spend some time with me. When Gervin called me it was arranged

4 – The Book of the Salmon Robe

with Prates that I would be excused from my normal duties for one or two hours.

When I visited his quarters in the enclave of the jewels, Gervin and I sat in the room where he received his visitors: the aquamarine chamber. It was an extremely holy place because built *so many lawful thousands of years ago*, and because the masters of the Brown Robe lineage had taught there before Gervin. In the charged presence held by the *living walls*, Gervin explained to me certain aspects of the Law that were not covered by the training of the Salmon Robe. Other times, we would walk together in the alleys of the temple and visit chapels, holy halls, shrines, sanctums and crypts. Some parts of the temple were such mazes of corridors! When I ventured out for a stroll on my own, it was not rare for me to get lost. *Thank the Lord Melchisedek*, there were plenty of helpful priests to walk me back to the quarters of the Salmon Robe.

Something that always amazed me was the power of the fields. Central to Atlantean technology, the fields were used for a great variety of purposes. The most lawful function of the fields was to establish strong spiritual connections within the perimeter of a chapel or holy hall. The effect was striking. As soon as you entered the chapel, you were filled with godly presence. Not all chapels felt the same, each was stamped with the presence of the god or angel to whom its altar was dedicated.

Entering an Atlantean chapel was magic – nothing short of an encounter with divine presence. This made walking through the temple an experience akin to travelling through the spheres.

One day, Gervin and I were wandering along an alley in the enclave of the thirty-three victorious gods, not far from his apartment. I suddenly felt a pull and my body came to a stop, right outside a chapel.

I could not take my eyes off the door of that chapel.

"I see!" Gervin burst out laughing.

I had no idea what he saw.

"Come!" he said, and as I was slow to respond he took my hand and walked me into the chapel.

It wasn't a very large chapel. The plass of the *living walls* shone with a special quality of gold, unlike the Spirit of any other building. As soon as I entered the field and saw the flame on the altar, I was so filled with awe that I became speechless (not uncommon for me), and on the edge of tears.

"Szar-ka," Gervin said – he often used the -ka of endearment when I became speechless – "would you like to know which god this chapel is dedicated to?"

I nodded anxiously.

"Lord Gana. A mighty god. One of those who were born at the very beginning of this cosmic cycle, long, long before human beings were created. He is venerated for his intelligence, and he is also said to be a great knower of the wisdom of the Dragon. Do you know what the Dragon is, Szar?"

I shook my head.

"The Dragon is an awesome, universal power. It permeates everything, not only the entire kingdom, the intermediary worlds and the worlds of the gods, but also the Underworlds and Further Down. The Dragon is fire – fire in the Earth, and fire beyond the heavens. It has many facets. Some are terrifying, even to the strongest of men; others are friendly and helpful, like the noble and magnificent Lord Gana."

Gervin paused, hoping that I would ask something. As I remained speechless, he went on, "Is Lord Gana calling you, Szar-ka?"

The idea that such a noble and magnificent god could be calling me filled me with wonder and bewilderment.

"How about I teach you the ritual way of greeting Lord Gana?"

I tried to say yes, but the emotion was too strong.

Gervin understood. *"Ha, Gana!"* he intoned in his strong ritual voice, lifting both arms vertically. *"Lobatchen Zerah!"* he continued, and as he finished the verse, he crossed his forearms on his chest, his fists clenched. *"Hera, Gana!"* he lifted his arms up again. *"Samayin ho Zerah!"* he concluded, his forearms crossed on his chest.

Copying his movements, I repeated after him, *"Ha, Gana! Lobatchen Zerah! Hera, Gana! Samayin ho Zerah!"*

"Very good, Szar-ka. Very good! Don't hesitate to come back here any time you like. Meditating in this chapel will be excellent for your spiritual development. Expect surprises, son!"

After this, the chapel of Lord Gana became my favourite inspirational hideaway. I often visited it, taking immense joy in offering some flowers on the altar and sitting in the light of the god, contemplating the *living walls*.

4.3 Wonder of wonders, the Law of Melchisedek

Not long after I arrived in Eisraim came the equinox of spring, the time of the yearly celebration of the Law of Melchisedek. The festival was comprised of a great number of ceremonies and rituals, and was attended by people of all castes. I had attended this festival every year since I was a little child. It was the great annual event of every village in the kingdom. But compared to the colossal ceremonies I was to witness in Eisraim, what I had seen up until then was nothing.

A few days before the equinox, delegations of priests and dignitaries from various castes began arriving at the temple. Long processions passed through the main portal. And the straight path of the Law – the temple's main alley – was full of people wearing robes of every imaginable colour. Rituals were conducted in all the chapels, and the fields were more highly charged than ever. The temple turned into a busy beehive, with priests and priestesses *lawfully mildly* hectically rushing in all directions. Lodging and

4 – The Book of the Salmon Robe

feeding so many people was no small enterprise! The logistics were significantly complicated by the fact that some visitors belonged to castes that were not supposed to come into contact with certain other castes. The enclave of lawful visitors and their adjacent dining halls therefore formed a perplexing maze where priests often got lost. The conflicting observances and requirements of these multifarious castes created an organisational imbroglio of cosmic proportions.

So many people gathered for the main opening ceremony that no hall was large enough to hold them. Instead, the Park of Lawful Congregations was used, and it took at least four hours before each person had taken position according to the Law of the castes (which dictated precisely where each group should stand in relation to each other group, and in what order people should arrive and leave).

Finally, Melchard, the high priest of Eisraim, made his entry. This was the first time I saw him. He was a tall man in his late forties. His curly brown hair and beard resembled a lion's mane. He walked slowly and with great dignity, flanked by two long lines of priests dressed in crimson robes and chanting the Law. For this special occasion, he too wore bright crimson garments, even though he was of the Brown Robe caste, like Master Gervin.

Having reached the altar at the centre of the park, he raised a loud voice, "*Praise the Lord Melchisedek!*" Spoken by this highly trained master of the Word, the enthralling magic of the Atlantean language took on yet a new dimension. The sounds that came out of his mouth were accompanied by sparks of bright white light that illuminated his aura.

The enthralled crowd responded, "*All glory to the Lord Melchisedek!*"

Melchard intoned one of the hymns of the Most Ancient and Holiest Body of the Law. "*He is the Lord of Lords, the King of Kings.*"

After each verse, the crowd repeated in one voice, "*All glory to the Lord Melchisedek!*"

"*He is our ancestor and our future, the father of all traditional orders in the kingdom.*"

"*All glory to the Lord Melchisedek!*"

"*The dawn of the gods he beheld, as he will contemplate the twilight of creation.*"

"*All glory to the Lord Melchisedek!*"

"*Shepherd of men, Spirit of the Law, priest of righteousness and lighthouse of all.*"

"*All glory to the Lord Melchisedek!*"

The ceremony was to go on for hours. But before long, I was so uplifted by the power of Melchard's voice that I lost touch with my body and fell into a swoon. Three priests carried me unconscious to the quarters of the Salmon Robe. It was a shame, for I was part of a large group of novices who had been duly prepared to carry on the chanting of hymns for a ritual to the Fertility of the Land later on. Unfortunately, I couldn't help it. Not just on this occasion but every time the spiritual intensity became high I fainted, which was in no way unusual for Atlantean people, whose consciousness was only loosely linked to their physical body.

When I woke up the morning after, I learned that I had missed *the night of the Law*, a moving ceremony in which all the delegations of priests walked to the nearby Holy Fontelayana river carrying torches and singing hymns to the Mother of the Endless Night. *Thank the Lord Melchisedek*, the yearly celebration still had many ceremonies to go!

That year, one of the highlights was the appearance of the Priestesses of the Dawn of Creation. Recruited from a particular caste that lived in the counties of the south, these women were the keepers of a primordial energy: the Spirit of Dawn, which vibrated in all things at the beginning of the world, but had long since disappeared. Apart from these priestesses, the Spirit of Dawn was known to less than a handful of high initiates in the entire kingdom.

This unique spiritual connection rested on an ancestral energy that the Priestesses of Dawn carried in their blood. The caste from which they originated was an ancient breed of small, dark-skinned, dark-haired people, whose stringent rules strictly forbade intermarriage with other castes.

The Law made it clear these priestesses fulfilled a critical function. They were the thread that linked the whole of humanity to the primordial Spirit of Dawn. Were this thread to be lost, the Law warned that the gods would have no choice but to give up on human beings, which would plunge the kingdom into unspeakable chaos. Thus the Law ordained that these priestesses be protected and cared for like the most precious of jewels. In order to preserve the purity of their space of consciousness, they remained secluded, refraining from any contact or interaction with all other castes save one: the Servants of the Priestesses of Dawn, who were dedicated entirely to their service and shielded them from the rest of the world.

A unique feature of these women-priests was that their faces could never be seen. On the rare occasions when one had a chance to approach them, only their body, limbs, and head could be seen, their hair remained covered by a shawl. But if one tried to look at their face, only a dark space could be seen. This, the Law explained, was because seeing their face was like seeing *that which is beyond the gods themselves.*

Only certain castes were allowed to attend this ceremony, which took place early in the morning in the fourth hall of Melchisedek, with all openings closed and the *living walls* dimmed so as to create semi-darkness. To begin with, as in all lawful functions the audience was left to wait for a few hours. The expectation was great. Public appearances of the Priestesses of Dawn were extremely rare.

When the precious women finally honoured the hall with their momentous presence, the audience let out a long, awe-struck "Oooh!"

There were perhaps thirty of them. Garbed in dark-orange dresses, they formed a tight cluster surrounded by at least twice as many attendants. In

4 – The Book of the Salmon Robe

the semi-darkness, it was difficult to judge if indeed their faces were invisible (a fact no one doubted, since it was ascertained by the Law).

As soon as they reached the stage, the priestesses started chanting the hymns of the Dawn of Creation, which were unlike any other chanting of the Law. This was yet another wonder of these priestesses: one might get to hear their chanting, but one would never be able to remember it. The hymns of the Dawn of Creation were a celebration of the unthinkable and unknowable. The Law said, *"Thou wilt listen, but thou wilt not hear, even less understand!"*

I fainted again. I was not the only one. At least a third of the audience fell unconscious. The effect was immediate: as soon as the chanting began, even highly trained priests lost touch with the kingdom, falling to the floor and into trance states of unfathomable depth. Many of them even wet their gowns.

Apart from wetting my gown, I slept an entire day and night. When I woke up, late the following morning, I didn't have the faintest recollection of what had happened, and I was surprised to find myself in bed. I thought only a few minutes had elapsed since the Priestesses of Dawn had arrived in the function hall.

A few days later, the climax of the yearly celebration was the ceremony of the Holy Blue Flame – one of the most magical wonders of Atlantean times. It was a large, predominantly blue flame, standing in a short chalice that rested on a broad triangular metallic plate, carried by three Crimson priests. The Flame was no fire in the physical meaning of the term. It did not burn the hand, it did not even warm the air around it. When beholding the flame, one could hear a special hissing sound – not a physical one, but a sound of energy.

The Holy Blue Flame was regarded as a direct manifestation of the Divine. *"The One God lives in the Flame,"* said the Law. *"Seeing the Flame is seeing God."* Lawfully understandably, before one could be allowed to behold the Flame, at least one day of fasting and lengthy purification rituals were required. The Park of Lawful Congregations was packed. When the short procession of the keepers of the Flame made its entry, a mighty wave of aspiration rose from the crowd. There it was, in front of all eyes: the Holy Blue Flame, shining with the Light of the One God.

"Stay with us, *my friend in the Law*! Stay with us!" good Prates whispered in my ear when he saw how aghast and abuzz I was at the sight of the flame.

I opened my mouth but was unable to answer him.

Melchard stood in front of the central altar and started a fire ceremony, pouring his Voice into the Flame.

The intensity of the ritual immediately transported me. From a distance, I vaguely heard Prates repeating, "Stay with us, Szar!"

I saw a great bright light, and fell to the ground.

Much later in the day when I woke up, I was in the sleeping quarters of the Salmon Robe where the security priests had carried me, as usual. It was then I learned that the equinoctial celebration of the Law was over. It had been a great success.

4.4 Fire rituals

During our talks, Master Gervin often exhorted me to speed up my studies. The concept was so foreign to me that at first I wondered if he meant I should try to make my sixteen years of training in the Salmon Robe pass more quickly. Speeding up was definitely not part of the teachings of the Salmon Robe. The Salmon Robes, like many other priestly orders, implicitly equated slowness with holiness. Nevertheless, I slowly came to the realisation that despite the fact that *sixteen years is what it takes to train a Salmon Robe priest*, I could perhaps digest the Salmon lore in fifteen, or even perhaps fourteen and a half years. The benefits of such an achievement were not obvious to me, but I loved Master Gervin dearly and desired nothing more in the kingdom than to come closer to him.

But what an effort it was to spend an hour with Gervin! He was so difficult to follow. I knew that he was a great doctor of the Law. Only great doctors of the Law lived in the enclave of the jewels. I had also heard that Gervin's lore was respected and admired as far as the neighbouring counties. Yet he often seemed to turn the principles of the Law upside down. He quoted verses that were never mentioned by the Salmon Robe priests, and that often seemed to disagree with their tenets. And when listening to him, I could never rest on what I had learnt and just relax. He kept asking me questions. These were not always complicated, but they often left me perplexed. And if by chance I came to fully understand what he meant, then he would show me some new aspect of the same topic that would leave me bewildered and yet again speechless.

"Do you understand why you really *need* to speed up?" he asked one day.

Even though we had discussed the topic many times in the last months, the answer to this question was still unclear to me.

As I remained silent, Gervin went on, "The reasons are as many as the chapels of our temple. For a start, trying to speed up your actions would greatly help your process of awakening."

The concept of awakening was so vague to me that Gervin preferred not to insist. "And how will you ever be capable of conversing with the gods if you do not speed up? *For the gods delight in that which is fast, and abhor slow contingencies.*"

The idea that I could ever converse with the gods sounded astonishing.

4 – The Book of the Salmon Robe

When he saw the stupefaction on my face, Gervin laughed. With his left hand, he picked out a large, juicy pear from a basket. It was one of those ambrosial *pears of the Law* that melted in the mouth. He threw the fruit in the air, caught it with his right hand, and then threw it to me. For he was worried to see me still so thin, and always liked to feed me.

Unfortunately, I missed the pear. The beautiful fruit landed on the plass floor with a thud.

Gervin whistled loudly. "We're going to *have* to do something, and it's going to *have* to be drastic!"

"I'll take care of it, Master Gervin!" I said, thinking he was talking about the juicy mess on the floor, and I immediately started cleaning up, using the bottom of my white gown as a rag.

"Mm..." Gervin took his head in his hands and contemplated the aqua-marine light of the ceiling, thoughtful. "A few thousand fire rituals, perhaps?" he murmured after a moment. "Do you know what fire rituals are, Szar?"

"*Thou shalt pour oblations into the fire, and thou shalt let the fire carry offerings to the gods,*" I recited.

"*Thou shalt indeed.* Extremely powerful rituals, these are. They raise the level of fire inside the officiating priest. They make his eyes and his aura shine. I think these rituals would do you a lot of good. I want you to start as soon as possible."

"But Master Gervin, the novices of the Salmon Robe are not allowed to perform fire rituals!"

"Well, then, tell Prates you don't want to be a novice any more!" Gervin answered in his jokingly serious voice.

I was speechless. Asking Prates for a promotion would have been outrageously unlawfully insolent.

"Ah, don't worry!" Gervin broke out into another of his smiles. "Let's go for a walk." When I completely ran out of answers his technique was to take me for a stroll, hoping the movement would help to activate my mind.

The following day to my complete surprise, Prates informed me I was to be initiated into my next degree. This was the end of my novitiate. I was no longer to wear a white gown but a light-pink one – the Salmon Robe! – like Artold and my other friends.

The ceremony was magnificent. Amidst hundreds of lamp oils, mantras were chanted for an entire day. Under the guidance of Prates, my young friends carried out many of the ritual performances in which the Salmon Robe priests excelled.

After only half an hour, I felt so high and so ecstatic that I fainted, as many other novices going through the same initiation had done before me. Prates, the *wise man in the Law*, used a special technique based on projecting forces into some of my gateways, or centres of energy. Soon, I was back in my body, and the ceremony resumed. Prates had to keep on repeating the technique throughout the day, but it worked wonders. Each time

I fainted, he brought me back to my senses in less than twenty minutes! And at the end of the ceremony (which went on until late that night, and had to be continued throughout the next day), I was entrusted with the secret symbols and recognition signs of the Salmon Robe.

In the days that followed, Prates began instructing me in the lore of fire rituals. There were hundreds of them, each dedicated to different gods and angels, and performed for a great variety of purposes: boosting the fertility of the land, clearing negative energies, blessing water streams, consecrating tree houses and filling them with angelic presence, blessing plass walls in a building, achieving longevity, asking favours from the gods, and so on. But the general principle of all fire rituals was the same: a fire was lit and oblations, such as spoonfuls of sacred oil, were poured into the fire while chanting powerful mantras. Often, the voice of the officiant priest became the oblation poured into the fire.

The fire and the sacred oils were but the external forms of extraordinarily powerful processes of energy. Each time the oblation reached the fire, a cosmic click took place. A Spirit impulse sparked the consciousness of the priest, resulting in a tangible change in the surrounding space. The chapels in which daily fire rituals were conducted were highly charged, and teeming with spiritual presence.

Encouraged by Prates and Gervin, I started performing fire rituals in great measure. I had to begin slowly and get accustomed to the spiritual intensity gradually – indispensable precautions without which apprentice ritualists could be stricken with fever, convulsions, madness, and even sudden death. But after a few months, I found myself practising on the fire seven hours a day, and a great result was achieved: I no longer fainted when the intensity of my rituals became high (although unfortunately I still fainted when attending other people's rituals). Nonetheless, Gervin regarded this as a major breakthrough, and he encouraged me to persevere relentlessly in my practice.

Once, as we were walking along the temple's alleys, he asked me, "Have you had any interesting experiences when meditating in the chapel of Lord Gana, lately?"

"Master Gervin, unfortunately I have had no opportunity to visit this holy chapel for weeks, as I am so busy performing the fire rituals."

"*How sad in the Law!*" Gervin looked straight in front of him, in a direction where I could see nothing. Then he declared, "I think it is time for you to start directing more of your fire rituals to Lord Gana." After a pause, he plunged his eyes into mine and added, "And ask him to help you awaken!"

We walked along a little further. "If Golden Cudgel was not such *a complete idiot in the Law*," Gervin went on in his exquisitely polite voice, "we could ask him to help you."

Golden Cudgel was the Dark-Golden Robe priest who held the office of high priest of Gana for the temple of Eisraim.

4 – The Book of the Salmon Robe

"But you would be better off asking old Gana-Gerent. He knows *an awful lawful lot* about Gana's lore."

4.5 The years of fire rituals

The next morning, Gervin arranged for Gana-Gerent to meet me in Lord Gana's chapel.

Gana-Gerent was a very old man with not one hair left on his shiny head. He wore a beige gown of an order unknown to me. This, by the way, was one of my dramas. While studying in Sheringa I had spent *years* learning about the Law of the castes, one of my favourite disciplines at that time. But after arriving in Eisraim I discovered to my dismay that virtually none of the castes of my native county were represented in the temple. The castes of the county of Eisraim were completely unknown to me, which often put me in the embarrassing situation of not knowing how to salute people the proper way.

"*Praise the Lord Melchisedek, Szar of the Salmon Robe!*" Gana-Gerent greeted me with an expansive smile that revealed the best of his four-and-a-half remaining teeth. "So I hear you are a great admirer of Gana the Wise! Come and sit with me, *my young friend in the Law*, I have many things to tell you."

Because he shone with the particular quality of golden light that glowed from the *living walls* of Lord Gana's chapel, I immediately took a liking to him.

Gana-Gerent started by teaching me some of Lord Gana's traditional attributes: his golden helmet of far-reaching vision and omniscience, and the occult cudgel with which he had slain many dark forces during the ancient wars in the heavens when the gods were fighting their titanic enemies, the asuras.

Particularly fascinating to me was the huge five-legged beast that was carved on the wall behind the altar. When I asked Gana-Gerent about it, he answered, "This white beast is called an elephanto. It is Lord Gana's friend. But the leg in the front is not a leg, it's his nose!"

"His nose?" I marvelled.

"Elephantos are huge, at least ten times larger than horses! They live in the world of the gods and in the fields of stars," Gana-Gerent elucidated.

The fields of stars were mentioned in many legends of the Law. They were dark spaces in which hundreds of tiny dots of light were hanging. No one could see them, for they lay beyond the thick mists that covered the kingdom. But the educated people who knew about these legends never doubted their reality, since they were attested to by the Law.

I looked skywards, trying to picture a white elephanto flying in a field of stars.

"According to some people," Gana-Gerent said, "there are also elephantos living in the kingdom, in the counties of the south. Anyhow, what matters is that Lord Gana's sense of smell is as powerful as that of elephantos. He can smell far down into the Earth and the Underworld."

My mouth dropped open in admiration.

The next thing Gana-Gerent taught me was how to perform fire rituals to Lord Gana. As I already knew a number of fire rituals, it was easy. All I really needed were the mantras to invoke Gana. The rest of the practices were somewhat similar with only variations in the type of hand-gestures, utensils, flowers, fruits, grains, coloured powders and other substances that were to be offered.

Yet the results were more spectacular than with any other rituals I had ever conducted. As soon as I started pouring my voice into the flame, I was transported high in Lord Gana's light, as if carried by some invisible elephanto. I completely lost touch with time.

When I came back to my normal self, I was lying on the floor. Good Gana-Gerent, who was sitting by my side, welcomed me back to the kingdom with his broad smile, *"Lawfully good?"*

"Mm..." I sat up, noticing the night had come. Trying my best to find words to express the ecstatic feeling and the explosion of light inside my heart, I hesitated a few seconds. "Lawfully good!" I finally answered.

Gana-Gerent understood.

After that day, most of my free time was occupied with fire rituals to Lord Gana. The priests of the Salmon Robe had many lawful duties and hours of ritual work to perform every day, but whenever I could I directed my offerings to the god with the golden helmet. And as Master Gervin often exhorted me to do, I prayed for awakening.

But what was awakening?

The more Gervin tried to explain it to me, the less I seemed to understand.

"When you practise your fire rituals, especially to Lord Gana, do you sometimes feel a *big* energy above your head?" Gervin asked me one day.

"Yes," I answered confidently.

"It is my hope that this energy will assist you in your effort of awakening," Gervin said. "But you must keep asking Lord Gana for his help, for there are many blissful sleepers who handle the Great Light of fire rituals daily, and yet never awaken."

I did ask for Lord Gana's help. But I could not grasp what it was that I was supposed to achieve. Month after month, Gervin pointed my attention to certain changes inside me which, he said, indicated that 'some awakening' was taking place. For instance, I fainted less often. A certain fiery quality had awakened in my body of energy (this was no wonder, since I spent more or less seven days a week sitting in front of a flame), and my voice had been significantly reinforced by the thousands of hymns I had chanted since my arrival in Eisraim.

4 – The Book of the Salmon Robe

"But, but, but..." Gervin repeated to me, "you still have no idea what awakening is about, have you?"

Each time he asked, all I could do was to remain silent and try to read the answer in his piercing grey-green eyes.

"Keep practising and praying, *my friend in the Law*!" Gervin encouraged me with his warm smile. "And remember that you can *be* anything, and you can *do* anything."

I could see he was waiting for some dramatic change to take place inside me. But what?

Following his instructions, I kept on and on with the fire rituals. I usually officiated in the chapels of the Salmon Robe priests, and whenever I could I went to do additional practices in Lord Gana's chapel, in particular at sunrise and sunset, times which Gervin had described as especially conducive to awakening. But hundreds of sunsets passed, and I still had no idea what awakening meant.

Quite understandably, after another year of constant practice I started mastering the process of fire ritual. Prates was happy with my progress. "Good spark! Good spark!" he would say. And after watching my efforts for a few more months, he invited me to become part of one of the teams of priests who officiated in the crypt of the Eternal Fire.

Located in the lawful centre of the temple, the crypt of the Eternal Fire was a very special place, in which *fire rituals had been performed without interruption for thousands of years*, said the Law of the temple. Priests from different castes took shifts to sit behind one of the three eternal flames and perform the amritayagya, or fire ritual of immortality.

The spiritual presence held by the *living walls* of the crypt was awesome. Each time a mantra was poured into the fire, huge sparks of light could be seen in the astral space. The crypt felt as if it was constantly being shaken by an earthquake of energy. During my first shifts, Prates stayed close to me to make sure I coped with the power of the amritayagya. But paradoxically, I never fainted when I was on duty down there. I thrived on the exalted Spirit that was vibrant in the crypt.

This triggered great hopes in Master Gervin. "When you officiate in the amritayagya," he explained to me, "you are much more awake than usual. If you could retain the state when you come out of the crypt, you would make immense progress."

I could relate to the fact that I felt different when I was in the crypt. But how? And why? As soon as I left the crypt, I went back to my normal self. Worse still, when I witnessed other ceremonies I kept fainting as usual. The truth was, I would have loved to follow Master Gervin's instructions, but I simply didn't know what to do.

"Keep on keeping on. Practise and pray!" Gervin encouraged me.

"*All glory to the teacher!*" I answered with hope. But months passed, and no decisive change took place. Master Gervin's awakening remained a complete mystery to me.

4.6 Darkness visible

One day, on his return from a journey out of the county of Eisraim, Gervin called me to the aquamarine chamber. As always, he started with praising the Lord Melchisedek and inquiring after my health, for I was still – by far! – the skinniest of all the Salmon Robe priests, despite everyone's insistence on feeding me all the *delicacies of the Law* the temple could offer.

"How long since you arrived at the temple?" Gervin asked.

"*Four springs and four autumns,*" I answered in lawful fashion.

"Mm..." Gervin closed his eyes and took his head in his hands. "If we do not speed up your awakening, we are going to end up running out of time."

I nodded in my *lawfully patiently* helpless way.

"Come on," he said, "let us try something radically different." And he invited me to sit in meditation position in front of him.

Often when I visited him we sat together and entered a contemplative state. That day while keeping eye contact Gervin projected a completely new intensity of consciousness into me. The light in the room went from aquamarine to dark. I felt a strong vibration between my eyebrows. My body became rock-still.

The feeling was not particularly pleasant. It reminded me of a painful experience two years earlier, when Artold and I had ingested mushrooms by mistake. The central kitchen, which supplied the fruits needed for our rituals, had wrongly delivered the mushrooms to us instead of to the order of the Wise Witches of the Law. After eating the mushrooms at the end of the ritual, we had been seized with violent hallucinations that had left Artold sick for a week and myself unconscious for a day and a half.

"Can you speak?" Gervin asked.

I couldn't. I had completely lost touch with the room. But I could still hear him. Instead of falling unconscious as usual, I found myself in a huge dark space.

"Darkness visible. The non-physical sphere that is the closest to the kingdom," Gervin explained.

The experience was not unfamiliar. It was reminiscent of my nightly drifting out of the body, but much less dream-like. It was the first time I found myself in the space whilst retaining some waking consciousness.

"Come on, move!" Gervin urged.

I found myself spinning forwards in darkness visible, as if caught by a powerful whirlpool.

"Very good, son! Very good! Now look at this. *By this symbol you will know me!*"

A magnificent golden shape was glowing in front of me. It was a complicated pattern of intricate geometrical figures.

4 – The Book of the Salmon Robe

"These are my recognition symbols," Gervin explained. "Now look at these."

Another set of golden geometrical shapes appeared in the space.

"*All glory to the teacher!*" he exclaimed. "These are the recognition symbols of Orest, who was my teacher in the Brown Robe. The fact that he left his physical body long ago does not make any difference, his recognition symbols have remained the same."

The former symbols reappeared. "If you ever happen to be in danger, bring this symbol to your mind and call on me through it," Gervin instructed me. Then he brought my consciousness back into the room. It was instant and painless, but I suddenly felt extremely sleepy.

When he saw the look of vagueness on my face, Gervin laughed. "I think we had better ask someone to escort you back to your quarters," he said, and went out to look for a *lawful attendant*.

That was the last thing I remembered from this meeting. I woke up in my dormitory the next day.

Every few days Gervin took me back into the space of darkness visible. He showed me different recognition symbols, and taught me how to use space-tunnels of energy in order to spin faster and faster. And the great progress was that I no longer fell unconscious at the end of the sessions. In most cases, I could walk to my dormitory by myself.

After a few weeks, Master Gervin announced that he was satisfied with my experiences and that the time had come for me to undergo a formal initiation into travelling.

"Let me explain how this will happen. On a certain day of the calendar, when all the rhythms of time are lawfully auspicious, you will be taken to a part of the temple that you have not yet visited: the travelling chambers. There you will be put in a mild state of hibernation. For your security, your body will be placed in a plass sarcophagus through which no foreign energies can penetrate. Then, once you are deeply asleep, your instructors will arrive. They will project you out of your body by activating certain gateways of energy, using their Voices. And then they will guide you and teach you how to find your way through the spheres."

To reassure me, Gervin added, "I have asked the White Eagles to take care of your travelling education, and very fortunately, they have accepted! Your instructor will be one of the most accomplished controllers of our temple – a woman of considerable travelling experience. She is one of the high priestesses of the White Eagle, and she was trained by the famous Lady Teyani herself.

Her name is Lady Elyani."

– Thus ends the Book of the Salmon Robe –

5

The Book of the Mysteries of Eisraim

5.1 Travelling, the first initiation

My first flight was to take place at night, in the enclave of the lawful physicians. At the end of a day of fasting, two priests from the healing chambers came to fetch me. I followed them through a labyrinth of alleys and corridors until we finally arrived at a strange building where the *living walls* of the hallways glowed with pulsing colours in the dark mauve, indigo and violet range. The priests led me to a room bathed in a dimmer pulsing light of the same colours. Lines of a spirit of chrysolite, emanating a dark orange glow, traversed the floor forming luminescent geometric patterns.

A lightly-built sarcophagus, made of thin, translucent plass, stood upon the centre of a fiery geometric shape in the middle of the room. I was instructed to lie in the sarcophagus, which remained uncovered until, as I was later to know, I could no longer perceive my physical environment. The priests began incantations of verses of the Law while pressing gateways on my body. The result was nearly immediate: I fell into a deep, trance-like sleep.

My next perception was that of strange sounds which, I learned later, were Voice-projections of Lady Elyani and Lady Seyani, her sister in the White Eagle. I found myself floating in darkness visible. The space was identical to the one where Gervin had taken me several times in the last weeks, but the difference was, I didn't feel sleepy at all. On the contrary, I was teeming with energy.

Looking around me I realised that the space was not as dark as I had thought previously. It was permeated by a diffuse purple glow, and in the distance I could discern faint lights of different colours.

5 – The Book of the Mysteries of Eisraim

"Szar of the Salmon Robe!" I heard a woman's voice summoning me. "I am Elyani of the White Eagle, your travelling instructor. I will be taking you for journeys through spaces, step by step. Follow my voice and my presence." Then she added, *"By this symbol you will know me."*

A set of geometric shapes appeared in front of me. Unlike that of Gervin, her astral signature wasn't golden but shining white.

"In most cases, you will just have to follow my light," the voice continued. As she spoke, a warm yellow light appeared in front of me. "This is not me," she explained "but a reflection of myself that I project in the space to guide you. Come, follow the light."

I moved towards the golden-yellow presence.

It was easy and joyful. Following her light I realised that when I had out-of-body experiences at night, I had absolutely no idea where I was going. I never chose my direction, being swayed by waves I did not understand. Now for the first time in my life, I was completely in control of my movements in the space.

"Szar, can you perceive the tunnel in front of you?"

"Yes."

"Go into it. Follow my light," the voice said.

As soon as I reached the tunnel, I was sucked into it and sent spinning forward at high speed. I soon emerged at the other end and found myself in a different space, in which the diffuse purple glow was slightly brighter.

"We are still in darkness visible, but higher up," Elyani explained.

I felt enthused, and *light as a bird in the world of the gods*.

"Now try to move up."

That was easy. I zapped upwards, leaving Elyani's light below me.

"Excellent!" the voice encouraged me. "Now show us what you can do. Try to move up as high as you can!"

I gathered my energy and let myself be pulled up by the space. There followed an exhilarating feeling of acceleration accompanied by ultra-fast spinning. And lo! I found myself in a completely different space.

No more darkness.

"*Oh my Lord Melchisedek!*" I exclaimed, profoundly moved by the incredible beauty of what was before me. "So this is what the fields of stars look like!"

In the kingdom, the furthest you could ever see was a few hundred lawful feet ahead, and in winter the mists were sometimes so thick that you could hardly see your feet. And there, in front of me, was a clear space of infinity. It was gigantic, mythical, *lawfully unreal!* Myriads of shining dots of all colours formed large clouds of light extending in all directions. But before I had time to contemplate the cosmic landscape, I suddenly lost my smooth trajectory. I was propelled to the right. Caught by violent eddies, I started rolling and tumbling like a ball of dust caught in a tornado.

It was only much later that I learned what had happened. Down below in the take-off room, when they saw the way I projected myself from darkness visible into the field of stars, Lady Elyani and Lady Seyani were pleasantly surprised. They beamed joyfully.

"This one is Gervin's man, isn't he?" Seyani asked.

"He certainly is! There is something about him, isn't there?" Elyani answered, looking through the thin translucent slab that covered the sarcophagus.

Surprised at her friend's enthusiastic tone, Seyani chuckled. "Lady Elyani! What do I see?" Quoting a chaperone's verse of the Law, she added, *"The man has charm, and is from the right caste!"*

Elyani blushed. "Seyani! What are you saying!" And for a moment she lost her concentration and let go of the trajectory control.

"Hold on, hold on!" Seyani burst out laughing, "You are losing him already!"

Up there, in the field of stars, as soon as I started rolling, something completely unexpected took place. Before I had time to be afraid, a voice made itself heard. Not Elyani's voice. An eerie whisper that seemed to come from infinitely far away. *"Fear not, traveller! Call on the Universal Knowledge Bank. Let it restore your trajectory."*

The voice had spoken in no time, as if all the words were uttered at once. It projected me into a different consciousness where thoughts moved incalculably faster than usual. I *knew* how to tap from the Universal Knowledge Bank. My trajectory was instantly stabilised.

The timeless voice continued, *"Move forth, child of the stars. The Earth's Dragon of the Deep is waiting. Only when you meet her will the sleeper awaken."*

Meanwhile, Lady Elyani had wasted no time in surrounding me with her light. But when she saw me flying straight, she refrained from intervening.

"Lawfully good!" she exclaimed with surprise. "In a space so close to us there was little risk but still... that was remarkably well done! Keep moving forwards."

It suddenly came to me that in the four years I had spent in the temple, this was the first time someone had told me I had done something remarkably well.

The faraway voice was still vibrant in my mind. It made me feel strange. As I kept moving in a straight line amongst the magnificence of the field of stars, it whispered again, *"Move forth, child of the stars. The Dragon of the Deep is waiting."*

"Enough for today. Now, start going down," Elyani instructed. I did as she said and after a short while I heard, "There is a tunnel coming on your left. Take it and move down."

The tunnel took me back to the dim purple space where I had started.

I felt heavier and heavier. The magnificent clarity of mind which I had enjoyed in the fields of stars eluded me. The further down I glided, the thicker my consciousness became.

Soon, I fell asleep again.

When I came back to my senses I felt dizzy but elated, vivid impressions of the field of stars flashing in front of me. The cover of the translucent sarcophagus had been removed. The two priests of the healing chambers were waiting for me.

I looked around for Lady Elyani, but there was no one else in the room.

5.2 Lehrmon of the Brown Robe

The next time I met Gervin, he kept eye contact with me for a long time. Then his voice became grave. "A change is taking place in you, Szar. Do you understand what it is?"

I didn't have a clue what he was talking about. I remained silent.

"A part of you is being called to awakening. It happened while you were travelling in the field of stars."

Was it the faraway voice? Or was it the elation that flared inside me when I zapped through the spheres?

Gervin continued, "You may not yet realise it but from here on, things are going to become radically different for you. All this will happen gradually, of course. It will not always make life simpler for you." After a pause, he added, "But who wants to remain asleep?" He hammered his words into me, branding my energy with his most penetrating gaze.

"You will continue your fire rituals and your travelling initiation. But the thing that matters most is neither of these. The one thing you need most in the seven spheres..." he paused.

I looked at him anxiously, wondering what was the thing I needed most in the seven spheres.

"...is to awaken!" he hammered again. "Stop being a sleeper!"

The perplexed look on my face made him smile affectionately. "Why don't we discuss this with Lehrmon?" he suggested. "You know who Lehrmon is, don't you? He is my disciple in the Brown Robe. In the last years he has mostly been at the temple of Lasseera, which is why you have not had the opportunity to meet him. But at the moment he is in the temple. It would probably do you a lot of good to see someone who has been working with me for..." Gervin closed his eyes. Then he smiled, "nearly twenty-five years. Lehrmon is an awakened one."

Gervin waited for me to go and get Lehrmon.

I remained at a loss, having no idea where Lehrmon was.

"If you go out and ask Shlsharan, he will tell you where to find him."

I didn't know who Shlsharan was.

"Walk out into the hallway," Gervin said patiently. "In the second apartment on the left, you will find Shlsharan of the Saffron Robe."

I smiled at Gervin and left the room. I turned left and found the second door.

It was open. I walked in, looking up to the doorway's arched ceiling. In the enclave of the jewels all doorways were twelve lawful feet high, so great sages with tall auras didn't bump their astral head in the plass walls when they walked into a room.

There was no one in the room, the *living walls* of plass mingled with yellow sapphire spirit. Captivated by the lemon glow, I waited for Shlsharan, pondering on Master Gervin's exhortations to wake up. Then my mind started drifting. Absorbed as I was in the luminescent spirit, time passed unnoticed.

How long did it last? I could not tell. Perhaps an hour, perhaps more. Finally, a man entered.

"*Praise the Lord Melchisedek, wise man of in the Law!*" I said, "Are you Shlsharan of the Saffron Robe? I am looking for Lehrmon."

The man frowned. He plunged his intense amber eyes into me for a few seconds.

He was in his early lawful thirties – far too young to be called '*wise man in the Law*'. Besides, I suddenly realised he was dressed in a brown gown, as only Gervin and Melchard wore.

"Hum..." I looked for an appropriate verse.

The man passed his hand through his thick fleece of dark-brown curly hair and smiled, "You are Szar, aren't you?"

"I... *I am, in the Law.*"

"I am Lehrmon. Of the Brown Robe!" he said, still smiling. "Now, follow me."

He didn't take me back to Gervin's room, but to one of the *lawful attendants of the enclave*. Time having passed, Gervin had been called to other occupations.

As I walked back to my room, it crossed my mind that Gervin may not have been very pleased with the way I had handled the situation.

5.3 Square, intermediary worlds, triangle

Every few days, in the middle of the morning, the two priests from the healing chambers came to collect me. They were tall, strong men whose function was to carry people who were unconscious, or too sick to move. They never said a word. They just called me with a gesture of the hand, and I followed them to the take-off room.

Lady Elyani was never in the room when I arrived. I lay down in the sarcophagus, and the two priests put me to sleep by activating gateways on various parts of my body.

Then while I was unconscious, Lady Elyani arrived and projected strong Voice frequencies onto me. At that moment I would always recover the thread of my consciousness and find myself in the purple space.

5 – The Book of the Mysteries of Eisraim

"Szar! *I greet you at the top of the square!*" Elyani saluted me.

"*All glory to the Lord Melchisedek, Lady Elyani of the White Eagle!*" I replied.

"No, this is not the way to salute me. You are now in the lower part of darkness visible, in the layer that is closest to the physical plane. The physical plane, or kingdom, is called the square," she explained. "You must greet me as I greeted you."

"*I greet you at the top of the square!*"

"Start moving up," she ordered. And while I ascended along a slow vortex of the purple space, she explained, "Darkness visible is one of the intermediary worlds, so called because they are located between the square (or kingdom), and the triangle (or worlds of the gods)."

In various teachings of the Law the 'square' was used to refer to the kingdom, but this was the first time I heard the word triangle being used to refer to celestial worlds. In the state of enhanced mental clarity I enjoyed when travelling, it made a lot of sense to me that the layers between the square and the triangle should be called intermediary worlds.

"The spheres in our lawful proximity are comprised of the square, the intermediary worlds and the worlds of the gods," Elyani went on, while her yellow light appeared in the space. "Come towards me. Take this tunnel."

I followed her light through a vortex-tunnel that led me to a different space.

"Keep spinning forwards!" she directed me to another tunnel.

When I came out of the spinning exercise, I found myself in a completely different space. It was much darker than the purple darkness visible where we had started.

"You are now in the second layer of the intermediary worlds," Elyani said. "As you understand, darkness visible is only the lowest echelon of the intermediary worlds. Now take the silvery vortex on your right."

What was exhilarating about these tunnel-vortices was not just the spinning, but the acceleration. It was like being projected from one space to another at increasing speed. The higher up I went, the faster it moved. At the end of the tunnel I found myself surrounded by a beautiful green astral light.

"The emerald intermediary world," Elyani commented. "Before we can go further, you must become expert at identifying these layers."

I hovered around for some time, letting the emerald light work on my consciousness.

"Now, let me take you straight to the upper limits of the intermediary worlds," Elyani said.

I followed her light through a sequence of increasingly fast vortices, until I emerged in a different region lit by a diffuse silvery light. Taking a closer look, I realised that the space was filled with silvery specks of light.

"Szar traveller," Elyani said, "*I greet you at the top of the intermediary worlds.*"

"*I greet you at the top of the intermediary worlds,*" I replied, copying her ritual voice.

"You are now at the great borderline between the intermediary worlds and the triangle," she advised. "If it were not for the symbols that I project around you, you would already have all the controllers of the kingdom after you. Only experienced travellers should visit these areas. Simple sleepers would lose their way, they would have great difficulties returning to their body from here. Now, get ready to cross the great borderline!"

I did not have to do anything, I was pulled up by Elyani's guiding power. And lo! I found myself in the field of stars once more.

"Szar traveller, *I greet you at the bottom of the triangle.*"

"*I greet you at the bottom of the triangle*," I replied.

But where were the gods? Were they the clouds of stars that filled all the directions of space?

"Move to your right and tell me, what can you sense, Szar?"

"Some kind of gentle draught."

"Right! This is called a stream. Look carefully and you will see thin particles of light flowing along the stream."

It was so subtle that it eluded me at first. But by concentrating, I began to discern the stream of light particles.

"Some people call them angel's hair," Elyani said. "Now, let the stream carry you."

As soon as I was close enough to the stream, I started moving at a steady pace. "Very easy!" I laughed with joy.

"All you have to do is hold onto the stream," she answered in a smiling voice.

I was gliding in the space, feeling very much at home among the eerie scenery of coloured clouds of stars, and marvelling at how clear everything was in this layer. Was this akin to the awakening that Master Gervin wanted me to find?

"If you want to you can speed up now," Elyani put to me. "But do it gently! The stream will exaggerate your acceleration."

Following her instruction, I found that the slightest impulse could speed up my movements dramatically. But even going much faster, I had no difficulty remaining stable, effortlessly being carried by the stream. It made me wonder what extraordinary speed a master traveller such as like Lady Elyani could reach when riding streams.

"Relinquish control," Elyani instructed me. "You are coming to a node – a crossing. I'll redirect your path."

A few seconds later I found myself abruptly shifting down and towards the right, zapping along on a new stream. Despite the mind-boggling speed, there had not been the least tremor while switching trajectories.

I felt different. When changing streams, my energy changed.

It was as if I had just gone from the field of one chapel to that of another.

5 – The Book of the Mysteries of Eisraim

I was left to continue my beam-riding for some time. Then Elyani directed me towards a vortex-tunnel that projected me back into the intermediary worlds. The field of stars disappeared, replaced by the dim glow of darkness visible.

I soon started feeling the heaviness that indicated I was close to my body. In a matter of seconds I fell unconscious.

When I came back to my senses, I sat up in the sarcophagus. Lady Elyani had gone, the two priests were back.

Slowly, I got up and followed the two men back to the quarters of the Salmon Robe.

5.4 The 'something' I was missing

A few days later, the meeting with Gervin and Lehrmon finally took place.

When I arrived at the aquamarine chamber, I found the two Brown Robes in the middle of an animated discussion. They stood up to greet me, and after we lawfully praised the Lord Melchisedek Master Gervin inquired about my health.

There was a special atmosphere in the room, not unlike what I had felt when I first met Gervin in the county of Sheringa.

"Szar," Gervin asked me after a few more lawful trivia, "have you noticed that when travelling in the spheres, you are much more awake?"

I nodded. Despite my vagueness, I could recognise that I was clearer when I followed Elyani's light in the spaces.

"Why do you think this is, Szar?" he asked.

Perplexed, I remained silent.

Gervin turned to his disciple in the Brown Robe, "Lehrmon, what do you say?"

Lehrmon smiled at me in such a friendly way that I was warmed from head to toe. "Like all of us when we travel, Szar escapes the sandman effect inherent to the kingdom," he said.

"A technical term referring to sleepy energies," Gervin interposed.

"Besides," Lehrmon continued, "it could well be that Szar's consciousness is stimulated by Lady Elyani's sharp spirit, since she projects her energy into him during the sessions." He sighed, "These high priestesses of the White Eagle are so awake! I myself find it frightening at times."

"And you lawfully know what you are talking about!" Gervin exclaimed, and they both burst out laughing.

Their outburst sparked a joyful wave. The aquamarine room was illuminated with empathy. *Sweet Lord Melchisedek*, these two men looked so happy to be together! The atmosphere they created was so warm, so strong, and so unlike the lawfully moderate human exchanges I was accustomed to.

This was a landmark in my quest. This warmth, I understood, was at the heart of the awakening Gervin wanted me to reach.

"*Rightly spoken*, man of Thunder! Travelling favours awakening, and so does the company of the White Eagles," Gervin said with authority. "But something else is happening to Szar. Something... mysterious. When he reaches the upper spheres, a particular force comes to meet him. If he could fully realise what this force is, then he would immediately become an extremely awakened person."

Extremely awakened? This sounded hopeful. The problem was, I had no idea what force he was talking about.

"Future will tell," Gervin concluded. Then he and Lehrmon went on discussing other matters that did not concern me. I resolved to observe the two bearded men the very best I could, looking for hints about awakening.

Something struck me. When he was in the company of Lehrmon, Gervin was different from the way I had seen him behave with other people, including me. He spoke faster, for a start. And he laughed a lot more. I kept watching intensely, hoping to find more clues.

As they were talking, Gervin and Lehrmon noticed that I was making great efforts, or what seemed to me like great efforts. They halted their dialogue and both turned to look at me. Then the three of us burst out laughing.

How precious that moment was! The aquamarine light was dancing with joy. The *living walls* held a space of feeling.

So different, and at the same time so simple.

Gervin stood up. "I have to go to a meeting with Lady Teyani," he announced. "Lehrmon, why don't you take our friend for a walk."

Lehrmon gave me that unique smile of his that made him shine *like a morning of the Law*. We took leave, and started our stroll in the alleys of the enclave of the jewels.

Lehrmon started by showing me a few odd places that I had never visited before. He mentioned that these had been his hiding places when he was a novice. He told me several anecdotes, starting with how he and Gervin had 'clicked' the very first day they had met. Remembering how I had been captured myself, I could fully understand what he was saying. I also learnt that Lehrmon was nine years older than me. He knew Lady Teyani and Lady Elyani quite well, and his favourite book of the Law was the book of Maveron. At the temple of Lasseera he worked with the Field Wizards and the Stone Makers, two castes which I knew nothing about, and with Master Esrevin of the Brown Robe who, like Gervin and Melchard, had been a disciple of Orest of the Brown Robe.

Lehrmon asked many questions about me – easy questions that I could answer immediately, so that I found myself having the most animated conversation of my entire life.

5 – The Book of the Mysteries of Eisraim

Was this awakening?

There was definitely a common point with travelling: I was being carried by him, as when Lady Elyani guided me through the spheres.

As we were walking down a small spiral stairway, he told me in his gentle voice, "What is waiting for you, Szar, is an Underworld of a lot more amazing than you think. You may think you are making incredible discoveries during your travelling lessons. *Man of the Law*, but let me tell you, these are *nothing* compared to what Gervin can teach you."

We had arrived in catacomb-like corridors, dimly lit by greenish glow from the plass walls.

"Have you come here before?" he asked.

"Never in the Law," I said, having no idea which enclave we were in.

Gods, what an unlawful smell!

Lehrmon pointed to a trickle of water, "Sewage. There are hundreds of bowels like this under the temple. Better not come here unaccompanied, though," he cautioned. "As long as people behave like sleepers, there is not much Gervin can do for them. To give him a chance to really engage the teaching with you, you must first shake yourself out of lawful dreamland. And if you don't, then Gervin will do it for you – and that will hurt."

I wasn't sure what he meant, but behind his word I sensed... something. Lehrmon was *not* like Artold. Not even like the wise Salmon priests who taught me the holy art of rituals. There was something different about him. And this something was so much like Gervin!

It became increasingly clear that during all these months in the temple, I had missed that essential something about Gervin.

It made me feel distressed.

"If you want Gervin to stop behaving with you as he does with sleepers," Lehrmon explained patiently, "you have to start asking him questions. In many cases if you ask nothing, Gervin will say nothing."

Questions?

What questions?

5.5 Space controller Fretcher

"*Szar traveller, I greet you at the top of the square!*" Lady Elyani's familiar voice woke me up from my torpor.

"*I greet you at the top of the square!*" I lawfully answered.

"Start with floating around in darkness visible," Elyani instructed. After a while she used her light to direct me to a vortex that spun me into a space of particularly bright purple.

"Lots of light around here!" I wondered.

"This space is connected to a lovely tirtha in the county of the Northern Lakes," Elyani explained.

I wondered if the space was special because of the place of pilgrimage, or if it was the space that made the place a tirtha.

All of a sudden, a man appeared in front of me. He was tall, in his late fifties. His dark-blue gown indicated he was from a caste of controllers.

"A beautiful space, isn't it? Do you like it, *my friend in the Law*?" he asked.

Not knowing the lawful way to greet him, I called on Lady Elyani for help.

"*Praise the Lord Melchisedek, controller Fretcher!*" Elyani exclaimed in a voice that sounded like a departure from the canon of lawful intonation.

"*All glory to the Lord Melchisedek, Lady Elyani, high priestess of the White Eagle,*" the man answered in an affectionate tone that didn't sound completely lawful either.

"How are you today, my good Fretcher?" Elyani asked.

"Having a quiet round, dear."

Such a relaxed conversation would have sounded quite odd in the kingdom, where lawful politeness demanded that people of different castes addressed each other with precisely codified formality. As I was discovering, in the non-physical spheres a number of things happened differently.

"Not many stray sheep at this time of the Moon cycle. And what about you and Lady Seyani?" Fretcher asked.

I was taken by surprise. I hadn't realised I had two instructors.

"Going well, Fretcher," a new voice made itself heard in the space.

"You're training a new apprentice?"

"He doesn't have his symbol yet," Seyani answered. "We'll probably start flying him under Gervin's symbols soon, so don't be too surprised when you next meet him."

"Under Gervin's symbols? Oho! Sounds interesting."

The White Eagles didn't comment.

Fretcher turned towards me, "What is your name, my boy?"

"Szar."

"Nice meeting you, Szar. You'll see me quite often if you happen to sweep the area, as you probably will." Then he asked the priestesses, "What about Gisya? Has she come back from her initiation in the Underworld?"

"No. She is dead," Elyani answered.

"Dead? Oh, gods! Teyani must be devastated."

"An unlawful disaster, Fretcher," Seyani said in a calm voice. "We have lost six priestesses in a row. In the last years not one has come back alive from the Underworld."

"Gisya was such a lawfully nice girl," Fretcher said, visibly upset. "Will you send my condolences to Teyani?"

"We lawfully will, my good Fretcher," Seyani answered.

"I'll probably see you later," Fretcher said, and he disappeared abruptly.

5 – The Book of the Mysteries of Eisraim

Immersed in the bright purple light, I wondered what it was like to die in the Underworld.

"Now Szar," Elyani asked me, "what do you think, is it the space that makes the tirtha, or the tirtha that makes the space?"

"*Oh my Lord Melchisedek!* She can read my thoughts!" I thought, terribly embarrassed. To make things worse I had no idea how to answer her question.

Elyani waited a few seconds, then explained, "Both are possible, really. Some tirthas have great healing properties because of their telluric energies. Others shine the presence of a god, or an angel of Highness. The angels imprint their presence in the astral space, and in turn the space creates a special atmosphere in the tirtha. Let me show you what darkness visible looks like in a tirtha of that sort."

Through a series of fast-moving vortices, Elyani led me to a completely different space of darkness visible. It was neither purple nor dark, but illuminated with shining white light.

"This is the astral space of a beautiful lake in the county of Perentie. A tirtha inhabited by the presence of the White Eagle. A famous place of pilgrimage in the counties of the north."

The light was magnificently warm – the same warmth that made Gervin and Lehrmon so special. This made me wonder. Who were the White Eagles, exactly? Lehrmon had said they were so awakened that he himself found it frightening at times.

What did someone frighteningly awakened look like?

When I came back to my senses in the take-off room, I looked for Lady Elyani. But as usual, the only people in the room were the two priests from the healing chambers.

I contemplated the slow pulse of the mauve luminescence of the plass.

"So much must be held by the memory of these *living walls*," I thought.

5.6 Sleeper, awaken!

Once every year the *Most Ancient and Lawful Orders* performed a ceremony called *the night of the transmission of the Law*. It involved novices and young priests as well as elders and the most respected teachers of the Law.

Around twilight, the elders formed a procession and walked to the Holy Fontelayana river, carrying torches. There they took boats and went for a short tour on the river. Three hours later the young priests formed another procession, but without torches. They walked to the pontoons on the edge of the river and waited for the elders who were to pass them the torches.

Despite the fact the ceremony took place at the New Moon we had no difficulty finding our way. The track which led from the temple to the river was one of those that glowed at night, due to a particular kind of field that was widely used in the kingdom. They were called the *paths of the rectitude of the Law*, because by following the astral glow on the ground one never went astray from the path.

Together with my young brothers in the Salmon Robe, I had been invited to join in. After chanting rituals for an entire day, we followed the procession and walked to the river with nearly a hundred priests of other orders.

When we arrived at the water we stood on the pontoons, silently awaiting the boats. Three hours passed, as was proper for a lawful function. But that night the mists were particularly thick and it took another three hours before the boats arrived.

When we saw the first glimmers of the torches, we all praised the Lord Melchisedek and began intoning the hymn of the birth of the light. In the space of a few minutes the mists were lit with a reddish glow from at least three dozen boats. A most lawful and inspiring sight.

I was standing on a small pontoon with a group of friends. When the first boat came to meet us we all clapped our hands with joy. More friends joined in, *lawfully mildly* anxious to receive a torch from one of the elders.

But the pontoon was so packed that it became unstable. Just as the first boat was drawing near, two young Salmon priests lost their balance and fell into the water.

In the misty orange glow, my friends and I looked at the two boys in consternation.

Had one of us given them a hand, it would not have been difficult to lift them up onto the pontoon. But none of us thought of the possibility. Faced with this highly unusual situation, we just watched in silence.

The boat was arriving fast. One of the torch-bearers on the boat yelled, "*For the Lord Melchisedek's sake,* do something!"

Bewildered, we looked at him, wondering what he might want us to do.

"Do something!" the man screamed at us.

We remained blank.

The boat couldn't be stopped in time. In a matter of seconds it hit the pontoon, crushing one of the boys with an ugly grinding noise.

No one screamed. We just watched the scene, blank.

Two of the senior priests on the boat jumped into the water and rescued the second boy. But the one who had been hit by the boat had disappeared. No one could find him.

There followed a great amount of confusion, with people shouting the news from boat to boat, and security priests racing towards our pontoon.

Master Gervin, who was on another boat, soon arrived on the scene. "Szar, are you all right?"

"*All glory to the Lord Melchisedek!*" I responded in a vague voice.

"Come on, get off this pontoon! Quick!"

5 – The Book of the Mysteries of Eisraim

I followed him mechanically, hardly aware of the agitated mob around us.

The ceremony was cancelled, and everyone walked back to the temple in a lawfully gloomy mood.

The next morning when I met Gervin, he invited me to sit with him. After inquiring about my health, he asked me how I felt after what had happened at the river.

I politely painted a sheep's smile on my face and uttered a common verse of the Law, "*The Law is my shelter*, Master Gervin. I am fine."

To my complete stupefaction, Gervin became *very* angry. "No, you are not fine!" he yelled at me. "Underworld and Underworld Further Down! You are *not* fine! And if you really believe that the Law is your shelter, well let me tell you, you are wrong! You are a complete dreamer! A drifter! The Law is no shelter to sleepers!" He paused, totally still, then started shouting again, "Right now, there could be great works for you to do! Important tasks upon which the very survival of our temple depends. But look at you! You are hardly capable of finding your way in the temple, and you need someone to tell you what to say each time you are to meet someone middle-caste or above. And when by chance you happen to say anything at all, all you can do is quote the Law like a puppet. You have *no idea* why you are here, or where you are going. Your days and nights pass one after the other in a complete waste of Spirit. And of course you don't even see there is anything wrong with all this. If it was to remain such a sleeper, you might as well have stayed in the county of Sheringa with all those Beige idiots. There was no point coming to Eisraim. I have enough puppets of the Law around me, thank you!"

Looking up to the ceiling, Gervin beat his chest with his fists, "Shame! Shame! Shame on this land for having begotten such generations of sleepers!"

Then he closed his eyes and remained silent.

His words left me speechless. Trembling. Utterly bewildered.

One of the most difficult things was, I could not see there was anything fundamentally wrong with my behaviour. All my actions were dictated by the Law. How could there be anything wrong with that? My deepest foundations were being shaken. But much worse even, was being yelled at by the man who was everything to me.

It left me completely shattered.

What followed was unexpected. Master Gervin's spiritual concentration brought down a momentous presence into the aquamarine chamber – a descending energy of massive proportions.

My first reaction was to pray to the Mother of the Light to help me stay conscious, for I hated to imagine what Master Gervin would say if I fainted again. So I forced myself to keep my eyes open and held fast to my body.

When Gervin reopened his eyes, what I saw in them was brighter than a field of stars. I started feeling strange energies and hissing sounds above my head, just as when he had boosted my consciousness to help me succeed in the grand competition of Sheringa city. In a state of limpid awareness I heard his voice calling, "*Sleeper, awaken!*"

His lips were not moving. Yet his voice repeated,

"*Sleeper, awaken!*"

Far above my head, a part of myself which I had never noticed before heard him.

We kept eye contact for a long time, while strong movements of energy kept taking place above my head. For nearly an hour, I felt as though a huge bottlebrush was moving to and fro above my head. Then the high presence faded, and the aquamarine chamber returned to its normal self.

With a nod, Gervin indicated that the meeting was finished.

As he walked me to the twelve-lawful-feet-high door, he placed his hand on my shoulder and said, "I will see you tomorrow morning."

This brought an immense relief. "*Praise the Lord Melchisedek!*" I thought as I was walking back to the enclave of the *Most Ancient and Lawful Orders*. "Master Gervin is still talking to me!"

5.7 The clear fountain

All glory to the teacher! This storm marked the beginning of a new phase. Awakening became an obsession. At last.

It was as comfortable as being stabbed in the heart. For days, I could hear the echoes of Gervin's harsh words resounding in my head. I felt stupid, and worthless. At the same time, I felt immensely grateful to the Mother of the Light that Master Gervin would still speak to me, and there was nothing I wanted more than to meet him in the space of awakening.

But where to start?

The only tangible direction I had was Lehrmon's advice: "If you want Gervin to stop behaving with you as he does with sleepers, ask him questions."

"*The Lord Melchisedek be my witness,*" I swore to myself, "I am going to ask Master Gervin a question."

But which question?

It had to be a really good question, for as the Law said, "*Well begun is half completed.*" I would have loathed to insult Gervin or waste his time by raising a point that was useless. I wanted my question to be an offering worthy of my master. But, Underworld and Underworld Further Down, what to ask?

My mind was blank.

The more I wondered, the less I seemed able to find a thread that could lead me to the right question.

5 – The Book of the Mysteries of Eisraim

There were no classes that day. The Salmon Robe priests were lawfully mourning their young friend. As I kept on walking through the alleys of the temple in search of inspiration, it came to me that perhaps Lord Gana could help. So I went and sat in front of his altar and invoked his name:

"*Ha! Gana! Lobatchen Zerah!*
Hera, Gana! Simayan ho Zerah!
Nama Gana, Nama Gana, Gana Gana Nam Nam."

I sat for hours in a state of profound contemplation.

The question still did not come.

Using the flame on the altar and my voice as an offering, I performed a long fire ritual, praying to the god for awakening.

When lunchtime came, I didn't go back to the Salmon Robe refectory. I kept on with the fire ritual, resolved to spend the whole day and the whole night if needed.

From time to time I stopped the ritual and listened inside, waiting for the god's answer. As no answer came, I started the ritual again.

It was around sunset that the miracle took place.

Suddenly, I had an idea! I knew what to ask Gervin.

I stood up and praised Lord Gana loudly. I touched the feet of the statue, and bowed to his golden helmet of omniscience.

I walked back to the quarters of the Salmon Robe, feeling extremely proud and fortunate that the god had responded to my prayers.

Paradoxically, this was my happiest moment since arriving at the temple. Of course, I did not show it. It was a day of mourning.

When I arrived at Gervin's place, the first thing he said (after praising the Lord and inquiring about my health) was, "Do you have a question to ask me?"

Underworld! How did he know? Had I been just a bit further advanced in my training, I would have burst out laughing (which, incidentally, would have made Gervin very happy). Here I was, trying to take my first step away from the highly predictable patterns of behaviour of sleepers, and here was Gervin, knowing in advance that I was coming to him with a question!

Gathering my thoughts and remembering the comforting presence of Lord Gana, I asked him the question,

"Master Gervin, when a man has no idea what he should say or do, as when the Law has not been taught to him about this particular point or course of action, what is it that he should do?"

Gervin listened carefully. He remained silent and thoughtful for a while, as if I had asked something deep – something that required serious consideration. Truly, this meeting marked a dramatic turning point in our relationship. The last thing he wanted that day was to discourage me by bursting out laughing, as he often did later when I asked him questions.

"This," he said, "is a really important question," and he paused again, thoughtfully twinging his beard. Then he answered, "When a man knows not what choice to make, he must listen to the clear fountain."

Gervin stopped and looked at me with a hardly disguised prompt that compelled me to ask, "What is the clear fountain, Master Gervin?"

Gervin smiled, satisfied at this bold step of mine. "The clear fountain," he said, "is an unlimited source of inspiration. It flows, always, and for all men and women, but few are those who know how to tap from its waters. And even among those who know how, few are those who remember to call on the fountain when critical situations arise. The more one listens to the fountain, the easier it becomes to follow its wisdom. But if a man is silly enough to disregard the wisdom of the fountain, then he becomes deaf to it. The fountain is still with him, but he hears it not, and so he wanders in darkness."

I was amazed and filled with wonder at the idea that there could be a clear fountain of wisdom that was always available to me.

"To hear the clear fountain," Gervin continued, "you must listen above your head. The flow of the clear fountain comes down vertically, from high above your head. You must listen, but not for words! For in most cases, the clear fountain does not speak in words."

This last sentence left me perplexed. How could the fountain speak without words?

"Sometimes," Gervin said, "you may hear words, and sometimes the fountain may speak to you through images. But words can be misleading, and images are not always simple to interpret. So the best way of listening to the fountain is by knowing. When tuning into the vertical flow of the fountain above your head, making yourself open and receptive, you will know what you have to do or say. But remember that it is only with a pure heart that one can hear the clear fountain. Those who listen to fountains without sincerity always end up understanding all the wrong things."

I immediately went above my head and tried to tune into the clear fountain.

"Let me help you," Gervin said, activating the energy above my head in a particular way. "Can you feel?" he asked.

It was miraculous. I could feel something. There was no flow of knowing yet, but I could definitely feel something.

We enjoyed a silent concentration, then Gervin grabbed a large pear from a basket, and placed it in my hand (he had given up his habit of throwing fruits for me to catch).

He took one for himself, and we ate the pears.

It was a special moment.

That evening, I returned to the altar of Gana and thanked the god for the treasure I had received from Gervin.

All thanks to Lord Gana's question.

5.8 Identifying presences and requesting access

In the following days, Gervin was away on a journey to the temple of the Western Plains (the monks of the Brown Robe were great travellers). All my efforts were concentrated on receiving inspiration from the clear fountain. I *had* to find new questions before he came back.

Meanwhile, the travelling initiation was continuing. As Gervin had pointed out, I felt much more awake when guided through the spheres by Lady Elyani. I therefore endeavoured to ask her questions too – probably the right thing to do with someone frighteningly awakened. It was somewhat intimidating, but Underworld! Hadn't I decided to become frighteningly awakened myself (whatever that meant)?

Interestingly enough, I found it much easier to ask questions when I was in the space.

"*Szar, traveller, I greet you at the top of the square.*"

Awakening to darkness visible, I answered Lady Elyani, "*I greet you at the top of the square.*"

"Take the vortex on your left and keep ascending through the intermediary worlds until you reach the emerald layer."

While following her instructions, I tuned into the clear fountain. So what was it exactly about Lady Elyani that was frighteningly awakened? Was it that she always knew which direction to take?

I began to feel my movements in the space were being hampered.

"Keep moving!" Lady Elyani said.

"I can't!" I had to report after a while. "I can move back, but I can't go forward."

"Why not?"

"There seems to be something blocking my way, like an invisible veil."

"Try to find your way through," she persisted.

It was like hitting a wall.

"Nothing seems to work! I simply cannot pass through that, whatever it may be. Should I go back?" I asked.

"Never!" my instructor answered fiercely. "Look for a presence."

This important point had been taught to me during the travelling sessions of the last weeks. When meeting a light in the space, the first thing to do was tune into it and try to sense a presence. This led to identifying beings. As soon as one saw the beings, the astral landscape changed. In darkness visible as well as in other layers, many beings were first perceived in the form of light or coloured glow. As Elyani had explained, the light was but the garment of the being. If one only looked at the light and forgot to tune into the presence, one missed the being. Even though I still did not know how to communicate with all these beings, learning to identify their presences had completely transformed my travelling experiences. It had helped me recognise a great multiplicity of forces in spaces which at first I had believed empty. How confused I had been during my first flights, thinking that darkness visible and other intermediary worlds were but uninhabited spaces! In reality, they were teeming with beings of various kinds.

Tuning into the astral veil blocking my way, I immediately sensed a presence.

"Identify the presence," Elyani ordered.

I applied a technique through which my occult symbols (which, at the time, were Gervin's) were displayed to the presence, and through which the presence's recognition symbols appeared in front of me.

"Szar," Elyani continued, "I want you to examine these symbols carefully. This particular type of presence is called a guardian, or threshold keeper. As the name indicates, its function is to guard the access to that particular area of the space."

"Why would the guardian want to keep me out of this space?" I asked.

"In many cases, guardians will *not* prevent you from passing. But you must approach them in a particular way. Technically, this is called 'requesting access'. Each time you meet a threshold keeper you must address him or her and formulate your request as follows: first, give your name, then the name of your spiritual teacher and your spiritual lineage, then ask for access to be granted to you. By the same token you must let the guardian see your astral recognition symbols."

Elyani gave me more details, after which I turned towards the guardian's presence and said, "Szar, disciple of Master Gervin of the Brown Robe, of the Temple of Eisraim, requesting access."

To my surprise, the presence immediately answered, "Access granted. Welcome, Szar, disciple of Master Gervin of the Brown Robe, of the Temple of Eisraim."

The veil disappeared. I found myself in a space of exalted emerald light abounding in presences.

"How can it be so easy?" I wondered, gliding effortlessly through the space. "Only a minute ago I was totally immobilised."

"That is what guardians are all about," Elyani answered my thoughts. "Had you not requested access, you could have stayed there a hundred years. Nothing would have happened."

"This sounds magic," I exclaimed naively, forgetting that my instructor was an accomplished priestess of the White Eagle, one of the most magical orders in the kingdom.

"Szar-ka, it is indeed!" she laughed. "But at the same time it is nothing more than knocking at the door. Even at the house of the most welcoming people, you will be left outside if you forget to knock at the door."

"Does it always work?" I asked, wishing Master Gervin could have seen me asking all these relevant questions. I was also starting to realise that Lady Elyani, like Gervin, spoke to me differently when I asked questions.

5 – The Book of the Mysteries of Eisraim

Instead of limiting herself to short instructions, she became much more talkative.

"Oh no! It certainly does not work all the time," she answered. "There are many places where the guardians will deny you access. It depends which door you are knocking at. There are myriads of worlds for which access is easily granted. And there are even more worlds that are difficult to enter. The higher you go, the harder it becomes. But ultimately, it depends on who you are. Master Gervin has access to just about any layer one can find in the creation."

I asked yet another question. "How does the guardian know who I am?"

"That is what being a guardian is all about, Szar! Guardians can tune into you and know immediately what kind of person you are. In many cases if they do not admit you it is simply to protect you, because you may not be able to withstand the intensity of their space. Some spaces are like burning fire. Mortal beings would crumble if they were allowed in. Elsewhere, access will be denied because the space contains powers that you may not have the wisdom to use the right way."

That day I felt unstoppable. "So there are many guarded thresholds, aren't there?" I asked.

"There are thresholds everywhere. As soon as you start recognising them your travelling experiences become much more varied. You become capable of entering all kinds of layers and worlds. But guardians do not always demand that you declare yourself before letting you pass their thresholds."

"Does this mean I have already passed many guarded borders without noticing them?" I wondered.

"Of course! Hundreds of them. Still, when meeting a guardian it's always preferable to tune in and request access in the proper way. When guardians let you in formally, they let you see more of their world. If you enter without the guardians' blessing you run the risk of moving through what appears to you to be an empty space when in reality it is full of forces and beings. *Having not entered through the right door, you pass but see nothing*. So whenever you land in a new layer, first look for the guardian and request access."

All this was so enlightening. I wished I could have thought of asking her these questions much earlier.

I spent the rest of the session looking for guardians. It worked like a charm. Each time I formally requested access, I immediately started seeing more lights and feeling more presences in the space.

"This is magic!" I exclaimed.

Elyani laughed. She seemed to enjoy the sessions more when I asked her questions, which led me to think that if I wanted to become frighteningly awakened, I too would have to learn to like being asked questions.

Later on, when I came back to my senses, I sat up in the sarcophagus. As usual, the cover had been removed. Timidly, I looked around, just in case my instructor was still in the room.

As usual, she wasn't.

I smiled at the two priests from the healing chambers.

They smiled back, lawfully polite.

I found their smile empty.

Lawfully patiently, they waited for me to come out of the sarcophagus and escorted me back to the chapels of the Salmon Robe priests.

5.9 The clear fountain knows the heart of the Law

"What has the clear fountain been telling you lately?" was Gervin's first question on his return from the county of the Western Plains.

I told him the question I had carefully prepared for this occasion (with Lord Gana's support):

"A great difficulty for me is that I am very unclear as to what it is that I am supposed to achieve. The fountain therefore suggested that if I could see the differences between sleepers and awakened people, it would bring much enlightenment. And a way of doing this would be to observe you and Lehrmon, and compare with other people."

Gervin's smile made me feel immensely relieved. Since he had yelled at me, I had been infinitely more cautious each time I spoke with him, making sure I meant what I said rather than quoting lawful platitudes.

"And what would you say is different about Lehrmon and myself?" Gervin asked.

I shared with him the conclusions of three weeks of intense searching. "You laugh a lot..." I began.

This made Gervin burst out laughing. Instantly, there was magic in the air – the same warmth I had felt when he and Lehrmon were together.

"Szar-ka," he exclaimed, "let these words be remembered. They are the best way you will ever define the initiates of my lineage: they laugh a lot! Now, what else did you find?"

"You speak faster than normal people," I said.

Gervin laughed again, then he looked at me with one of his intensely serious looks. "This," he said, "is only half correct." Then he changed the tone of his voice, making it exaggeratedly slow and monotonous, "The truth about this matter is that sleepers speak ve-ry, ve-ry, ve-ry slo-o-ow-ly, which is ni-i-ice of them, be-cause it leaves you ple-e-enn-ty of ti-i-ime to un-der-sta-a-and what it is that they are sa-a-ay-ing."

Deep Underworld! As he was speaking, I recognised the intonation of so many people I knew. It made me shudder.

5 – The Book of the Mysteries of Eisraim

I had carefully prepared another question: "Will you give me some more clues, Master Gervin?"

"Certainly!" He thoughtfully twinged his beard, "Sleepers rarely try to do anything new. They know how to perform their tasks as prescribed by the Law of their caste, but they never venture into unfamiliar territory. What they have been taught to do, they repeat until the end of their life. What they have not been taught to do, they never attempt. And so they never really strive for anything. To stop being a sleeper, you must strive for awakening. But in reality, striving for *anything* will take you closer to awakening."

On one hand, what he said made a lot of sense. But on the other hand, all this was so difficult to reconcile with my understanding of the Law. The idea that a man could need anything more than what the Law prescribed for him was shocking, to say the least.

Seeing my disarray, Gervin explained, "There are some greater things in the Law, Szar."

Holding onto the clear fountain, I tried my best to follow.

"The Law has many facets, but men know them not. Many pundits are nothing but *parrots of the Law*, as the Law itself calls them. You have heard this expression before, haven't you?"

I nodded.

"It comes from the book of Maveron, a highly enlightened part of the Law that is particularly dear to the priests of my lineage. *The parrots of the Law* are the people who only know how to repeat verses by heart. Often, *by following the letter of the Law, they betray its spirit*. The book of Maveron also says, '*Sleeper, awaken! Change your ways, open to the light of the Lord!*' and '*True to the heart of the Law, you will have to walk away from the trodden paths.*'"

Sweet Lord Melchisedek! Was *that* part of the Law? Never before had I heard anything remotely as daring as this. Had it not come from Master Gervin – a highly respected doctor of the Law – I would have called it a sacrilege.

When he saw how horrified I was, Gervin burst out laughing. Then he asked me, "When you were in Sheringa, did you ever have classes of politics?"

"Yes, Master Gervin," I sighed, remembering how painful they had been.

"Then you must know that one of the beauties about the Law is that a verse can always be found to justify what one wants to do. If you have watched politicians when they indulge in their wicked art, you must know how the letter of the Law can be manipulated in a way that betrays its spirit."

How could a doctor of the Law possibly say things like that?

Of course I had noticed there was something wicked about politicians. But suggesting that their art was a departure from the Law was... unlawful!

Enough to be thrown in jail for! Moreover, it implied that I myself had broken the Law when following classes of politics.

The very thought that I may have broken the Law turned me blank.

Gervin gave me a minute to recover my spirits.

"The Law is immense, like an ocean," he continued. "But as an ocean is made only of water – everywhere the same – so there is only one essence of the Law."

This, I could follow. The essence, or heart of the Law, I knew to be the presence of the Lord Melchisedek.

"But in order to know the essence of the Law, you must awaken. If instead of applying the letter of the Law like parrots, people were to strive to know its essence, then they would awaken. *But they hear not, and time is passing – much faster than they think.*"

All I could do was remember these words by heart, hoping that one day their meaning would become clear. There seemed to be such a gap between Gervin and myself. Would I ever be able to cover all this ground and comprehend his thinking?

Compassionately, Gervin went on giving me instructions that I could understand and relate to. "Szar," he said, "I want you to find things which seem difficult for you. Then I want you to try hard to achieve them. It doesn't matter what they are. Just try hard." Looking deep into my eyes and using a near-Voice threshold, he repeated, "Try hard!"

"Let me explain something else to you," he went on. "The only way sleepers know how to conduct their life is by following routines. So many people in the kingdom repeat exactly the same activities every single day, from their fourteen-year-old birthday ritual to the moment of their departure for the Great Journey.

If you want to become an awakened one, you must learn to *take sleep by surprise* (another expression from the book of Maveron). Taking sleep by surprise means doing something unexpected. Something no one, not even yourself, knew that you were about to do.

Sleepers are desperately predictable. One can always know in advance what they are going to do or say. Whereas if you follow the clear fountain, you will do things that no one can predict. And yet these things will be lawful in a superior way, for *the clear fountain knows the heart of the Law*. By letting yourself be guided by the clear fountain rather than by the verses you know by heart, you will start abiding by the heart of the Law."

Seeing I could not possibly absorb anything else, Gervin signalled the end of our meeting.

When I walked back to the dormitory of the Salmon Robe novices, I felt completely overwhelmed, and once more shattered. Once again, Gervin had shaken the very foundations of my world.

The pain in my chest was so bad that I burst into tears.

Since my early childhood I had found my security, like all Atlantean people, in the perfection that I saw in the Law. In the kingdom every man

5 – The Book of the Mysteries of Eisraim

knew where his place was. To accomplish his daily duties, all he had to do was follow the example of his father, and let himself be guided by the verses of the Law. There was *no doubt and no hesitation*, and no one had to worry about the possibility of making the wrong choice. This made the world so safe! And so perfect. A magnificent dance in which every movement was precisely ordained.

Could it really be that this perfection was but a sleepers' dance?

"Can it really be that they are all asleep?" I asked myself while eating dinner with my fellow Salmon apprentices. "That simply cannot be!"

But for the first time, looking around me I saw a group of young men mechanically putting food in their mouth. They moved slowly, and they did not talk much. And when they spoke, all they did was to repeat a verse of the Law.

Gervin was right, it was all so predictable.

From the clear fountain, it struck me that this meal scene had been repeated exactly the same way day after day. Year after year. And quite likely, generation after generation.

But so what? Wasn't that what the perfection of the Law was all about?

Two priests started chatting:

"*Motser, my friend in the Law! How are you today?*"

"*All Glory to the Lord Melchisedek! Ram, my friend in the Law, I am well indeed. And you?*"

"*I am well indeed, Motser, thanks to the Good Lord Melchisedek! And how are your parents?*"

"*They are well, thanks to the grace of our Lord Melchisedek. And how are your parents, my friend in the Law?*"

They sounded so much like Gervin's caricature of sleepers who spoke 've-ry, ve-ry slo-wly' that it was frightening. Especially because I myself behaved exactly the same way.

More than painful, the experience left me crushed.

The thought started to haunt me, "Asleep! They are all asleep, and so am I!"

The village in which I had spent my early years, the school where I had been educated, all the places I had visited – whatever memories I recalled, all I could see were sleeping people moving like puppets.

5.10 The blob-men and the roots of the Law

In the days that followed, I tried hard to find something I could do to *take sleep by surprise*.

One evening as I was overwhelmed again by the vision of the meal scene, a deep wave arose inside me, "I *must* find a way of following Master

Gervin's instructions." And I turned to the clear fountain with such entirety of soul that an answer immediately came to me.

Following the impulse, and perhaps for the very first time in my life, I did something completely unprescribed and unpredictable.

It was sudden and short. I lifted up my bowl of soup and dropped it on the table, bursting out laughing loudly. Not a joyful laughter. My heart was broken.

The room became dead silent.

A few faces turned in my direction, gazing at me vaguely, hardly noticing the lawful soup splashed all over my Salmon gown.

After a few seconds, everything went back to normal. Same routines. Same voices. Same lawful babble.

"They *are* asleep," I realised.

I felt confused, irritated, broken. Something extremely deep was being cracked inside me. I didn't feel like dying, I *was* dying. My world was being pulled apart.

I got up, went straight to Lord Gana's chapel, and cried.

When I next met with Gervin, I voiced my disarray, "Master Gervin, I am *terribly* confused."

"I much prefer this," Gervin smiled. "At least, you are something."

I was too overwhelmed to try to understand what he meant, so I continued, "*I have abided by the Law every day of my life.* I have done everything the Law prescribed for me. It cannot be that there is something wrong with the Law! And how can I be a sleeper if I do all the right things of the Law?"

A deep expression appeared on Gervin's face. If I hadn't been so depressed, it would have made me feel ecstatic. I had found a question that meant something to my master.

"Szar," he asked after a moment of silent concentration, "where did the Law come from?"

After a few seconds of inner deliberation, I decided the proper way to answer this point was to recite carefully chosen verses of the Law:

"*Long ago, when water and fire covered the surface of the Earth,*
When the Earth was fresh and men were young,
When the One Ocean was teeming with the seed of all the creatures,
The Lord Melchisedek gave the Law to the gods,
Who gave it to the Elders,
Who gave it to men."

"*Right and righteous*, my young doctor of the Law!" Gervin gave a smile which conveyed the warmth of these beautiful verses. "Tell me, Szar, have you ever heard of the blob-men?"

The blob-men were an oddity sometimes mentioned by storytellers. I had never known whether they were real. "Do they truly exist?" I asked.

"They lawfully definitely do! I have seen them myself."

5 – The Book of the Mysteries of Eisraim

This awoke something in me that was as close to curiosity as a young Atlantean sleeper could manage.

Gervin continued, "They live on the warm beaches of the distant sea. Small people with very dark skin and small round faces. Their bodies are soft, with no proper solid bones. They do not speak, but they sometimes utter strange sounds. They lie down and sleep all day, hugging one another, except for when they copulate or when they crawl on the sand to collect jellyfish, which they eat raw. They pass stools and urine under themselves without even noticing it. Sometimes the waves come and wash their bodies."

"Do they never do anything else?" I asked.

"Ne-ver!" Gervin mirrored my astonishment by gazing at me with wide eyes. "Except for when one of the females gives birth."

"Have you seen this?" I asked.

"I have!" he answered. "The baby just fell slowly on the sand, and the woman hardly seemed to notice it."

Speechless I was indeed.

Gervin raised his voice, "Szar, there was a time when all men were blob-men! *When the Earth was fresh, your ancestors, and mine, and those of all those kings* – all were blob-men. And do you know what made them change gradually and become people like you and me? It was the Law, Szar, the Law that the good Lord Melchisedek sent to human beings through the Elders."

This, at last, I could understand.

Gervin went on, "Through the Law, each man found a task and a place in the world for himself. It had to be very simple and devoid of any ambiguity, for the blob-men and their scions were unable to make any decision for themselves. They knew nothing, not even how to stand on their feet. The Law taught them everything. By following the Law and constantly chanting its verses, the Spirit of Melchisedek came to flow through their blood, and they rose from their deep sleep into a lesser sleep. Now, Szar, tell me, *how many Laws are there?*"

To this traditional question, which pertained to *the Most Ancient and Holy Body of the Law*, I responded by chanting,

"There is, there has been, and there will be only one Law,
As there is, there has been, and there will be only one God.
Praise the Lord Melchisedek!"

"*Very right and righteous!* But then tell me, Szar, do you think that your needs are the same as those of the blob-men? And if the good Lord Melchisedek were to speak to you, do you think he would do it the same way as if he were speaking to the blob-men?"

"No," I said, "the blob-men were too different. They could not even speak. There would have to be a different discourse for them than for me."

"And yet," Gervin continued, "*there is only one Law, which is the Word and Voice of our Lord Melchisedek.*"

There I was, cast into the throes of perplexity again.

"The Law," Gervin explained, "is like a great marketplace. All come to it, and each takes according to his needs. Remember when you went to the marketplace as a young child. What was it that interested you the most?"

"Honeyed apples!" I replied without any hesitation.

"And now," Gervin pursued, "do you still look for honeyed apples when you go to a market?"

"No," I said, "it has been years since I even thought of looking for one." The clear fountain flowing, a question arose, "Gervin, do you mean to say there are parts of the Law for children, and others for adults?"

Gervin gave a handclap, "Precisely! But there is more to all this." He paused, holding eye contact with the aquamarine *living wall*. "Time has passed," he said, "but men have not grown up. They still look to the Law like little children. The Law they believe to be the Law is not the real Law. Remember the words of the book of Maveron, Szar: *The parrots of the Law are true to the letter, but they betray its heart, and great darkness overtakes them.*"

All this started making sense to me, and I wanted to know more. "What could men do in order to look to the Law like grown up people, and not like children? What is it they are doing wrong?"

"They use the letter of the Law to comfort themselves in their sleep. Sticking to the letter of the Law blindly was fine for the early scions of the blob-men, who could only be sleepers. But it is not the will of our Lord Melchisedek that men should sleep forever. Time has passed," Gervin reiterated, "but men have not changed. If they keep on behaving like sleepers, they are bound to be shaken by a painful awakening. And it will happen much faster than they think. For they wrongly believe that *the Law is their shelter*. They have departed from the heart of the Law. The Law will not protect them much longer."

I understood that Master Gervin was referring to his frightening prophecies of chaos and destruction – nothing short of the end of the kingdom.

I felt carried by Gervin's awakened mind as by Elyani's presence during the travelling sessions. "Do you mean to say that when our ancestors were abiding by the Law, they were following the heartness of Melchisedek. But when present people repeat the ways of their ancestors, they depart from the heart of the Law, even though they are doing exactly the same things?"

"*Right and righteous!*" Gervin answered gravely. "For our ancestors, following the Law required courage. They were emerging out of nothingness, and to them the routines prescribed by the Law were an enlightenment. By repeating over and over again the things which the Law had ordained for them, they became peasants, cobblers, plassers, priests, husbands and wives, whereas their close ancestors were but blissful blobs wallowing on sandy beaches. They went from the deepest sleep to being dreamers in the Law, which was an extraordinary step forwards. Now the

5 – The Book of the Mysteries of Eisraim

time has come to take a further step towards awakening. But the tragedy is, men use the Law to mask their sleep."

"How can I know what the Law wants from me?" I asked.

Gervin answered by quoting Maveron, *"The clear fountain knows the heart of the Law."*

A long silence followed, during which Gervin and I kept eye contact.

Then he changed the subject. "In three weeks, there will be a special fire ceremony in the second hall of Melchisedek. I will be taking part in it. It will be followed by a reception in the enclave of the High Priest, with some of the wisest people in the temple. Would you like to accompany me?"

My mouth dropped open with bliss.

As I was walking back to the quarters of the Salmon Robe, it flashed into my mind that it was because I had started asking questions that Master Gervin had invited me to that reception. Lehrmon was right. Gervin was now behaving towards me in a completely different way. And our meetings lasted much longer.

I wished Master Gervin could have yelled at me much earlier! And the knowingness of the clear fountain suggested that I should perhaps ask him to yell at me more often. On reflection, I decided against this suggestion.

It was lawful dinnertime. The idea of finding myself once more in the same sleeping refectory killed my appetite. Instead, I went to Lord Gana's chapel and I prayed.

"Help, Lord Gana! Help! Master Gervin wants me to strive for things and make efforts to achieve them. But I don't even know what to strive for! How will I ever be awakened?"

"Ha! Gana! Lobatchen Zerah! Hera, Gana! Simayan ho Zerah!"

I stayed in front of the altar until late in the evening, desperately trying to find something I could strive for.

The answer came to me when I was walking back to the Salmon dormitory: "I will not faint during the reception with Master Gervin!" I decided. And in the following days I invoked the Mother of the Light seven times a day, and Lord Gana, and all the gods which the Salmon Robe priests honoured through their rituals, "Please, give me the strength not to faint during the ceremony."

These were sad days. The more I observed my Salmon Robe friends, the more I found them to be sleepers. Even among the Salmon teachers, the only one that was a bit like Gervin and Lehrmon was Prates. All the others spoke ve-ry slo-wly, and only through predictable verses. And despite the fact that they were quite friendly, warmth wasn't part of their world.

My world?

I felt totally defeated. If even the teachers were sleepers, then why would I not be a sleeper myself at the end of the Salmon training (of which I had only completed four-and-a-half years out of sixteen)?

Thank the Mother of the Light, there was Lord Gana. When I felt too cold I could always go to him in the enclave of the thirty-three victorious gods. I contemplated the beautiful light on the altar, let it warm me a little, and prayed for awakening. And I cried, hoping this nightmare would come to an end.

5.11 The White fruit

The ceremony to which Gervin had invited me was magnificent.

The hymns were the same as those we chanted at the chapel of the Salmon Robe. But through the power of the voice and the spiritual dimension of the priests, they became so much more alive. It brought down an awesome quality of presence in the hall. With more than one hundred of the most experienced male and female priests of Eisraim, the hall was vibrant with the heartness of the Law.

But when the chanting finished, I realised with consternation, "*Oh my Lord Melchisedek*, I forgot to try not to faint! How could I be such a sleeper?" and I thanked the Mother of the Light for not letting me pass out.

People formed small groups and walked to a reception hall in the enclave of the High Priest, where food and drink were waiting. The atmosphere was joyful and animated.

I was escorted to the reception hall by Master Gervin and one of his friends, Master Esrevin of the Brown Robe, who had come to visit from the temple of Lasseera. He was a medium built stocky man in his mid-sixties, with piercing black eyes and short white hair. And like all those of the Brown Robe he wore a beard. He was very friendly, calling me his *dear friend in the Law* and complimenting me for having changed so much since the last time we had met (two years earlier, in a ceremony where I had fainted after only ten minutes). Like Gervin he spoke fast, said weird things, made jokes that I did not understand, laughed a lot and radiated warmth – this warmth which was so painfully missing in sleepers, and which I was starting to enjoy more than anything else in the kingdom.

As we entered the reception hall, a young woman with brown, curly hair walked towards us. After exchanging lawful greetings with Gervin and Esrevin, she turned towards me, "*Praise the Lord Melchisedek, Szar of the Salmon Robe!* Do you not recognise me?"

The presence felt familiar, but I could not remember ever seeing this person. With some embarrassment, I turned towards Gervin for a hint.

Amused, Gervin looked up to the gods.

I tried to guess her caste. She was wearing a long, elegant white dress.

Before I had time to collect my thoughts, she suddenly changed the inflection in her voice and commanded, "Szar traveller, spin forwards into the silvery vortex! And hold on to the stream!"

The flabbergasted look on my face made her, Gervin and Esrevin burst out laughing.

5 – The Book of the Mysteries of Eisraim

"My travelling instructor!" I muttered.

"Brilliant!" Gervin exclaimed. "You have identified the presence almost immediately."

I started laughing with them.

"This lucky man," Gervin told Esrevin, "is being taught travelling by the powerful Lady Elyani of the White Eagle. I hope he will be up to her." Then he turned to the young woman, "Lady Elyani, how is my apprentice doing?"

"Brilliant!" Elyani echoed Gervin's voice.

So was this what a frighteningly awakened person looked like! I was astonished to see how young she was. After hearing Gervin repeatedly praise her masterly skills, I had imagined her as a grey-haired wise woman. And here she was, looking younger than myself, and beautiful and *fresh as a morning of the Law*.

Master Esrevin put his hand on my shoulder. He made his voice jokingly compassionate, "These two form a dangerous pair, Szar! But I am sure you will survive their teachings."

Lady Elyani and Master Gervin laughed again.

"Come on, Master Gervin," said Lady Elyani, "let me abduct your protege for a lawful moment. Lady Teyani wants to meet him."

Underworld! Was I really going to meet the famous Lady Teyani, the head of the order of the White Eagle and the grand master of all the female orders in Eisraim?

"By all means, Lady Elyani," Gervin answered in a lawfully diplomatic voice. "If you can bring him back from the remote spheres, I have no doubt you will bring him back from Lady Teyani."

That sounded frightening enough, and surely there was no need for Master Esrevin to add with faked pity, "Farewell, Szar!"

"Master Esrevin!" Elyani reprimanded him, and the three of them laughed again.

"Awake!" I thought, "these people are awake." All around us in the room I could hear lively voices which spoke fast, and people laughing – a refreshing change from the sleeping refectory of the Salmon apprentices.

"Follow me, traveller!" Elyani set off across the large hall.

A wave of anxiety swept my chest. What if I made a huge blunder with Grand Master Teyani? I felt insecure, inadequate and out of place. Suddenly I wished I had stayed with the Salmon sleepers. "The clear fountain," I kept repeating to myself, "I *must* hold on to the clear fountain!"

We came to a corner of the hall where a group of women dressed in white were chatting.

Lady Elyani addressed one of them in a formal voice, "Lady Teyani, let me introduce to you Szar of the Salmon Robe, disciple of Master Gervin of the Brown Robe."

Sweet Lord Melchisedek, was *this* Lady Teyani?

She was nothing like the old witch I had imagined. She was a tall, beautiful woman perhaps in her mid-forties, with long dark hair arranged about her head in a complicated manner, then falling to her waist. A whitish glow shone from her skin. But what struck me most was her stillness. This woman was grounded like a mountain. It looked as if nothing in the seven spheres could have shaken her.

"*Praise the Lord Melchisedek*, Lady Teyani, Grand Master of the order of the White Eagle."

She remained silent for a second, plunging her gaze deep into me. The intensity was such was that I immediately started losing touch with the room.

"Oh, no!" I called inside with all my strength, "Mother of the Light, *please! Please!* Do not let me faint!"

To my great surprise I heard Elyani's voice, as when she was guiding me through the spheres. "Don't worry, we are taking care of you."

Everything had become dark. And silent. I was no longer in the reception hall but in the space. Everyone had disappeared but Lady Teyani, who was shining in front of me.

"Welcome, Szar," she said in a serene voice. She smiled, radiating white light and warmth. "Welcome," she repeated. "The White Eagle has told us you were coming, and we have been waiting for you. And now, you have come."

In this exalted light, her words made sense to my soul.

"*Greetings, White Eagle!*" the clear fountain replied through me.

"Szar, you must hurry! There is a long way to go."

"Where shall I go?" the fountain asked through me.

"Awaken, Szar! Awaken! Waste no time."

Before I could ask more, I abruptly found myself back in the reception hall with people talking all around me.

Praise the Mother of the Light, I was still on my feet! But stunned as I was, all I could see were Teyani's eyes. Bright, dark eyes.

Lady Teyani picked up a small white fruit from a dish by her side, and she took my left hand. Looking straight into my eyes she placed the fruit on my palm, and closed my hand on it. Then she held my hand for a few seconds and put force into me.

Again the hall became dark.

"No! Please!" I called inside, recognising the only-too-familiar precursory symptoms of fainting.

"Trust the Eagle!" Elyani spoke to me through the space.

A few seconds later I was back in the hall, and still standing.

Lady Teyani nodded to indicate the end of the meeting.

I opened my mouth but could not find anything to say.

She smiled. An incredibly warm smile. Totally like Lehrmon's.

As I was slow to move, Elyani gently pulled the sleeve of my gown and escorted me back to Master Gervin.

5 – The Book of the Mysteries of Eisraim

When they saw the shining glow in my eyes, Gervin and Esrevin exchanged an amused glance.

"That was a very long meeting," Esrevin commented.

I frowned. It had only seemed like a few seconds to me.

"And the grand master of the White Eagle has made you a present," Gervin exclaimed with satisfaction, taking my left hand.

I opened my hand and looked down at the small white fruit.

"Szar, do you realise this fruit was given to you by one of the most dangerous women in the kingdom?" Master Esrevin said in a teasing voice. "Lady Teyani is said to be the reincarnation of a great magician of the Ancient Days. The priestesses of the White Eagle are famous for their charms."

Elyani laughed.

"What if this white fruit contained a sweet, bewitching magic that will make you a pawn in their hands?" Esrevin kept on. "What are you going to do with this fruit?"

Elyani stopped laughing and gazed at me.

This was a test. By saying the wrong thing I could offend her and her master.

There was a silence. Esrevin and Gervin were looking at me, waiting for an answer.

"Clear fountain," I called inside, "help!" Instantly, the light that Teyani had projected into me became vibrant above my head. And lo! a miracle took place: I knew what to say! I remembered the legend of the Law which told how the White Eagle of the gods came to pick up heroes fallen on the battlefield, to escort them to the celestial regions.

Looking down at the fruit, I uttered the words the heroes were supposed to say as they exhaled their last breath, "Let the White Eagle take me!" Boldly, I placed the whole fruit in my mouth and started chewing.

The result was beyond my expectations (in more than one way). Pleasantly surprised by my answer, Elyani, Gervin and Esrevin laughed and applauded. But something else also took place. I realised that there *was* magic in the fruit! In a matter of minutes, I completely lost touch with the reception hall, and was projected into a distant space.

"No! Please!" I called inside as I felt myself going. "Don't let me faint this time!"

Elyani's peaceful voice came to me in the space, "Szar, you have my word, you will remain on your feet! Don't resist the power of the fruit. Let it carry you into the light."

Far Underworld! Where was I? Looking back, probably in one of the spheres of the triangle. But the hallucinogenic power concentrated in the fruit made the experience completely different from the travelling sessions with Elyani.

My body had become immense. Vaster than all the intermediary worlds. And it kept growing. Soon it encompassed all the spheres of the triangle too. Gigantic white clouds were drifting through me. Down below, at my feet, was the kingdom of Atlantis, minuscule and insignificant. And even more minuscule was Szar, standing somewhere in the county of Eisraim.

And lo! soon after, he appeared to me: the White Eagle of the gods. A stunningly beautiful being of light. He was carrying me up into the spheres, rising to higher and higher intensities of light. The exaltation that accompanied this ascension was beyond words and through the clear fountain, high mysteries were being revealed to me.

The more we ascended, the vaster I became. Soon, we reached a sphere so high that I completely lost touch with all manifested things and entered a state of ecstatic communion with the Eagle.

5.12 To the awakened one there are many paths

Upon waking the next day, the first thing I did was to ask my Salmon friends whether I had walked back to the dormitory or had been carried unconscious.

Unfortunately, none of them could remember.

I was quite stunned, and not yet completely back in my body. For at least two days I felt quite remote from my daily priestly routines. Words came out of my mouth and the rituals were being performed but I was looking at the world as if from a distance, still caught in the after-effects of the momentous journey with the Eagle.

When I next met with Gervin, his first words were, "I am glad to see the White Eagle brought you back!"

"Did I faint?" I asked anxiously.

"You didn't!" Gervin answered, to my immense relief. "You were remarkably well behaved. You just looked a bit vague, but so what! It's the lawful least one could expect after such a dose of White Eagle magic."

"I'm glad I did not embarrass you by collapsing on the floor," I did my best to speak faster than usual so as not to irritate Gervin by mumbling like a sleeper. "That fruit was not at all what I thought it was."

Gervin laughed, "Master Esrevin had warned you, hadn't he?"

"I guess he had," I said. Then I immediately asked the question I had prepared for the meeting: "Master Gervin, a few times you have mentioned that there are works waiting for me. Will you tell me more about these?"

Gervin remained silent for a while. Then he took on a soft gentle voice, "Great changes in the kingdom are coming, Szar. There will be upheavals of unprecedented magnitude. A harsh transition towards a new world – a *very* different world. The time is coming, and much faster than they all think. In this transition I have a role to play. When the time comes, perhaps you will want to help me."

5 – The Book of the Mysteries of Eisraim

The idea that I might be of any help to Master Gervin sounded odd indeed, but it filled me with joy. "Gervin," I exclaimed, "I will do anything I can to serve you. But I have great difficulty finding out what it is that I am supposed to do even now." Then my ideas got mixed up and I asked, "Do you think I would have been capable of staying on my feet during the reception the other night had Lady Elyani not been helping?"

Gervin laughed and patted my shoulder, "Perhaps not, but so what? When I was a young apprentice in the Brown Robe, I myself used to go into deep trances that made me roll on the floor."

This I found immensely reassuring. Yet I confessed, "Gervin, I have great doubts about my capacity to ever become awakened."

"I would rather regard this as an excellent sign!" Gervin approved.

"I can't even find what it is that I am supposed to strive for," I lamented.

"Before a cup can be filled with divine nectar it must first be emptied. This is just what we are doing at the moment. We are deconstructing all sorts of ideas that you have about yourself and about the world, so as to make space for new realisations. You are in between two worlds, Szar-ka. The old is gradually letting go, but the new has not arrived yet. This phase is most uncomfortable, but it cannot be avoided."

"Can you tell me if I will succeed?" I asked.

"No!" Gervin was adamant. "No one can know these things. You have to trust me when I tell you that you *can* be anything, and that you *can* do anything you want. But whether you will end up doing it or not depends entirely on you." Quoting the book of Maveron, he concluded,

"To the sleeper, there is only one path, only one destiny.

To the awakened one, there are many paths, many destinies. Nothing is fixed."

I sighed, remembering with a touch of nostalgia my early days in Eisraim, when I had believed that by becoming a Salmon Robe priest I had engaged in a simple and direct path to lawful fulfilment.

Sensing the despair which was welling up inside me, Gervin stopped his teaching for the day. Encouragingly, he said he found I was starting to understand a number of things about sleepers. He invited me to persevere relentlessly in my striving for awakening. And we sat and kept eye contact in silent concentration because, Gervin said, a few things needed to be rearranged above my head after my encounter with the White Eagle.

5.13 Unlawful panic

While going through my *lawful daily routines* I was doing my best to follow Gervin's instructions. I kept watching the people around me. What was it about them that showed they were sleepers? In many situations, I found them just... normal! Yet it was becoming more and more painfully obvious to me that, compared to Gervin, sleepers spoke 've-ry, ve-ry, ve-ry slo-wly'. And the predictable nature of their behaviour was becoming more conspicuous by the day.

I realised that if I tried to, I could nearly always figure out what the people around me were about to do or say. At times I even started to find it aggravating. But at the same time, I found it safe. What if they all were as unpredictable as Gervin? The idea made me shudder. Gervin's teachings were so different and hard to follow. I usually came out of the aquamarine chamber feeling shattered, and often even sick.

Gervin had instructed me to conduct a frightening experiment. He had said, "Take one of your sleeper friends completely by surprise. Do something unlawfully unexpected. And you will see, he will become blank. He will look straight ahead as if you were not there, and after a moment he will resume his activities. As if nothing had happened."

Invoking Lord Gana for courage, I resolved to do what Gervin had said.

He had suggested I abruptly interrupt the course of one of these codified conversations which formed the social modus operandi of the Law. The problem was, I *liked* these ready-made dialogues. I found them lawfully nice. And they were so convenient! Thanks to them you were never embarrassed by not knowing what to say, or what to answer.

One morning, I approached my dear friend Artold,

"*Praise the Lord Melchisedek, Artold! How are you, my friend in the Law?*"

"*All Glory to the Lord Melchisedek! Szar, my friend in the Law, I am well indeed. And you?*"

"*I am well indeed, Artold, thanks to the Good Lord Melchisedek! And how are your parents?*"

For years Artold and I had had the same conversation every morning. For the first time, I was about to break the rule.

A rule established by the Law!

No, I couldn't possibly do that!

Yet it was an *order*, from Master Gervin.

Didn't the Law say, "*Serving thy master is serving the Law*"?

Strange feeling. Gripping anxiety. My stomach, an Underworld hell. But could there also have been a touch of excitement?

My plan was to act at the end of the following sentence.

Artold was lawfully serene, "*I trust they are well, even though I have not heard from them for some time. And how are your parents, Szar?*"

The tension inside me reached a climax.

For a fraction of a second, I thought of pulling out. I felt *compelled* to tell Artold that I trusted they were well, even though I hadn't seen them for some time.

But I didn't.

I dared.

5 – The Book of the Mysteries of Eisraim

Holding fast onto the clear fountain, I refrained from answering. Instead, I loudly clapped my hands just in front of Artold's nose.

Artold was stupefied. But he did not react. He became blank. Just as Master Gervin had predicted. He remained silent, motionless. His vague eyes looking through me rather than at me.

Then he walked away. As if nothing had happened.

He resumed the lawful course of his activities. And I was left alone amidst the auburn glow of the dormitory's *living walls*.

Suddenly, I realised that I was no longer part of Artold's world.

It triggered an irrational wave. Sheer panic. "Help!" I called inside, "Help! Help! Help! Gervin!" I burst into tears, shocked beyond understanding. "Artold is my best friend, this can't be! They're *all* asleep! Gervin, help! What's left?"

To my great surprise, I received an answer. Gervin responded through darkness visible, "Come, Szar, let us have one of our talks. Come right now."

I was so distressed and out of my mind that I ran all the way to the enclave of the jewels.

Wherever I looked, I saw only sleepers. That made the panic worse.

When I arrived at the aquamarine chamber I was trembling.

Gervin first looked at me silently for a few seconds. Then with his unique irony he greeted me by starting another of those codified conversations: *"Praise the Lord Melchisedek! Szar, my friend in the Law, welcome and sit down. I am glad that you came to visit."*

As I was sitting down, the lawful words of answer choked in my throat, *"All gl..."*

I couldn't. I just *could not* say the words.

There was a short silence. Then out of nowhere, Gervin and I exploded into laughter. Or rather, Gervin laughed, and I was taken by convulsive spasms that sounded like laughter, while tears kept pouring from my eyes.

The spasms lasted for perhaps as long as five minutes and then, just as abruptly as they had started, they stopped.

And the silence that followed was beyond description.

Gervin and I kept eye contact.

I was no longer trembling. All the tension had dropped.

There was nothing but a huge void, a holy nothingness. And the presence. As on the first day, when Gervin had come to fish me from the county of Sheringa. It came in a unique flavour of eternity – a time crossing. The moment felt like it had never started and would never end. There was the real Gervin in front of me, and I knew my Self for knowing him.

"Sleeper, awaken!"

I had no idea how long it lasted. When Gervin finally broke the silence, he said, *"The Lord Melchisedek does not rejoice in sleepers, but in those who strive for awakening."*

He kept speaking to me, to help me come back to my body. "Something about sleepers is that they are unable to make choices or decisions. When faced with a situation for which they have been taught a response, they repeat that response. But if the situation is new or unusual, they are so completely taken aback that they just switch off and there is nothing left of them. It's as if they were dead, for *sleep is the sister of death*. And this is why sleepers can never invent anything new, nor even see the need for innovations."

The words sank in, but I was too overwhelmed to respond. Often, when I stopped asking questions and became silent, Gervin discontinued our conversation and politely sent me back to my quarters. But that day he was particularly patient with me. "Now, this tells you what you have to do in order to awaken: never take any situation for granted. Never rest on your habits, or on what has been taught to you. Always be ready to take sleep by surprise. To decide on a course of action, rely on nothing but the clear fountain."

Gervin picked a pear from a basket. In a glance, he judged I was too overwhelmed to eat. So he bit into the fruit instead of handing it to me. "I see you are making great efforts, and I appreciate it," he said. "Let me give you another tip. When you really do not know what it is that you are supposed to do, ask the clear fountain, 'What would an awakened one do in this situation?'"

And he ate the pear, leaving me plenty of time to recover my spirits.

At the end of our meeting, he suggested that the time had come for me to undertake a three-week contemplative retreat in the first hall of Melchisedek. "That will do you a lot of good. It will help you understand what awakening is about," he concluded.

5.14 Prepersonal bliss in the light of Melchisedek

With Prates' permission, I spent three weeks meditating in the first hall of Melchisedek.

It was one of the most ancient (and therefore most sacred) buildings of the temple – as ancient as the Law of the temple, which meant *lawful tens of thousands of years in plenty*. The inside of the hall shone like liquid gold, the glow from the *living walls* mingling with the Holy Light of the Lord Melchisedek and his angels.

There, meditation was so easy! All I had to do was sit in the light, and I was transported to the heights of the Law. It made my heart radiant like a Sun. Every morning, just by walking into the field of the chapel I felt infinitely wise, and divine. Rivers of devotion flowed through me. What more comfort could a servant of the Law ever wish for? What greater bliss? *Right and righteous* was the Law when it proclaimed,

5 – The Book of the Mysteries of Eisraim

Nothing can bring more fulfilment to a man
Than praising the Lord Melchisedek
And paying all glory to him.

The three weeks passed like a lawful dream. I came out of the retreat feeling regenerated – a perfect break after these terribly difficult months during which my very foundations were continually being shaken. My self-doubts had been washed away, my confidence restored. *Unshakeable is the man who is supported by the Law.* This verse reflected exactly how I felt. The light was back with me. How wise of Master Gervin to have recommended this retreat.

During our following meeting, Gervin first asked if I had enjoyed my contemplation of the Lord.

"*Lawfully magnificent*, Master Gervin. I feel so much stronger now."

Gervin remained silent for a while, contemplating the aquamarine light of the ceiling. Then he lowered his eyes onto me and in one sentence delivered a devastating blow.

Holding my gaze, he said, "Now what you must understand is that the connection you had in the hall of Melchisedek was a sleeper's connection."

I could hardly believe my ears.

"Like a dream, these experiences happened totally out of your control," Gervin continued, "and not much of them will be retained when the painful twilight of the kingdom comes."

Deep Underworld!

I was blank for at least five minutes.

The experience of the light of our Lord had been amazingly powerful. If *that* was unreal, then really there was nothing left for me to rest on.

The gnawing anxiety was back, like a huge splinter in my heart. My distress was total.

From somewhere the words pushed themselves out, "Isn't the light of our Lord real?"

"Good Lord Melchisedek!" Gervin laughed. "Of course He is real! *He is the One that is, that was, and that will be.* It is not with the Lord Melchisedek that there is something wrong, it is with you!"

How could I be erring just when I felt the strongest and the surest of myself? Tears sprang from my eyes. I felt completely emptied out. I wished I could be dead.

Gervin's next words brought my confusion to a climax, "Right now, Szar, I think you are more ready for awakening than ever before."

"Help! Gervin!" I said, reeling, "I need help! My world is collapsing. I just can't understand what it is I'm supposed to do."

"My son," he said in a gentle but firm voice, "if you want to tread the path of an initiate you must learn to face such moments where everything seems to give way under your feet. It is often when you come closest to your goal that you have to bear with the greatest darkness. Now, let me try to explain to you what I mean.

Imagine a fool who can never remember anything for more than an hour. During the day, the kingdom is lit by the Sun. The fool believes the Sun will be forever warm. Yet a night follows. Everything becomes dark and cold, and the fool can't remember that the Sun ever existed. The fool becomes a non-believer in the Sun. He can't even imagine its existence.

Today the light of the Lord Melchisedek is all around us. Sleepers take it for granted that his presence will forever be with them. But when the twilight of the kingdom comes, they will be left in the cold, overtaken by darkness. The Law, they will forget, and some will even disbelieve that the Lord Melchisedek exists."

That was, lawfully, too much! Hadn't Master Gervin been a famous prophet of the Law, I would have shouted blasphemy. To every soul in the kingdom, the Lord Melchisedek was the most solid and tangible reality. It was the foundation stone of the Law, and of the entire world. The idea that one day – be it one hundred thousand years from now – men would not believe in Him, sounded as unlawfully unreal as it was unacceptable.

"When you were in the chapel," Gervin hammered his words into me, "you were basking in the light of our Lord like a tree under the midday Sun. If you remain a sleeper... just wait till the night comes. There will be nothing left of your faith and devotion to the Lord."

Gervin waited.

There did not seem to be anything left for me to believe in or rest on. My mind was void. The clear fountain was all I had left.

"Clear fountain, clear fountain, help!" I called inside.

Gervin fixed his gaze above my head.

Miraculously, the fluttering turmoil started calming down. The aquamarine light in the room became brighter. My breath slowed down.

A question came to me. "Then... there must be a different way of knowing the Lord. There must be a way of connecting, a way that does not fade when the night comes," I said.

"Of course there are other ways."

For the first time that day, I saw a light in Gervin's eyes indicating I could be on the right track. "But still," I went on, "what you say means the kingdom is full of sleepers who believe they are seeing the Lord Melchisedek when in reality they are blind."

"Szar," Gervin was emphatic, "they *do* see the Lord, and many of them have a profound knowledge of his ways and of the cosmos which is his playground. But the time will soon come when the warp of fields collapses and all their knowledge is lost." Gervin's eyes were now fixed on that corner of the room where so much seemed to be happening, even though I could never see anything. "For me, Szar, this is the greatest of all tragedies. I see these brilliant learned men, these inspired prophets and high priestesses, and I admire their lore. But I also see that in no time their power will be reduced to naught. Some of the greatest of them will be reborn as insane fools, wandering far away from the paths of the Lord."

5 – The Book of the Mysteries of Eisraim

This was the closest to being distressed I had ever seen my teacher. Deeply moved, I asked, "Gervin, will you teach me how to see the Lord in a way that does not fade when the night comes?"

"It is one of my deepest wishes that you may behold the Lord beyond all appearances," he answered. "But for this you must first awaken."

Awaken! There was nothing I could want more, yet hearing this word was like being stabbed in the chest. It made me feel totally powerless, worthless, useless... More than four years had passed, and I still couldn't tell what the word meant. Often I thought that all my efforts, instead of leading me to awakening, had only contributed to turning my sleep into a nightmare.

"A clue, Gervin! Please, a clue!" I begged him.

"In the coming weeks," he said, "I will have to spend some time with several high priestesses and prophetesses of the temple. Some of them are highly awakened initiates, and others are complete sleepers. Yet all are extremely divine. Would you like to accompany me? You and I could share our impressions as to what sleeping means to them."

How could someone be divine and yet be a sleeper at the same time? That blew the Underworld out of my mind. But the idea of spending time in Gervin's company instantly rekindled my spirits, making me forget the beating I had just taken. Almost.

"I would love that!" I said.

5.15 The eyes of Marka

Early one morning, I met Gervin at his apartment and we walked from the enclave of the jewels to the female wing of the temple, the secluded buildings where the orders of female priests had their quarters. It was the first time I visited that part of the temple. We entered through a portal flanked by high columns, which led into a large hall. No one guarded the threshold, yet only authorised people ventured through.

As soon as we entered, I was surprised by the intensity of the energy field. In this the domain of Lady Teyani, the atmosphere of consciousness was deep, and radically different from that in the Salmon priests' premises. It was like entering another world. Every nook and cranny was alive with the magic of lawful hymns, and the air resonated with spells and invocations.

From the first hall we walked through a complicated maze of corridors, patios and alleys. I followed Gervin, admiring the great diversity of glow from the walls, astral lights and fields, each with its own presence. It felt *so* lawfully ancient! But the walk proved much longer than I had anticipated. At the end of each corridor, there was always another corridor. The maze seemed by far the most complicated of any in the temple. After walking up and down several stairways, we finally entered a small room where a group of women were waiting for us. One of them was Lady Teyani. Around her stood three priestesses wearing the dress of the White Eagle, surrounded by a few other priestesses clad in gowns of various colours.

There was also a dark-skinned woman in her late fifties, sitting on the floor, leaning against a *living wall*. She looked extremely tired. She wore an orange gown. A long shawl was draped over her head, covering her hair. Her eyes were closed.

"*Praise the Lord Melchisedek!*" Gervin greeted the priestesses.

Lady Teyani answered, "*All glory to the Lord Melchisedek*, Gervin of the Brown Robe, and to you Szar," and she smiled at me.

I smiled back but did not greet her. Master Gervin had instructed me to keep my mouth lawfully shut throughout the visit.

Gervin sat by the woman in orange. "How is she today?" he asked.

"Not very well," Teyani answered. "She won't eat."

Turning towards an elderly priestess who was standing close to Teyani, Gervin asked, "What do you think, my good Mouridji of the Purple Robe?"

"I am afraid Marka is doing just what you predicted she and other priestesses would do when the warp of fields deteriorated beyond a certain point," Mouridji replied.

"Mm..." Gervin delicately took the hand of the Orange priestess. "Marka..." he called in the softest voice I had ever heard him use.

Marka did not answer.

"Gervin, this means we are coming one step closer to the fulfilment of your prophecies. Aren't we?" Mouridji asked.

Gervin nodded gravely.

Mouridji turned to the younger priestesses, "Long ago, Master Gervin predicted that when the fields lost their purity, the high priestesses of Malchasek would become ill and drift away from their body, one after the other."

Another priestess quoted Gervin's words, "When the seventh energy field of darkness visible becomes corrupt, Malchasek the great angel will call back his seed, and you will know that the time is coming."

"None of the hymns of the Law, and none of our healing charms seem to be able to restore their health," one of the White Eagle priestesses said.

"And when they speak, they say that Malchasek is calling them back to the spheres of Highness, and that they no longer have a mandate in the kingdom," Mouridji added.

"Should we try something else, Gervin?" Teyani asked.

Gervin shook his head slowly.

All became silent.

"Marka, it's me, Gervin," my teacher half-whispered into her ear, and he activated a particular gateway close to her left clavicle.

There was an immediate response, like a descending breath of light.

5 – The Book of the Mysteries of Eisraim

Surprised, I looked up to the ceiling, but could see nothing out of the ordinary.

A lofty presence made itself felt in the room.

I noticed a tear in the corner of Gervin's eye. It immediately made me cry.

The presence became stronger, and Marka opened her eyes.

What I saw then was to remain one of the most extraordinary experiences of that entire life. Dragon's Word and Deep Underworld, the Lord Melchisedek is my witness, during these years I saw some *really* strange things – but not many like Marka's eyes! The feeling that illuminated the room as she slowly opened her eyes was beyond description. Nothing I had encountered while travelling in the spheres of the triangle could compare with the light in her eyes, not even the glorious fields of stars.

Then and there, I exited time completely. Teyani, Mouridji, Gervin, the small room, me in my apprentice's pink gown – all disappeared. At the onset of the experience, a verse came to me: *Far beyond the nothingness which is beyond the gods themselves.* Everything was transcended. There was but the Silence of a gigantic Beingness.

I had no idea how long it lasted. I completely missed the rest of that meeting. When I recovered my normal awareness, I was walking with Gervin through the maze of corridors, back to his apartment.

"*Thank the Mother of the Light!*" I thought. "I didn't faint!" It was quite unexpected, with such an out-of-the-seven-spheres experience. Had the White Eagles helped?

As soon as we crossed the portal and I was relieved of the injunction to keep my mouth shut, I asked Gervin, "Is Marka a sleeper?"

"Oh, no, my son! Marka is an awakened one. She belongs to the spheres of Highness. And I am afraid, she won't be with us much longer."

A feeling of infinite sadness swept my heart. It wasn't difficult to see how dear this woman was to Gervin.

"A great saint, she is. When she was a young priestess, I had the immense privilege of being her travelling instructor, as Elyani is now for you," Gervin smiled. "And she helped me a lot, when I had to travel far, far away. She took care of my body when I went for my first long journey beyond the spheres of Melchisedek. That was... nearly thirty-five years ago."

We walked in silence for a while. Then I asked him, "Should I strive to become an awakened one like her?"

To my surprise, Gervin burst out laughing, as if I had said something really funny. "Szar-ka, Szar-ka, your confusion is great! Come, follow me. Let us go and have some lunch in the aquamarine chamber, and I will *try* to explain to you a few more things about awakening. Then we will go back for another meeting with Lady Teyani."

5.16 The Blue priestesses

One of the reasons why I particularly enjoyed being taught by Gervin during a meal was that I did not have to produce many questions. While I was busy chewing, Gervin continued talking, whereas normally if I remained silent for too long, he would pause and wait for me to ask something. I always chewed a lot when eating in his company.

That day, the space between us was particularly warm.

"Marka is not a good example of either sleep or awakening for you," Gervin began. "Her enlightenment is from a different epoch. The priestesses of Malchasek are the keepers of an extremely ancient light. They are unique women. Their energy is completely different from that of normal people – even high initiates."

This reminded me of the priestesses of the Dawn of Creation, another order which was the recipient of ancient energies.

"You or I could never become priests of Malchasek," Gervin continued, "as Malchasek's servants are exalted Spirits who have descended from the spheres of Highness, and who help to incarnate his Light in the kingdom. What has been happening in the last years is that the quality of the energy fields in the kingdom has deteriorated so much that the priestesses of Malchasek cannot maintain their presence among us. The rampant corruption that is gradually infiltrating the warp of fields is incompatible with the purity of their souls. Alas, when high priestesses like Marka depart from the kingdom, so will the protective light of their great angel. This will only make the fields worse."

The warp of fields was still mysterious to me. All I understood was that the godly presence in chapels rested on the fields. Once, I had also heard someone say that if the fields were to lose their mind, then all plass buildings in the kingdom would melt *like snow under the lawful Sun*, and so would *an awful lawful lot* of other things.

"But let us return to sleep and awakening," Gervin went on. "Perhaps a breakthrough for you could come from pondering on what happened when you were meditating in the hall of Melchisedek. Compare how you felt then with how you are now. Right now, you are listening to me and trying to find questions you could ask me."

Conscientiously chewing, I looked lawfully thoughtfully to an aquamarine *living wall*.

Gervin smiled, "And so you are actively with me, giving me the best of your presence. You know that you are Szar, listening to Master Gervin. When you were in the hall of Melchisedek, the situation was very different. There was nothing but the Lord. You were so absorbed in the contemplation of our Lord that you did not even know who you were. You were not in the hall, because there was no 'you' in the hall. There was only the presence of our Lord Melchisedek."

5 – The Book of the Mysteries of Eisraim

Gervin paused, watching me eat. Then he went on, patiently, "You, Szar, were no longer. Instead of Szar there was a blank, passively lit by the light of our Lord. That blank was divinely lit, and the light awakened a high Spirit inside you. But this was nothing more than a sleeper's connection. The experience was not of your making. It came from outside, and you had no control over it. Were it not for the power of the fields, you would have been unable to reach the light of our Lord."

Gervin finished his cup and went on, "Awakened people remain aware of their own Self while knowing the divine presence. Through their own Self, they know the presence. Sleepers, on the contrary, lose all self-reference when tuning into the Divine. The Divine knows Itself through them."

By that stage, I could do no better than make sure I remembered Gervin's words by heart, so I could meditate on them later.

"The Blue priestesses, whom we will be visiting this afternoon, are typical sleeping prophetesses. Observe them carefully. When they tune into their deities, they *evaporate into a lawful mist* – there hardly seems to be anything left of them. Then something very high and beautiful comes down to reach them, and it inspires them to speak words of great wisdom."

Following this Gervin made a joke about my thorough chewing, and we walked back to the female wing of the temple.

As soon as we passed the portal, I felt again the dense field loaded with presence. We had to walk for more than twenty-five minutes. I admired the ease with which Gervin found his way through the mysterious labyrinth.

The walk ended in a dim, medium-sized room where Lady Teyani was waiting for us in the company of a dozen women clad in light-blue gowns.

After duly praising the Lord Melchisedek, Gervin addressed the group, "*What can I lawfully do for you, wise women in the Law?*"

"*Praised be the gods of the great ocean, the gods of the air, and the gods of the earth,* Master Gervin of the Brown Robe, an unlawful pollution is disturbing *the peace of our recitations of the Law* and of *the rituals to the gods above, the gods below, the gods which are and which will be...*"

I was struck by how slowly she spoke.

Teyani interrupted the litany. "Elemental muck from a corrupt field. Only a trickle, but enough to disturb their rituals."

"Can't my Field Wizards fix it?" Gervin frowned.

"They've already fixed it three times, but it keeps coming back," Teyani answered.

"We clear the pollution, we offer it to the Mother of all Compassion," another Blue priestess declared (even more slowly), "but, the Law of the Blue priestesses says, *no fish can drink all the waters of the ocean,* and *who can tell how many grains of sand...*"

Gervin and Teyani were holding eye contact.

Mother of the Light! So much warmth between these two souls.

It took me by surprise. I hadn't realised they were such close friends.

"...and, when the recitation ends, *the nectar of the Law* no longer *flows from the heavenly spheres*, unless *we keep a flame, burning in each corner of the chapel*, which is prescribed only in *the rituals to the gods of...*" the Blue priestess was going on, and on, and lawfully on. And I thought the Salmon sleepers were bad!

Teyani's light was extraordinarily beautiful. The way she looked at Gervin fascinated me. He and she were flying together in some mysterious sky.

Oh, how I wished I could be part of their world!

If *only* I could understand.

"Clear fountain, help! Show me the way to awakening," I prayed.

When the Blue priestess finally became silent, Gervin gave her a polite nod. He spoke unusually slowly, "Mm... I shall ask Master Woolly to visit this chapel and *give you his lawfully expert advice*."

"Master who?" Lady Teyani asked.

"Master Woolly of the Cream Robe," Gervin answered her, speaking normally.

"Never heard of this one," she sounded surprised. "Who is he?"

"He's *a character in the Law*," Gervin grinned. "I just fished him from the temple of the Western Plains. I enrolled him in the team of Field Wizards."

"What does Woolly do?"

"Stones. Mind-blowing stones," Gervin said, enthused. Turning towards the Blue priestesses, he resumed the lawfully slow parlance, "I think, it would be best, for me, to see you perform one of your rituals, and make a first-hand assessment of the situation."

The Blue priestesses agreed, and prepared themselves for a prophecy session.

The grand-White Eagle lawfully excused herself. Before leaving she gave me a strange smile that made the energy above my head hiss like a hundred snakes.

Gervin instructed me to sit on the floor and observe the session carefully.

I was puzzled by the paleness of these Blue priestesses, and their incorporeal energy. Their feet hardly seemed to be touching the ground.

It took nearly half an hour before the ritual could begin. It was a slow, repetitive chant of some part of the Law unknown to me. The voices were magnificent. They brought down a powerful presence into the field of the room. I had to make a great effort to avoid fainting. For a moment I thought I was in the fields of stars, but the experience lacked the sharp clarity of my travelling lessons with Elyani. It was like being in a misty cocoon of astral lights, in which I felt completely safe and protected. But I saw that I was about to lose consciousness, so I opened my eyes and forced myself to stay present in the room.

One of the priestesses started a strange incantation in a dialect I had never heard before, "Arken... groser... vatan..."

5 – The Book of the Mysteries of Eisraim

"She is prophesying," Gervin whispered in my ear. When he saw the perplexed expression on my face, he added, "This is no Atlantean dialect. She is speaking in tongues."

The Blue priestess continued her monotonous monologue for what seemed a long, long time.

"Get the message?" Gervin whispered to me.

I shook my head.

"Keep your eyes closed and let the voice take your consciousness into the spheres," Gervin advised.

The result was immediate: bright symbolic images erupted into my mind. First I saw a black swan diving into the waters of a lake. Then a fabulous landscape. Then the golden statue of a god. The images were absolutely superb, they looked more real than anything I had ever seen in the kingdom. The depth of the colours and the richness of the light filled me with wonder.

"The oracle is speaking to you, Szar. Open your heart, and listen to the message," Gervin whispered.

I could intuitively sense that the images carried a message. But how to decipher it? I was projected from image to image, completely absorbed in them. Even if my mind had been available for comment, it was hard to see how an intelligible meaning could have been extracted from the visions. Following Gervin's suggestion, I tried to open my heart more, but all it did was to speed up the succession of oracular images.

Before long, I completely lost touch with the room, the voices, and with the images... and entered a deep state of trance.

It was the next morning before I recovered my senses. I was in the dormitory of the Salmon Robe priests.

"Oh, no! I did it again!"

Artold came towards me, *"Praise the Lord Mel,chi,se,dek, Szar! How, are, you to, day, my, friend, in, the Law?"*

That day was not a good day.

5.17 Faraway voices

During the following weeks I kept asking the clear fountain to inspire me and suggest things to strive for. This was no easy task. I came to the conclusion that basically I didn't want anything, and it made me feel like dying.

Once in Lord Gana's chapel, it came to me through the knowing of the fountain that the problem wasn't that I didn't want anything, but that I didn't know what I wanted.

Perhaps I wanted impossible things, such as understanding Master Gervin or enjoying the company of awakened ones. The warmth in Lady

Teyani's eyes when she looked at Gervin, *that* was something worth living for. But that was so far away.

Now, what could a failure like me strive for?

Late one evening, after finishing a fire ritual in the chapel of Lord Gana, an idea finally came to me.

It was not just something that demanded a lot of trying, it was also something that I *really* felt like achieving. During our conversations, Gervin had often stressed that the more I wanted to succeed, the more awakening the striving exercise would be.

I decided I would strive to surprise Lady Elyani at the end a travelling session by coming back to my senses early enough to greet her.

This proved a terribly difficult, painful and frustrating exercise. At the end of each session, I tried to pull from all my resources to project myself back into waking consciousness. But each time I fell unconscious.

I tried to prepare myself in advance. During my daily priestly activities, I often recalled my resolution and prayed to the Mother of the Light. And in each fire ritual I asked for Lord Gana's assistance.

Nothing worked. Despite all my efforts and invocations, and despite my earnest desire to contemplate Lady Elyani's beautiful White Eagle energy again, the travelling lessons systematically ended in a black hole. When I emerged out of the sarcophagus, I would find the two boring sleepers of the healing chambers. Silently they smiled back at me in their boring empty way, as if to punish me for having failed again. And they escorted me back to the boring sleepers of the Salmon Robe.

So I tried a powerful technique of the canon of the Law, in which a fire ritual and a high invocation to *all gods* were performed at the time of the New Moon, to declare the wish to the universe. It was followed by a series of rituals performed at sunrise and sunset every consecutive day for two weeks, so as to build up the intensity until the Full Moon, the time when the gods would respond or not respond, depending on factors beyond the understanding of mortal beings.

Whether they did or not, this I never knew, due to a near-disaster of my own making. During the session that took place on the day of the Full Moon I was travelling along a stream in one of the fields of stars of the spheres of the triangle, when Lady Elyani instructed me to speed up.

Forgetting how powerful the streams can be, I initiated far too strong an impulse. The result took me completely by surprise – an incredibly violent acceleration which projected me far, far away.

Elyani shouted, "Hold on to the stream, Szar! You're losing the stream! Hold on!"

It was already too late. Before I could realise what was happening, I found myself in a strange space completely devoid of light. Quite different from anything I had visited before.

"Where am I?" I was distressed, slightly stupefied by this unlawful jump into nothingness.

5 – The Book of the Mysteries of Eisraim

"You've passed the edge of the spheres of Melchisedek. You are in the wrong space, Szar! You can't stay there. Follow my light, let it bring you back."

I heard her words, but found it difficult to move.

"Elyani, I think I must have made the... the wrong connection. It feels so weird, around here... and heavy... I can't move."

"Szar you *must* hold on!"

"Elyani, I'm feeling heavier and heavier. I'm losing control. There is a strong wind..."

"Oh, no! Szar, resist the wind!" Elyani's voice was faint. "It moves infinitely faster than it seems. If you let it take you..."

I was succumbing to sleep. "No!" I called, "Help me, Gervin! I don't want to die a sleeper!" But a thick sandman effect overtook me. I lost consciousness and started drifting, carried away by the winds.

Down in the take-off room Seyani shouted, "We're losing him!"

Elyani, the master traveller, did not waste any time. "I want four men, immediately," she ordered.

She sat on the floor leaning against a *living wall* and instantly projected herself out of her body. She forced her way through all the controlling procedures and without any transition crossed the limit of the spheres of Melchisedek.

Seyani, despite her own high level of expertise, could only admire the ease with which Elyani was speeding through space. "*Hail, White Eagle of the gods!*" she chanted, "*Behold thy servant maid. Protect her with thy wings.*"

In a matter of seconds, Elyani reached the grey layer in which I was stranded. But to her surprise, the winds had stopped. The space was perfectly quiet.

"Szar?" she called.

There was no answer.

For the first time in all these travelling sessions she came close to my astral body. She called my name again and she used the Voice to wake me up, but without success. I was totally unconscious.

She was about to 'carry' me back when she heard the whisper. A strange voice, unlike anything she had encountered during years of travelling.

"*Fear not!*"

The whisper seemed to come from far, far away.

"*Fear not! Space Matrix is watching.*"

Elyani tested the voice for identification symbols, but received no answer.

Instantly, she became a different person. Calling on all the powers that Lady Teyani had bestowed on her, she shielded her energy and charged her Voice. And in that nowhere space she stood close to me, like a panther ready to strike.

"*Fear not, White Eagle! Space Matrix is watching.*"

Still, silent, contained, Elyani held the instant as only initiates can do.

She waited, but the voice had stopped. So she attached me to her energy and started moving slowly.

Another voice. A whisper. Strange.

Hardly discernible.

The first voice resumed, "*Space Matrix priority access granted. Engage remote guidance through intention.*"

Elyani stayed still and tested the voice again. They did not respond to any of the identification devices she had been taught.

She waited a few more seconds. The space was peaceful.

What miracle had stopped the winds?

Elyani started moving back to the spheres of Melchisedek, pulling my astral body.

No other voice made itself heard.

Soon, Elyani was back in her body. She clicked her fingers, opened her eyes, and immediately stood up.

As she had commanded, four men were waiting in the room.

"Take him to the healing chambers!" she told them. "Quick!"

The light translucent slab that covered the sarcophagus was removed. The men lifted my body, and the small group hastened to one of the healing chambers in the nearby enclave.

Lady Teyani was very pleased when she heard how her disciples had handled the matter. Not one minute lost, not one useless word, not one uncalculated move. Having reached one of the healing chambers, the two priestesses used standard healing techniques, projecting the Voice on various gateways of my body.

It quickly appeared that my energy hadn't suffered any damage. After implementing a few more healing techniques, the two White Eagles left.

When I opened my eyes, my first thought was, "Am I dead?" But the plass ceiling of the healing chamber looked nothing like my ideas of the first stations in the Great Journey. It just dispensed a pale whitish glow.

Turning my head to the right, I saw the familiar faces of the two escort priests.

As usual, they did not say a thing.

I looked around. No Lady Elyani.

I closed my eyes again, and I cried.

5.18 Revelation sky

During these months, Gervin was frequently called to the female wing of the temple. Many orders of priestesses were experiencing difficulties in relation to the deterioration of the fields. He often took me with him,

5 – The Book of the Mysteries of Eisraim

inviting me to carefully observe the priestesses' energy and attempt to judge their degree of awakening.

It was still difficult for me to understand how someone could be highly connected to divine spheres, and yet be a sleeper. Nevertheless, these *wise women in the Law* were not all the same. The differences often had to do with the order they belonged to. Some of them spoke ve-ry slo-wly and hardly seemed to notice my presence in the room, while others had a sharp glow in their eyes and moved fast, like the priestesses of the White Eagle. When Lady Teyani spoke I could never know in advance what she was going to say, and I often missed the meaning of her words. Besides, she laughed when I really could not see anything funny.

As weeks passed, I reached the dramatic conclusion that there were many people in the temple who spoke ve-ry, ve-ry slo-wly. Even more dramatic was the fact that the Salmon Robe priests showed *all* the symptoms of being asleep. When I watched them – students and teachers – I found myself predicting what their next move would be. "Now Ram is going to walk to the doorway... done! Now, Motser is going to ask Ram, '*How are you to-day, my friend in the Law?*' Done! Now Ram is going to ask Motser about his parents... done!" And I loathed myself for not being fundamentally different from them. What used to be a peaceful routine of study and ritual practice had turned into a nightmare.

My travelling lessons were refreshing breaks. Apart from Gervin, Lady Elyani was the only person I could speak to at a normal pace. But I hated to imagine what opinion she had of me – probably a boring sleeper who rarely understood her jokes and never had anything interesting to tell her.

I felt like a stranger among the Salmon priests, but I didn't belong anywhere else.

"*Szar traveller, I greet you at the top of the square!*"

"*Controller Elyani, I greet you at the top of the square!*"

"Let us go straight to the triangle," she directed.

Trying to pre-empt her instructions, I swiftly spun into a silvery vortex that lifted me out of darkness visible. A sequence of fast-moving vortices led me out of the intermediary spheres, and I soon found myself in a glorious field of stars.

"*Controller Elyani, I greet you at the bottom of the triangle!*"

"*Szar traveller, I greet you at the bottom of the triangle!*"

"Elyani, why do I never see any gods when you take me to the spheres of the triangle?"

"I was waiting for you to ask me that," Elyani said.

It made me realise I could have asked her the question months ago.

Elyani immediately felt the wave of sadness inside me, "Hey, what's happening to you?"

"I'm all right. So what should I do to see the gods? Each time I move in the upper fields of stars, I look for guardians. But I never seem to find anyone I could request access from."

"This is because we usually travel in quite high areas where the gods do not like to be disturbed by visitors," she explained. "But I could try to arrange something for you if you want."

After a few seconds of silence, her light appeared in front of me in the space.

"Follow me, traveller!"

She took me to a large golden stream, and invited me to ride it.

"Speed up!" she instructed, promptly adding, "Carefully!"

"I know. I've learnt my lesson."

"Faster, faster."

This was *no problem in the Law*. The stream was massive, yet extremely stable. Soon, I noticed that huge clouds of blue, orange and yellow light were moving towards me.

When I told Elyani about them, she replied, "Just keep moving."

"But these clouds are coming straight at me! Very fast!"

"No, Szar traveller. *You* are going straight into them."

"Mother of the Light!" I exclaimed in horror.

Before I had time to think, I hit the first cloud.

The field of stars instantly disappeared. Without any transition, I found myself in a completely different landscape, a green valley surrounded by rolling hills.

"Elyani?" I called.

There was no answer.

"Where the Underworld am I?" I thought. I started walking, stunned by the extraordinary quality of light that illuminated the valley.

An astonishing landscape, without mists!

In the kingdom, wherever you went, you were immersed in the mists. The fact of being surrounded by such a spectacular view opened a completely different state of mind. And the trees were amazingly beautiful. They were not just shining, they seemed to be made of light.

I kept calling, "Elyani! Elyani!" but no response came. "That's it!" I thought. "I must have done something wrong again and killed myself. This must be the first station of the Great Journey, or perhaps even the Fields of Peace."

Not far in front of me was a small stream. When I reached it, I plunged my hand into its crystal water and drank.

"Oh my Lord Melchisedek! How incredibly delicious!" I exclaimed. Then I thought, "If I can drink, then perhaps I am not dead after all."

"Szar!" I heard a woman call my name.

It was not Elyani's voice. "Underworld Further Down! If they know my name here then it must be the Great Journey. I am dead."

A woman was walking towards me. She wore a long emerald-green dress, and waves of reddish hair fell down over her hips. As she came nearer, I was struck by how amazingly beautiful she was.

"Are you Elyani?" I ventured to ask.

5 – The Book of the Mysteries of Eisraim

"No, I am a friend of hers," the woman smiled. "My name is Mareena. Elyani has sent me to tell you that you are perfectly safe here."

"Ah?" was all I could answer. I did not dare ask where I was, but the woman must have read my thoughts. "You are in one of the worlds of the triangle," she said. "To return to Eisraim, all you have to do is lie down and fall asleep. Elyani will take care of you."

"Ah?" Inside myself, I thought, "Gervin, I know I'm not supposed to, but still, I wish you could tell me what I should say to this person."

"Just lie down, Szar!" Mareena instructed.

I did as she commanded. But as I lay down my eyes beheld the sky. "Oh my Lord Melchisedek! This is... This is..." Never in my entire life had I even imagined that something as magnificent as that sky could exist. The blue was so clear, so alive that my heart was shocked and I started crying.

The woman sat down on the grass beside me. She slowly passed her hand over my forehead and gently closed my eyes. "Fear not, Szar. You will return here, and sooner than you think."

And I fell asleep.

When I woke up, I was back in the take-off room. The slab of the sarcophagus had been removed. The two priests were waiting for me.

"Oh, no! I missed Elyani *again!*" I thought with consternation. It was at least my twentieth unsuccessful attempt at remaining conscious while returning to my body.

I sat up for a second. Then I lay down again and closed my eyes.

I tuned in and asked, as if the travelling session was still going on, "Elyani, where was I?"

To my great surprise, she answered through darkness visible, "Szar?"

"Where was I, Elyani? I *need* to know!"

"Catching glimpses of the world of the gods. Nothing more, nothing less."

"Elyani, it was so beautiful. That sky... I never suspected the world of the gods or anything else in the creation could be so beautiful. Can I go back there?"

"I am sure it will happen," Elyani answered. "Are you going to be all right, Szar?"

Stupidly I said yes, and Elyani terminated the conversation.

When I returned to the dormitory of the Salmon Robe, all I could do was collapse on my bed and cry.

Good Artold came and sat by my side. "*Praise the Lord Mel,chi,se,dek, Szar, my friend in the Law! How are you to, day?*" his desperately monotonous voice droned.

"Artold, please, leave me alone!" I cried.

Taken by surprise by this *unlawfully unusual* answer, Artold left the room. As if nothing had happened.

I couldn't stop sobbing.

It lasted for hours. I had no idea what was happening to me. I felt completely devastated. I couldn't find the strength to get up and resume my normal occupations.

Flat on my bed with my eyes closed, I tuned into the space and called, "Elyani, where are you?"

Through darkness visible, Elyani's answer came immediately. "Not far, *my friend in the Law*. Not far."

"Elyani, what is happening to me? Why do I feel so miserable?"

"Your soul is longing for the world of the gods," she said in a soft voice.

"How can I be crying for a place I don't even know, Elyani?"

"This longing for the Light, it is in everyone," she answered. "It is like a wound – the wound that came when we were separated from the Divine."

"How can it hurt so much?"

"There is nothing that can hurt more than this."

"Was this woman a goddess?" I asked.

"Mareena? Of course she is a goddess!"

"She was so amazingly beautiful."

"Szar-ka, all gods are amazingly beautiful."

"And that sky was... Why does everything look so grey down here?"

To this, Elyani had no answer. She just surrounded me with her presence in darkness visible.

So peaceful, and beautiful.

"What should I do now?" I asked.

"Just lie down," she said. "I'll help you fall asleep."

Sleep, sleep... always sleep!

5.19 Led by the Mother of the Light

It was early in the morning. The Salmon Robe priests were about to perform a special ceremony under the guidance of six of their teachers. In a large chapel of the enclave of the *Most Ancient and Lawful Orders*, the floor had been covered with carefully arranged flower petals and grains. There were dozens of fruits of all colours, and at least two hundred flames.

My young friends were starting to be well trained. Every one knew exactly which part to play, and the lengthy preparations were silently carried out like a fine piece of choreography.

Not long before sunrise we each sat in our allotted place, and the singing began. It was a ritual to the Mother of the Light, the facet of the Universal Goddess who, said the Law, had *unfolded the early stages of the creation*. She was also regarded *as the highest principle of compassion*, the one who blessed and protected the children of the Law, that is, every living soul in the kingdom. Some of the most moving hymns of the Law, and also some of the most tremendous rituals, were dedicated to the Mother of the Light.

5 – The Book of the Mysteries of Eisraim

After completing the opening hymns all the priests started chanting in one voice, "*To the Mother of the Light, I give, I give.*" With each "I give," precious oils were poured into the fire, making hissing sounds which added rhythm and magic to the incantations. The combination of mantras, occult forces and high surrender to the Universal Deity created an exceptionally powerful and vibrant space.

"*To the fresh Waters from which the Fire sprang, I give, I give.*
To her who chanted the Dawn of Creation, I give, I give.
To her who is the Molten Sea and the Sea of Lightning, I give, I give.
To her who is the beginning and the end, I give, I give.
To the Great Dragon, the Mother of the Endless Night, I give, I give.
To the feminine who is the creation, I give, I give.
To the source from which all the gods arose, I give, I give.
To her precious essence of fluid immortality, I give, I give.
To her who stood before time, I give, I give.
To her who gave birth to the stars, I give, I give.
To the primordial substance which was before the Earth, I give, I give.
To her who was the Magic of the Ancient Days, I give, I give.
To her who breastfeeds the child, I give, I give.
To her who is the compassion and the Mother of all beings, I give, I give.
To the night to which all the gods will return, I give, I give.
Unfathomable is thy name, limitless thou shinest.
To the Mother of the Light, I give, I give."

The presence brought down by the fire ritual was massive. It triggered a profound wave, which rose from the depths of my being. Something inside me exploded. My heart flared. I started feeling vast, as if my body was spread for miles around the temple, with my head high in the mists of the kingdom's sky.

"Please, Mother, help! Help me awaken," I asked with all the strength of my despair. And in this expanded state, I drew from huge forces and kept calling, "Let me not remain a sleeper! Please, Mother, help!"

A response came.

A presence of infinity turned her face towards me. And the certitude materialised inside me, "If I stay with the Salmon Robe priests, I will *never* become an awakened one."

It was absolute. Not like an idea or a human decision. A clear fountain of divinely gigantic proportions. As if time and its secrets had been condensed in one point of complete knowingness, at the core of my being.

It was limpid, obvious and final.

If I stayed with them, I would *never* awaken.

"Well then, let us take sleep by surprise, and go!" my clear fountain responded. "Walk out!"

Was I about to make a cosmic mistake?

In this heightened state, I couldn't care less.

So I did it.

I did something which only a few months earlier I would have found inconceivable. I stood up in the middle of the ritual, and slowly walked towards the door of the chapel.

Completely unacceptable, according to the rules of my priestly caste. Abandoning a ritual for no lawfully acceptable reason was an offence against the gods. But it came as a total surprise, both to my fellow apprentices and to the elder priests who directed us that day. True to their sleeper's nature, they ignored my move. They all kept singing their ritual, invoking the Goddess and pouring oblations in the fire. And this only added to the unreality of the situation.

"I can walk out and never come back, and it will not make any difference to any of them, or to anyone else. Another priest will take my place, chant the hymns I would have chanted, do the tasks I would have performed, and the world will be exactly the same." And the Mother of the Light whispered to me that being a highly replaceable pawn was one of the hallmarks of a sleeper.

The time it took to reach the door seemed to stretch into an aeon. My self-awareness was total, effortlessly noticing every single detail in the room all at once: the way each person sang, every ritual gesture they performed, every attitude on their face.

"These people are *so* asleep! *So* asleep!" the realisation hit me again. "*Mother of the Light, protect my way!*"

When I finally reached the door, I felt like a different man. A part of me was being left behind. A chapter of my life had ended.

I walked along the colonnade that bordered the building, sat in the garden, and listened to the magnificent singing. From outside.

I was light. Free. Infinite.

The splinter had been removed from my heart.

I called through darkness visible, "Gervin, I must speak to you. Can I come *now*?"

"*Now?* This sounds serious!" Gervin answered. "Come right now, then."

On my way to the enclave of the jewels it crossed my mind that Gervin might not be very pleased to see me walk away from the training in which he had enrolled me.

"*Mother of the Light, protect my way!*"

It was as clear as the fountain. After explaining to him what had just happened, I simply said, "Gervin, I walked out of the class. It's finished. I cannot go back there."

Gervin did not react. He just asked, "Why?"

"Gervin, they are completely asleep. If I stay with them, I *know* that I will not become awakened. But it's more than just this. From the deepest of myself, I know it is wrong for me to be with them. I cannot explain why, but I *know* I have to leave."

5 – The Book of the Mysteries of Eisraim

Gervin looked at me with a touch of irony in his smile. "Oho!" he said, in a way that didn't tell me much. "Do you know what you want to do next?"

This took me completely by surprise. In a world where all people believed their destiny to be fully traced from the moment they came out of their mother's womb, this question *never* arose. Had I been normal, I would have followed the line of my parents. Having become a priest, I should have followed the rule of my order. But now...

"What do I want to do next?" I echoed. The situation was so odd that all I could do was let the clear fountain take over.

"I want to awaken, Gervin," I finally answered.

Gervin, still smiling, asked, "And what else do you want?"

"That's all I want, Gervin, but I pray to the Lord Melchisedek he will not take me away from you."

Gervin's laugh signalled he was happy with my answer. "That's it," he joked, "you are already trying to bargain with the Lord!" Then he became serious, "What do you think the priests of your caste will say when they learn that you are leaving them?"

"Probably nothing. My behaviour does not fall into any of their categories, same as when I clapped my hands in Artold's face. They will keep going. As if nothing had happened. Or perhaps they will say I am sick in my mind and badly in need of a healing."

"Do you think that by walking out you have taken sleep by surprise?" Gervin continued.

I spoke from the clear fountain, "The Mother of the Light has taken *me* by surprise!"

"Mm..." Gervin nodded. To my immense relief, looking deep into my eyes he declared, "You are right, Szar, there are probably some more awakening challenges for you than spending another ten years studying in the company of parrots of the Law."

The instant breathed infinity. It was simple and vast like the Mother of the Light.

But everything suddenly became more complicated when Gervin asked, "What caste of priests do you think would suit you the best?"

The idea that a man could decide for himself which caste he would join was completely out of the Atlantean world! I remained silent, not just because of the absurdity of the question, but also because one of the things I wanted the most in the kingdom was to deserve to wear the same brown robe as Gervin. But his order was mysterious, and probably reserved for awakened ones, like Lehrmon, Master Esrevin, or Melchard the high priest.

I was sinking into an abyss of sadness. "Have my failed efforts of awakening made me an outcast?"

"Who says you are failing?" Gervin replied vigorously. "Remember when Szar-ka arrived at Eisraim. What do you think he would have done if the Mother of the Light had knocked at his heart and inspired him to walk out in the middle of a master ritual?"

I sighed, "Szar-ka would have patiently waited until the revelation passed, like some kind of headache, and then he would have gone on with his daily routines."

"As if nothing was," Gervin smiled, the compassion of the Mother of the Light shining in his eyes.

Abruptly, he clapped his hands right in front of my nose. "Very true! So you are no longer Szar-ka, and perhaps I have not completely wasted my time with you."

"I am no longer Szar-ka," I said with tears in my eyes, "but it hurts, because I am nobody else either, and I don't even know who it is I am supposed to be, or if I will ever be that."

"There, there, my son," rock-solid Gervin replied, "I could probably pat your back and make you feel better, but I don't know that it would help you. When a man undertakes the journey to awakening, he must unequivocally face the possibility that he may never get anywhere, and that unless he reaches his final goal, he will have lost all the comfort of his former condition for nothing." Looking straight into my eyes, Gervin gently hammered, "This is true for you, as it was for me before you!"

Containing my tears, I held onto the clear fountain. Then with a tempter's voice, Gervin asked, "Do you sometimes regret the time when you were about to become a noble of the administrative castes, with a loving wife and a comfortable, simple life in front of you?"

"A simple life indeed! But then how would I have ever known how beautiful the fields of stars are? And that which I saw in Marka's eyes, I would never have known either."

"Yes. But now that you have seen these things, would you like to go back to life in the lay world? If you wanted to, it would be very possible, you know. You could return and claim the high position you earned for yourself in the games. I could help you. And with all the things you have learnt here, you would be a real tiger among men. Princes would compete to have you in their court."

"Never!" I clenched my fists, "Never, never, never! If a man disregards the clear fountain, then he may lose it and never find it again!"

"Very true," Gervin grinned. "Lawful thanks for reminding me."

I smiled at myself giving lessons to Master Gervin. But my heart was not merry.

"Gervin," I begged him, "will you give me some direction?"

Gervin spent a few seconds looking intensely at one of the *living walls*. I looked there too, but could only see the aquamarine glow. Finally he said, "I have a mission for you, Szar. I need someone to go and collect a soft stone, a field amplifier. Fior, a brother of our temple, has prepared it for me. It is a precious object. You will have to take great care of it. Fior is staying in a small hermitage in the mountains of Lasraim. I suggest you

5 – The Book of the Mysteries of Eisraim

take advantage of this mission to make a tour of a number of places of pilgrimage in the forests of Nadavan. There you can rest your mind, and let the clear fountain inspire you."

I couldn't have imagined anything more reviving and exciting.

"As for now," said Gervin, "why don't you go and meditate in the chapel of Lord Gana? And *get some lawful rest*. I will meet you tomorrow to give you instructions for your journey."

I thanked him wholeheartedly. But as I was about to walk out, it occurred to me I no longer had a place to sleep. Or was I to return to my former quarters? Holy Underworld! I hoped not!

I turned to Gervin and tentatively asked, *"Get some lawful rest... where?"*

"Where? Mm..." Gervin smiled and pretended to be looking to the magic *living wall* where much seemed to be happening, judging by his intense gaze and serious beard twinging. Then he answered, "Third door on your right, coming out of here. It's Lehrmon's apartment, but I am sure he won't mind if you stay there while he is away. For your meals, just turn up to the refectory of the building next door. I will tell them you have moved here."

Lehrmon's apartment? In the enclave of the jewels! This sounded like an incredible promotion.

When, I walked out of the aquamarine chamber, aghast and abuzz, I told myself, "Good Lord Melchisedek, Mother of the Light and Far Underworld! I wished I could have walked out of my class long ago!"

5.20 Robed

I was woken up in the middle of the night by an anxiety attack.

Which caste did I belong to?

In the deep blue glimmers of the sapphire room I sat up on the bed, catching my breath.

There was something eerie about the silence – the first night in five years without the snoring of the Salmon sleepers. And this room, with its crystal-like asperities on the walls and high vaulted ceiling that made it look like a huge sapphire geode, was just too big and beautiful for me. So much space all for myself made it difficult to breathe. It wasn't the kind of premises prescribed for apprentices by the canon of the Salmon Robe.

"If I am a Salmon Robe priest, then I am breaking the Law!"

Breaking the Law! Just thinking of the possibility made me shudder.

But I had just walked out of the Salmon Robe. I was no longer to follow their Law.

"But if I am no longer a Salmon priest, then... what am I?"

It was plainly unthinkable for a man not to belong to a caste!

Which verses of the Law would I be chanting in the morning? How was I to salute people in the temple? What was I going to wear? How was I to look and speak?

I was paralysed with fear. In the kingdom, people found their roots and their identity in the social group they belonged to. The Law said, *"A man's nature is the nature of his caste,"* and,

"Fear not, doubt not, man of the Law!
Just walk along the path of your caste,
The Law takes care of those who care for the Law."

"I am no one, nothing, nowhere!" Feeling like a complete failure, I sobbed, unable to find rest. The ugly splinter was back in my heart, feeling worse than ever. I envied Artold and the sleepers of the Salmon Robe, and a part of myself could not avoid wishing that none of this nightmare had ever happened.

When dawn finally came, I did not even dare to go out of the room, for fear of being seen wearing the Salmon gown. And what if I met one of the Salmon priests? I did not go and get any food, I just hid until it was time to see Gervin.

When I arrived in the aquamarine chamber it did not take long for Gervin to realise I was in deep turmoil. As he inquired about my health, I said, "Gervin, I am losing my mind. I no longer know who I am."

Gervin took me completely by surprise, "And what if this was part of your training, Szar? And by the way, tell me, who were you exactly?"

"I was Szar, apprentice of the Salmon Robe priests and student of the Law."

"Nonsense!" Gervin thundered. "Only sleepers think of themselves in that way. You are a spark of the Divine Spirit, beyond all castes and beyond all forms. You can *be* anything, you can *do* anything!"

That, again, was completely beyond my mind. All I could do was to hold onto the clear fountain – which, incidentally, brought an immediate reconnection. "Ah! The clear fountain!" I thought. "How come I did not remember to draw from its waters last night?

How could I forget?"

I tuned into its pure verticality and instantly felt lighter.

Out of nowhere, Gervin asked, "Szar, do you know which is my caste?"

I remained silent. High Atlantean initiates like Gervin had the privilege of not revealing their caste to anyone. One referred to them simply according to the colour of their gown. Thus my master was Gervin 'of the Brown Robe', and it would have been unacceptably rude of me to ask any further details.

"Well, I will tell you which is my caste," he said, leaving me breathless.

I could hardly believe this moment had come. Rooted like a gigantic fig tree, he raised his voice,

"I am Gervin, of the Masters of Thunder."

Mother of the Light, was that possible?

5 – The Book of the Mysteries of Eisraim

The Masters of Thunder were a legend. The most incredible rumours of miracles circulated about them. For hundreds of years, they had accomplished feats that defied the imagination and had changed the course of history. Some of them had even taken part in the revelation of the Law! The idea that I could be standing in front of one of them left me more speechless than ever.

With my eyes open wide, I must have looked so stupefied that Gervin burst out laughing, "Do you have such a low opinion of your teacher that you should become dubious when you hear this?"

I tried to say no, but my voice choked and my mouth stayed open. Moreover, I had no idea of the lawful way to address a Master of Thunder.

"You see, Szar-ka," Gervin twinged his beard, "here we have a problem. I personally think that spending a few years without a caste would be excellent for your spiritual development."

Had I not been paralysed, that thought would have sent me gasping and convulsing, for sure.

"But there are too many technical difficulties associated with that," Gervin went on, "and also, this part of the kingdom is not warm enough to let you wander around undressed. The problem is, you do not really fit into any of the castes of the temple, even though, looking at you right now, I think Blue priestess might perhaps be just what you need."

I didn't find that funny.

"There could be a possibility though," Gervin kept twinging his beard. "But I don't know that I should advise you to take it. You see, we Masters of Thunder sometimes take apprentices. As a last resort, we might consider dressing you in the Brown Robe."

Mother of the Light, where was I?

Gervin smiled at me, "Do you think you would like to become an apprentice of the Masters of Thunder?"

I was compelled to shake my head, "No! That can't be!" Then, holding onto the clear fountain, I immediately said, "I mean, yes! Yes!"

Gervin pulled a face, "Contrary to what you may believe, it is not such a rosy prospect. You thought that being caste-less was bad... well, let me tell you, in many respects, being an apprentice of the Masters of Thunder is much worse. If you decide to take this direction, I must warn you that some hard and painful trials are waiting for you."

Gervin the rock gazed at me.

The anxiety and the dark thoughts of the night rushed back into my mind. "I would love to follow you, Gervin, but I don't know that I will ever be capable," I whinged.

"Unrepentant sleeper!" his voice held an infinite softness, "Why do you think I have been spending all this time with you?" With feigned harshness, he added, "And when will you remember that you can be anything, and you can do anything? Thus says Gervin, Master of Thunder, engaging the Word of his lineage. Do you think he is a liar? From now on, each time you doubt yourself, you will be insulting me and my lineage by challenging my words!"

Lawfully bewildering, that sounded.

Gervin looked straight into my eyes and asked in a solemn voice, "Szar, now for the first of three times, I ask you, will you accept my offer to become an apprentice of the Masters of Thunder?"

I was too annihilated to speak.

"Yes!"

It was not me who had answered. It was the clear fountain.

Gervin looked through me. "Only after the third time will this acceptance become binding for you and for me. And by then, *a lot* will have happened." There was a long silence. "Now go back to your apartment. I will get a *lawful attendant* to bring you a brown gown. Put it on and *for the Lord Melchisedek's sake*, go and have some food, and *get some lawful rest*. You will need it before your journey."

5.21 Starting a new life in the Law

Later on that day, I went for a travelling session with Elyani. Gervin had told me this was to be the last lesson, at least for some time. To mark the occasion, I decided to walk to the take-off room by myself, rather than wait for the two sleeper priests of the healing chambers.

Now that everything was becoming so different, I was not sure if I would ever see Elyani again. I was going to miss hearing her voice.

As I was strolling along the alleys of the temple's lawful centre (I hated walking fast) it came to my mind that this was my last chance to succeed in my 'striving exercise' and surprise the White Eagle by not losing consciousness on my return to the kingdom.

How was I to tell her farewell?

How was I to tell anyone anything? Now that the colour of my gown had changed, I didn't even know how to salute people. In the last months, I had often thought I would have been immensely proud to wear the brown gown, because Lehrmon, Esrevin and Melchard were highly awakened people, like Gervin. Now that it had happened, I felt immensely embarrassed.

I didn't even know how to walk! Each order of priests walked in a particular way. They did not have to learn these things, they came to them with time, through etheric osmosis. And there were a thousand other little things dictated by your caste: how to sit, how to clear your throat or blow your nose, and even how to go to the toilet!

No one had told me how to do these things with a brown gown. It made me feel like an impostor.

"*Praise the Lord Melchisedek, Szar of the Salmon Robe!*" a priest saluted me.

5 – The Book of the Mysteries of Eisraim

"*All glory to the Lord Melchisedek, Golden Cudgel of the Dark-Golden Robe,*" I replied with a lawful smile. Then, gripped by a wave of anxiety, I looked down to make sure I hadn't forgotten to put on the brown gown.

Thank the Lord Melchisedek, there was nothing pink left on me!

But then why had he called me Szar of the Salmon Robe?

"This Golden Cudgel is such a hopeless sleeper!" I thought as I watched him walk away. The encounter made me feel more secure. The people who knew me – there were not many of them – were unrepentant sleepers. None of them would even notice that the colour of my robe had changed.

"*Oh my Lord Melchisedek!*" a voice filled with incredulity called me, "My little Szar? Is that you?"

"Hum... Praise the Lord Melchisedek, Mouridji of the Purple Robe."

"Congratulations, son! Don't you look handsome!" the short old woman took my hands. "And I knew it. I *knew* Gervin was making a *big* mistake when he sent you to the Salmon Robe. I told him, by the way. The very day you arrived here. So he has taken the advice of Mouridji the prophetess, at last!"

"Hum... yes... *And how are you, my friend in the...* I mean, yes, Mouridji of the Prophetic Robe."

"I am so happy, son!" and in her joy, the *wise woman in the Law* stood on her toes and kissed me on each cheek.

I blushed. It was the first time someone had kissed me since my parents' farewell when I left for boarding school.

"Everyone in the temple is going to be *so* happy!" Mouridji exulted. "I can't wait to tell my friends."

"Ah?"

"I'll let you go. You must be very busy. The priests of the Brown Robe are always so busy. But if you ever need something, don't hesitate to come and ask me. Mouridji knows *everyone* in this temple, you know."

After this friendly exchange, I left the alley and descended into the catacomb-like corridors of the under-temple. It was a longer way to the take-off room, but there was plenty of time. And it was so quiet down there.

5.22 Skeleton in the sarcophagus

It was the end of the session. The insidious heaviness of the sandman effect was overtaking me, as usual.

"No! I will *not* sleep!" I pulled on my resolution, and recited to myself verses of the book of Maveron that Lehrmon had taught me,

"*Of all needs, the need for sleep is the most irresistible.*
Some can resist desire.
Some can resist hunger, and even thirst.

Some can even resist death.
But who can resist sleep?
He who never sleeps, never dies."
I felt heavier and heavier.
I called inside, "Help! Help! Gervin, help!"
The space was thick and dark. The black oblivion was so tempting that the challenge seemed impossible. For a second, I was tempted to give up.
"No! Help! Please, help!"
But who can resist sleep?
Succumb... heavy!
Sleep, like an infamous beast, was calling me into its arms.
Succumbbb... heavy! Succumbbb...
The wanting for slumber was so enormous that I was no longer myself. The pull turned into pain.
"Help! Where is my body? If only I could find my body!"
Every fibre of my being was aching. It became unbearable.
But who can resist sleep?
Uniting every part of myself, I launched a desperate call, "O, Mother of the Light, he-e-e-elp!"
From far away, a strange voice responded. It was so feeble that at first I couldn't hear what it said.
"Whoever you are, help! Please help me! Let me not fall unconscious."
"*Space Matrix access granted*," the voice whispered. "*Engage travelling through intention.*"
"My body!"
Instantly, I was back in my physical body.
The pain was excruciating, as if every single muscle was being branded by thousands of tiny red-hot needles.
I opened my eyes. The plass sarcophagus was closed.
I tried to move my arms, but it hurt so much that it forced a muffled cry out of me. This started a loud burst of coughing, which caused a fit of lacerating pain in the muscles of my chest.
What if Elyani had already gone?
Drawing from my last resources, I half-sat in the sarcophagus and started pushing the light slab with my hands and my head.
Elyani and her friend Seyani were on their way out. When they heard the coughing, they quickly turned back, watching with perplexity as the slab moved.
Still spluttering, I managed to thrust my head out of the sarcophagus.
With a stunned smile on her face, Elyani came and helped me push the slab. She stood close to me.
I sat up, panting, and looked up at her.
There was an interesting silence.
"Lady, Elyani... I really wanted to thank you..." I was interrupted by a violent fit of coughing. When I finally managed to control it, I panted,

5 – The Book of the Mysteries of Eisraim

"Thank you for all the time and the care... It has been a privilege..." But the coughing took over again.

Elyani was so close she could have touched me. She contemplated me – pale as a corpse, thin as a skeleton, and coughing like a filosterops.

She waited for me to catch my breath, then started a lawful answer, "*Farewell, my friend. The Law has brought us together, now it takes us apart...*" But she interrupted herself. She dropped her formal voice and just said, "It's been very good for me too, Szar," and she gave me a smile.

A beautiful smile, luminous and warm like the White Eagle.

It made me forget to cough. I didn't know what else to say.

For a moment, neither did Elyani.

Of course, we didn't look into each others' eyes. It would have been unlawful.

Lady Seyani waited tactfully.

"Congratulations on your Brown Robe," Elyani said tentatively.

"Thanks," I nodded.

She hesitated a few more seconds, then she quickly added, "For a long, long time, the Brown Robes and the White Eagles have been friends. Farewell, friend." And she turned round and left the chamber.

Seyani followed her silently.

I waited a few seconds, just in case they came back.

Then I let myself collapse in the sarcophagus.

"Brown Robe, hey!" I snapped my fingers joyfully. But it triggered another violent coughing fit.

5.23 Tirtha tour

I took a boat on the Holy Fontelayana river, then another one on the Ferex river. It took me to the edge of the forests of Nadavan. From there, I walked.

The first of the places of pilgrimage I was to visit on my way to the mountains of Lasraim was a small lake nested in a clearing. When I reached there the first thing I did was look at myself in the water. Szar of the Brown Robe! I could hardly believe it was true. Only a few days ago, I was Szar, the apprentice ritualist. And now... who was I exactly?

This was the question Gervin had suggested I keep asking myself during the pilgrimage. And he did not want me to define myself according to the image of *any* caste, even the Masters of Thunder (which was just as well, since I really could not imagine myself as one of them).

"You can be anything, you can do anything," I tried saying to myself over and over. But I couldn't get it to ring true. So instead, I told myself, "The clear fountain can be anything. The clear fountain can do anything." That made sense to my soul.

As I headed north, I began to feel stronger. I was gradually getting used to seeing myself dressed in brown. The atmosphere of the tirthas I passed on my way washed away the sorrows of the last weeks. It was exciting to sleep in tree-houses again. There were always plenty of them in places of pilgrimage. They were surrounded by orchards laden with luscious fruits. And thanks to the good works of the warp of fields, the weather was always kind.

I finally reached the first spurs of the mountains of Lasraim, so called because they stretched from the county of Lasseera in the north to the county of Eisraim in the south. Brother Fior's hermitage was not located very high up in the mountains. I was a slow climber, so it took me a whole day to reach it. The landscape was most inspiring. Going higher, the mists became sparser. I could sometimes see as far as a thousand lawful feet in front of me.

I reached Brother Fior's around sunset. I was charmed by the clever troglodytic construction. Its tree-house facade, woven by branches, grew to resemble a temple frontispiece. Fior, who had sensed my arrival, was waiting for me at the portal-style entrance. He was a short, fat, elderly man with a jovial smile and not much hair left. He was dressed in a worn-out dark-grey robe, and welcomed me warmly, *"Praise the Lord Melchisedek, Szar of the Brown Robe, disciple of Master Gervin!"* seeming glad to have a visitor.

Following a short and lawful exchange, he took me for a quick tour of his hermitage, which was dug far deeper into the rock than could be suspected from outside. At the end of a vast entrance hall, a corridor led to several other rooms. The stone walls were lined with plass, making the troglodyte construction a lawful dwelling with *living walls*.

After giving me a strange hot brew made of mountain herbs, Master Fior took me to one of the rooms at the back of his hermitage. There the precious egg-shaped stone, about half an inch long, was resting on a stone altar in the middle of the room. It was one of those jelly-like soft crystals that were used to draw power from the warp of fields.

Fior was proud of his work. "You will have to take care of this thing, my boy. It has taken me four months to crystallise it."

"I shall take care of this thing indeed, Master Fior. Shall I carry it in my bag?"

"In a special box, that I will give you tomorrow." He stood still, letting me contemplate the fruit of his labour.

"Have you ever used a stone like this?" he asked.

"I have never used any soft stones, Master Fior."

He half-whispered in a tone of wonder, "A stone of this calibre can do extraordinary things."

"Like talking to people through the voice channels of darkness visible?"

"Any common stone can do that. The one before your eyes can draw awesome powers from the fields. You should ask Master Gervin, he knows

5 – The Book of the Mysteries of Eisraim

a great lawful deal about stones. And his Field Wizards! Some of the best stone-makers in the kingdom. Have you met Master Woolly?"

"No."

Seeing my complete ignorance, Master Fior refrained from saying more.

He had prepared a copious dinner, which we ate silently. Then he showed me to my room.

As I was falling asleep on my couch, I thought of Elyani. Her fresh smile had been with me since I left the temple.

Would I ever see her again? I had tried to speak to her through darkness visible a few times, but with no success. Could Master Fior's soft stone connect me to her?

"Elyani?" I tuned in and tried to rest on the stone's energy.

The result was instant. A voice channel was open.

"Elyani?" I called.

I heard an unknown voice shouting, "What is *that*? Someone is breaking into the field of the chapel. Shall I call Namron?"

"No, wait!" Elyani's voice came through. She addressed me, "Szar, I don't have time to speak to you now, please disconnect. I will contact you later."

I immediately let go of the connection.

Had I committed another blunder?

In the morning, after I finished eating the huge breakfast that Master Fior had piled on the table for me, I stood outside the troglodyte dwelling, contemplating the mists. It had rained during the night. The open landscape of the last evening had been replaced by the usual Atlantean fog.

When everything was ready, Master Fior called me into the room where the altar stood. I watched him place the soft stone into a small plass box, the inside of which was lined with a thick dark-red velvety padding.

"The plass-field blocks the radiation of the soft stone, so no one can detect it while you are carrying it," Fior explained. "Now listen, my boy, last night I heard you testing the soft stone for long-distance communication. That was all right because you were here, but be very careful not to do anything like this once you are on your way. If for any reason you were to activate the stone, or if you opened the box, you would immediately be detected. There are thieves in this region. Do not talk to anyone on your way, and when you reach Eisraim, go straight to Gervin. Do not mention the soft stone to anyone. Lawfully understood?"

"Yes, Master Fior!"

"Now off you go, my boy. *The Lord Melchisedek be with you on the path!*"

I thanked him lawfully for his hospitality and for the food he had put in my bag, and I set off down the mountain. Inspirited by the serious nature of my mission, I walked faster than usual. It only took me half a day to reach the forests of Nadavan. From then on, I spent my days tuning into the spirits of the trees, sometimes remembering Lord Gana, sometimes wondering what Gervin had in store for me next. I slept in hidden corners of the forest, avoiding the tree-houses for fear of meeting other pilgrims.

The third evening, when I was perhaps half way to the river, I came across a splendid little lake – not one of the tirthas I had been told about, but still a highly inspiring spot. I decided to camp there and, after a dinner of grains and berries, I fell asleep with my head on my bag.

Every night I made sure the bag touched my body, so no one could take the box without waking me. There was little chance anyone could have found me, lost as I was in these forests where I never met a human soul. Still, *one can never be too cautious in the Law!* I thought of using my bag as a pillow.

It was the first time I slept with the box so close to my head. It produced strange results. I spent the whole night having the most bizarre, vivid dreams, as if a whole assembly of Blue priestesses were prophesying for me. At times, it was as if I was travelling through the spheres and meeting the White Eagle. Extraordinary images cascaded into my consciousness. It went on without interruption until dawn. I woke up feeling strange, but energised and joyful.

I dropped my robe and skipped over to the lake. Making silly loud noises, I rushed into the fresh water and swam, thanking the Lord Melchisedek for this *beautiful morning in the Law*.

But as I was swimming, something unexpected took place. Louder than ever before, I heard Elyani's voice calling me: "Szar, Szar, be careful! You are in danger!"

I tried to respond to her, but without success. I couldn't find the sphere from which the voice channel was coming.

Was there a dangerous animal in the lake?

The waters were as tranquil as they were clear.

Tuning into the clear fountain, I asked myself, "What would an awakened one do in this situation?"

The obvious answer flashed through my mind, "The box! What is happening to the box?" Gathering all my energy, I made a dash for the shore and ran full speed back to my things.

I found the bag open, the food thrown onto the ground, and no box!

"Oh, no!"

I hit my chest with my fist and yelled under the misty sky, "No! No! *Oh, Lord Melchisedek!* Not that!"

In a fraction of a second it all became clear. Sleeping with my head on the box had been a capital mistake. Without realising it, I had activated the soft stone, which had caught the attention of a thief. It had probably not been difficult for him to locate me. My amplified dreams had gone on all night.

I quickly got dressed. Holding on to the clear fountain, I became dead silent, listening for sounds that could indicate the direction taken by the thief.

5 – The Book of the Mysteries of Eisraim

But the forest was perfectly quiet and peaceful. There was not even the slightest hiss of wind. Only a few birds could be heard singing and twittering in the distance.

I looked on the ground for tracks but could not find any. I ran in one direction, then another, searching for clues.

Nothing.

Finally I collapsed pitifully on the mossy ground, and I cried. "Wake me up from this nightmare, Lord, do not abandon me!" I sobbed, hitting the ground with my fist, and praying the Lord Melchisedek that this day had never come to be.

It was the pit.

Black despair.

No way out.

"This time, I am finished."

The shame was more than I could bear. I could not see myself ever going back to Gervin, or even calling Elyani.

Dying was the only way out.

Succumb... heavy!

Slowly, I walked to the lake.

My mind had turned murky like a stagnant pool of the dark Underworld.

The truth was, I had failed. I had failed to become a public servant in Sheringa. I had failed to become a Salmon Robe priest. And now I had failed the mission that perhaps would have led me to become an apprentice of the Masters of Thunder.

"*Die with ease*," said the Law. "*The tie that binds the children of the kingdom to their body is loose.*" Already half-gone, I waded into the water slowly, ready to let myself drown and end the agony.

Who cared? I was such a highly replaceable pawn.

The murky pool was calling me.

I had water up to my chest when the clear fountain made itself felt.

"Clear fountain, my beautiful, I wish I had thought of listening to you this morning, before jumping into the water like *an idiot in the Law*."

"Then why not listen to me now?" the wisdom of the fountain answered. "By killing yourself, you will betray your master, and abandon the friends who need you."

"Who needs a fool like me? All I can do is bring shame to my master!"

There was a loaded silence.

I kept moving forward.

But as the water reached my mouth, a magnificent symbolic image appeared. The Eagle's shining Spirit of Whiteness.

The White Eagle of the gods was flying towards me, calling, "Help, Szar! Help me!"

The picture was surprisingly vivid. I shook me out of the insidious torpor into which I was sinking. For the first time ever, I interpreted an oracular image. It was limpid, obvious.

"Elyani!" There was not a shadow of a doubt. "Elyani is in trouble!"

I found myself at a crossing of destinies. On one side there was little Szar-ka. He was drowning, his consciousness engulfed by unclear spaces. On the other side, there was a man decidedly walking back to Eisraim and facing the destiny of the Brown Robe.

"Elyani! I don't want you to die!"

Deep.

The feeble murmur.

The wheel of destiny had turned.

Little Szar was dead. I had become the man in the Brown Robe.

I spat the water out of my mouth and started walking back to the shore. I gathered the food that had been spilled on the ground and threw it into my bag. And without even drying my robe I started the journey back to Eisraim.

With all the strength I could gather, I called through darkness visible: "Elyani! I am coming back. Wait for me! Whatever may be happening to you, wait for me."

There was no answer.

5.24 Surprises

When I arrived in Eisraim, I went straight to Gervin's apartment, and after lawfully paying my respects to him, declared immediately that I had lost the stone.

Gervin closed his eyes and took his head in his hands.

He was silent for a few seconds, then he looked at me in a puzzled way, "You mean you can make such a huge mistake and look me in the eyes, and speak like you do?" he said without anger.

I did not know what to do with this response. Did he mean that my incompetence was topped by outrageous arrogance?

I spoke from my heart, "Gervin, after nearly killing myself, I left Szar-ka's grief in the waters of the lake. The clear fountain inspired me. Now is no longer the time to cry, but to repair the damage. I have come to beg you to instruct me how I can recover the soft stone, or make another one. But there are other pressing matters. As I was about to give up, the White Eagle of the gods came to me and informed me that Lady Elyani was in grave danger. I request your permission to go and inquire after her health."

Gervin pulled his beard with surprise, "What has happened to Szar-ka? Where is my whingeing little boy?"

"Perhaps he is a bit less of a little boy," I sighed. "Have you heard from Lady Elyani?"

"I saw her only two hours ago. She is shining, as ever."

5 – The Book of the Mysteries of Eisraim

It was my turn to be surprised. I was utterly convinced that great perils were upon the lady of the White Eagle.

Thoughtful, I called onto the fountain.

Seeing me so perplexed, Gervin suggested, "Why don't you call her? You are becoming familiar with the voice channels of darkness visible, aren't you?"

So I sent a call. In the temple, the fields were so powerful that no soft stone was needed to access a voice channel.

Elyani answered immediately, "*All glory to the Lord Melchisedek, Szar, man of the Law.* Welcome back to the temple."

"Are you well, Elyani?"

"*Lawfully certainly well.* What about you? I was very worried about you three days ago. I tried to send you a signal. Did you receive it"

"I did, and may the Lord Melchisedek be thanked for it. Unfortunately, I wasn't wise enough to benefit from it. But please tell me again, is everything right with you? The White Eagle of the gods came..." I stopped there, as it came to my mind that perhaps I had simply misinterpreted the vision.

"I am *as lawfully fine as one can lawfully be*, Szar. Ask Master Gervin. I just saw him."

I lawfully ended the conversation.

I felt the need to sit down. It was now my turn to hold my head in my hands. My superb momentum was fast vanishing. The self-doubts were back. An impulse had pulled me away from the lake and saved my life, and that impulse was proving to be an illusion.

What, then, was left?

"I don't know, Gervin, I don't know!" The familiar flavour of despair was insidiously slipping back into me. "I don't know that I will ever make it to awakening. There seems to be such a gap! Perhaps after all I am not fit, and the reality is that you must find another candidate. I have wasted a lot of your time already. I can't see any sign that I will ever be of any help to you."

"Do you think there is something wrong with you?" Gervin asked.

"A few things, to say the least! For a start, I am... no one. I feel like a nothing, completely insubstantial. There is nothing solid inside for me to rely on, or trust. My resolves are useless. My thoughts are naive and fleeting. My vision is non-existent. And after all these years in the temple, I am still incapable of interpreting one oracular image the right way!"

"Well, my son, this kind of realisation is the beginning of wisdom! Sleepers never think there is anything wrong with themselves. They can't even imagine they could ever become different from what they are. They know that one day their hair will turn grey and their teeth will fall out, but they can't imagine that a transformation other than ageing could take place inside them. See what a long way you have come!"

What a magnanimous soul Gervin was.

I wished I could have thanked him, or even perhaps laughed with him (he particularly enjoyed it when I could laugh at my own misery). But I was sinking into the murky whirlpool, as if the waters of the lake had finally got me. "The only thing I have learnt is the taste of defeat," I whispered, and I started crying.

"I know that taste well, my son, much better than you think," Gervin replied in a soft voice. Then to my complete surprise, he asked, "Now, Szar, the time has come for me to ask you for the second time, will you accept my offer of becoming an apprentice of the Masters of Thunder?"

This could not have arrived at a worse moment.

Stunned, I stood up and looked at him, "Why would you want me?"

"This is for me to decide. Will you answer me?"

Tears were pouring from my eyes. "If I listen inside, I cannot believe that I will ever be the man you need."

"Nonsense!" Gervin yelled at me. "At the moment, all you are listening to is despair! *Wake up, man of the Law!*" Using a near-Voice threshold, he projected at me, "Szar, you can be anything, you can do anything!"

The power of his Voice shook me out of my sunken gloominess. In a solemn tone, I asked him, "Gervin, *great prophet and knower of future events*, do you really believe I will awaken?"

"That is entirely up to *you*, Szar. The archives of time cannot foretell such things, for awakening is an act of free will. If the names of those who will awaken were written in advance, then there would be no free will."

What could I do but tune into the clear fountain?

Again, I found myself at the crossing of destinies.

Two time tracks were laid in front of me – two distinct lives, each waiting for me. On one side, the murky whirlpool was taking me towards endless wandering. On the other side, Szar of the Brown Robe was standing, grounded like a rock. I could not step in one direction without letting go of the other.

Who decided?

Who had decided while I was at the lake?

A wave rose inside me, "Yes, I want to become an apprentice of the Masters of Thunder."

Gervin nodded, welcoming me high in the light.

It was warm and beautiful, and completely unknown.

"I will ask you this question a third and last time, Szar, and then it will become binding both for you and for me. By then, a lot more will have happened," he declared solemnly.

A lot more? The very thought made me shudder. As I was starting to realise, Gervin never said things like this lightly.

This time I spoke not from despair, but from what seemed to me pure objectivity. "Gervin, I really do not know what to do from here. I think I have exhausted all my resources."

5 – The Book of the Mysteries of Eisraim

The Master of Thunder burst out laughing so loudly that I had to smile myself, despite my state of annihilation. And he kept laughing. And laughing.

Until a great opening took place.

The aquamarine chamber became an awesome temple, filled with light and presence.

Everything stopped. Gervin and I became one.

A moment of eternity.

The Master of Thunder was communicating some of his power to me.

An aeon later, when the kingdom became the kingdom again, Gervin said in a gentle voice, "Szar your training has hardly begun. In a few days I will tell you what is coming next." My curiosity was aroused, but Gervin's tone clearly indicated that I should wait.

"Now..." Gervin took on a jokingly serious voice, "now, I have something to tell you."

The intonation was unmistakable – something unexpected was about to fall on my head. I slightly tucked my head in my shoulders, waiting for the blow.

"Golden Cudgel, the high priest of Gana, left his body ten days ago," Gervin began. "As you know, next week will be the celebration of the thirty-three victorious gods, those who are honoured for having triumphed in the wars against the asuras, the ancient dark forces. Now that Golden Cudgel is no longer with us, the masters of the halls of Melchisedek need another expert in Gana's lore to officiate in next week's ceremony. I told them you were the man."

My eyes staring wide, I choked, "But I know nothing about Gana's official rituals! How could you tell them that?"

Gervin pulled a face, "I did not actually say it like that. I just suggested they ask the oracle if the man could be you. And the oracle said yes! And see how you are... each time there is a little bit of challenge, you start whingeing again!" And he laughed.

"But! But... Gervin, that is not funny at all. What if I mess up the ritual to Lord Gana?"

Pointing his finger up towards heaven, Gervin said, "It's *his* problem! After all, *he* answered yes through the oracle. If you want to complain, please complain to *him*, not to me!"

Sweet Upperworld! Who else in the entire kingdom but Gervin could make jokes like this one?

5.25 Send them to hell, and they don't know how to thank you

*G*ang! Gang! Gana!

Thank the sky of the gods, brave old Gana-Gerent was there to help! The *wise man in the Law* knew every lawful thing about the rituals to Lord Gana, and six days were plenty to learn the hymns I was supposed to chant. I rehearsed frantically, starting every day before dawn and flooding my consciousness with the god's arch-mantra: *Nama Gana, Nama Gana, Gana Gana, Nam Nam*. Spending so much time in the Lord Gana's chapel was a divine treat. The more I chanted, the more I was in love with the god.

There was only one difficulty. As part of the ceremony, I was supposed to perform a dance. For Lord Gana is a great dancer among the gods. Just seeing him move his arms is enough to fall into an ecstatic trance.

Gana-Gerent tried his best to teach me the movements of Gana's ritual dance but the results weren't up to celestial standards, to say the lawful least.

When he first saw me practise, Gana-Gerent burst out laughing. "Szar of the Brown Robe, you are lucky! Lord Gana is famous in the seven spheres for his sense of humour. And contrary to other gods, he very rarely curses those human beings who worship him the wrong way!"

I found his comments only moderately reassuring.

After half an hour of exhausting practice, Gana-Gerent became impatient, "It's because you're too thin. That's what it is, *far* too thin! You'll never look like a dancer. You know that, don't you?"

"So what shall we do, *wise man in the Law*?"

"Move only your arms," he suggested.

I tried to let the god inspire my arms.

"It still doesn't work, but it's much better," Gana-Gerent conceded. "But can't you try to move your arms faster? Gana is a swift god. He does everything divinely fast. Now try to do the jump."

I jumped as high as I could.

Gana-Gerent burst out laughing again, "Don't worry, my boy. I'm sure it will work out, since Gana has named you through the oracle. *Those who have been chosen by the gods always succeed.*" And he advised me to discontinue all dancing practices once and for all. "Just let yourself be inspired by the god during the ceremony," he recommended.

Following his advice, I focussed on the recitation of the hymns, and prayed to the god for inspiration.

The celebration of the thirty-three victorious gods went like a dream. In the central crypt I found myself on a large stage in the company of some of the most respected priests of Eisraim. Thirty-three fires were lit, and the rituals were superb. Thank the Mother of the Light, I didn't faint! (It was easy, because I had to officiate the whole time.) As to the dance part, everything went fine. It just happened that when I had to dance, the audience was in far too profound a spiritual concentration to notice what was happening on the stage. Later when I asked Gana-Gerent what he had thought of my movements, he said he had preferred to keep his eyes closed through that part of the ritual.

5 – The Book of the Mysteries of Eisraim

During the celebrations I gathered some of the most beautiful of the fruits that had been presented to the thirty-three gods. When the last practice was completed I placed everything in a huge basket, which I decorated with leaves and flowers.

The following day, I took the basket to Gervin. And I greeted him by chanting verses of the Law – not like a parrot, but with spirit.

When I finished, he closed his eyes and he exclaimed, "*All glory to the teacher!*" and he directed loving thoughts to Orest, who had been his master in the Brown Robe.

"*All glory to the teacher!*" I said. "This time I have not come to ask you anything, Gervin, just to say thank you. Thank you for allowing me to serve Lord Gana, thank you for the brown robe, and hundreds of thank you's for all the rest."

We kept eye contact for some time, and there was fullness.

Finally, Gervin broke the silence, "Now, now... I have some good news that you are not going to like, and some bad news that is going to make you very happy. Let me start with the good news. I have arranged for you to go and visit certain friends of mine. They are called the Sons of the Dragon. Exceptionally powerful initiates, they are. And quite original, moreover. I am sure you will find them... interesting."

That sounded exciting, especially knowing what it took for Gervin to consider that someone was original. His next sentence, however, came as a cold shower, "But the thing you are not going to like very much is that they live quite far away, and I cannot go with you."

"How far?"

"In the county of the Red Lands, in the south."

From Eisraim, it took at least three weeks to reach the sandy deserts of the Red Lands.

I took a deep breath. "How long shall I stay with the Sons of the Dragon?"

"Well, son, this will depend on you. If you do well down there, then it may take some time."

"One hundred days?" I tentatively asked.

"Perhaps a few times one hundred days."

When he saw me containing my tears, Gervin immediately added, "But not one hundred times one hundred days!"

A few times one hundred days sounded like hundreds of long times! Master Gervin was right, I didn't like this news at all.

"What is the name of that place I must go to?" I asked.

"The temple of Vulcan, also known as the temple of the Dragon. Some extraordinary things happen over there, miracles such as you would find difficult to imagine. The Sons of the Dragon are great initiates of the Underworld."

"And what do you want me to do in that temple?"

"Mm..." Gervin sighed, and went on explaining, "Remember your words when you came back from Fior's hermitage? You described yourself as... insubstantial. Well, that was a very insightful comment, son. There is a certain..." Gervin carefully looked for his word, "a certain denseness that is missing in you. For you to be able to work with me and join the Masters of Thunder, you need to become solid as a rock."

I nodded silently. I understood exactly what he meant. "If this is what it takes to be able to work with you, then I will be glad to go, Gervin," I said in a voice that wasn't glad at all.

"Now," said Gervin with a touch of his magic wit, "let me tell you the bad news – the part you are going to like. Before you can go to the temple of the Dragon, you must undergo a preparatory journey, a short descent into the Underworld. There are some unlawfully nasty places down there, and I hate the idea of asking you to descend. But you must trust my word, it will prove quite helpful for what you have to do next." He waited a moment, then dropped the rest, "And Lady Elyani will be your guide."

When he saw my face lighting up with a joyful smile, Gervin teased me, "I knew it! This is the way apprentices are, these days. Send them to a temple to prepare them for the Fields of Peace – doom and gloom. But send them to hell, and they don't know how to thank you!"

Gervin suddenly became grave. "Now young man, beware! You will have to be thoroughly prepared for this descent, which will be *no holy day in the Law*. Elyani and I will be in charge of instructing you. And another thing: when you come back, I will ask you for the third and last time if you want to become an apprentice of the Masters of Thunder. If you say yes, then it will become binding for us both."

"Uh oh!" I thought. "Each time this has happened before, I've been in for a complete disaster. What am I going to mess up this time?"

5.26 Prepared to die

When I arrived at the portal of the female wing, a short, plump woman dressed in the white gown of the Eagles welcomed me, "*Praise the Lord Melchisedek, Szar of the Brown Robe!* I am Lady Pepni of the White Eagle." Before I had time to reply, she turned around saying, "Follow me!" and started walking fast.

"That's why the Brown Robes are friends with the White Eagles," I thought, rushing behind her. "They move fast."

Good Lord Melchisedek, how complicated this part of the temple was! There were so many corridors turning and bifurcating, all looking the same, that I doubted I would ever be able to find my way back on my own. It took at least twenty minutes before we arrived at a small inner courtyard where Elyani was waiting for me.

5 – The Book of the Mysteries of Eisraim

Pepni left, and I greeted my travelling instructor, "*Praise the Lord Melchisedek, Lady Elyani, high priestess of the White Eagle.*"

"*All glory to the Lord Melchisedek, Szar of the Brown Robe,*" she gave her unique smile.

It was the first time I could really look at her. In the reception hall I was far too surprised and intimidated, and in the sarcophagus I was far too sick and intimidated. This time, I was just intimidated.

I barely established eye contact with her (it would have been unlawful), just enough to fix her brown eyes in my memory. A bright, witty gaze – the least you could expect from someone frighteningly awake. Her curly brown hair did not reach her shoulders, which the dress of her order left half-uncovered. Her skin was shining – probably some charm that the priestesses of her order learned from Teyani the great magician.

"Congratulations on your nomination as a high priest of Gana," she said to begin the conversation. "I went to watch the fire rituals to the thirty-three victorious gods. Your performance was excellent."

"Hum..." I hoped she hadn't seen the dance.

"The way you were dancing was so different from Golden Cudgel's style," she said. "I found it fascinating."

"*Oh my Lord Melchisedek,*" I thought.

"And what about your pilgrimage in the forests of Nadavan. Did you enjoy it?" she asked.

"Nothing short of a disaster, Lady Elyani. After I received your emergency signal at the lake..."

"I know, I know," she interrupted me. "Szar, look at this place, do you like it?"

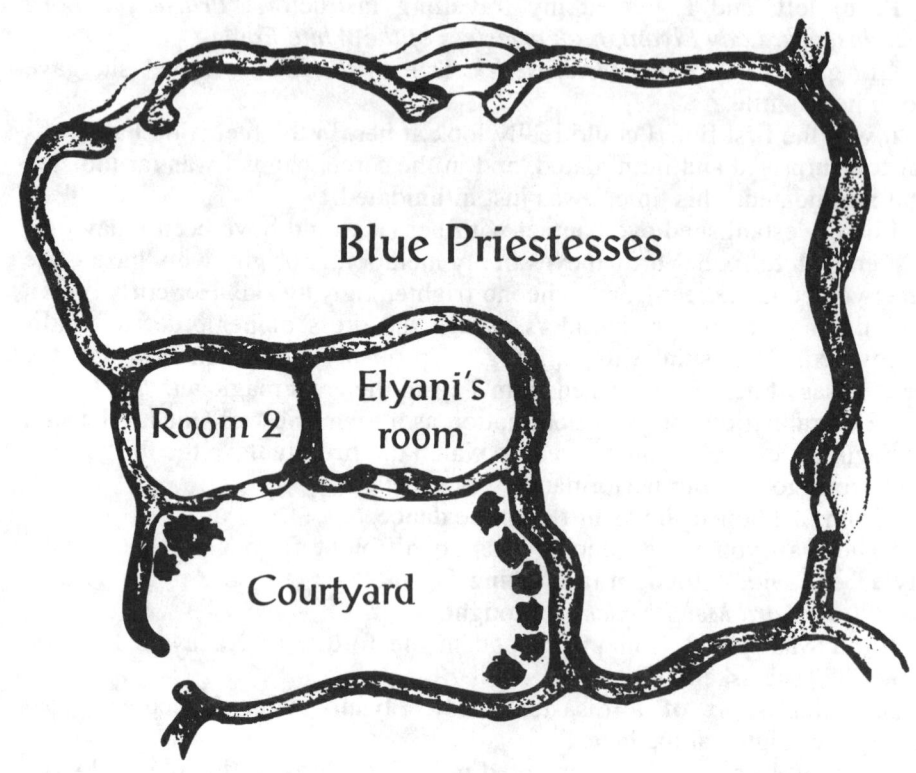

Elyani's courtyard

Inside the courtyard was the most *lawfully delightful* little garden, with high laurel trees and a lawn made purple by myriads of tiny violet flowers.

"Beautiful! Is this where the descents into the Underworld take place?"

"It is not the usual place," she said, "but it is the one I have chosen for you. Here, the *living walls* hold special forces. When I was a child, I often used to come and hide in this courtyard."

"Did you arrive at the temple when you were very young?"

"I was born in the temple," she smiled.

"Maybe this is why I am always one hundred lawful leagues behind you, Lady Elyani! It has not always been easy to follow your instructions while travelling in the spheres."

"But you have done so well! It has been a joy to watch your progress, Szar."

She invited me to sit down with her on the purple lawn.

If she was to be my instructor, then maybe after all it was lawful to keep eye contact with her. I wished I could have thought of asking Gervin about

5 – The Book of the Mysteries of Eisraim

this important point of etiquette. Meanwhile I kept looking through her, rather than at her.

"Szar, this time I am not taking you to a nice place," Elyani pulled a face. "When I went there myself, it made me... it made me quite sick. And so Master Gervin has asked me to take care of you, during and after the descent."

"Thank you, Master Gervin," I directed a loving thought to the enclave of the jewels. Yet I was starting to wonder what the Underworld was going on in the spheres below. "Lady Elyani, will you tell me what the Underworlds are like?"

"The Underworlds are the garbage bins of the Earth. All the nasty things, all the sorrows that are too heavy for people to carry in their hearts, all the grief, and all the plagues fall down there. Remember the verses of the Law,

That sorrow which I had buried in my heart and forgotten,
I met with again when travelling through Hades."

I was still more curious than worried, "And what am I supposed to do when I am down there?"

"You can't do anything while you are down there," answered Elyani. "But you must hold on to a symbol, so as not to lose your Spirit."

"How could I lose my Spirit?" I began, naively. But remembering the beatings I had taken in the last months, I said, "Yes, I see. There are many ways by which a man can lose his Spirit, aren't there?"

Elyani enveloped me in her gentle presence, "You have just been through a difficult time, haven't you?"

I nodded. For a short second – so short that it couldn't possibly be unlawful – our glances met.

She definitely had that warmth that made awakening worth fighting for.

"You know, becoming a priestess of the White Eagle was not always easy either," she said.

"What sorts of things do White Eagle priestesses do? Is it extremely secret, or can you tell me about it?"

"Perhaps both," she said, waiting for a question.

Mother of the Light! She and Gervin were so much alike. At times, I wondered if she was his daughter.

"Tell me for instance," I immediately asked, "what was the most difficult thing you ever had to do?"

Elyani answered without any hesitation, "Descending into the Underworld."

I swallowed hard, wishing I hadn't asked this question.

Seeing my disarray, Elyani quickly went on, "We can discuss the priesthood of the White Eagle another day. For now, let us focus on the descent. As you go down, you will encounter people and forces that will make you feel... uncomfortable. And many latent emotions will burst inside you – grief, and doubts. These may cause you to lose your way."

She pointed her finger at my heart, "This is the main danger, down there: losing your way! If you lose your way, then you can remain stranded for a long, long time. It all becomes frozen. Worse than death! And so your instructions are:
Keep walking, hold on to your symbol!
Never stop on the way!
Never walk back, never look back!"
"Did you lose your way when you went down?" I asked.
"Yes," she said.
Remembering how safe I felt when travelling under her guidance, I was perplexed, "How could I get lost if I follow you?"
"The problem is, in the Underworld you can only be accompanied down to a certain point. Then you have to travel on your own. For one is always alone in those spheres. Everyone. Always."
This journey sounded less appealing by the minute.
"There is a secret," she said. "In order to keep your thread and not lose your way, you must pick a symbol that has real meaning for you and remember it all the time. Whatever you see, whatever idea or memory comes through your mind, you must remember the symbol. You must promise yourself to cling onto it, and not allow anyone or anything to make you forget."
"What sort of symbol should I choose?"
"Something which has real meaning for you. Instead of a symbol, some people remember the presence of their teacher, or of someone else they love and care for. You can also use a resolve on which you have set your mind. You must find the thing you are the least likely to forget."
I had no idea what such a thing could be. And I was feeling less and less confident. "Elyani... in the tasks that Master Gervin has set for me in the last years, I have not succeeded many times. Why should I not fail again?"
"Mm... Do you know what Lady Teyani says when one of her priestesses speaks like this? She yells at them." Elyani raised her voice, "This is sleeper's talk! Are you a White Eagle or a white goose? *Wake up, woman of the Law!"*
I smiled. The loud imitation was very well done. "Doubts..." I muttered.
"Teyani says that the part of you which has doubts and likes to whinge is the part that is longing to return to the state of complete sleeper."
That sounded astoundingly true. I had to stop and think.
"Well, perhaps I need to be woken up, then," I exclaimed with a thoughtful frown.
"All right," she said. And she unlawfully yelled at me, "Szar, this is sleeper's talk! *Wake up, man of the Law!* Are you a Master of Thunder or a brown chicken?"
So she knew about the Masters of Thunder!
Being yelled at left me so stupefied that Lady Elyani burst out laughing.

5 – The Book of the Mysteries of Eisraim

"Perhaps I..." the image of the brown chicken loomed large in my mind and interrupted my flow.

Elyani was watching the reaction on my face, deciding which direction to take next.

"All right! All right!" I raised my voice, "Forget what I said! I won't go down to the Underworlds like a brown chicken. And I'll move so fast that I will be back here before Lord Gana has time to realise his high priest has disappeared *under the lawful violets.*"

"Mm..." was all she answered. She changed the topic, "By the way, Szar, one of the priestesses of the White Eagle will be descending at the same time as you. Her name is Vivyani."

"Really?" I said, *"How lawfully wonderful!* We might even meet down there."

"Unlikely," Elyani pulled a strange face.

The only other person I had ever seen pull faces like this was Gervin.

"No one ever meets anyone down there," she went on. "There are but lonely shades that are always looking for other souls but can never find them."

Fearing another wave of retaliation if I let her words get to me, I opened a wide smile, "Sounds wonderful, Lady Elyani, I can't wait! And how long is the descent going to take?"

"A few days, or perhaps a few weeks."

Far Underworld! A few weeks? I nearly choked again.

"Am I going to remain lying on the lawn for weeks?" I asked.

"No. You will start here, so the last image you take with you will be beautiful. The last thing that is on your mind before dying stays with you forever. And after a few hours, your body will be carried to this room," she indicated one of the two doors that opened onto the courtyard. "You will be lying on a special mattress stuffed with herbs that can work magic as in the Ancient Days, *when the Earth was fresh and men were young.* You will not be alone. Another such mattress has been put there to receive Vivyani of the White Eagle, so I can look after the two of you at the same time."

"Will I meet Vivyani of the White Eagle?"

"Of course. As soon as you come back. At the moment she is undertaking the preparatory training. She will be descending the day after you. Let us see which one of you can come back first!" With a spark in her eyes, she added, "It is really good of Vivyani to let you start one day earlier than her. But then of course, that could make it embarrassing for you if she was to return before you."

"Don't worry about that, Lady Elyani!" I resumed my fully optimistic smile. "I've had plenty of preparatory training in embarrassing my lineage."

Each time I heard her laugh, I felt stronger.

5.27 Initiatory death

"The great paradox is, the more you die, the more you become alive. And awake!" Gervin started briefing me on how to behave in the Underworld.

"There is much more to dying than people think. When you die you must let go of everything. This creates a state of total opening in which anything becomes possible. The Lords of Destiny can set you on a new trajectory. The gods can bestow unsuspected gifts upon you. The divine spark inside you can flare. Someone who would never die would be like a chicken that never hatches out of its egg."

I pondered on the image of a brown chicken hatching. Gervin went on, "Dying, though, can happen in many ways. When the Mother of the Light made you walk out of the Salmon Robe, a part of yourself died. When you decided not to let yourself drown in the lake, another part of you died. And before that, when you were travelling in the spheres, you underwent a few deaths barely noticing them." Gervin plunged his gaze into me, "As your Spirit awakens, dying becomes a permanent state of opening that brings more joy than words can tell."

The power behind his words awakened a buzzing vibration in the space of the aquamarine chamber.

"So the best you can achieve from this descent – apart from coming back, of course! – is to dive into the death state like an initiate, with a positive attitude of joy and opening to infinity, instead of resisting every bit of the disintegration. But at the same time, you must hold onto your symbol, so as not to lose your way."

"Which symbol shall I choose, Gervin?"

"Let me give you a clue about this. The symbol with which you will start your descent may not be the appropriate one to help find your way back to the surface. The secret is, find a new symbol at the time of the great letting go, when your little self explodes. The symbol will be revealed to you from the deepest of yourself, and this is why it will have the power to guide you, even through the desolation of the Underworld."

"And what am I to do if I lose my way?"

With the thunderous power of his lineage Gervin hammered into me, "You *must not* lose your way! If you were to lose your way, there is no guarantee anyone would be able to bring you back, and so you will *not* lose your way! Lehrmon went before you, I before him, and my teacher and others before me. None of us lost our way, and neither will you."

"Yet Elyani lost her way," I pointed out.

"Nearly, that is right, and this is why she insisted so much on taking care of you."

"Mm..." I thought, "so *she* insisted – not Gervin."

5 – The Book of the Mysteries of Eisraim

"But the priestesses of the White Eagle have a very strict rule," Gervin went on. "They must descend *one hour before the New Moon, when the Underworld opens its deepest and most frightening passages, and when all the souls in its cold bowels enter the gloomiest despair.* You, on the other hand, will be leaving one day before the New Moon, which will make the journey softer. Yet, beware! There is no easy way of descending into the Underworld."

All this left me thoughtful. "How should I prepare myself?"

"Ponder over what we have discussed today. Choose your symbol carefully. And spend some more time with Elyani. It will be excellent for your spiritual development."

I frowned. What the Underworld did he mean?

Probably that I should try to observe her carefully, and endeavour to become as frighteningly awake as she was.

For no reason whatsoever, Gervin burst out laughing.

5.28 The descent

It was early in the morning, the day before the New Moon. This time Lady Elyani herself came to the portal of the female wing. As I was following her through the labyrinth of corridors, I asked her, "Should a man be feeling something special before he begins the descent?"

"No. Now isn't the lawful time to worry," she answered.

Just as well. My mind was rather blank. Lawful business as usual. Would I have felt more fear if I had been less of a sleeper?

To divert my attention, Elyani said, "Vivyani was *delighted in the Law* when she learned that Gervin's apprentice would be hibernating in the same room as herself. She looks forward to meeting you, as soon as you are back. She is a joyful little soul, you know."

"...and I have to hurry up and come back within decent time," I said, "otherwise she may not have the patience to wait for me. I know."

"I taught you travelling, I did not teach her," Elyani said in her joking voice. "You have to make me proud and return way before her!"

A brown chicken like me beating a priestess of the White Eagle in travelling... that would have *surprised the kingdom out of me.*

We arrived at her courtyard. I contemplated the fragrant little violet flowers which thickly covered the lawn. "And so, what shall I do now?"

"Go to the bathroom!" Of the two doors that opened into her courtyard, she pointed to the one on the right.

"She *is* taking care of me," I thought. When I came back I asked her, "Is this the room where my body will be kept?"

"No, this one is my room. You and Vivyani will be in the other one," she pointed to the door on the left, by the laurel trees. "Come and sit on the lawn," she said, "I have something for you to drink."

I sat close to her on the carpet of purple flowers and took the large cup she handed to me. Seeing the milky liquid, I smiled, "A white beverage, of course! What else?" and started drinking. But the concoction was so incredibly spicy that I choked, "What is *that*?"

"Dragon's milk," she answered candidly. "Very secret, and totally magic. It will save your life, as it has saved many others. If you come back really quickly, I will consider passing on the recipe to you and your lineage."

"Lady Elyani, if one thing could motivate me, this is the one for sure!" I forced myself to swallow the magic drink.

It took a while.

When I finished, I loudly exhaled the fire.

"Now," she said, "I have a favour to ask. You know, the last thing that is in your mind before dying is extremely important. The Law of the Eagles says it stays with you forever. Well, I would like you to take this garden with you. Will you *really* look at it, please?"

I just could not believe what was happening in my body after drinking that dragon's milk. There were tongues of fire dancing in my belly, and tingling raging in every cell of my body. I felt such a rush of energy in my head that I could have jumped and roared. Yet, strangely, I found it difficult to move.

Collecting my spirits, I followed Elyani's instruction.

I started with the laurel trees on the left, and slowly turned my head.

Elyani's eyes were shining more than ever.

Was it the dragon's milk? I completely forgot about not keeping eye contact.

"Will you remember my garden?" she smiled.

Such a beautiful smile. Warm.

Warm like Teyani when she contemplated Gervin.

"Elyani," I said after one or two minutes, or perhaps three, "I am starting to feel very dizzy. I can hear this loud hissing sound in my head."

"Don't worry, all this is very normal with dragon's milk. Just lie down with your head over here," she said.

I could hardly feel my body. I had to drag myself to the spot Elyani had indicated, and I fell flat on my back.

Elyani placed a white blanket over my body and sat on the ground behind my head. In her softest voice, she asked, "Are you ready?"

I looked deep into her eyes, "Let the White Eagle take me!"

Returning my smile, she placed her hands on two gateways located in my temples, and operated a quick manipulation which projected me out of my body into darkness visible.

My clarity of mind was instantly restored.

5 – The Book of the Mysteries of Eisraim

In the space, I heard Elyani's voice calling, "What is your symbol?"

"I will start with Gervin's travelling symbol," I answered, "and perhaps I will take another one later."

The beginning of the descent was similar to the travelling I had undertaken before, with one exception – the perception of going down. After a short time, I heard Elyani say, "We are now leaving darkness visible and entering the outskirts of the Underworld," but as yet I couldn't detect much difference.

Until then, I had been falling down at a very gentle speed. "We are now going down into a shaft," Elyani instructed me.

Abruptly, it was like free-fall. It lasted less than three minutes, and yet I covered a huge distance.

Elyani's voice was still with me, "Take your time. Take a good look around you."

This space was different from the spheres in which I had travelled before. The atmosphere was cold, and the darkness was thick – nothing like the astral glow of the intermediary worlds.

"I will take you into another shaft," Elyani said after a few minutes.

Another free-fall followed. It took me to colder and darker spaces.

"*Good Lord Melchisedek*, Elyani, I had never realised that space could be so dark!"

"How are you feeling, my friend of the Brown Robe?"

"Challenged, Lady of the Eagle. I don't want to be a sleeper this time. Have you ever heard of the book of Maveron?"

Elyani responded with a quote, "*The day of the sleeper is darkness. The darkness of the awakened one is day.* That sounds exactly like what we need, doesn't it?"

"*Beware, the time is coming!*" I quoted back, holding onto the clear fountain.

"Now, you must move down from shaft to shaft rapidly. Be ready for the jumps."

I fell and fell, swallowed by increasingly ominous darkness. It seemed to go on for an *awful lawful lot* of time even though, as in the spheres above, I could sense that time was not the same as it was in the kingdom.

Finally, I landed in what seemed to be a large cave, dimly lit.

"This is it," Elyani said.

I was no longer falling, and I could no longer float. I had to walk. Something immediately struck me, and I stopped to call Elyani, "The clear fountain... I can't feel it any more!"

A prompt response ensued, "*Keep walking, Szar! Never stop on the way!*"

As I started walking again, she explained, "A number of things are going to fall off you, one after the other. It's the way it happens in the Underworld." After a moment, she asked, "How are you feeling?"

"Heavy. But I think I don't mind the challenge," I said. Collecting all my will, I hammered into myself, "I do not want to sleep!"

To my delight, Elyani responded with what I felt was the most beautiful verse of the book of Maveron, and perhaps even of the entire Law,

"He who never sleeps, never dies!"

I kept advancing, pushing step after step. Elyani repeated her set of instructions over and over again, *"Keep walking, hold on to the symbol! Never stop on the way! Never walk back, never look back!"*

My mind steadily fixed on Gervin's symbol, I kept going.

Soon, I met other people. Some were walking slowly. Others were sitting, or lying on the ground. They looked quite miserable. They did not speak to each other, and they hardly seemed to notice each other. Yet a number of them were talking to themselves. Some were involved in imaginary conversations, others were completely incoherent. Many of them had a halo of darkness instead of a face. I was starting to understand why the Underworld was called the kingdom of the shades.

"There seems to be quite a lot of madness going on here," I said to Elyani.

When she answered, her voice was worryingly faint, "Szar, I am not going to be with you much longer. Even if I could be with you, you would not see me."

Still walking, I spoke in a reassuring tone, "Believe it or not, I feel rather more awake than when I got out of bed this morning." Then I added, "And make no mistake, I have not forgotten your promise."

"What promise?" said the distant voice.

"As soon as I get back up there, I want the recipe of dragon's milk!"

"Promise!" was the last I heard from her.

"Oh, no!" I thought, suddenly gripped by anxiety. "This time I am right in it!" But this was no time for Szar-ka to be whingeing. With my mind fixed on Gervin's travelling symbol, I plodded on, repeating Elyani's instructions as a mantra, *"Keep walking. Hold on to the symbol. Never stop on the way! Never walk back. Never look back!"*

The more I walked, the sicker the people I met. Some were screaming in terror. Others yelled like animals. Others ran as fast as they could, panic-stricken, as if harassed by invisible enemies.

As I advanced in the semi-darkness, I was hit by a torrent of grief. The nostalgia for the kingdom I had left behind me combined with the horror of what I was discovering. Tears were pouring from my eyes.

"But what am I doing here?"

"Keep walking!"

The atmosphere was defeated and thick with deathly despair, insanity and disease. Wherever I looked there were grotty people, deformed animals and monsters, all contributing to the loud, ugly clamour.

"Oh, gods!" I looked up, but all I could see was darkness.

"Hold on to the symbol!"

5 – The Book of the Mysteries of Eisraim

I tripped over a body. A naked old woman, dried out and skeleton-thin. When she saw me she curled up. She pulled her hair and screamed in terror.

"I'm not going to hurt you!" I shouted.

She screamed so loudly that she could not hear me.

"Never stop on the way!"

I tried to walk away but she clung to my leg.

Frightened, I kicked her.

She wouldn't let go.

I kicked harder, in the face.

She fell unconscious.

I ran away, as fast as I could.

"Oh gods!" I exclaimed in horror. "What am I doing?"

I felt a strong pull to run back to her and comfort her.

"Never walk back, never look back!"

As I slowly forced my way through the rabble of people and beasts, a passage of the Law ran through my mind,

Kingdom of Hades, kingdom of the shades,
World without hope,
Endless void where great and small are reduced to nought.
O, Knight of the East and the West,
Take one step, and another step,
Looking neither to the left nor to the right,
Lest thou see the darkness and despair.

After an endless march, I arrived at a large archway which separated this cavern from the next. The stench became intolerable. It took my breath away.

A small man ran towards me, "Walk back, friend!" he shouted. "Don't go in this direction! This cavern is worse than anything you can imagine!"

Pleasantly surprised to see someone who spoke coherently, I saluted him, *"Praise the Lord Melchisedek, friend in the Law!"*

He fell on his knees and cried, "You have no idea what I have seen!"

"What have you seen, *friend in the Law?*"

The small man bashed his head on the stony ground and cried, "No! No! No! No..."

I watched him silently, hoping he would return to his senses.

He hit his head harder and harder, shouting, "No! No! No..."

"Keep walking!"

The man had spoken the truth. What I discovered there was worse than anything I could have imagined.

"Oh gods! Is this really part of your creation?"

I completely lost my focus and started sobbing like a child.

The cavern was filled with the mutilated bodies of people and animals, piled together on top of each other.

I vomited.

"Hold on to the symbol!"

So many corpses covered the ground that I had no choice but to tread on them. On the slippery maelstrom, I had to watch my steps carefully.

"Oh gods! No! This can't be!" I cried, realising that many of the bodies were still moving. Some were calling for help, desperately trying to extricate themselves from the heaving mass of putrid flesh and thick black worms.

"Never stop on the way!"

It seemed to go on forever. At times, some of the grossly mutilated bodies called me by my name, "Szar, please don't leave us here. Take us with you."

I stuck to my instructions, *"Never walk back, never look back!"* and tried to ignore them.

"Please Szar! Stop! You are our only chance to ever get out of here! Please!" they kept calling me.

I finally arrived in another cavern where thousands of insane people and beasts were running in all directions. The pandemonium of howling, screeching and wailing was so unbearable that I had to plug my ears. But it made no difference to the deafening cacophony.

"Keep walking!"

But how?

I had to jump fast to dodge the living projectiles.

As I advanced, the cavern became pitch-dark. Many times I was knocked to the ground by people who ran into me.

Each time, I stood up and started walking again.

I wasn't yet feeling any pain in my body, but the sorrow was overwhelming. "Gervin!" I cried. "What am I doing here? What is all this for?"

"Hold on to the symbol!"

I arrived in an area lit by a dim glow. I thought I recognised some of the faces I had passed hours earlier.

Was I running round in circles?

Perhaps I was getting confused. I found it increasingly difficult to think straight.

"Never stop on the way!"

I decided to ignore what I saw.

But after some time, I recognised the naked old woman that I had kicked in the face. She was still screaming in terror and pain, pulling her hair.

I didn't want to see. I tried to shut my eyes, but it did not hide the scenes in front of me.

The insanity of the situation was starting to get to me. What was the point of walking if I was going around in circles? I might as well have tried to return to where I had started.

"Never walk back, never look back!"

I went on. And on.

5 – The Book of the Mysteries of Eisraim

The pandemonium never ended. Fatigue was starting to take its toll.

How long had I been walking? It felt more like days than hours. But how to know, in these dark caverns?

"*Keep walking!*"

My body ached.

My feet were full of blisters. My legs were seized by cramps.

Fatigue turned into exhaustion.

Like a miserable wretch, I walked more and more slowly, my face contorted with pain, my arms jerking out of control. But nothing hurt more than the noise. A symphony of hell, the dire clamour of millions of souls in pain.

"*Keep walking!*"

As I was fighting my way through a narrow bowel that forced me to bend my head low, I was suddenly struck by a horrible vision: my feet! My feet had been eaten away. I was walking on maimed legs!

The realisation made me collapse on the stony ground, my face against the rubble.

"Elyani, I just can't walk any more!" I yelled.

I heard her voice, and I saw her face, but she was no longer a young and beautiful priestess of the White Eagle. She was an old wrinkled witch, wearing rags and screaming at me in anger, "Never stop on the way! Never stop on the way!" Seeing her so hateful and furious at me hurt more than anything else. "No! No! That can't be you!" I cried.

"*Hold on to the symbol!*"

As I tried to crawl my way forward, I realised something terrible had happened. I had lost Gervin's symbol!

Where was it?

I couldn't remember its shape.

"No! No! No!" I cried in despair.

5.29 In the kingdom

Lady Teyani walked across the purple lawn and entered the room where the two bodies were being kept in hibernation. They hardly breathed, looking like children deeply asleep. The air in the room was vibrant with the power of the Voice, which Elyani had to use intensively in order to keep the two bodies alive. There were strong fragrances of herbs, and clear signs that the presence of the White Eagle had been invoked – definitely a room where Teyani felt at home.

After a quick lawful greeting, she asked, "How are our beautiful sleepers today?"

Elyani pulled her breath, "Vivyani looks all right. But there are signs that Szar is suffering. His body is so weak and sickly. If he was to stay in hibernation more than three weeks, there wouldn't be anything left of him."

"Didn't you say he did very well when he arrived at the caverns' rim?" Teyani tried to encourage her.

"Yes, he remained remarkably clear. Much clearer than Vivyani, who was deeply distressed when she caught her first glimpses of the caverns of sickness."

Teyani changed the subject, "Look at this huge brown birthmark on Szar's left cheek. Not very beautiful! Let us see if we could get rid of it while he is hibernating. We should try some of the herbs that Pepni and Afani brought back from the county of Perentie. They make remarkable balms."

Elyani smiled thoughtfully.

"You have invoked the White Eagle, haven't you?" Teyani asked. "What did he tell you?"

In a depressed voice, Elyani answered, "The White Eagle told me that Szar is undergoing great trials, and that Vivyani is still walking but will soon be stopped."

Teyani did not like the news, of course. But there was nothing anyone could do. She went and sat on the floor, gently caressing Vivyani's face while she scanned her centres of energy. After inspecting Szar's main vital gateways, she complimented Elyani, "Voof! What a remarkably well-monitored hibernation state! You have become a master in the art. I will have to come back to you for some lessons."

The thought of giving lessons to the great Lady Teyani, magician of the Ancient Days and Grand Master of the White Eagle, made Elyani laugh. A little.

5.30 Underworld Further Down

"*Keep walking! Never stop on the way!*"

By then, I seemed to have forgotten everything else.

The clamour was unbearable.

Miserably crawling over the rocky ground through dark, narrow bowels, I clung onto the verse in desperation.

"*Keep walking! Never stop on the way!*"

I was being harassed by terrifying faces. Some were grotesque monsters, others were people I had known during my life, and who now seemed to enjoy terrorising me by screaming insults at me.

All the sleepers of the Salmon Robe were after me, "You thought you could escape us? Poor idiot in the Law!" they sneered. "Now, we are going

5 – The Book of the Mysteries of Eisraim

to make you pay for walking out on us!" And they kept beating me, and trampling on my maimed limbs.

"Keep walking! Never stop on the way!"

A gigantic Artold, his face contorted with hatred, shouted, *"And how are your parents, my friend in the Law? And how are your parents, my friend in the Law? And how are your parents..."* And like a wild beast, he bit me.

My charcoal black body was gradually falling to pieces. I had lost my feet long ago, and then my left hand. Then I had spat tooth after tooth. More and more dents were being chipped off my body. I had to bear the horrendous vision of myself slowly crumbling.

Together with the stench, thick toxic fumes made me choke and gasp. But of all things, the most painful was the noise – the deafening clamour of all the souls in pain. It never stopped. The despair it conveyed was beyond words.

I reached a point of total exhaustion where I could no longer move.

I whispered, "Elyani, forgive me! I just can't go on any further! Elyani, I am dying!" As I called her name, the old witch reappeared and started nagging me again.

But as the idea of death came into my mind, a whole chain of thoughts were triggered. Deep inside my psyche, Gervin had implanted forces which, as he had planned, reappeared at this crucial moment.

"Death!" I thought, "that's what I need! No more fighting. Just death."

I stopped trying to crawl, stopped trying to keep the substance of my body together, stopped trying to push those dreadful faces away, and the pain, and the stench, and the clamour. I totally, unrestrictedly and irreversibly let go and stopped trying.

A momentous opening followed.

Within a few minutes, my body disintegrated completely.

So what?

Seeing myself without a body made me feel immensely free. I lost touch with the narrow cave, and I entered a vastness of a new kind.

Where was I?

The monstrous shapes had disappeared. So had the stench and the clamour.

There was nothing like floor, ceiling or walls – just Light. White Light.

And lo! Gervin appeared, walking towards me in his brown robe. And he spoke to me. "See, it was really simple. All you had to do was stop trying!"

Transported by the Light as I was, it felt very natural to see him. "Yes, you are right, it was really simple!" *I answered with a smile, and I believed what I said.*

Gervin went on, "Now of course, if you had tried to stop trying, that would never have worked."

Everything felt so simple in this White Light. "Of course!" *I said.* "But Gervin, didn't you teach me that in order to become awakened, I should try to do things – anything?"

"That is because you need to do a lot of trying before stopping the trying brings you to awakening."

"Of course!" I exclaimed.

"As soon as you are back in the kingdom, you will have much more trying to do. But for now," said the Master of Thunder, *"you must find the symbol that will take you back to the surface."*

Then he just added, *"I will see you in the kingdom,"* and he walked away.

"Not a problem in the Law!" I thought, *"I will find that symbol."*

The light changed. It was less bright, and a gentle breeze could be felt. I found myself in a large empty room where all kinds of events that had happened in my life were laid in front of me.

"Now, that!" I exclaimed at one stage, "*that* is really beautiful!"

It was the time when Gervin had explained to me the verse,

One Law, one way!

"Sleepers believe that their destiny is traced right from the moment they are born," Gervin had commented. "*One Law, one way!* What else could they do but follow the Law of their fathers? They never have any doubt or hesitation. They blindly repeat the example of their ancestors, believing they follow the real Law.

But when men shed away the grossest hazes of sleep, they are no longer bound by their limited understanding of the Law. They realise that there are many paths they can follow. This often causes great doubts about which direction to take.

But to the awakened ones who know the heart of the Law, the path becomes simple again. It no longer matters if there are many options, and many time tracks laid in front of them. They know how to recognise where Truth lies, and they can follow it straight. *One Law, one way!*"

"This is my symbol," I thought without any hesitation, "for *he who never sleeps never dies*."

It was as simple as that. Having found my symbol, I endeavoured to walk back.

As I was advancing straight in front of me, the light gradually became dimmer and yellowish. There was a drowsy heaviness, so different from the White Light, which had neither heaviness nor lightness – absolutely nothing but Light. I started meeting people again, and they called me by my name, "Szar, please come here, I want to show you something."

"Stop, Szar! I have something to give you."

I did not listen to them, repeating to myself, "*One Law, one way. He who never sleeps, never dies!*" Sometimes, people even tried to touch me and catch hold of my arm. I just had to remember the Light from which I was coming, and they faded in front of me.

I strode forwards. This time it was easy not to let myself be distracted by the crowds and the beasts. After seeing the Light, all the rest appeared to me insubstantial and unreal. I could sense that the people in these caverns

5 – The Book of the Mysteries of Eisraim

were in great turmoil, but their distress was pure illusion. I knew that only the Light was true, and that only the Light existed. At one stage I even thought of telling them, "Stop this mockery! Even your thoughts do not exist!" But what was the point? It would have been a complete waste of time, since anyhow everything around me was illusion.

I kept walking, holding on to my symbol, "*One Law, one way. He who never sleeps, never dies!*"

I got to a hall where many sick people, adults and children, were lying. I could see all sorts of injuries on their bodies: burns, sores, putrid wounds, maimed limbs.

A man called for help. A woman echoed him, and soon there were hundreds of people wailing and calling my name, "Szar! *Please*, take us with you. Don't leave us here!"

I walked, untouched.

"*Please*, Szar! You could help us if you wanted to. *Please!*"

"*One Law, one way. He who never sleeps, never dies!*" I ignored them, until my attention was drawn to something completely unexpected.

I stopped, hardly believing my eyes.

In a corner of the hall, amid many bodies, Elyani was lying, deeply asleep. This was no illusion like the old wrinkled witch. It was the real Elyani, the magnificent soul, sleeping amongst the filth.

I came close to her and, to make sure I was not being confused, I tested for the recognition symbols used in travelling. And there it was in front of me, the beautiful occult symbol of the White Eagle!

"Sweet Elyani," I gathered her in my arms, "this is the first time I see you asleep. How beautiful you are! But this is no place for a lady of the Eagle."

I tried to wake her up, with no success. So I decided to carry her with me. Her body was completely cold. In such a place of death, that did not seem strange to me.

Many in the crowd kept on wailing, "Szar! Please, take us with you too! Lead us out of here!"

"*One Law, one way. He who never sleeps, never dies!*" I started walking again, with the beautiful White Eagle in my arms.

We went from hall to hall and then reached huge caverns, meeting crowds of various kinds. We waded through rivers that did not make my body wet, because I remembered the Light. We had to walk through fire, and it did not burn me. A few times, I even had to walk in the air across deep chasms where no one had bothered leaving a bridge for us. "Illusions," I kept on thinking, "all this is illusion. Only the Light is real."

Elyani, the pure soul, was so light in my arms.

We walked for days, or was it weeks?

She moved her hand for the first time, showing me for sure that she wasn't dead. Only deeply asleep.

Why would I be worried about her being dead, anyway? Wasn't I dead myself?

"*One Law, one way. He who never sleeps, never dies!*"

Hours went by, and she started making slight movements. Her body was getting less cold.

I walked and walked. There seemed to be no end to it. That did not worry me. I knew that only the Light existed, and that worry was illusion.

Further along the way, Elyani turned on her side in my arms, and for the first time she looked as if she was breathing. Not long after, she placed her arms around my neck in her sleep. She had a smile on her face.

For the first time in an eternity, I remembered what warmth in the heart felt like.

As I kept advancing, I thought, "Shall I love this woman?" and my heart said "Yes! Of course I love her!"

But what was this? I had spent aeons walking past agonising crowds and saying to myself, "Their suffering is an illusion." I had walked through fire, and that was an illusion. I had crossed dozens of illusory water streams and precipices. "Only the Light exists. Only the Light is real," I thought, and remembering what the Light felt like, I saw that this was the truth, "Love is an illusion!"

"Love is an illusion."

Like the rest.

"Why carry her body, then? She does not exist and I do not exist! Nothing exists but the Light!"

Shrugging my shoulders, I knelt down. I laid her sleeping body on the side of the path. Her arms were soft. I untied them easily from my neck.

Without looking at her, I stood up again. And without turning back, I left.

And I kept walking. And walking. And walking. For what seemed like another eternity.

"*One Law, one way. He who never sleeps, never dies!*"

5.31 Hopes

When Lady Teyani entered the sleepers' room, she only had to take a look at Elyani to know that some good news had arrived. She smiled, and without any formal greeting inquired, "Elyani, what has the White Eagle told you?"

"A miracle has happened, Teyani! The White Eagle said that Szar will be back in two days. He said Szar had found Vivyani and picked her up on his way."

"What? Do you mean he found Vivyani?"

"The Eagle said he led him to her."

5 – The Book of the Mysteries of Eisraim

"*Praise the Lord Melchisedek!* So the Eagle's word is being fulfilled! Szar is the one we have been waiting for." The two women hugged each other with joy. "Gervin and Lehrmon are going to be so happy!"

"How are the bodies?" Teyani asked.

"Vivyani's is still fine, but Szar's body has suffered a lot. If he is really back in two days, then everything should be all right. But I don't think he could take much longer than that."

"This bad birthmark is not responding to our balms," Teyani gently caressed Szar's cheek. "Can you think of any other remedy?"

Elyani shook her head. "Teyani, I really wish it was all finished. I think my patience is coming to its limits."

With a reassuring smile, Teyani sealed Elyani's lips with her index, "Hush, Lady of the Eagle! Don't you know that the patience of the White Eagle is infinite? And what are two days, after more than six weeks? What do you think his first words are going to be?"

"I don't know. His last words were... Teyani, I am embarrassed! I said I would give him the recipe of Dragon's milk if he came back quickly, and he reminded me of it just before disappearing."

Teyani burst out laughing, "As if the Masters of Thunder did not already know enough of our secrets!"

5.32 Illusions

I walked.

"*One Law, one way. He who never sleeps, never dies!*"

There were fewer and fewer people. The clamour was fainter. I didn't care. I just walked.

Then out of nowhere, I heard the voice calling me, "Szar! Szar!"

"Now," I thought, "I know this voice."

But who could it be?

It felt like so long ago.

"Szar!"

There was life in the voice. "I remember," I thought, "that was what life felt like."

But I couldn't really feel it. I just vaguely remembered.

Could it be that the nightmare was going to finish? I didn't care, I just kept on walking.

"Szar, I can feel your presence. Please, answer me! It's me, Elyani."

"Elyani..." The long-forgotten name was surfacing in my mind.

"Szar," the voice called, "just stay where you are. I'm coming down to pick you up. I will be with you in one minute."

"Stay where I am?" I thought, "*Never stop on the way! Keep walking!*"

One minute later – what was a minute, compared to the endless journey I was on? – she was standing in front of me.

"Szar?" she said. "Oh, my Lord Melchisedek, you look..."

What did this person want?

Was she not unreal like all the others on the way? I kept walking.

But as I passed her, she grabbed my arm.

"Illusion!" I thought.

Seeing the state I was in, Elyani knocked me unconscious by activating centres of energy in my head, and she carried me back up to the surface.

-o0o-

When I first regained some consciousness, I was in the small room, and somewhat in my physical body.

It felt strange.

I looked at the ceiling. For some time.

White.

I turned my head to the side. She was there.

I closed my eyes again.

Deep, deep sleep.

-o0o-

The next time I woke up, Elyani was singing into my ear.

Strong vibration. Voice. Sometimes just voice.

The words make no sense.

She is soft. So soft.

"*One Law, one way. He who never sleeps, never dies!*"

Falling asleep again.

Called back by her voice.

So soft. Does it really exist?

Darkness.

-o0o-

"Szar!"

A whisper in my ear. So soft.

"Szar, you must drink."

Lips.

Strange.

Warm.

"Have a little bit more!"

Sleep. Dreamless sleep.

-o0o-

Philadelphia.

Fire. Lots of fire.

"No! No!" I screamed.

"Szar?"

"No! No!"

5 – The Book of the Mysteries of Eisraim

"Szar," she Voice-projected in the night. "Wake up!"
Violently pulled into my body.
Her face. "Yes... I recognise you. Elyani. Are you real?"
"Of course I am real!" she gently caressed my hair.
"But I thought you were down there."
"Where?"
Greyness. Despair. Never ends.
So the woman I had met in the cavern of sickness was not even Elyani. An illusion. I knew. Just as well I had dumped her body.
She Voice-projected a few low-pitched sounds.
"One Law, one way. He who never sleeps never dies!"

-oOo-

"The time has come to pull him back into his body!"
Voice-projection. Two Voices. Loud. Strong. Alive.
Bright light.
Tunnel.
Lady Teyani was in the room. "Did he say anything about Vivyani?" she asked.
Elyani answered. I couldn't hear the words.
"Vivyani," I thought. "I remember... Am I going to meet her?" I opened my eyes and turned towards the women. "How long ago did she come back?" I asked.
Teyani and Elyani interrupted their discussion and looked at me.
Teyani knelt close to the mattress. *"Praise the Lord Melchisedek, traveller!"* she smiled. "Do you remember me?"
Warm.
"All glory to the Lord Melchisedek, Lady Teyani!"
"Szar, it is better if you do not speak too much. Still, we must ask you about Vivyani. Do you remember Vivyani, Szar?"
"Has she already gone, or will I get to see her?" I asked.
There was a heavy silence.
Teyani broke it. "Szar, a few days ago, the White Eagle of the gods came to tell us that Vivyani had lost her way. But he said that you had found her, and were bringing her back. Yet she was not with you when you arrived here. If you could remember what happened to her, it would help us to locate her."
"No. I can't remember." I closed my eyes. But in one second, memories flashed back to my mind. "Did the White Eagle say I was carrying her?" I opened my eyes.
Elyani answered, "The White Eagle said he had led you to her in one of the caverns of sickness. He said you were bringing her back, and that she was nearly revived from the infinite coldness."
The sinister truth struck me. The person I had met in the caverns of sickness was not an illusory Elyani, she was the real Vivyani!

Shocked out of my torpor, I took my head in my hands. "No! No! No! No!" I cried in despair. "What have I done? I could have brought her back! I had her in my arms, and I have abandoned her!"

There was a moment of surprise at seeing my near-corpse so suddenly revived. Lady Teyani came closer and held me in her arms, gently rocking me like a child. "Peace, Szar, peace!"

"I want to see her. Where is her body?"

Teyani helped me to sit up and pointed behind her.

A young woman was deeply asleep on a mattress. I didn't recognise her.

"I had her in my arms," big dry sobs shook my body, "and I have abandoned her. I have forsaken love! I thought it was an illusion. And now she might die. Because of me!"

Adding to my distress would have served no one. The White Eagles kept their sorrow to themselves and remained silent.

"*One Law, one way. He who never sleeps, never dies!*" I collected what was left of my spirits, putting memories together.

"I want to go back," I said in a cool voice. "I remember exactly where I left her. If I return down there right now, I can bring her back."

Teyani used a voice channel to call Elyani, "Could his body cope with another descent?"

"Don't even thought-form it!" Elyani voice-channelled back. "The six-and-a-half-week-long hibernation has left him completely exhausted. And the week of delirium after it hasn't made him any better."

"Listen!" I said. "I know exactly what you are thinking, but I can do it. I know I can do it."

There was another heavy silence.

"Please," I asked, "call Master Gervin!"

"All right," said Elyani, "we will call Master Gervin immediately. Meanwhile, you lie down again and *get some lawful rest*."

So soft.

I collapsed in the bed.

"*Oh, Lord Melchisedek!* Feels so good to be horizontal again."

Sleep. Oblivion.

-o0o-

I woke up when Gervin and Teyani came in.

Gervin did not speak. He just kept eye contact with me.

Feeling the presence of my old friend immediately revived my life force. I smiled.

"Gervin," Teyani said, "have you ever seen a man who has just returned from the Underworld and wants to descend again?"

"Ne-ver!" exclaimed Gervin. "We are impressed, Szar. Really. A sleeper could never have done it like you did."

I knew that he meant his words, yet my heart was not happy. I looked at him silently. He understood exactly what I was asking.

Using a voice channel, Teyani pleaded, "Gervin, this man has heart. I believe he could find her. Will you allow him?"

"I can't see that happening," Gervin answered through darkness visible.

"*My Word,* Gervin!" Teyani insisted. "If you let him go down, let it be recorded in front of the Archive council that I will engage *all my lore* to protect his life force."

"*No way, woman of the Law!* It is not even an option," Gervin was categorical. "Look at him! He is half-dead already. Even for Vivyani, we cannot take the risk of losing him. There is too much at stake."

Addressing me, Gervin went on, "Szar, your mission was to descend and find your way back. This you did and you did well. No one had instructed you to go and rescue Vivyani, and so no one will blame you if Vivyani does not come back. What you need now is a good rest." The glorious Sun shone through his smile, "No doubt Lord Gana, in his infinite bounty, must have highly commended your soul to the White Eagle of the gods. And see the result! You have landed in the most beautiful niche in the entire temple. Let yourself be spoiled. Enjoy your convalescence. Otherwise Lord Gana will think you don't know how to appreciate his gifts."

Lord Gana! Hearing the magic name revived me a little further.

But what about Vivyani?

"You have completed this trial, Szar. It is finished," Gervin said in a tone that left no space for discussion. "Now, and for the benefit of all, including the White Eagles, the best thing you can do is recover your strength, and your joy."

5.33 Troubled times

Each time I woke up, I sat up and turned towards Vivyani.
Her blond hair was tied behind her head. I couldn't see if it was long.
It was hard to believe she was dying. She looked so peacefully asleep.
One morning, I asked Elyani, "How old was she?"
"Nineteen."
"No signs that she is coming back?"
The question sounded futile. Elyani shook her head silently.
I closed my eyes and hid inside.
But the next time I woke up, Vivyani's body was no longer on the other mattress. Elyani anticipated my question, "She has been taken into another room. Lady Teyani is taking care of her. Lady Teyani is a great magician. I have seen her do many incredible things."

I sighed. I could not find words to answer her.

I didn't feel like drinking the sweet, milky brew that she presented to my lips.

I sank into unclear spaces where the dull greyness of the kingdom mingled with the nightmare visions I had brought back from the Underworld. I drifted in and out of sleep without even noticing the borderline. Each time I could have woken up for good, the sorrow of having abandoned Vivyani hit me and I preferred to hide in numbness.

An image constantly came back to my mind: the soft, warm body which I had left on the side of the path. The last thing I wanted was to forget the shape of the dark rocks on the side of the winding path, the brownish hue of the pebbles, the precipice in the distance. For she was still there. I knew. Branding the scene in my memory was the only chance of ever finding her again.

Finding her again.

It became an obsession.

I feared that by waking up I would lose my thread to her.

I didn't want to come back to the kingdom.

I stayed somewhere. In between.

When I woke up and opened my eyes, there was often a moment of confusion during which I could not figure out where I was. Some cavern?

Illusion? On all sides. Always. For ever and ever.

It went on and on.

Elyani was always by my side. But that was the other side. I couldn't get there without letting go of Vivyani, abandoning her a second time.

I preferred to stay with the nightmares and the stench. Loyalty does not care about stench. Down there, there is stench in plenty.

That became safe. The other side wasn't.

One night I woke up and in the dim glimmer of the *living walls*, I saw Vivyani on her mattress.

"Have you come back?"

Disoriented, I crawled towards her and called her name, "Vivyani! Vivyani! Don't die! Wait! Wait for me!"

But the body was not Vivyani's. "Szar! Wake up! It's me, Elyani. I was just resting. It's very late, you know."

She covered herself and sat up.

I knelt by her side and looked through her and nowhere.

She put her hand on my shoulder and burst into tears, "Szar, please, stop this. Please! I beg you."

My mind was back in the Underworld. I had just dropped Vivyani, and I was walking away without turning back.

"No! This is not right!" Elyani shouted. She shocked me by projecting the Voice with full intensity, "Back! Back! Come back!"

It dragged me out of my dream violently.

Back!

"Stop it!" Elyani shouted and sobbed at the same time. "Stop it! It is finished! You are back, and she's dead. She is dead! Dead! There is nothing anyone can do about it!"

5 – The Book of the Mysteries of Eisraim

For the first time, I saw her.

She was in tears and wearied, dressed in a light nightgown, half-shivering in the cold night.

So soft.

She covered herself with a blanket and cried. "Szar, do you realise what I have been doing in the last nine weeks? Absolutely nothing but cleaning your body and looking after your energy! That was fine when you were down there, but now there is something that is just not right. You are indulging in your grief Szar, and that is not doing any good to anyone! Stop it! Please, stop it! It hurts. I can't take any more of it!"

For the first time, I was with her.

"I am sorry," I whispered.

I realised that I had been taking in her warmth like a sponge, and not giving one thing back. For nine weeks.

Seeing myself so totally selfish brought about a powerful awakening.

Back into the room.

For the first time, I felt what she felt.

She sobbed. The shadows of my Underworld reflected on her face.

"I am sorry, Elyani," I finally said. "I can see that what you say is true. I am doing... something not right."

Surprised to feel my presence, Elyani unlawfully plunged her eyes into mine. "Are you back, Szar?"

I did not avoid her gaze. "Back."

She could not stop crying.

"Elyani, I see I have taken an incredible amount of your time and energy. Tomorrow I will go back to the enclave of the jewels, so you can return to some normal life."

"What do you mean, you are going back to the enclave of the jewels? *No way, man of the Law!* This is the convalescence, Szar. It was supposed to be the fun part! I have done all this work thinking of the good times and the laughing we would have after you came back, and now you owe me!"

I was so moved that I couldn't answer.

In this kingdom of sleepers, no one had ever cried for me. And apart from Gervin, no one had ever cared for me. What was I to tell her? I didn't even think of taking her hand, and the Underworld had left me too dry to cry. So I tuned into the verticality above my head, seeking for inspiration. And lo! there it was!

"The clear fountain!" I exclaimed, "It is back with me. The first time I have felt it since I drank your dragon's milk."

"Blame my dragon's milk!" she smiled. "What does the fountain tell you?"

I remained silent.

She did not insist.

I didn't want to let her down. "It is time to start the second part of the journey, this is what the fountain tells me. Something important," I whispered.

"What is in the second part of the journey?"

"I don't know," fatigue was taking over. "Something important."

"Will you let me take care of you, Szar?"

I closed my eyes. "I feel I have nothing to give."

"But being taken care of is not about giving, it's about receiving."

"It must have been exhausting for you to spend your days giving to someone who never gave anything back."

"No!" she answered. "It's when people do not know how to receive that giving becomes exhausting. Otherwise it is a joy."

"Receiving," the fountain whispered through me. "That is what I have to learn." My eyelids were heavy. I couldn't open my eyes.

"Let me take you back to your bed," Elyani took my arm.

I let myself be filled with her White presence.

She smiled. I couldn't see it, but I felt it.

When I reached the bed, she tucked me in and stayed by my side. As before, but completely different – I was there for her to be there for me.

So soft.

5.34 Cosmological glimpses

After that night, everything changed. The nightmares receded. Each time the dark under-gloom caught me, I called Elyani. She spoke to me. I opened to her and let her in, and she knew how to dispel the bad dreams.

She chanted hymns of the Law and projected the Voice on my gateways. She anointed my hands and feet with precious oils from distant counties. She fed me strange foods I had never tasted, with subtle spices and rare herbs in plenty. And she prepared dozens of even stranger drinks, mainly white, which made my energy bubble and my mind go tipsy.

She knew how to take care of someone. She created a warm nest, a small one-bedroom world in which I felt totally protected and safe, strong enough to learn to walk again, free enough to say silly things and cry when I needed to.

Soon, she started laughing again. She was such a joyful soul. It didn't take long before I laughed with her. I didn't have anything to do, just let myself be carried by her enthusiasm. It was so easy that it made me ask myself questions about awakening.

Gervin had often explained that laughing was one of the things that sleepers were not good at. What was I to make of the fact that I was laughing more and more, as Gervin soon noticed? Was I being awakened by Elyani? It sounded too easy. I was not doing anything.

5 – The Book of the Mysteries of Eisraim

Could awakening be received?

That did not go well with the fact that awakening had to do with free will. Surely one could not receive awakening.

But could it be that through receiving, one could awaken?

"A whole new world is opening to you," Gervin told me during one of his visits, and it seemed to make him quite happy. "This is the second part of your journey, and perhaps not the least important," he added.

Then there was discovering the joy of discussing all sorts of topics, not all lawfully enlightened. Before descending to the Underworlds, I had never really discussed anything with anyone. I had often spoken with Gervin, of course, but that was not the same. When I talked with Elyani, a new state of mind awakened inside me. I never ran out of questions, and all sorts of strange new ideas came to me. Of course in the beginning, I was somewhat inhibited by the fact that she was so much more knowledgeable in the Law than me, and so much more trained in the mysteries of her order, and so much more awake. But the gap soon stopped being frightening, thanks to Elyani's softness and sense of humour. Each time my mind froze, she knew so well how to pull a face that reflected exactly how I felt. She made me laugh, and the discussion opened in a new direction.

So we discussed and laughed about many orders in the temple, and about places in the kingdom she had visited, about *wise men and women in the Law* she had met in her life as a White Eagle priestess, about my schooling years in Sheringa, my frustration at Artold's slow parlance, my despair at losing the stone in the forests of Nadavan, and about whether I would ever awaken, as well as the pet filosterops of Mouridji's neighbour (an old lady who was becoming as blind as the oracle of the King of Atlantis), and Gervin's predictions of looming disaster, and hundreds of other fantastic and insignificant things.

One day Gervin came to visit and was pleasantly surprised to find me not in bed, but sitting on the lawn. After lawfully praising the Lord Melchisedek, he turned to Elyani and applauded her work.

"You look much better, son!" he told me. "No wonder, though, with all the white beverages you must have been given!" He sat with us on the violet lawn, and from one of the pockets of his gown took out two large *pears of the Law*, which he gave to Elyani.

"Gervin," I asked him, "after discussing things with Elyani, there are hundreds of questions I would like to ask you."

"Hundreds?" Gervin opened his eyes wide and turned to Elyani.

Elyani chuckled.

I pretended to take no notice, "Gervin, when I met you in the White Light after dying in the Underworld, was it a dream or was it real?"

"Real. Much more real than here, actually."

"Which part of the Underworld were we in? It felt completely different from all the other places I saw down there."

"That was no longer in the Underworld, but in Highness." Gervin could see that the concept of Highness was vague in my mind. "You should take advantage of your convalescence to ask Elyani about the ladder of the worlds. The White Eagle is a great traveller among the gods, and so his servant maids know everything that is worth knowing about journeying through the spheres."

"The spheres of Highness..." I mused, "are very high. How can a man go straight from the deep Underworld to the lofty spheres of Highness, and be back in the Underworld in no time?"

"At the moment of dying," Gervin explained, "it is not rare for people to connect with the White Light of the spheres of Highness. This is part of the magic of dying. It doesn't matter where you are, whether in the kingdom, in the worlds of the gods, or in the Underworld. Dying can immediately transport you into the Light. And when you become a fully awakened person, then you die a new death every second. You can dwell in the Light of the spheres of Highness forever."

Eternal Life through a permanent state of death. It left Elyani and myself thoughtful.

Then I risked a burning question, "Gervin, suppose I had not been a sleeper at all, and had undertaken my descent into the Underworld like a *really* awakened person."

"Suppose!" echoed Gervin.

"Would I have been able to bring Vivyani back?"

"Yes," he answered, matter-of-fact, "very likely so."

"So, really, it is this important to become an awakened one."

This was spoken from the heart. It made Gervin shine one of his enlightening smiles. "You understand that the White Eagle guided you to her, don't you?"

I nodded silently.

"Gervin, will Szar learn more about the Underworld when he goes to the temple of the Dragon?" Elyani asked.

"That could well be. No one in the kingdom knows more about the Underworld than the Sons of the Dragon."

Despite my gripping desire to find Vivyani, the idea that I might have to go down a second time made me feel sick to the stomach. Elyani, who understood, gently called on the presence of the White Eagle for me.

It was magic. Each time she invoked the Eagle, I felt serene again.

Gervin, who had been watching her, smiled affectionately. And he started telling us about Lehrmon, who was working hard at the production of extraordinary soft stones in the temple of Lasseera, together with Master Esrevin and the *soon-to-be-famous-throughout-the-entire-kingdom* Master Woolly, the stone-maker genius.

After Gervin left, I engaged in a discussion of the spheres with Elyani. "So the kingdom, the intermediary worlds, the worlds of the gods and the

5 – The Book of the Mysteries of Eisraim

spheres of Highness are all part of the spheres of Melchisedek, is that right?"

"Right!" she replied.

"And where do the Underworlds fit in all this?"

"Also part of the spheres of Melchisedek, but below us. And there are plenty of Underworlds! What you saw during your descent was only a superficial crust. Underneath, there are layers upon layers. It goes down as deep as the spheres above are high."

I shuddered at the thought of what I had escaped. But what would happen to me at the temple of the Dragon? I swallowed hard. "Do you think the Sons of the Dragon will ask me to go down again, and perhaps even further down?"

"I don't know. Perhaps you should ask the White Eagle of the gods through me?" she said to divert my attention.

The stratagem worked instantly. "Do you mean you could prophesy from the White Eagle for me?" I asked with surprise.

She pretended to be offended. "Of course I can! Szar-ka, what do you think? I am a high priestess."

"Be careful, White Eagle, I might take you up on this one!"

"Ask me. Any time," her voice was honey-sweet. "But for now, let us return to the spheres. Which sphere are we in now?"

"Now we are standing in the kingdom, below the worlds of the gods and the intermediary worlds, and above the Underworlds."

"Lawfully so!"

"Tell me, what's the Upperworld, exactly?"

"Another name for the world of the gods, which we sometimes call the triangle."

"Simple," I gave a handclap.

"Simple," she smiled. "In the ladder of the worlds, which is the first layer that comes after the kingdom?" she asked.

"Darkness visible, the first of the intermediary worlds."

"*Right and righteous.* And why is it called darkness visible?"

"Visible, because it can easily be seen from the kingdom, and darkness, because when one looks into it, the atmosphere suddenly becomes dark. And by the way, Lady Elyani, I know very well how to recognise when people are talking through the voice channels of darkness visible so I can't hear what they are saying!"

She looked up to the spheres with a dignified attitude on her face, pushing her lips forward and playing with her hand on her chin just like Master Gervin when he pulled his beard.

What else could I do but burst out laughing? She followed.

When we recovered some seriousness, I asked, "And who lives in the spheres of Highness?"

"Great sages and angels. Those who never die."

"Aha!" I said. "That sounds exactly like what Gervin wants me to strive for, because only *he who never sleeps, never dies*."

"Exactly. Gervin's words were clear, weren't they? As soon as you start dying every second, you are fully awakened, and then you never die! Got it?"

"Mm..." I pondered, "but I thought the gods were immortal?"

"Not completely. Their worlds are located below the spheres of Highness. The gods live hundreds of hundreds of hundreds of times longer than us, which is why they are called immortal. But they must leave their body and die at the end of a cosmic cycle, and be reborn at the beginning of the following one. Anything below Highness is subject to death."

"Really," I observed, "the more you go down, the more death there is. In the spheres of Highness they never die. In the worlds of the gods they don't die very often. In the kingdom we die quite a bit. But it's nothing compared to the Underworld I saw, where everyone seems to be dying a lot. Makes you wonder what happens further below."

"But it's obvious," she said with a mischievous smile, "they must be dying all the time! Which means that if we could go there, we would be fully awakened."

"And then we'd never die?" I asked in a perplexed voice.

"Szar-ka," she said, "isn't it time for you to go and *get some lawful rest*?"

"But what about the spheres of remoteness?" I asked.

"They are very far. Not at all like us. Totally different."

"What sort of people live there?"

"Other forms of intelligence. Not at all like us human beings." The lady of the Eagle slowly waved her arms around me, swelling her cheeks and letting a mysterious whisper blow through her rounded lips. "Flying Dragons. Great clouds of blue consciousness that make 'ffffooooohhhh' sounds when you tune in and listen."

I was fascinated.

"A while ago," she added, "I heard Lady Teyani prophesy that one day, you would tell us many secrets about the spheres of remoteness."

"Lady Teyani was prophesying about me? How come?"

Elyani shrugged her shoulders innocently. "We have to talk about *something* in our temple meetings."

"Elyani," I frowned, "you won't get out of this one so lawfully easily!"

She saw it was the truth. "All right," she admitted. "It was when I reported to her after you had that travelling accident, when you lost consciousness and I had to go and pick you up. Remember?"

"Of course I do. That was when I was always trying to catch you before you left the take-off room, but each time I finally managed to open my eyes you were already gone."

When Elyani was moved, the light of the White Eagle shone through her. This time so much light shone that she was nearly embarrassed. "I wonder

5 – The Book of the Mysteries of Eisraim

what projected you into a sphere of remoteness," she went on. "Lucky it wasn't too far. But you know, when I arrived there something very strange happened. Those deadly winds of space had miraculously stopped, and I heard a feeble murmur. I tried all the known types of identification symbols, but it didn't respond."

"Was it threatening?"

"Not at all! *I* became threatening, because I was scared it would attack you. Nothing like it. The voice just whispered to me there was nothing to fear because 'Space Matrix' was watching. And another voice heralded the return of a Flying Dragon."

"Far Un..." I began, but I stopped, having promised myself never to say these words lightly again. "And what did Teyani have to say about that?"

"She said it was an extremely significant connection, and that one day you will have much more to tell us about it. She also suggested that this connection could well be the reason Gervin chose you as his apprentice."

"I don't see the link, there."

"Flying Dragons, Space Matrix, and being looked after in remoteness," explained Elyani, "all this sounds like travelling in large measure. You may not have realised it yet, Szar, but the Masters of Thunder are fantastic travellers. People like Gervin and Lehrmon have explored the spheres up and down and in every other direction. Some of these spheres have so many directions that they can become extremely confusing. The mind cannot cope with them. And so the Masters of Thunder have developed a supermind process for travelling in multi-dimensional spaces, and applied it to extravagantly distant explorations – the kind of journeys that sound far away even to gods."

I looked at her eagerly, waiting for more.

"No! That's it, I'm not saying one more word!" she looked up towards heaven, "O, White Eagle of the gods, forgive me! I am supposed to be stealing all the secrets of his order, and here I am, explaining to him what his teacher has not had time to tell him yet. Help! Should I try dragon's milk?"

I rolled on the purple lawn, "No, not that! Lady Elyani, I'll say anything you want, but don't do that to me!"

"You mean you didn't like my dragon's milk?" she looked as if her heart was broken.

Mother of the Light, what had I said? I sat up immediately. "Of course, I loved it! It was the most fantastic, unique dragon's milk I had ever drunk. And the Lord Melchisedek is my witness... what a day I had afterwards! I can't wait till I deserve another one."

5.35 Welcome to the personal stage

For the first time since the descent, I was to go and visit Gervin in the enclave of the jewels instead of him visiting me in Elyani's courtyard.

The lady of the Eagle escorted me through the maze of halls and corridors. When we arrived at the portal of the female wing, she quickly checked my energy before letting me go. Satisfied that I could cope with walking, she gave me a cautious blessing.

I went straight to the enclave of the thirty-three victorious gods. I *had* to pay a visit to Lord Gana's altar.

As I was walking, I realised this was the first time in weeks that I had left Elyani. Some strange feelings accompanied this realisation, so strange that I couldn't really tell what they were. And everything around me felt so different. "What the U... has happened to me?" I thought, as I lawfully greeted people on the way. Why do I feel like I am living in a different world?

As always, paying my respects to Gana was like greeting an old friend. "*Ha! Gana! Lobatchen Zerah! Hera, Gana! Samayin ho Zerah!*"

At least he had not changed! "Oh, Lord Gana," I thought, "what would I do in this world if you were not here? But what is happening to me?"

The light around the altar was as sweet as Elyani's white drinks. "The white drinks..." I thought, "perhaps this is what is happening: I'm not coping with so many white drinks. Too magic for me. What do you think, Lord Gana?" I asked through the fountain.

The knowingness of the fountain, however, rather indicated that the white drinks were excellent for me.

I sighed in relief.

All sorts of questions came to my mind at the same time. It made me smile, remembering the times I used to come here desperate to find questions I could ask my master.

I wondered if it would be possible for me to prophesy from the wisdom of Lord Gana, just as Elyani prophesied from the White Eagle. Perhaps if I watched her officiating, I could find clues on how to do the same with Gana. Prophecy sounded exactly like what I needed to answer all my questions. More than ever before, I needed the wisdom of the gods.

By the time I arrived at Gervin's, many more questions had popped into my mind. The *wise man in the Law* greeted me warmly and lawfully and as always, he inquired about my health.

"I don't know!" I said, "My body is fine, but all sorts of strange things are happening inside me, Gervin. I wish I understood them better."

"What do you think could be happening, son?"

"It's all so different, Gervin. Would you believe it, there are times when I have so many questions that I don't even know which one to ask Elyani first. And I feel regrets about many things I have done in the past, and

5 – The Book of the Mysteries of Eisraim

which now appear to me to have been gross mistakes, and missed opportunities. And my mind is often preoccupied with wishes and emotions – hopes and feelings like I never had before."

"Do you think sleepers have regrets and wishes like these?"

"I know they don't. But I can't help thinking that my life used to be so much simpler before. Gervin, there are even times when my own wishes contradict each other! I can see no wisdom in that."

"Aha!" Gervin laughed. "Like what, for instance?"

"I wish I didn't have to go to the temple of the Dragon. And I hope no one ever asks me to go down into the Underworlds again," I shuddered. "But I wish the Sons of the Dragon could tell me how to descend and find Vivyani. I know she is dead, but so what? Whether her body lives or not does not change the fact that her soul is still frozen down there. Who will take care of her?"

"So you are becoming a man of compassion."

"Compassion sounds like the wisdom of great sages. What I am talking about is much more simple. I am just starting to understand the value of being taken care of, and that has made me think about a lot of things. Perhaps, after all, having been taken care of by Elyani has taught me even more than descending into the Underworld did."

"Perhaps!" Gervin twinged his beard, signalling that our discussion had depth, "but then of course if you had not gone to the Underworld, there would not have been an opportunity to be taken care of. And if you had not died in the White Light, perhaps you would never have been capable of letting someone take care of you."

"Perhaps," I answered, wishing I had a beard like Gervin and Lehrmon, so I could twinge it and reach great depths of thinking like them. To my dismay, the five or six thin blond hairs on my chin never seemed to grow. I wondered if the White Eagles had special brews for growing beards. Even though, why would they?

"Now," I continued, "I have come to tell you one thing, Gervin. If, for the third time, you ask me to become your apprentice, I will not hesitate. I will say yes. I have given it a lot of thought in the last weeks. I am still not at all sure that I can follow you, but if by the grace of the gods I could ever become a Master of Thunder, then perhaps I could find Vivyani. And deep inside I still believe there was some truth in the vision I had at the lake. One day our good Lady Elyani will need help, and I want to be there for her. But what help could I give her now, ignorant and powerless as I am? If you make me strong, then I can help her. And also, perhaps one day I will be able to give to someone, a bit like you have given to me, and that would be the greatest of all gifts."

Gervin and I looked at each other silently. I could feel his warmth – the warmth I had admired in him ever since I met him. But now, I could also *receive* the warmth, as when Elyani was taking care of me. And in this receiving, there was giving. It was a marvellous experience. For the first time, I found myself shining warmth into Gervin, just as when I sat and did eye contact with Elyani.

It was simple and full. A magic instant. "Gervin's warmth is so much like the White Eagle's," I thought. Or perhaps was it the other way around?

"Something I have found about sleepers is that they do not understand what warmth is about," I said. "They are cold, a bit like the people in the Underworld, but they do not even realise it."

"Very true, man of the Law!" answered Gervin who, I was discovering, knew extremely well how to receive the warmth I was sending him.

"Now, I also have something to tell you," Gervin said after a while. "Remember when I said that a lot would have happened by the time I asked you a third time, which will be binding for us both? In fact, so much has happened that I believe there is no longer the need for me to ask you. This warmth, of which you speak well, will be our binding. Still, there is a formal way of doing things by which we must abide, so as to help the power of our lineage flow from me to you. Tomorrow morning, you will meet me at the door of my room two hours before sunrise, and I will conduct a ceremony in which I will formally invite you to join the Masters of Thunder."

I shivered. Shame on me, my only thought was, *"Good Lord Melchisedek,* what will have happened to me by tomorrow morning?"

Gervin read my thoughts. He promptly raised a protective hand towards my heart. "It's all right! It's all right! This time I am not sending any disasters your way," he said quickly, making me laugh.

5.36 White Eagle prophecy

Elyani was waiting for me at the portal of the female wing of the temple.
"I haven't seen you for ages!" I exclaimed.
"Three hours at least," she smiled.

As I followed her, I feigned exasperation, "This is getting to be ridiculous! There *must* be a way for me to find my direction in the corridors of your temple!"

The lady of the Eagle chuckled. "Of course, there are ways. Plenty of ways."

"Magic?" I asked.
"Of course!"
"Do you think a few hundred more white drinks could help?"
"Funny you should say that! I have just prepared a really special one."

"Sweet Upperworld!" I thought, "I knew that something was going to happen to me." As I believed I recognised a hallway, I asked, "Didn't we just walk past here three minutes ago?"

"No."

5 – The Book of the Mysteries of Eisraim

"Gervin and Lehrmon can do multi-dimensional travelling through the spheres of remoteness," I said, "and I can't even find my way to your bedroom. I have a lot of catching up to do."

We walked down a small stairway. I was sure we had already passed it. I didn't even bother mentioning it to my guide. "Elyani," I said, "there is a question I have had in my mind for some time. Are you Gervin's daughter?"

"Ouch!" she exclaimed, "Szar, what are you asking!"

Realising I had made a blunder, I immediately said, "Sorry! I won't mention it again."

"That's good." She paused. "Gervin is not my father, but I am very touched that you thought he was."

When we finally arrived at the courtyard, Elyani suggested I *got some lawful rest*.

"I'm not tired at all. Listen, something has happened. Gervin has announced to me that tomorrow at dawn he is going to initiate me as his apprentice in Thunder."

"Lawfully wonderful!" It was clear Elyani loathed this news. "And did he say when you would be going to the temple of the Dragon?"

"Probably not long after that. You have healed me so well. Sometimes I wish I could have been sick a little longer."

"Oh, really?" Elyani shone with the light of the Eagle.

"Really! Can't you poison me a little with one of your drinks? Tomorrow during lunch, perhaps."

Elyani did not laugh. She bit her lip and contemplated the mists, pulling herself together.

The silence was broken by a few drops of rain that started falling into the courtyard.

"What do you think is waiting for me at the temple of the Dragon? Probably nothing I should be looking forward to. Are there any high initiates of the Underworlds here, in the temple of Eisraim?"

"Not that I know of."

"Are there no orders in Eisraim which descend to the Underworlds like you and I had to do?"

"Only a few. It's too dangerous. Most of them are just accompanied to a cavern like the one I dropped you in. Then they are led by the hand for a short visit, until they start yelling, '*Oh my Lord Melchisedek, what is that*?' Then they are taken back to the surface, and they call themselves great initiates of the Underworld."

"And what about the White Eagles. Do they all have to go down?"

"All of them," Elyani answered, pulling one of her delicate faces. "It is one of the essential trials to become a high priestess of our order, and we accept it and are proud of it because we like to be known as the order of the White Eagle, not the White Goose. But in the last years the casualties have been horrid. Gervin must have spoken to you about the deterioration of the warp of fields."

"Which is why *he* asked you to look after me," I caught her.

She pulled another quick face at me. "In the last three years not one of the White Eagles has returned. Sending someone down has become like proclaiming a death sentence. Each time, it leaves Teyani devastated. If it continues like this there will be nothing left of our order."

"Maybe I am being presumptuous," I just had to say it, "but I'm sure that if I had gone down again, I would have found Vivyani."

"Szar, I believe you. But your body was at the limit of exhaustion. It would have died while you were down there."

"All right, all right! I accept that." Looking at my skinny body, I grinned, "I just need another one hundred thousand white drinks, and who knows? Maybe I will be fit enough to try again."

When I mentioned Vivyani, Elyani often changed the topic. This time she passed her hand close to the large birthmark on my left cheek and sighed, "When you were asleep, Teyani and I tried a balm on this, but it didn't work. Though I have thought of other herbs that may prove more efficient."

Looking straight into her eyes, I said, "I want to ask the White Eagle of the gods if there is something I can do at the temple of the Dragon to bring Vivyani back. Will you be my prophetess?"

We had long passed the stage of wondering whether eye contact was unlawful. Holding the intensity in my eyes, Elyani nodded, "I will. But will you *get some lawful rest* first? The prophecy could take a long time."

The drops had turned into rain. I capitulated and went to take a nap that lasted four more hours than I had expected. Despite the fact that I felt stronger than ever, my sleep patterns were still irregular.

When I re-emerged, it was already sunset. It was still raining. I went to knock at Elyani's door.

"What have you been doing?" I exclaimed with surprise when I saw her. "You are shining!"

It made her shine a little more. "Come on, we have to take the herbs."

"You mean you are drinking this one with me?"

"Yes. It's prophecy-time!" She handed me a large cup full of a pinkish-white liquid. I sat on the floor and took a sip while she was adjusting the flame on her small bedroom altar.

"Half!" she said, "You must drink half."

I did as she ordered and handed the cup back to her, "This one is all sweet and bubbly."

Without a word, she expedited the other half in one draught. Then she turned towards me with a vague look in her eyes, as if the oracle was already talking to her.

"Bizarre," I thought. "This brew seems to be having more effect on her than on me."

5 – The Book of the Mysteries of Eisraim

Then, looking up as if through the ceiling, she started making sounds like I had heard other prophetesses utter, "Zar-Zarra... Elva... Roh!" And the sequence of unintelligible onomatopoeia – or was it an old Atlantean dialect? – went on.

"Oh, no!" I thought. "She is one of those prophetesses that only the gods themselves can understand!" As Gervin had instructed me to do in similar situations, I remained very still, trying to open to the oracular flow. But the sounds went from bad to worse, and her body started to shake.

At first, I was concerned for her. But the oracular sounds turned into such a cacophony that I started having my doubts. "Elyani," I thought, "you are playing one of your tricks on me!" There was a difficult moment during which I wondered what to do. "If she is *really* prophesying and if I start laughing, then she is going to be very hurt." But the noise kept degenerating to the point where I could no longer contain myself, and I exploded with laughter.

Suddenly quiet, Elyani looked up to heaven, "That's it! He doesn't believe me! I knew he did not trust me to be his prophetess."

That's when I realised there was more in the herbs than I had thought.

I couldn't stop laughing. Shaken by violent contractions, I had to hold my belly with my hands, and I could hardly breathe. The power in the herbs took over. I got completely carried away and started rolling on the floor.

Elyani was sitting close to me. She laughed a bit too, to keep me company.

I had no idea how long it lasted. I completely lost touch with time.

Finally, I rendered my last laugh and collapsed in a foetal position. Elyani gently passed her hand through my hair, as she used to do when I was very sick.

"I'm dead!" I whispered with a long, long sigh of relief.

"Just stay very quiet like this for a while, and you will be ready to meet the White Eagle."

I made myself baby-soft, receiving the incredibly high quality of light she had brought down into the room. And the warmth.

When she invited me to sit up, I was completely out of my head.

My eyes were captured by hers. I had never seen eyes shine like this. It was like contemplating the fields of stars.

I was about to tell her how fascinated I was. With a hand gesture she indicated I was to stay quiet. "The White Eagle is with me. I will be speaking as he commands me to. You can ask any questions you want, but you must know that all the priestesses of the White Eagle will hear his answers."

The White Eagle! His presence was so much like Elyani's.

Or was it the opposite?

I was direct. "I want to know if there is a power I can gain at the temple of the Dragon that would allow me to find Vivyani."

The prophetess answered immediately, and in her normal voice, "When facing misfortune, what can a little boy do but hold his head in his hands and cry? Only great warriors have the power to change the course of destiny. If Szar is given a chance to become a great warrior, let him not turn back. There will not be a second chance."

This did not make much sense to me. "Could I know more?"

The prophetess shook her head. "The White Eagle does not want to say more on this. If you insist, he will speak words, but these will be so confusing that they will poison your mind."

I swallowed and promptly changed the topic, "When I was at the small lake in the forests of Nadavan, after losing the precious soft stone, I had a vision of the White Eagle coming down to me and asking for my help. I want to know if that vision was real."

"It was real, and sent by the White Eagle himself," she said.

This unambiguous answer made my heart burst with joy. Basking in the lofty presence of the Eagle, I remembered how I had doubted myself, and all the sorrows I had created for myself by not trusting the vision, and I smiled.

But if the vision was real, what was going to happen to Elyani?

I didn't want to frighten her by implying she could be in danger. So I asked, "How could I make myself strong enough to serve the Eagle? What do I have to do to become a giver?"

"Ride the Dragon. Fulfil the will of your father."

My father? That did not make sense. The *old man in the Law* had died so long ago. How could I ever know what he had willed for me?

"Can I ask more on this?"

Elyani shook her head silently.

Perplexed, I wondered how to rephrase the question.

Elyani shook her head a second time.

I heard the warning and gave up on this point. Contemplating the extraordinary light in her eyes, I asked, "I already owe so much to the White Eagle. How will I ever be able to thank him?"

"Ride the Dragon! Fulfil the will of your father!"

I let the words work on me for a moment.

My father... What the Upperworld had my father to do with all this? Perhaps the White Eagle was referring to Gervin.

That was when I made a capital mistake. I interpreted the repeated answer of the Eagle as a sign that I was running out of meaningful questions. I decided I had asked well, and I was satisfied with the precious answers I had received, even though they did not make much sense to me just then. So I signalled with a nod that I had no further questions, and I entered a contemplative state.

What a young fool I was! The White Eagle of the gods was there for me. Had I been discerning enough to figure out the right questions, the prophecy could have gone on all night, and completely new horizons would have been opened to me. Elyani had even sent me a clue. She had warned, "It could take a long time!" and she had insisted I *got some lawful rest*. If only I had remembered to tune into the clear fountain!

None of this came to my mind. I just sat silently in front of Elyani, enjoying the lofty presence in the room and the splendour in her eyes.

After perhaps half an hour, the presence became fainter and Elyani closed her eyes.

I thought she probably needed *some lawful rest* and some time for herself. So I walked out of her room quietly.

5.37 The abandoned priestess

It was early in the night. Droplets of rain were falling into the courtyard. The moonlight, reflecting through the mists, created the silvery atmosphere so characteristic of Atlantean nights.

Elyani came out soon after me. She sat close to me on the lawn. "There are a few things I must explain to you about prophecy. For a start, after receiving the oracle, a prophetess is fragile. She should not be left alone!" Her voice sounded patient, not angry. Still, it was clear I had done something wrong.

I woke up from my misty contemplation, "I'm sorry! Are you all right? What was I supposed to do?"

"Yes, I am all right. The prophecy session was very short. But you must understand what usually happens to a woman when she receives an oracle. Her Spirit must ascend high in the spheres, it can be a great effort. When the session finishes she is left with her Spirit high above and far from her body. This, combined with the fatigue – prophecy can be exhausting! – leaves her in a state where she does not have full control over her body, and where she is extremely open and vulnerable, like a little baby. If she is left alone and not cared for, she feels nothing but desolation. As if she was abandoned somewhere in the cold regions of the Underworlds."

"*Sweet Lord Melchisedek*, is this how you are feeling?"

"No, not really." There was just enough light for me to guess she was pulling one of her sophisticated faces at me. "There are several types of prophecy. With the connection we established tonight, I remained in my normal self, more or less – especially because it was so short."

"One day will you tell me more about the different types of prophecy?"

"For sure. If I'm still talking to you by then, of course."

"Oh, I'm sorry! I'm sorry! I'm sorry! Now I remember Gervin telling me that priestesses who had just prophesied needed protection. But I never thought of asking him how to do it. Elyani, please, will you tell me? What would be the best way, I mean the most special, the warmest and sweetest way, of taking care of a priestess of the White Eagle – suppose – who had just finished a lo-o-ong and exhausting session of prophecy, in which her Spirit had spread all over the spheres?"

"Suppose!" she echoed, and from the tone of her voice I figured out I was already a quarter forgiven. "But that would be very easy! You would just have to look after her as if she was a baby. What would you do if you were taking care of a one-year-old little girl?"

The last one-year-old I had seen was my little brother, when I was four years of age. "Mm..."

Elyani gave a deep sigh, as if I had even more things to learn than I thought. "You would make sure that everything was taken care of for her, and you would *really* be with her. You would be specially nice to her and talk to her. Perhaps you would even hold her hand."

After a tentative silence, she continued, "You would feed her if she needed to eat. And most importantly, you would create a safe and warm atmosphere around her."

"A bit like you were doing when I was sick?"

"Yes. But don't worry. Tonight I'm all right." She waited a few more seconds and she repeated, "I'm all right."

That made me feel much better. I remained thoughtful, wondering what to do next.

Elyani preferred to change the subject. "What did you think of the answer about the great warrior?"

I shrugged my shoulders. "I don't know! Look at me! I'm all skinny, I have always hated running, and it took me three times longer than all the other children at school to learn swimming. I remember once when I was sixteen, I was catching my breath after climbing up and down a stairway. My physical education teacher took a long look at my body and said if I wanted to be given a wife, I should try my utmost best at the grand competition of Sheringa."

Elyani chuckled.

"That man felt so much contempt for me that he never spoke to me again," I sighed. "I can't imagine myself having anything to do with great warriors. Perhaps the meaning of the words was symbolic."

"Perhaps."

"Listen," I asked, "I was fascinated with how your eyes looked when you were receiving the oracle. It was... amazing! Is the art of prophecy one of the protected secrets of your order, or can I ask you about it?"

"Both!" she answered. The clouds had thickened and I could not see her face, but I knew exactly how she was smiling. "But another time!" she said. "It's a long story. I want you to be fully rested for your initiation. I gave Master Gervin my word that I would make you fit, and I intend to keep my word."

"So you won't poison me tomorrow at lunch? What a shame!"

She remained silent.

5 – The Book of the Mysteries of Eisraim

"You know, thanks to all your magic drinks, and your care, I have developed a supernatural power in the last weeks."

She could not get her voice to sound merry. "Really! Which one?"

"I can read the mind of the priestesses of the White Eagle. Especially one of them."

"And what can you read, O Master of Thunder, Ambassador of the Lord Melchisedek?"

I had never heard this expression. "What's an Ambassador of the Lord Melchisedek?"

"It is one of the titles of the Masters of Thunder, one that is given to them when they go and visit the inhabitants of the spheres of remoteness. And so, ambassador, what can you read?"

I had to search for my words. "It is the last night, isn't it? As soon as Gervin initiates me, he will send me to the temple of the Dragon."

"Yes."

"It is not going to be a safe journey, is it?"

She did not answer.

"Elyani, I know you have asked the White Eagle about this. What did he tell you? I could well die over there, couldn't I?" I had to force the answer out of her, "I *need* to know Elyani, please! What are my chances?"

"Fifty-fifty. This is what the Eagle said: *'So much for yes as for no – like the purple blossoms of the alohim tree after the first storm in spring: half remain on the branches, half fall on the ground.'*"

We spent a long time listening to the droplets of rain falling into the courtyard.

"Elyani, thank you. Thank you for what you have done for me. Now I know for sure, what I have gained lately has not come from visiting the Underworld. It's come from the way you have taken care of me. Being sick with you has been the most special time of my life."

Realising what I had just said, I promptly tried to correct my words, "I mean, being sick in your company..."

"That's it, Szar-ka," the lady of the Eagle teased me. "That's all you have to do when you meet the Dragon. Just tell him one of your jokes and in the earthquake-laughter that follows, you won't have any difficulty escaping!"

Facing the Dragon! So was that what Gervin wanted me to do? No wonder the Eagle had compared the odds of my death to the blossoms of the Alohim tree. Had he been over-optimistic, so as to reassure Elyani?

"Can you imagine a brown chicken like me riding a dragon?" I questioned.

"Yes of course I can." She sounded like she believed her words.

"If only you could come with me. How am I going to survive without your white drinks?"

"Before Gervin brought you to me, you lived well without them, didn't you?"

"Precisely, I didn't! I had no idea how frozen and dead I was before you brought me back from the Underworld."

It was the second time she cried because of me. I couldn't see her face, but I could feel. Big tears of sorrow, rendered shameless by the night. But her grief sent me silent and shy like *a young idiot in the Law*, just when she wanted me to speak to her the most.

After a while she stood up and walked to the end of the courtyard. "Will you come and sit close to my favourite laurel tree?" she asked.

I followed her voice and, groping in the dark, lightly touched her hair to know where to sit.

"This tree is special to me. My mother planted it," she confided.

I caressed the leaves with my hand. She couldn't see, but she could feel.

"I want to thank you too," she said.

"Me?" This sounded grossly undeserved. "But what for?"

"For the things you have given me in the last weeks."

I had no idea what she meant.

Or perhaps I did know what she meant. But I did not know what to answer. So I remained silent as if I didn't know.

She understood, and she remained silent too.

There was fullness.

Much later in the night, she asked if I wanted to *get some lawful rest*. I said no, but she insisted, because she had given her word to Thunder, and she sent me to sleep.

5.38 Apprentice in Thunder

It was so early in the morning that all the alleys of the temple were still empty. As I was about to knock at Gervin's door, I tuned into the clear fountain and prayed to the Mother of the Light not to let me faint during the ceremony.

A familiar voice called, "Szar!"

It was Lehrmon.

"*Praise the Lord Melchisedek, Szar of the Brown Robe!*" he joined his hands and laughed with excitement. And he ran towards me, and hugged me.

"*All glory to the Lord Melchisedek, Lehrmon of the Brown Robe!* Have you come all the way from Lasseera for me?"

"Of course! I wouldn't miss a moment like this one."

The door opened, but to my surprise it was not Gervin who stood in the doorway.

"*Praise the Lord Melchisedek, Melchard of the Brown Robe!*" Lehrmon exclaimed with enthusiasm. Melchard responded with a joyful voice, and the two men hugged each other.

5 – The Book of the Mysteries of Eisraim

"*Praise the Lord Melchisedek, Sir Melchard, High Priest of Eisraim and Grand Commander of the Law...*" I started saying.

"No! No! No! No! No!" the broad-shouldered man interrupted me. "This morning, I am Melchard of the Brown Robe." With a smile that shone the warmth of the Eagle, he took my arm and walked inside with me.

The light in the aquamarine chamber was the brightest I had ever seen it.

"*Praise the Great Apollo, Gervin, Grand Master of Thunder! All glory to the teacher!*" Lehrmon joined his hands in a prayer gesture and bent his head with reverence.

So Gervin was the grand master of the Brown Robe?

"*All glory to the teacher!*" Gervin responded, keeping his eyes closed for a few seconds. Then the two men laughed with joy and hugged each other.

Master Esrevin, who had travelled from Lasseera with Lehrmon, made his entry. He gave the same salute, his hands joined in front of his heart, "*Praise the Great Apollo, Gervin, Grand Master of Thunder!*"

Melchard saw that I didn't know what to say. He invited me to salute Gervin the same way. And they all welcomed me and hugged me as if I was their brother.

When all the greetings had been exchanged we sat in a circle, with Gervin in front of me.

Gervin looked straight into my eyes and declared in a grave voice, "Szar, for the third and last time, I ask you, will you become my apprentice in Thunder? Before answering, think well. If you accept, you will become bound to a new destiny, and to the lineage of Thunder. This is no easy path. Several before you have failed, and fallen so deep into the pit that aeons will elapse before they see the Light again."

I shivered. Master Gervin, as I had discovered in the last months, never spoke words of warning lightly.

"Yes."

"Why do you wish to accept my invitation?" Gervin asked. "Speak from your heart."

I frowned in surprise. This was no ordinary novitiate ceremony, where candidates learned their lines by heart months in advance and were lawfully warned of all surprises awaiting them, so as to be prepared to give lawfully satisfying answers.

In the vibrant aquamarine atmosphere of the room, listening to the knowingness of the clear fountain was easy. "If I walked away now, my life would lose all meaning," I said. "Now that you have given me a glimpse of what awakening can be like, I will never find peace as long as I am a sleeper."

"Do you realise that in this quest, you will have to make great sacrifices, and lose many of the things which are dear to you?"

This was easy to realise, for it was happening already. In a matter of hours, I would have to leave the temple, and Elyani, and journey to a terrifying destination.

"Yes."

Gervin turned towards Esrevin, and Esrevin said, "Yes." Then he turned to Melchard, who likewise said, "Yes." Lehrmon, in turn, gave the same, "Yes."

Gervin fixed his flamboyant grey-green eyes on me, and the energy in the room became even sharper. Faces appeared on his face, men who looked at me gravely and said, "Yes."

"These are Masters of Thunder in the Fields of Peace," Gervin commented.

When his face reappeared, I was hardly in my body. High above my head, an explosion was taking place. But it was so remote from my normal self that it eluded me.

Through eye contact, rock-solid Gervin projected my consciousness into these high and mysterious energies and declared, "Today, and in the presence of my brethren, I, Gervin, Grand Master of Thunder, accept you as my apprentice and invite you to learn the secrets of my lineage."

Gervin kept pouring energies into me, making me feel as if an enormous fire had been lit high in the sky, above my head.

Then he smiled, and in one second I was back in the room.

"Well done, son, well done!" Esrevin congratulated me.

Was it already finished? I was surprised, finding it difficult to believe how easy it had been not to faint.

"Szar is used to lengthy ceremonies," Lehrmon told Esrevin. "Nearly five years of training in the Salmon Robe has made him a fine ritualist."

"Szar, we forgot to tell you that this was no ceremony," Melchard laughed. "In our lineage, there is only one initiation by which you become a Master of Thunder. A powerful ritual."

"Far more powerful than anything you could ever have seen, even if you had become the highest initiate of the Salmon Robe," Gervin added matter-of-factly.

"You won't be disappointed, Szar!" Lehrmon confirmed.

From an altar behind him, Gervin took a basket of fruits, mainly *pears of the Law*. The shining hues in the fruits' aura showed that they had been offered during a fire ritual. He gave one fruit to me, one to each of the others, and took one for himself. "But before we can raise you to this sublime degree, we need you to become much stronger, Szar." Turning towards Melchard, he added, "The White Eagle has worked on him a lot in the last weeks."

"Elyani told me all about it," Melchard smiled affectionately, biting into his juicy *pear of the Law*.

So Elyani knew the high priest of Eisraim and reported to him! That sounded worrying, to say the lawful least. She and I had discussed so many topics in the last weeks!

Melchard shook his head, as if he could read my thoughts and wanted to reassure me. Which of course made me feel even more embarrassed.

5 – The Book of the Mysteries of Eisraim

"Is there something you need to ask us before going to the temple of Vulcan?" Gervin asked.

"Yes," I said, contemplating the pear and remembering Elyani. "You haven't told me what you wanted me to achieve in that temple."

"Szar, the Masters of Thunder are involved in a great task, a secret enterprise of far-reaching consequences, which I have been supervising for nearly thirty-five years with the help of Esrevin and Melchard, and more recently our good Lehrmon."

During the last weeks, one of the things Elyani had communicated to me was her love of secrets. This one sounded like a momentous secret. I bit into the *pear of the Law*, and listened.

"As I told you before, I would like you to help us in this great task."

"The one that is so secret," Esrevin added with a witty smile, having noticed the shining glow in my eyes.

We all laughed.

"But before you can help us," Gervin continued, "we need you to become fully awakened, of course, but also more... mm..." Gervin searched for the appropriate word.

Was it because he did not want to hurt my feelings?

"Dangerous," he finally said, "that's the word. We need you to become dangerous!"

Sweet Lord Melchisedek, if there was one thing I was not, it was dangerous!

"A powerful man you must become, if you are to help us fulfil my prophecies. In the temple I am sending you to, there will be opportunities for you to gain great strength. Do not miss your chance!"

From the deepest of myself, I heard the warning.

I was starting to know the value of a chance.

– Thus ends the book of the Mysteries of Eisraim –

6

The Book of the Great Dragon of the Deep

6.1 The Sons of the Dragon

What incredible scenery the mountain range in the south of the county of the Red Lands unfolded before my eyes, with its short plateaus, red cliffs, narrow canyons, and sand dunes with sparse spiky shrubs of a kind totally unknown in the north. The dusty, arid landscape was so unreal that I would hardly have been surprised to see an elephanto's trunk rise from behind the dunes. I wished Elyani could have been with me to see it all.

When I finally arrived in the vicinity of Lohrzen's mountain, I stopped at a distance to contemplate the huge reddish cliff in which the entrance to the temple was carved. "Lawfully unreal!" was my only thought. As I came closer to the massive doors, I mumbled to myself, "I know I am not supposed to, but I wish Gervin could have told me what to say when I arrive at my destination." The temple of Eisraim, with its unguarded entrances through which people came and went as they pleased, seemed painfully far away.

Before I even had time to knock at the portal, a loud bass voice accosted me, "Who are you, *stranger in the Law*?"

I could not see who was shouting. The only opening in the huge doors was a minute hole. Holding on to the clear fountain, I called back, "I am Szar of the Brown Robe, sent by Master Gervin of the temple of Eisraim."

"Are you a Son of the Dragon?"

The question left me perplexed. I tuned into the clear fountain, trying to figure out what an awakened person would answer.

Fortunately, another voice shouted, "The temple of Eisraim, you said?"

I threw a half-proud, half-cautious, "Yes, Sir!"

"What kind of robe is he wearing?"

"Monk's robe. Brown. Dirty," answered the first voice.

6 – The Book of the Great Dragon of the Deep

"Let him in."

"Here we are," I thought. "Gervin, look at me! I have already made it inside."

With unlawfully ominous creaks, the huge doors began to swing open. They seemed to take forever. Gradually a dark hall appeared in front of me. Bravely, I walked in.

My first surprise came when I realised how big the two men were. I had rarely seen such tall, broad-shouldered people. They did not look particularly amicable. They stared at me, while the doors closed behind me. I began to feel less and less comfortable.

The creaking concert finished with a loud bang, as a hefty transversal log sealed the portal. One of the giants grabbed me by the shoulders. Examining me as if I was a chicken in a market place, he asked the other giant, "Do you think he is any good?"

His acolyte looked thoughtful and muttered a dubious "Mm..."

Then they started discussing my physique. "He is awfully skinny. Do you think our god might take offence at him?"

"Could be..." the other one answered.

Then the man pushed me quite roughly towards his friend. I nearly choked when I heard him say, "Perhaps we should throw him into the pit with the Nephilim scum."

"Lawful Sir," I tried to tell them, "I came with friendly intentions..." But as I was speaking I realised it was a rather silly thing to say. The second giant mimicked the tone of my voice sarcastically, "He came with friendly intentions!" and they both burst out laughing, "Ha! Ha! Ha! Ha! Ha!" The thunder seemed to roll on for aeons.

Trying to fight against such mountains of muscle was not even an option, especially as I had never fought anyone in my entire life. As the clear fountain was telling me nothing, I saw myself in a bad position. "That's it, Master Gervin," I thought, "I will die a sleeper! I wish you could have told me how I was supposed to face death this time." As I was collecting my spirits, wondering how I could send a last communication to the lady of the Eagle, another man turned up.

"What's your name, my boy?"

"Szar, Sir, sent by Master Gervin of the Brown Robe of the temple of Eisraim."

He was not as tall as the other two but just as bulky, and his voice was even lower-pitched than the others. "I expected you, my boy. You have been announced."

"Right," I told myself. "They must have received a message from Gervin through darkness visible. If they have soft stones here, there must be a way to speak to Elyani," who had made me promise to call her as soon as I could get to a voice channel.

The man gave his orders and the two gatekeepers took me to a cold, bare room adjacent to the entrance hall.

Strange place. The walls didn't glow. They were dead – not made of plass, but of rough stone. The only light came from the few torches fastened to the walls.

A fourth man, also a colossus, appeared carrying water and food.

"Mother of the Light!" I thought, contemplating the bizarre charcoal-like chunks on the plate and already remembering Elyani's white drinks with nostalgia. "Where have I landed?"

Looking as innocent as I could, and making sure no one was looking at me, I started extending my consciousness all around me, sweeping the space of darkness visible in quest of a soft stone.

There was a knocking at the gates. For one second I thought of shouting to the poor soul, "No! Go back!" but I decided I had been brave enough for the moment, so I contained myself.

"Who are you, *stranger in the Law*?" demanded the voice I had first heard.

"I am Phileon, son of Phileon."

"Are you a Son of the Dragon?"

The man outside sounded quite confident, "I am not yet, Sir, but I aspire to become one of them, as my father is, and as the father of my father was."

"Enter, candidate!" the guard replied, and the doors creaked opened again.

"That's what Gervin forgot to tell me to say!" I thought, making sure I remembered the words, just in case someone else in this madhouse asked me what kind of a son I was. Yet I quickly realised that the magic words, even though they opened the temple's doors, were no guarantee of safety.

Through the large passage opening into the entrance hall, I saw a young man walking in. The two giants started again, "Do you think he is any good?"

"Mm..."

"He is awfully skinny. Do you think our god might take offence at him?"

"Could be..."

They started pushing their new victim around, asking each other whether they should throw him into the pit with the Nephilim scum. Seeing I was not the only one to be received in this fashion made me feel only moderately better.

After a few minutes the third man, who seemed to occupy a higher position in the temple hierarchy, reappeared. This time he did not say that the newcomer had been announced, but asked him in a ritual fashion, "*Candidate, can you give me the word which you have received from your father, as he received it from his father?*"

A bit shaken, but still quite together, the young man answered "*Yes, I can.*"

"*Very well. Whisper it in my ear,*" which the young man did.

"Brethren," exclaimed the chief, "*this is the genuine son of a Son of the Dragon. He should therefore be given a chance to walk in the fire and*

6 – The Book of the Great Dragon of the Deep

demonstrate through various other trials whether, by his endurance and courage, he is worthy of becoming one of us."

I hated the sound of what I was hearing.

"*Let it be so!*" answered the two giants, one after the other.

"Phileon," said the chief, "*you are but at the portal and can still walk away if you wish. But if you decide to stay, know that there is no turning back.*"

To which Phileon, in well-prepared fashion, replied, "*I shall not turn back, as my father did not turn back, nor the father of my father.*"

"Well then," replied the chief, "*enter, and think not of turning back.*"

How come no one asked *me* if I wanted to turn back?

Before I had time to figure out what I would answer if such an offer were made to me, the chief brought Phileon into the room where I was toying with my drink. "Phileon," he said, "this is Szar, another candidate. You will undergo the trials together."

Still scanning the space, I could find no trace of the presence of a soft stone.

6.2 Phileon, son of Phileon

Phileon, like me, was given food and drink. We both waited in the side room for an hour or so without exchanging a word, until another man came to fetch us. He too was a colossus, with a huge hairy chest and tree-trunks for thighs and arms.

"I'm Brother Floster," he said. "Follow me, candidates!"

As Phileon and I started walking behind Floster, I observed him carefully. Like the others, he was wearing dark leathery clothes: a pair of shorts and a shirt. His wrists were circled with tight strips of some kind of thick, black, scaly leather. He had a neatly trimmed beard and long black wavy hair. Walking behind him, I was fascinated by the sight of his hairy legs.

I tuned into him, asking myself, "How much of a sleeper is this man?" It immediately appeared that his sleep was no usual sleep. There was a solid, grounded force in him, different from anything I had observed before.

Floster took us through a network of corridors and hallways dug in the rock. There was no plass in the walls. The place was unlawfully dark. I made sure I carefully memorised the way, just in case I had to leave the place in a hurry. The temple looked vast but quite simple compared to the bewitched maze leading to Elyani's courtyard. After a few minutes of climbing up and down stairs, we arrived in a small cave lit by two tiny windows opening onto the cliff.

"Sons, you will stay here for the duration of your trials," our guide said. "Now get some rest. There's plenty of water in that jug, and a brother will bring some food for you this evening. *Tomorrow morning at dawn, I will come to take you for the passage through the first gate.*" He looked at me for a few seconds with his deep black eyes, then he looked at Phileon. And he walked out, banging the door closed behind him.

The first thing I did was to inspect the windows. I was so thin I would have had little difficulty climbing out. But thrusting my head through it, I realised that the room was at least three hundred lawful feet above ground level. Contemplating the steep cliff left me with an uncomfortable feeling. Unless some flying chariot of the gods came to fetch me, there was no hope of escape. I sighed, "The White Eagle, perhaps?"

Such weird walls in that cell. Same as in the rest of the temple: only stone, no plass. Completely dead. Without plass glow, the only light came from the narrow openings that were the windows. Unlawfully gloomy, and cold!

Phileon sat on one of the mats on the floor, I sat on the other, and we looked at each other for some time. Then I finally engaged one of the pre-established conversations of the Law through which people came to know one another.

My companion was the son of Phileon the potter. Naturally he was becoming a potter himself, learning the trade from his father and his three uncles. As we talked, I soon realised Phileon had been prepared to come here over a number of years, yet he had only a vague idea about what was going to happen. His father, when he had told him about the temple, had said more than once, "Not what you think, my son! Not what you think!" which was reminiscent of the warning issued by Gervin before I left, "*Expect surprises!*" But the more I discovered about this temple the less I savoured the prospect of being surprised by the Sons of the Dragon.

As the lawful chat with Phileon went on, I learned that visiting this temple was part of the Law of potters, because their trade dealt with fire. The members of several fire castes – craftsmen who worked with fire, one way or another – came to the temple of the Sons of the Dragon to receive their initiation. Phileon's father had instructed him that as a result of becoming a Son of the Dragon, many gestures and techniques he used daily in the art of pottery would take on a completely different meaning. Only then could he become a real knower of his craft.

"How did you discover that your father was a Son of the Dragon?" I asked, wondering if there were things I had never found out about my father.

"During my *birthday initiation of seven years of age*, he first told me about it. Then during my *birthday initiation of eleven years of age*, father communicated to me the secret words and symbols by which the Sons of the Dragon know each other."

For Phileon, coming here was the great adventure of his life, perhaps the only time ever when his daily routine of pottery work, leisure time and sleep would be interrupted. The excitement of this journey was indeed a

6 – The Book of the Great Dragon of the Deep

great awakening for Phileon. "This young man in the Law," I thought, "is less asleep than ever before in his life."

I was eager to know more about my short-term destiny. "Did they tell you what was going to happen?" I asked.

"We are going to be told secrets that men of other castes will never know. Secrets about fire and the god Vulcan. We are going to be initiated so we become real men," Phileon said with a definiteness that I felt touching.

"Real men... What's a real man?" I asked myself. "Can a sleeper be a real man?"

"*Which is your caste, Szar, my friend in the Law?*" Phileon asked.

"*I belong to the Brown Robe, Phileon.*" Even though my young *friend in the Law* had already told me all about his caste, I continued the normal course of the lawful conversation so as not to disorientate him, "*And which is your caste, Phileon?*"

"*I am from the fire-caste of the potters. And how old are you, Szar, my friend in the Law?*"

"*I have known twenty-four springs and twenty-three autumns, Phileon. And you?*"

"*I have known seventeen springs and seventeen autumns.*"

"I too was just turning eighteen," I thought, "when I first met Gervin."

"*Szar, my friend in the Law,*" Phileon continued, "*has your father, through the grace of our Lord Melchisedek, bestowed the gift of a wife onto you?*"

"*This joy in the Law is not yet known to me, Phileon. And you?*"

Phileon smiled with a touch of excitement in his eyes, "My father said that when I return home, I will be a Son of the Dragon. Then he will find me a wife!"

I had mixed feelings at the idea of Gervin finding a wife for me on my return to Eisraim. Anyhow, Gervin had never told me if being married was part of the rule of the Brown Robe. If Elyani was not his daughter, then perhaps he himself had never been married. Were Lehrmon and Esrevin married?

After talking with Phileon for an hour, I already knew all about his family (including his brothers, sisters, uncles' families and all his other friends and relatives), together with the duties of his caste, whereas I didn't even know if I was ever to be married! Conversations of this kind made me nostalgic for a simple life, a nice little time track where everything was straightforwardly traced and decided for me. How complicated my position was, and what embarrassing situations it created at times! When asked how my days were occupied, what was I to say? I could but smile when imagining Phileon's face if I had described my descent into the Underworld to him. Holding fast onto the clear fountain, I had to make up seemingly lawful answers such as, "*I follow the duty of my brown priestly caste, invoking the gods and serving the glory of our Lord Melchisedek, day after day, night after night.*" Lucky I had learnt such a vast repertoire of verses of the Law when I was at school! I could pick bits of them and recombine them into nice-sounding sentences. All this painfully resembled the classes in politics I had had to endure whilst studying in Sheringa.

"Here I am," I thought, "whingeing again! What would an awakened one do in this situation?" I tuned into the clear fountain and recalled Elyani's eyes when she was prophesying from the White Eagle of the gods, and I soon forgot my regrets.

Phileon was unusually perky, curious and talkative. A normally lawful sleeper-boy would just have sat with his eyes wide open, staring at the dead wall in front of him, waiting for the Sons of the Dragon to give the next instruction. Clearly, this initiation was doing him a lot of good. "You ask so many questions, Phileon," I complimented him, "I didn't know potters were so clever."

"That's because my father is no common potter, but an advanced initiate of the caste of the fire-potters, Sons of the Dragon. But you see, I can only tell you this because you are about to become a Son of the Dragon yourself. If it were not for the grace of Vulcan, you could not be here."

Vulcan, the god of the last hour... as part of my training as a priest, I had heard the name of this god but had never been involved in any of his rituals. "Phileon, who is Vulcan?"

He replied by chanting verses of the Law of his caste:
"*He is the tutelary god of my father, and of my father's father.*
Vulcan, Vulcan, Lord of the fire!
Vulcan, Vulcan, Lord of the anvil!
Irresistible is his power,
Great and mighty are his works,
For he is the god of the last hour."

"My father," Phileon spoke with awe, "he is a very powerful man! He says that *all the men who work with fire are worshippers of Vulcan, but they don't all know it*. And he says that Vulcan's power is as great as the power of the Dragon,
The Great Dragon which encompasses
That which is beyond the gods themselves."

"That sounds amazing, Phileon."

"Yes!" he exclaimed proudly. "My father told me, if it becomes tough for me at the temple, then I should call Vulcan and open to his power so he can help me, and *everything will spin like a smooth pottery wheel!*"

"No one told me anything!" I started thinking. But I quickly brought myself back to the awareness of the clear fountain. "Right," I told myself, "if Phileon can cope with the trials, then probably so can I. After all, I've survived the horrors of the Underworld and death in the White Light of the spheres of Highness, not to mention Elyani's dragon's milk." Still, I took a close look at Phileon, whose body was smaller but much stronger than

6 – The Book of the Great Dragon of the Deep

mine, and further doubts crept in. "If the trial involves running – running away from the Dragon, let's say – I am done."

The conversation had gradually drawn to a close, and Phileon sank into a doze. I took advantage of this quiet time to extend my consciousness in the space around our little room, searching for the unmistakable energy that would have signalled the presence of a soft stone. I felt all sorts of weird presences and heard bizarre non-physical sounds, but could find nothing that would have allowed me to engage a voice channel in darkness visible.

Beginning to feel the insidious pull to let myself drift into vagueness, I promptly called onto the clear fountain, "What would an awakened one do here? O Lord Gana, inspire me! Let me not miss the chance." Seeking inspiration, I remained with my mind vacant under the pure vertical flow of the fountain for some time, and finally thought, "If Gervin sent me to the temple of *Vulcan, Lord of the fire*, he must want me to learn about the power of this god."

Later I asked, "Your father, who is such a powerful man, told you to call on Vulcan's help. Did he tell you how to do it?"

"He said I should invoke him with the verse of the Law, *Vulcan! Vulcan! Lord of the anvil!*"

I let the verse and its rhythm sink into my energy. Then, establishing a vertical flow of connection as the Salmon Robe priests had taught me, I tuned into the presence of the temple and started the incantation,

"*Vulcan! Vulcan! Lord of the anvil!*
Vulcan! Vulcan! Lord of the anvil!"

Something startling happened, something I had never experienced before: a powerful wave of energy swept my belly, accompanied by a kind of tremor. "*Good Lord Melchisedek*, what is *that*?" I thought, taking a break from my recitation of the mantra. The tremor was so foreign to my usual palette of bodily sensations that for a moment I doubted whether it had really happened.

But to my great surprise, as soon as I resumed the incantation of the verse of the Law, the same "vroof!" took place in my belly. "Far Un..!" I started thinking. "The god is answering me!" I could still hardly believe what was happening, so weird was the feeling.

Vulcan! Vulcan! Lord of the anvil!
Vulcan! Vulcan! Lord of the anvil!

Each time I resumed the invocation, I received a "vroof" in response, accompanied by a slight but distinct twitch in my abdominal muscles. It did not feel at all bad, just strange. "What a curious place," I thought, "where the gods talk to mortals directly without the need for prophets. And moreover, using their guts as an oracle!" I wondered if the White Eagles knew about this kind of prophecy.

Cautiously, I kept on experimenting with the power of the invocation until the fatigue of the journey overtook me and I fell asleep.

6.3 Dragon dance

Next morning at dawn Brother Floster came to get Phileon and me for the first of our trials. He loudly kicked the door open, then stood in the doorway, torch in hand, staring grimly at me for an interminable minute with the deep, Volcanic look of a Son of the Dragon. "*Follow me, candidate,*" he threw at me. "*Now there is no turning back.*"

In true Atlantean fashion he stared at Phileon with the same look and for just the same amount of time. Then he told him, "*Follow me, candidate. Now there is no turning back.*"

Outside the door another priest of Vulcan was waiting, just as big as Floster, and carrying a torch like his. We started walking behind Floster, and the other priest followed. Our small procession wound its way through many corridors and halls without meeting one living soul, gradually descending deeper and deeper into the rock. There was no plass in the walls, and no windows or openings. Had it not been for our guides' torches we would have been in complete darkness.

Unlawfully terrifying!

In a lawful building you could *never* find yourself in complete darkness. There was always a friendly glow coming from the plass walls.

Here the only light came from flames, that created macabre shadows on the walls – shadows as in the caverns of sickness. Never had I seen something so macabre in the kingdom.

After a long and tiring walk, our guide stopped in front of a low door. "*Now, candidates,*" Floster announced, "*you will enter this Dragon's cave into which the light of the day never reaches, and you will implore the help of our Lord Vulcan for the trials which are coming, for there is no turning back.*" He opened the heavy gate and with a gesture of the hand indicated that Phileon and I were to go in. Bending our heads, we did as he said, and the door was slammed loudly behind us.

The world turned black.

I closed my eyes, reconnecting with darkness visible.

I heard the men lock the door and walk away.

The room was quite chilly. I slightly withdrew my energy from my physical body, as prescribed by the Law to alleviate the discomfort of cold or pain. But I didn't find myself surrounded by the familiar purple glow of darkness visible. Instead, the astral atmosphere of the room resonated with the most superficial layers I had encountered while plunging into the Underworlds – not the caverns of sickness full of wandering souls in pain, but the dark empty spaces in the descending shafts under darkness visible. Nothing to worry about. But I could feel that Phileon was becoming unlawfully nervous.

"How are you, Phileon, *my friend in the Law?*"

"I am... I am... I am not afraid," he answered.

6 – The Book of the Great Dragon of the Deep

I thought of comforting him, but the wisdom of the fountain advised against it. This was the adventure of his life, the one that would make him a 'real man'! It was better if it remained strictly between Vulcan and him.

I sat in what I believed to be a corner of the room, waiting. The astral atmosphere remained mild and very tolerable, nothing more than an Underworld's breeze. It did not get worse as time passed. Anyhow, we were not even out of our body! "All glory to the teacher! Gervin, this is child's play," I though with gratitude for the training I had received. And I probed darkness visible once more, in search of a soft stone to voice-channel Elyani.

But as my perception was sweeping through the intermediary layers, I was hit by a heavy wave of venomous energy. It took me completely by surprise, and before I had time to think of what to do, a second and stronger wave came rushing through me, not unlike some kind of foul black pus. Instantly, I gathered myself back into my physical body.

As I went from the diffuse light of astral worlds to the total darkness of the room, everything appeared to be back to normal. But I immediately guessed that I had been sensing the astral pre-wave of a force about to hit us physically.

I sent a warning to Phileon, "*My friend in the Law*, I think the time has come to do as your father instructed you, and invoke all the help you can get from the Lord Vulcan."

"I already am, *my friend in the Law!*" he answered in a shaky voice.

A few verses I had heard long ago came back to my mind,

Those waves of infinite darkness,
Those foul fumes which erupt from Dragon's breath,
Throw men and gods alike into oblivious sleep.

"It's coming!" I thought. "I know. This time whatever happens I want to retain my connection to the clear fountain *that knows the heart of the Law.*" With every single spark of energy I could call upon, I hammered into myself, "I do, not, want, to sleep!"

The room was still silent and peaceful. What would it feel like to be hit by the foul wave? Would I cope with it, or faint and miss my chance?

I tucked my head up towards the clear fountain. It brought back the strange effect that had taken place in my belly the day before. I tried the same invocation:

"*Vulcan! Vulcan! Lord of the anvil!*
Vulcan! Vulcan! Lord of the anvil!"

Vroof! Again, my belly was shaking. The god was speaking to me, but this time much more strongly. "Not a bad feeling!" I thought, and I continued, this time putting more of myself in the invocation.

"*Vulcan! Vulcan! Lord of the anvil!*
Vulcan! Vulcan! Lord of the anvil!"

The reply came in the form of a mighty vroof – so strong that it took me by surprise. For a second I wondered if it was the foul wave hitting me. Not at all! I felt fine, grounded like a rock.

"Not a bad feeling!" I thought. And as I kept on with this strange practice, the effect built up. It became exhilarating, as if my body had become larger and much stronger.

When the first of the foul waves finally hit the room, I was just in the middle of a big vroof. As the wave rushed violently through my body, I recognised the same force and flavour I had identified earlier while scanning darkness visible. It was it! But something weird and completely unexpected took place. I wasn't thrown to the floor. No black pus was poured into me. My energy wasn't devastated. Instead of hurting me, the wave sparked an incredibly massive vroof inside me, which left me intoxicated with power.

Phileon, unfortunately, did not seem to enjoy the wave as much as I did. He screamed in agony and collapsed on the floor with a thud. Unconscious. Serene and blissful like a sleeping toddler. And as I was looking at him affectionately, it suddenly dawned on me, "But I can see! *I can see through the darkness of the night!*"

"*Vulcan! Vulcan! Lord of the anvil!*" I praised the god.

A second wave hit me, slightly less intense than the first one. I received it joyfully. Together with the grounded vastness, I felt tingling in every cell of my body. My belly sent a call, wishing that a new and even bigger wave would hit me, bringing more ecstasy,

"*Vulcan! Vulcan! Lord of the anvil!*"

I had to wait for a hundred years, but when the wave finally arrived I heard myself shout a loud "Ooohh!" with delight.

Then my body spontaneously began to move. I found myself waving my arms around in a slow, strange dance. Wave after wave pounded me, feeding the vroofing ecstasy, and words started flowing through my mouth,

"*Vulcan is in me! Vulcan is me!*
I am dancing with the Dragon!
Vulcan is in me! Vulcan is me!
I am dancing with the Dragon!"

Through a superior knowingness, each and every movement of the dance seemed to be precisely determined. I felt sure and confident that every step was right, even though I had never seen anything like it. Drunk with presence and with power, I lost all sense of time. I danced and danced like an inspired madman of the gods, shouting strange words I had never heard before.

How long did this go on? That I will never know. My next glimpse of normal consciousness took place when I was shocked out of my trance by a loud yell, "Szar, stop! That's enough! Don't do too much! Stop!"

Phileon was no longer in the room. In front of me stood a tall man with a pair of torches instead of eyes. I remained still a few seconds, gazing at

6 – The Book of the Great Dragon of the Deep

him. But I was so intoxicated that my body started the slow dance again, and I laughed. There was so much of the god's power in that laugh! The man was compelled to laugh with me, and his eyes flared.

We danced together and chanted,

"Vulcan is in me! Vulcan is me!
I am dancing with the Dragon!"

Then he said, "Now that's enough, my boy," and he knocked me unconscious in no time by delivering two precisely measured blows on gateways of my neck.

6.4 Dragon hangover

When I recovered my senses, I was back in the small room. Good Phileon was calling me, "Szar! Are you waking up at last?"

His voice was reaching me as if from far away. I felt exactly as if I had just been run over by Zarbelros and Zonoteros, the twin sixteen-legged giant bulls of the revengeful gods. Every single muscle in my body was aching. But that was nothing compared to the headache. With a great effort I managed slight movements of my lips and fingers, until I was finally able to say in my just-back-from-the-Underworld voice,

"Oooh! I need a drink."

Kindly, Phileon went to the jug and brought me a cup of water.

Looking at him and seeing only a vague haze, I mumbled, "No, that's not exactly what I meant, but thank you anyway." I drank a sip, which made me realise how much my mouth was on fire. The water was so divinely refreshing that I finished the whole cup in one go and gulped down another as soon as Phileon refilled it.

"Did they torture you a lot, Szar?"

"Eh?" I said, moving my arms and legs a little bit, trying to decide if I was already launched on the Great Journey or if I had some more time to go in the kingdom. "Torture?" I said, "Nah! Nothing like that. Did they torture you?"

"They burned me!" Phileon said, proudly exhibiting a mark on his forearm, "and I did not feel any pain, thanks to Lord Vulcan. I was praying very hard. Now I am a Son of the Dragon. Did they take you to the room with all the torches?"

"No." I said, "I don't think I remember that. But wait a minute... How long did I sleep?"

"You slept for two days and one night, Szar."

"What?" I sat up abruptly, making my headache throb excruciatingly. Vigorously pulling my soul back into the body, I asked, "Do you mean I have been sleeping all this time, while you were being initiated?"

Phileon gave me his most amicable smile, "*It very much looks like it, my friend in the Law.*"

I fell back on my mat, which did not improve the headache one bit. I stared at the ceiling, then closed my eyes again, "Oh, no! No! *No!*"

"I can't believe this!" I thought, "I can't believe I've done it again! Gervin sends me here to be initiated and what do I do while the ceremonies are taking place? I sleep! Underworld, Underworld Further Down and Underworld's Bottom! Gervin, I'll never dare to present myself to you ever again. I failed. I failed again!" Totally overwhelmed, I had an image of Elyani agonising in front of me while I held my head in my hands, crying like a pathetic little boy.

"Where is the clear fountain?" I thought. It had not disappeared, but I felt like I was looking at it from the bottom of a deep well. I tried to tune into it, but before I knew it I was asleep.

I next woke up when brother Floster came to bring us some dinner. When he saw me sitting up on the mat, he exclaimed with his deep, Son-of-the-Dragon voice, "Ah! *Praise the She-Dragon, Mother of the Endless Night!* Our great dancer of the Dragon dance is back! How are you, my boy?"

"I am alive," I heard myself reply. "Sort of."

He came closer. "That's very good, my boy," and he laughed, "Ha! Ha! Ha! Ha! Ha! See what happens when one wants to do too much in a day!"

Floster's attitude was quite different from when I had last seen him, two days ago. He was now smiling and friendly (in his dragon's way). He looked satisfied, "Sons, you have both done very well. Have your dinner and *get some lawful rest*. There's more to come tomorrow."

Total surprise. Done well?

Feverishly, I asked "Do you mean I have not failed the trials yet?"

The mountain-looking priest took a surprisingly gentle voice, "Not at all, my boy! Var, the high priest of Vulcan, was extremely pleased with you. He said he enjoyed the Dragon's dance with you very much."

I felt like a man summoned back to life by the power of a great hierophant.

Floster laughed loudly and went on, "Don't feel offended if he knocked you down flat like a bag of turnips. He had to do it for your own good. You see, Dragon's dance is powerful medicine. If you take too much of it the first time, you find yourself dead asleep for an entire Moon cycle. Ha! Ha! Ha! Ha! Ha! And then when you wake up..." Floster held his head with his hands and mimicked an agonised groan, "Oooh!"

"I know exactly what you mean," I said.

"Ha! Ha! Ha! Ha! Ha!" When this man laughed, the walls trembled.

He pointed to a cup on my dinner tray. "You drink that red stuff after you finish your dinner, and you'll be much better tomorrow morning. But be careful my boy, don't drink it before you have food in your stomach, or it will make big holes in your guts. Ha! Ha! Ha! Ha! Ha!"

6 – The Book of the Great Dragon of the Deep

"How funny," I thought.

"Anyway," he concluded, "you will see Var again tomorrow. For now, both of you eat your dinner and *get some lawful rest*." He raised his left forearm and clenched his left fist in front of me with an I-know-that-you-know kind of look, then did the same to Phileon, and left.

"I can't believe all this!" I thought, ravenously attacking the dinner on the tray that had been left close to my bed. Ten minutes ago I was feeling destitute and so ashamed of the embarrassment I had caused my lineage that I preferred to be a derelict of the Law rather than return to Eisraim and face Gervin. And now, I was a 'great dancer of the Dragon dance', waiting for my initiation into the mysteries of Vulcan. Lucky I had waited till dinner before killing myself!

"Phileon, I have never been so hungry in my entire life!" I said, and it was true.

Phileon was genuinely pleased to see me cheered up, "My father, he is a really powerful initiate of Vulcan. He told me that *when the fire in the belly is awakened through the initiation*, you feel like eating lots of food. I am very hungry too, you know... brother!" The emphasis on this word showed that Phileon had been waiting a long time to call someone 'brother', as only fellow initiates do.

"Well then, good appetite... brother!" I answered, devouring the strange food that was on my copiously loaded tray. Most of it looked like heavy charcoaled pieces of something difficult to identify. It was not exactly the light food that was served to the priests of Eisraim, to say the least, and even less like the subtle dishes full of precious herbs that Elyani had been cooking for me in the last months. But still, what a feast! I could hardly remember enjoying eating so much.

When I was finally satisfied, I lay down on my mat again, then remembered the drink Floster had brought for me. I took the cup and cautiously smelled the red liquid. Nothing extraordinary. I drank a little, and as the bizarrely-flavoured beverage appeared tolerable, I asked Phileon, "Want a sip, brother?"

Phileon, remembering what Floster had said, replied in a lawfully polite manner, "*Many thanks, my friend in the Law, but the Lord Melchisedek has already quenched my thirst.*"

I smiled and, thoroughly exhilarated, finished the cup in one draught. I tucked my head in my shoulders, waiting to see what was going to happen to me.

Nothing. And just as well.

I was exhausted, but I decided to take some time to prepare myself for the next day. Resisting the pull of sleep, I went inside and thought, "Now this time... I can't afford to faint or fall into a trance again. This time, whatever happens, I must find a way to remain on my feet. How would an awakened one do that? As I concentrated hard, the space in front of me became dark and, to my surprise and delight, the face of Gervin appeared in darkness visible.

Master Gervin!

The softness on his face warmed up my heart. I could see him. I could feel his presence. Since it was my question that had brought him to me, I asked again, "Master Gervin, what would an awakened one do now?"

"*Right now?*" he asked.

Whenever I had heard him say these words, he had really meant business. With a Son-of-the-Dragon voice, I answered, "*Right now!*"

Gervin looked at me intensely for a few seconds, then with his Underworld of a sense of humour, he said, "Sleep!"

Mountain-Floster's laughter resounded in my head, "Ha! Ha! Ha! Ha! Ha!"

It was just after sunset. The room was turning dark. I soon fell asleep.

6.5 Relax, and miss your destiny

At dawn when Floster returned and stood in the doorway, torch in hand, he looked delighted to see me on my feet. After a loud, "*Praise the Great Dragon, brethren,*" he turned towards me, "Brother, I see the drink has worked wonders on you. How is your head doing my boy?"

"*Praise the She-Dragon, Mother of the Endless Night!*" I answered. "Your drink did indeed work wonders, brother Floster. My head feels *as fresh as the first spring blossom on the alohim tree.*"

Floster raised his left forearm and clenched his fist. "Ha! Ha! Ha! Ha! Ha!" Then his raucous laughter gave way to a grave expression, indicating that a ritual procedure was being engaged. He stared at Phileon for some time, then said in a near-threatening tone, "*Follow me, brother. There is no turning back.*" He proceeded to stare at me in the same manner and issued the same warning, "*Follow me, candidate. There is no turning back.*"

Again we formed a small procession. The other priest, who had been waiting outside holding a torch, walked behind us. As we were descending into the rock, I asked myself, "*Sweet Lord Melchisedek*, what are they going to do to me today?" I recalled the White Eagle's words when asked about my chances of surviving the temple of the Dragon: "*So much for yes as for no – like the purple blossoms of the alohim tree after the first storm in spring.* Fifty-fifty!" Yet I thought, "Strange! Somehow I can't really feel threatened by the energy of this place." The deeper we descended into the mountain, the more vibrant the rock was – the same energy as I felt in my belly when I invoked Lord Vulcan. My belly *loved* that feeling. Had I not been on guard, I would have let out a loud "Ha! Ha! Ha! Ha! Ha!" just like Brother Floster.

6 – The Book of the Great Dragon of the Deep

My body was vibrant with a new life. Some kind of continual sub-vroofing was ready to spark any minute, especially if the Dragon sent one of its blissful waves. "I could like this place, after all," I thought. "But then of course," my mind went back to the charge, "if they ask you to run, you spastic brown chicken, don't even think about fifty-fifty."

I called onto the clear fountain and hammered into every cell of my body, "I do, not, want, to sleep!" The rhythm of my steps brought back the precious symbol, *"One Law, one way. He who never sleeps never dies!"* But as we kept going down through the rock, the vroofing effect reappeared: belly waves and twitches, some of them rising all the way up my spine like a soft warming breath. This time the Vulcan vroofing happened by itself, I did not even have to utter the invocation. But I contained myself, holding onto the clarity of the fountain. "If I get drunk again, the Dragon knows what might happen!"

The deeper we descended, the stronger the belly waves, which were spreading into my thighs and chest. "Vul-can! Vul-can!" the name resounded inside me. I could hear the entire mountain in which the temple had been carved repeating the name, "Vul-can! Vul-can!"

This time the journey was not tiring. It seemed much shorter, and even quite enjoyable. "Underground bowels and Vulcan vroofing go together well," I thought. After all, the stone walls without plass also had some good sides. There was something raw about them. Totally uncivilised, but vroofingly interesting.

We arrived in a high cavern, at then end of which was a huge portal guarded by five mountain-priests. These ones were not only carrying torches, but also maces.

Floster went up to one of the guards and ritually whispered a few words in his ear. Then a small door on the side was half opened for him, and he disappeared through the doorway.

I watched my shadow on the wall. Unlawfully bizarre! Inside a normal building you never saw shadows on the walls, only plass glows. Here, wherever you went the Underworld followed you.

A minute later, I heard two loud knocks resounding from the other side of the large portal doors.

One of the guards looked me in the eyes and asked, *"What is your name?"*

The priest who had been walking behind us during the descent answered for me, *"O guardian of this holy threshold, his name is Szar."*

"What have you come to seek?"

Again, the priest spoke the ritual words for me, *"He has come to seek the light of our god, for his dearest wish is to become a Son of the Dragon."*

"Enter, and know that there is no turning back!"

"I do not want to be a sleeper!" I shouted to myself. "Gervin, inspire me! Let me not go through this ceremony like a sleeper. *One Law, one way! He who never sleeps, never dies!"*

Atlantean Secrets

The portal was slowly opened, revealing a huge cavern decorated as a temple hall. As I was taken inside, I was dazzled by the light. Perhaps as many as fifty priests of Vulcan lined the sides of the cavern, each bearing a torch in his right hand. The walls were studded with dozens of torches, and at the back of the cavern I saw a raised altar surrounded by four large furnaces. At first I felt slightly disconcerted by the smoky atmosphere and the Deep-Underworld-sounding chant that the priests intoned as I was being escorted through the temple. But there was a now-familiar Vulcan-vroofing feel to all of this. Highly exhilarating, and quite comfortable.

I beamed when I recognised the man with torches instead of eyes, the one who had Dragon-danced with me two days earlier (before knocking me down flat like a bag of turnips). Var, the high priest of Vulcan! It was like meeting an old friend.

Standing behind the altar, he welcomed me with a brotherly smile. "Enter, Szar!" he called out in a deep, ritual voice. "I am glad to meet you again. You have given satisfaction to the Lord Vulcan our god with your dancing. Now has come the time for your initiation as a Son of the Dragon. Phileon will be allowed to stay and watch, as he became a Son of the Dragon yesterday."

As I was led towards the altar, I thought, "Var does not look very old! Hardly thirty-five, younger than Floster." I was taken to stand opposite him, with the four glowing furnaces around us.

The priests continued their chanting until Var began the initiation ritual,

"First, Szar, I will instruct you on the nature of the Dragon.
Through Fire, the Sons of Vulcan worship the Dragon.
The Dragon is Fire,
And wherever there is fire, there lies the Dragon!
The Fire is above, and the Fire is below.
All things are Fire, and the Dragon is every thing.
The Fire above is Cosmic Fire, and the Fire below is Cosmic Waters.
The Cosmic Fire has risen from the Cosmic Waters,
And the Cosmic Waters are but concealed Cosmic Fire.
The Dragon is above, and the Dragon is below.
The Dragon below is the She-Dragon, Mother of the Endless Night.
Limitless is her power, she who puts men and gods alike to sleep.
She holds the treasure, the one stone of those who live forever.
He who can descend into her bosom and withstand her infinite darkness,
Is he who will rise.
In the Fire he will rise, and never again know death.
The great She-Dragon is waiting.
Dragon below awaits Dragon above,
For the accomplishment of the one thing."

The chanting went on. Then Var instructed me about Vulcan-vroofing. "The waves that you have felt when calling on our Lord Vulcan are the

6 – The Book of the Great Dragon of the Deep

jerks of the Dragon. Now I reveal to you that a reference to these tremors is concealed in a well-known verse of the Law:
When the Great Dragon moves,
And a breath is exhaled upwards through the gate of the waters,
Tremble, man of the Law!
As a Son of the Dragon, you will tremble indeed, but with ecstasy, not with fear, as the ignorant do."

Hearing these words, I couldn't help feeling the excitement of vroofing tremors in my belly, together with the blissful tingling throughout my body. The gathering of priests intoned another mesmerising hymn of their Law. Var's eyes shone even brighter. Using the Voice, he projected onto me, *"Know that you are a Son of the Dragon!"*

At times, Gervin had projected words at me from a space of Voice, but never anything like this. Var's Voice was magical, bewitching, stupefying... incredible! It had depth, and life, and it moved every single cell of my body. I did not just hear it, I also *saw* it as flames of light coming out of his mouth. It triggered a seismic vroofing wave that started from below my feet and went up, slowly sweeping through me, finally flourishing above my head. I was so stunned that my legs started wobbling, and I had to hold on fast to the clear fountain to keep myself up, *"One Law, one way. He who never sleeps, never dies!"*

Pointing to a cauldron full of hot charcoals that sat on the altar, Var directed, "You will repeat the secret oath of the Sons of the Dragon after me, at the same time sealing it by applying the inside of your left forearm onto this red-hot vessel."

Two men walked towards me, and as I began to repeat the oath after Var, I understood they were going to hold my arm against the burning cauldron.

I felt a pressing urge to step back. But I clung to the fountain, asking, "What would an awakened one do, now?" And lo! I knew what to do. *Dragon below, Dragon above!* I looked into the eyes of Var the high priest and before the two men had reached me, I had moved my left arm and applied it to the cauldron, in the same place I had seen Phileon proudly exhibit his marks.

There was a hissing sound as my flesh was burnt, and for a fraction of a second I feared I was going to lose consciousness, again. But touching the cauldron created a paradoxical reaction, a massive vroofing explosion in my belly, which saved me! Suddenly, just like during the Dragon dance, I felt huge, and fantastically grounded. I could feel the pain in my arm, but it was completely insignificant compared with how vast and exhilarated I felt.

Projecting the Voice, Var repeated, *"Know that you are a Son of the Dragon!"* And as the two priests pulled my arm away from the cauldron, the whole audience chanted, *"Vulcan! Vulcan! Lord of the anvil!"* And the vroofing went on.

When it finished, there was a pause in the ritual. Throughout the hall I heard the men whispering to each other and changing places. Var took advantage of this to kindly tell me, "That's it, my boy. Now you can fully relax and let things unfold gently in front of you. No more trials."

Had I done as he suggested and stopped holding fast onto the clear fountain, I would have missed my destiny!

Var continued with the ritual. *"Let me now instruct you in the secret signs of recognition of our order. When a Son of the Dragon wants to test you and probe your origins, he will say, 'There is no turning back.' If you wish to disclose your identity as a Son of the Dragon to him, you will hold your fist in front of him, showing the part of your forearm where your secret oath of a Son of the Dragon was sealed with fire. And you will repeat, 'There is no turning back.'"*

The high priest and I exchanged the signs, after which he continued in a routine ritual voice, *"Praise the Great Dragon! Now, Szar, Son of the Dragon, here is the time where your destiny must be sealed. Solemnly, I ask you, will you tread the path of the Great Warrior?"*

I could hardly believe my ears. "The path of the Great Warrior!" I thought with amazement. "Is that what the White Eagle meant?"

The high priest of Vulcan continued, "As your father could not instruct you on these matters, let me tell you what the ritual way of declining this invitation is. You will just say,

All glory to the She-Dragon, Mother of the Endless Night!

Many thanks in the Law, your highness, but I must decline your invitation. I will not tread the path of the Great Warrior.

I will return to the ways of my fathers.

Having contemplated, thanks to you, the greatness of the Dragon,

I will now apply myself to serving the Dragon above and the Dragon below.

Of this, I now give my Dragon's word,

That I may be worthy of joining the Sons of the Dragon during the Great Journey, after departing from this mortal abode."

While he was speaking, I remembered the words of the White Eagle: "If Szar is given a chance to become a Great Warrior, let him not turn back. There will be no second chance." Tuning in as high as I could, I prayed, "Gervin, let me not miss this moment as I have missed so many others before!" But what the Underworld was a Great Warrior? What would an awakened one have done here? What was I supposed to say?

As I hesitated, Var gave me a kind smile and whispered, "Just repeat the words I said, my boy."

From the purest and highest streak of the fountain I could receive, and with more boldness than ever before in my life, I looked at him and said,

"Many thanks, your highness, I will accept your invitation to tread the path of the Great Warrior. *Of this I now give my Dragon's word.*"

There was a Dragon-charged silence. Var spoke, his voice gentle, "Son of the Dragon, you do not have to tread this path, as it is full of dangers and burdens. If you simply wish to return to your peers, there will be an honourable place for you in the hierarchy of the Sons of the Dragon."

I prayed, "Clear fountain, inspire me! Let me say the right words, so they do not reject me from the path of the Great Warrior. When Elyani needs me, I want to be there for her."

And the words came to me,

"*I will not return to the ways of my fathers.*
I will stay and contemplate the greatness of the Dragon.
My Dragon's word I have given.
And the She-Dragon knows there is no turning back!"

I could see in Var's eyes that, lawful or not, my message was coming across.

There followed a longer, even more charged silence.

Finally, Var broke it with a momentous, "Vulcan! Vulcan! Vulcan!" Compelled by the power of his Voice, the entire room followed him, "Vulcan! Vulcan! Vulcan!" A superior elation spread throughout the temple. These men's bellies started all vroofing together, and the god was with them.

The waves inside me quickly became so violent that my body felt like rocking again. Carried away by the exhilaration of the moment, I slowly started moving my hands, ready for another dance. But when he saw what was happening to me, Var immediately whispered, "No, Szar! Don't start again! Not now!"

Suddenly remembering how I had felt when waking up after that first dance, I promptly shook myself out of the intoxicated state, holding on to my symbol, "*One Law, one way! He who never sleeps never dies!*"

The ceremony continued with a lengthy chanting of the Law of the Dragon, and finished with a few minutes of silence. Straight afterwards, all the priests came and personally congratulated me, welcoming me as their brother. Many of these mountains of muscles hugged me fraternally, making all my vertebrae crack as if my neck was being broken – certainly not the least of my trials!

The joyful company then began to find its way back to the surface through the bowels of the mountain, talking and laughing loudly. As I walked, I could not help asking myself, "*Dear Lord Melchisedek*, what am I in for next? What are they going to do to me?" But I was proud to walk back from the ceremony instead of being carried unconscious. "Gervin! I am not sleeping!" I trumpeted. "Even though, of course, there are so many ways of being asleep while being awake."

Phileon and I went to rest. While we were in our room, the young potter asked me, "My father, he had told me the ritual words to decline the invitation, so I repeated them. Who told you the words to accept it?"

"No one, Phileon. I just thought it would be the right thing to say, and so I said it."

Phileon did not follow. He became mute. What I was saying simply did not fit with his world. He could not take it in. This marked the end of our conversations. There was nothing like envy, bitterness or disapproval on Phileon's side. The young man had simply switched off. He had wiped me out of his universe, just like Artold after I clapped my hands in his face. Phileon just sat facing the wall, his eyes open, his mind blank – the great Atlantean pastime. It worked even without plass.

Following an afternoon of recuperation (all these adventures were exhausting!) we were to attend the ritual banquet which was customary for candidates just initiated as Sons of the Dragon. Floster, with his perky earthquake laughter, came to take us to an important part of the temple we had not seen yet: the dining hall. It too was dug in the rock, but with wide windows that let the daylight in. The fifty or sixty brothers who had attended the morning initiation took their seats along large tables. More charcoal delicacies were served to us, and there was lots of laughing. Then the men chanted hymns together, and Phileon and I were invited to join in. There was some serious vroofing going on, and some of the men even started dancing. But Floster came over to me, "No, no! Not you, brother Szar! You must keep your energy for what is coming next! Remember how your head felt last time."

So I sat back and watched the mountains of muscles dancing, wondering what the dance looked like when performed by a skinny brown chicken like me.

When the banquet ended, Floster accompanied Phileon and me to our room. There he announced, "Szar, take your bag. It is time to say farewell to your friend Phileon. From now on, you will be sleeping in another room. Phileon will *return to the ways of his fathers* tomorrow morning."

I turned to Phileon, adopting the lawful face, "*Farewell, my friend. The Law has brought us together, now it takes us apart. All glory to the Lord Melchisedek!*" And Phileon parroted back. Then I followed Floster to another cell, pretty much like the one I had just left.

"Floster," I asked, "can you tell me what a Great Warrior is?"

"Ha! Ha! Ha! Ha! Ha! You mean you don't even know what a Great Warrior is? Ha! Ha! Ha! Ha! Ha!"

I was starting to like Floster. He was no common sleeper.

"*My friend in the Dragon,*" Floster's huge chest expanded even further, "the only thing I can tell you is that last time I saw a candidate become a Great Warrior, he was just about as crazy as you are! Ha! Ha! Ha! Ha! Ha! For the rest, Marek the Indestructible will come and speak to you tomorrow morning." Then he gave me another of those brotherly hugs that made all my vertebrae crack and he bade me good night, lifting his left fist upwards in the ritual fashion.

I found Floster's words only moderately encouraging. What an Underworld of a day this had been! I could have done with a white drink. What was to come next? I decided the best thing I could do at this stage was to follow Gervin's last instruction – sleep!

6.6 The man with a dangerous smile

He was tall, about the same height as I was, but broad-shouldered and chiselled like a tiger. He was perhaps in his mid-thirties. The first thing that struck me about him was his eyes. Piercing dark eyes, ablaze with awakening. The vroofing energy of the Sons of the Dragon was with him, but he also looked exceptionally sharp. He wasn't wearing leather shorts like the others, but a shirt and pants made of thin black cloth, and a black cap. He had entered without knocking at the door or saluting me in the lawful manner. He just sat in front of me and stared at me.

"My name is Marek, son," he announced after a while. "I was told that you want to become a Great Warrior."

As I remained silent, he asked me, "Do you know what a Great Warrior is?"

Not knowing what to answer, I just shook my head.

His forearm flexed to the horizontal position, Marek looked down to his left fist, which he slowly opened, then clenched. He asked in a purely matter-of-fact tone, "Who instructed you to accept the high priest's invitation?"

He did not look like someone who wanted to hear lawfully nice verses, just the truth. So I told him, "When he sent me here, my teacher, Master Gervin of the Brown Robe, instructed me to become dangerous. The path of the Great Warrior sounded like the right choice to fulfil his command. And," I pursued, "an oracle once informed me that I should take up this offer if it were ever made to me, as there would be no second chance."

"True, son! True! Yesterday was your one and only chance to become a Great Warrior. But tell me, inside yourself, what is it that you want?"

What else could I do but hold onto the clear fountain. "I want to stop being a sleeper, that I may become worthy of the lore of my teacher, Master Gervin."

"There are many dangers associated with becoming a Warrior," Marek went on in his matter-of-fact tone. "Do you know that you might be dead as early as tomorrow?"

The man was not joking, that I could tell. A chill ran through my body, the echo through my mind, "...as early as tomorrow." The voice of the beautiful White Eagle resounded in my head, "Fifty-fifty!"

"Marek," I said, "it is a long road that has taken me here. I have made many mistakes, and wasted many opportunities. Once, I even let someone die, stupidly, simply because I was not up to my task. I know that I may die in this trial but if there is a chance I can become a Great Warrior I am going to take this chance and not turn back. Better be dead than a sleeper, and have to look on helplessly while your friends die in front of you."

Marek remained silent, looking down to his left fist.

After some hesitation, I asked him, "Will you tell me what a Great Warrior is?"

Marek gazed at me, "I am a Great Warrior. A Great Warrior is an advanced initiate of our temple, someone who has seen the Dragon face to face and who has heard *her Word, which is the thunder of the Earth. A Great Warrior knows the power of the Voice.*"

"Are all the priests of this temple Great Warriors?"

"Oh no!" Marek answered. "To become a Great Warrior you must ride the Dragon and survive. Few can do that."

Ride the Dragon! So the White Eagle's word was being fulfilled.

There was a silence, which I broke by asking, "What do I have to do to ride the Dragon?"

Again, Marek looked down to his left fist, which he kept clenching and unclenching, creating impressive ripples in the muscles of his forearm. Then he intoned a slow recitation of the Law,

"*Only those whom the Dragon herself has chosen*
Can become Great Warriors.
Into the bowels of the Earth you will be taken,
And offered to the Dragon.
If the Dragon accepts you, a Great Warrior you will become.
If she rejects you, you will die.
There is no preparation and no man can give help.
You must now stride forward, or renounce.
There is only one trial, one attempt.
You pass the trial or you die."

Marek's face lit up with a dangerous smile, "Many of those who say they want to become Great Warriors are nothing more than madmen. The Dragon knows how to sort them out! Son," he added, "if you wish to leave the temple now, no one will know. There will be no blame. You will still be a noble Son of the Dragon, and you will be free to serve the Dragon in your own way. There may be a nice life waiting for you outside. Why waste it?"

"Marek," I told him, "I am not beyond fear. But I will not give up." I was starting to understand that when I felt weak, I could now turn to my belly and rest on the Vulcan effect. So I vroofed myself a wave, looked him in the eyes, and slowly articulated the words that came to me straight from the fountain, "Marek, there is no turning back! If the Dragon wants to get rid of me, he will have to kill me. I will not walk away. Dragon's word!"

Marek's dangerous smile reappeared for a second. "Say 'she', son. When Great Warriors talk about the Earth Dragon, they say she, not he." Still looking down to his fist, he added, "Gervin was right, you are no ordinary dreamer."

After a pause, he winked at me, "So be it! I see you are not going to run away like a rabbit." His voice became grave. "So it's like this: tomorrow before dawn, you will be taken far down into the bowels of the Earth, to a place where the She-Dragon will have no difficulty finding you. When she comes to you, you will hear her Voice, which is the thunder of the Earth. And all you have to do is one thing," he clicked the fingers of his right hand and aimed his index finger at me, looking straight into my eyes, "survive!"

I swallowed. "How will I recognise the Voice of the Dragon?"

Marek showed his dangerous smile to me again, "Don't worry son, you can't miss it!"

Remembering all the opportunities I had missed with Gervin because of being too dumb and forgetting to ask questions, I persisted, "Can you give me any hints on how to survive once I hear her Voice?"

"Remember your initiation about *the tremors which are the jerks of the Dragon*? There'll be lots of these tomorrow. But really, no man can help you down there. Whether you live or die is entirely up to her."

Marek would say no more. He invited me to move freely around the temple during the day, and go and visit the dining hall for my meals. He also informed me that Var the high priest wanted to see me. A brother would come to take me to him. Then he gave me the ritual salute and with a menacingly feline walk, made his way to the door.

"*By the way, man of the Law,*" he halted in the doorway, "if you make it tomorrow, I will be in charge of teaching you a few things that Great Warriors are supposed to know." And he left.

6.7 The legend of Lohrzen

One of Var's attendants came to fetch me while I was having lunch in the dining hall. He took me for a short stroll up the stairways until we reached a terrace on the cliff. Climbing a few more stairways carved out of the edge of the cliff, we finally reached a room where the high priest of Vulcan welcomed me, "*Praise the She-Dragon, Mother of the Endless Night, Szar.*"

"*All glory to the She-Dragon, Mother of the Endless Night, your highness.*" Like Marek, this man had fire in his eyes. Like a field of stars, but one below the earth.

"Have you fully recovered from your Dragon dance, *my friend in the Dragon?*"

"Nearly, your highness."

Var gave a friendly grin.

"The man has class," I thought, admiring the way he combined kindness with the dignity of his function.

"Look at the altar on your right, Szar. On the shelf, there is a small plate made of orichalc, attached to a necklace. Go and look at it."

I went to the altar and contemplated the finely-wrought silvery chain and the metallic plate on which strange signs were engraved.

"Take it, Szar," Var said. "Take it in your hand."

I did as he said, and he explained, "This relic was worn by a Son of the Dragon named Lohrzen. He was a Great Warrior, one of the most powerful of all times. He lived long ago, in the early days of the kingdom when the mists were so thick that day and night were not clearly separated. Those were the days that followed the revelation of the Watchers. Have you ever heard of the Watchers, Szar?"

"I have heard old legends mentioning their name, your highness, but my master has never instructed me on this topic."

"No doubt Master Gervin will teach you about them, as his lore is vast. The Watchers were powerful angels of fire who descended from the spheres and incarnated in human bodies. They came to educate men, who were then still young, resembling the blob-men of our distant shores. Have you heard of the blob-men?"

Remembering a particular discussion with Gervin, I said, "Those who sleep on the beach all day and make children without even noticing it. Yes, I have heard of them."

"A lot of the knowledge of the Great Warriors came from the Watchers. Powerful indeed were the Watchers, more powerful than the mind can conceive. They taught men several arts and sciences, in particular those relating to the use of fire. And they married with the daughters of men, and had children with them, and the children were called the Nephilim. The first of the Nephilim became champions and princes among men, having inherited the extraordinary powers of their fathers. But they were a doomed breed that soon degenerated into the most revolting scum, monsters and giants who eat human flesh, turn their daughters into whores and indulge in all forms of depravity."

'Nephilim scum' was an expression I had heard a number of times since my arrival at Mount Lohrzen. If they were a race of cannibals and prostitutes, no wonder the brethren sounded so disgusted each time they uttered their name.

Var continued, "Soon the Nephilim slime started fighting wars against each other, using men to fill their armies. These were the first wars in the kingdom. Many men and women died, and there were famines and plagues."

It was during those troubled times that Lohrzen was born in the county of the Red Lands, in a village only a few hours from this temple. He was an extraordinary child who could speak to the gods and thus heal people. Once, just after his eleventh birthday initiation, a plague devastated the county. A third of the men and women in his village fell, and the priests declared them dead. But Lohrzen told them, 'No, you are wrong! It is not the will of our Lord Melchisedek that these men and women should die!'

6 – The Book of the Great Dragon of the Deep

He called onto the powers of the Earth, and the men and women woke up, and they said they had returned from the Underworlds."

"Now," I thought, "that sounds exactly like what I want." But even with my newly discovered vroofing arrogance, I didn't dare interrupt Var with a question.

"The viciousness of the Nephilim knows no limits, so wars kept on raging. Villages were burnt. Crops were destroyed. Women were raped and their children killed in front of them. Seeing the despair of his fellow villagers, Lohrzen endeavoured to become strong, so he could defend them. Bold, this Lohrzen, he approached one of the Watchers named Verzazyel. Verzazyel was a formidable angel, a prince of fire who had descended from high spheres and lived in a cave in the red canyons, not far from this temple. Lohrzen went to Verzazyel's cave, where he disappeared. People thought he had been killed. Those who try to conquer the power of the Watchers often lose their life.

But to everyone's surprise, after seven years had passed Lohrzen reappeared. Having conquered some of the fire of Verzazyel, he had become a Great Warrior. He came straight to this temple and chose a number of brethren, to whom he taught new and secret ways of fighting. Together they set out to kill a great Nephilim prince called Percipion. They took his personal guards completely by surprise. The Great Warriors were but six, yet they killed the prince and more than a hundred men in one night."

That sounded dangerous.

"Then Lohrzen spoke to the remaining commanders of Percipion's army and convinced them to switch allegiance to him. And they followed him! Lohrzen trained more Great Warriors among the Sons of the Dragon, and together they killed Nephilim prince after Nephilim prince. They never fought battles, they just came in the night, dressed in black like the emissaries of death. They used their superior cunning to find their way to the princely apartments, and then..." Var drew his flat hand sharply across his throat with a short whistle, "striking like lightning, they killed everyone in sight."

"Sounds very dangerous!" I thought, still holding the orichalc plate in my hand.

"Each time, Lohrzen spoke to the army of the prince he had just killed. They admired him, and followed him. The Great Warriors soon became known as 'the nightmare of the Nephilim', as they always struck during the night and never failed to kill. It then happened that the commanders of two armies, fearing Lohrzen, whom they knew was coming, rebelled against their Nephilim masters and killed them. They surrendered to Lohrzen, who was now at the head of a huge army.

Had he wanted to, Lohrzen could have become the prince of this part of the kingdom. But he was very wise, and when he had rid all the neighbouring counties of the Nephilim scourge – not one of the Nephilim warlords was left! – he took the commanders of his army to the King of Atlantis and made them surrender to him. 'Here is my present to your supreme highness!' he announced. And ever since, the Great Warriors have been legendary for their unforgettable presents. The king appointed a wise man among Lohrzen's lieutenants as the new prince. And Lohrzen and his Great Warriors returned to the Temple of the Dragon, where they continued to enjoy the ecstasy of the She-Dragon of the Deep and trained more brethren in their secret arts.

Szar, the plate that you have in your hand was the one Lohrzen obtained from the Watcher. He wore it every single day of his life and placed it on the altar three days before he died."

Startled, I swallowed and called onto my fountain, hoping I was not going to make a blunder with the plate and offend such a dangerous being.

Var was amused at my reaction. He went on, "Lohrzen left an instruction, which he spoke with the Voice: that no one should ever touch this plate until the day a young warrior not sent by his father came along and surprised the priests by insolently demanding to see the Dragon face to face."

Var paused. "The plate is yours, Szar. Put it on!"

When this man spoke an order, he left no space for hesitation. Yet when my hands reached my neck, I felt compelled to pause and ask, "This relic is worth a lot, and not just because it's made of orichalc. What if I die tomorrow?"

Var laughed dryly. "Then the plate will remain buried with you in the bowels of the Dragon until the end of time. Lohrzen will not mind that. But *there is no turning back*. Lohrzen's words were spoken from the Voice and must be fulfilled. Put it on!"

I obeyed. The plate felt cool on my throat.

Var resumed, "Now, Szar, you must hear the end of Lohrzen's prophecy. One day, the Great Warrior who wears this relic will fight a great battle against the magic of the Watchers. When everything seems lost and his last companion is dying in his arms, the plate's power will save him."

Immediately I asked, "Does this mean I will survive tomorrow?"

Var responded with the same dangerous smile I had seen on Marek's face, and never before in the kingdom, "Only the Dragon knows that!" Watching me shiver, he added, "When you hear *the thunder of the Earth, which is the Voice of the Great Dragon of the Deep*, then you will know."

Var called a priest who escorted me back to the dining hall. But I was no longer hungry. After a short stroll through the corridors of the temple I went back to my room and *got some lawful rest*.

And the night came.

6.8 Eisraim, chapel of the White Eagle

"*W*ho, sent by the Lord Melchisedek, is knocking at the door?"
"It's me," Elyani replied unlawfully. "Can I speak to you, Teyani?"
"Come in, my love."
Lady Elyani entered, pushing the hood of her white cape back onto her shoulders. She looked tired. "Teyani, something is going to happen to Szar. Very soon, I know. I have come to ask for inspiration and for help, wise woman!"
In a glimpse, Teyani remembered the first time she had taken Elyani into her arms. Elyani was three days old. Her mother Adya, dear friend and White companion of Teyani, was dying. Teyani gave her Eagle's word that she would look after the child, and she had always done so, first as a mother, then as a teacher, a friend and a mother.
"Come, my child. Sit with me. Do you know what is waiting for him?"
"It is one of those impossible initiations where they put the candidate in a death-like trance and throw him to the Dragon. Then they come back three days later to see if the candidate is still alive. And if he is not, they just shrug their shoulders and wait for the next candidate."
"Szar is a powerful soul," Teyani's voice was soft.
"His body is weak! We think that our Underworld descents are bad, but what they do over there is much worse – completely insane! They expose the candidates to Dragon intensities that can make every bone in their body crumble into dust – the kind of Cosmic Fire that comes straight from the Furnaces of Doom. No wonder those who survive are called the Vulcans of the Law."
Teyani placed her magic hands on Elyani's shoulders, letting a subtle healing influence flow into her gateways. *"Peace, my child, peace!"* she called high into the White Eagle's fountain.
Tears were rolling down Elyani's face. "Forgive me, wise woman, for being so impatient. It's just that... I don't know what to do."
Teyani took her in her arms, "I know, these are difficult times," she whispered, thinking of all the White Eagle priestesses that had been sent down into the Underworld in the last years. Not one of them had returned. "Come, *my friend in the White Law*" Teyani said, "stay with me. Let us perform the ritual together."
When they had finished preparing the room, the two women took their positions behind the altar. Before intoning the first hymn, Teyani declared emphatically, *"The gods never owe the mortals, ever!* And I am but the servant maid of the White Eagle. Yet, because of certain things that happened before you were born, I was granted the immense favour to be heard by him when I knock at his heavenly gates. Tonight, I will speak to him and try to reach his heart. But do not expect anything.
Far beyond the minds of the mortals are the ways of the gods,

And even further beyond the reach of the gods are the ways of the Lord Melchisedek."

And Teyani began the ritual.

6.9 In the bowels of the Dragon

"Mother of the Light, what is happening to me?"

It was very early in the morning. I could hardly believe how clear I felt.

I had spent the whole incredible night dreaming of the White Eagle of the gods. The Eagle had been carrying me into the spheres, holding me in his wings, and telling me legends and secrets about the gods and their worlds. At each station we stopped to contemplate the magnificence of the fields of stars. And each time, we met Elyani. She smiled at me with cosmic kindness and handed me a white beverage. Each time I drank, I felt stronger. Then just before I woke up, the White Eagle made me an awesome gift: one of his feathers of light. Amazed, I took it in my hand, and my energy suddenly exploded with White Light – light such as mortal beings can rarely contemplate.

"I wish Floster had given me this room earlier," I reflected, sitting up on my bed.

The room was totally dark. There was no moonlight. "Today will be the New Moon!" I realised. "That's why they want to offer me to the Dragon so quickly." As Gervin had explained, the Underworlds are at their gloomiest just before the New Moon. Inundated with White light as I was, the realisation did not affect me in the least.

The door opened. Marek and three of his men made their entry. They were dressed in black, their heads covered with a cap made of the same thin cloth as their shirts and pants. All but Marek were carrying torches.

Looking at me with his cool Great Warrior's look, Marek whistled. "Dragon's womb! What a light! What have you been doing?"

"I dreamt of friends of mine."

Walking towards me in his slow, feline way, he said, "Sounds like you have powerful friends, Szar. I'd be interested to meet them."

I smiled. He did not.

"Look at these men," he pointed to his companions. "They are Great Warriors. Some of the best in the kingdom."

They stood in front of me, impassible, and still as the mountain. They were young, two of them in their twenties, the third in his mid-thirties. As I was tuning into them, asking myself whether they were awakened or asleep, Marek said, "Come on, son, we're going for a walk. Let's move."

We formed a small procession. Two of the Warriors led the way. I followed them, while Marek and his other friend walked behind me. They did not talk, but soon they intoned a slow litany,

6 – The Book of the Great Dragon of the Deep

"Farewell, man of the plains.
The time has come to leave everything behind you.
The Dragon is the gate."

Holding onto the clear fountain, I let my steps be guided by my favourite mantra, *"One Law, one way. He who never sleeps, never dies!"*

We walked down into the rock, through long serpentine tunnels and down endless rough stone staircases. For the first hour, I was comforted as usual by the Vulcan vroofing that each stone in the mountain conveyed. But as we kept descending, I was gripped by an increasingly heavy and oppressive feeling that made it difficult for me to breathe.

After we had been going down for at least three hours, Marek noticed it was becoming more and more difficult for me to walk. For the first time since the descent had begun, he spoke. "What you are feeling at the moment is the *venom of sopor, the heavy fumes that come from the Dragon.* This part of the mountain is charged with very special forces."

I held fast onto the clear fountain, praying to the Lord Melchisedek to keep me on my feet, for I remembered the verses of the Law only too well:

Those waves of infinite darkness,
Those foul fumes which erupt from Dragon's breath,
And throw men and gods alike into oblivious sleep.

Gradually, the thick inertia and the heaviness became so oppressive that I could hardly walk. I forced myself to go on, step after step, recalling Elyani's instructions before descending into the Underworlds, *"Keep walking! Never stop on the way!"* But finally, in the middle of a narrow tunnel, I had to stop, trying to catch my breath.

Marek came close to me, "We have entered the bowels of the Dragon, son."

"I can't breathe."

"That's because *you* are trying to breathe, and *you* are trying to walk. But here, there is not much left of you, there is just the Dragon!"

"What do I do?"

"Don't do. Let the Dragon do it for you."

I was panting, wondering how I could let the Dragon walk for me. Marek flexed his left forearm horizontally and, as he liked to do, contemplated his fist while slowly opening and clenching it. He started uttering a low-pitched sound that he gradually built up with Voice power, and that penetrated deep into my belly.

Taking me by surprise, he projected his fist straight into my solar plexus.

The punch left me gasping, reeling from the blow. I fell on my knees, holding my sides with my hands.

"Now, you let the Dragon breathe, or you die!" Marek yelled at me. He resumed his low-pitched Voice projection, then, *"Don't think, just do it!"* Gradually, a massive wave rose inside me, coming up from the rock below. My body was still gasping, but something else was taking over. I recognised the feeling of the Dragon dance and the blissful jerks. For at least a minute, I felt I still couldn't breathe. But I didn't need to. I was fine! I felt like laughing. I stood up, as if in a trance, and slowly, slowly, I waved my arms and rotated my body, guided by the knowingness of the dance.

Marek grinned. Gesturing at me with his thumb, he commented to the others ironically, "He's a good dancer, you know!"

"That's it!" I realised. "That's the way to do it! Find the Vulcan vroofing and gear the clear fountain directly into it." And it worked. Connecting the vertical energy above my head with the waves from below my body, I could breathe again.

Marek gave me sufficient time, then asked, "Can you walk now?"

Intoxicated, I answered, "I can't walk, but I can dance!" and I found myself looking at him with the same dangerous smile I had seen more than once on his face.

He winked at me and gently tapped my shoulder, "Good boy!" Then, addressing the small troop, "Come on, let's do it!" And we resumed our way down.

The rest of the journey was unreal. I walked and walked for hours, but I hardly felt time pass. It was all so simple! The fountain activated vroofing waves below my body and, for reasons that were completely beyond my mind, my shadow and I kept trotting behind them like a filosterops.

A few times we came across human skeletons. At first I had to swallow and hold on fast, *"Never stop on the way! Never look back!"* Then I shrugged my shoulders, letting the vroofing elation take over. "Vul-can! Vul-can!" I chanted. No longer bothering to think about the piles of bones of my predecessors, I just danced my way along.

At long last we made it to a small chamber. In the middle, there was a grave dug in the rock. Seeing it, I chuckled foolishly.

"Lie down in the hole!" Marek pointed to the grave.

The four men placed their torches in rings that were attached to the walls. Then they sat at the four corners of the grave and chanted two short hymns of their Law.

Marek leant forwards towards me. *"Praise the She-Dragon, Mother of the Endless Night,* you made it! Not bad, son! Many men have died before they reached here. Now your part is finished. There is not much more you can do, it's all up to her. So... enjoy! The Dragon will come to you and you will hear her true Voice, as few men in the kingdom have heard. You're a lucky man! Maybe that will kill you, but there are sillier ways of dying, believe me," he laughed, and because I was drunk with the force, I found it funny too.

"Now listen. Once the grave is covered with the slab, no man can help you. But until then, *we* can. We must make you presentable for the Dragon, you see. Enjoy what is coming, son. If you survive you'll remember it."

I gave him a blissful smile as he took his position back at one corner of the grave. The four men remained silent for a minute, and then together they started projecting the Voice at me.

6 – The Book of the Great Dragon of the Deep

Marek was right. It was unforgettable! A few times in my life, I had heard the Voice, but Voice like this, never! As soon as the loaded sound waves sent by the four men hit my body, the dreamy intoxication of the journey was dispelled and my mind cleared. With total self-awareness, I felt the low-pitched vibrations rushing into my system, saturating my energy with Dragon power. As they kept on, I began to feel like a dragon myself. I roared loudly. So much force was building up in my body that at first I thought I was going to explode. But Master Gervin's teachings on death came back to me, and with this extraordinary simplicity that I had already experienced once, I just... let go! I let myself die in the living power of their Voices.

This time, dying was even easier than during my first descent into the Underworld. Something inside me remembered and knew exactly how to do it. I did not have to think, or try anything. It just happened by itself, and at the right moment.

The result was an immediate enlargement of my energy, like an explosion into vastness. My last normal thought was, "Holy Underworld! Marek, you are right, this is well worth dying for!" My energy started expanding in extravagant proportions. I seemed to be spreading through the rock for miles and miles around. Soon I completely lost touch with the room where the men kept projecting the Voice onto me, loading body part after body part.

I never knew how long the four Warriors continued, nor when they finally covered the grave and left. I no longer had a body. I was no longer Szar and his little fountain. There was just a fantastic force, alive inside the Earth, and vast.

But the expansion did not stop there. Soon, I became larger than the kingdom itself, and my presence reached into the spheres. This was very different from the travelling I had done with Elyani. This time there was no guidance, no controllers, no destination – just expansion. There was not me in space, exploring the spheres; I *was* the spheres! I swelled and swelled, first encompassing the intermediary worlds, then the worlds of the triangle, and continuing far beyond. The experience was one of phenomenal vastitude, with stars, beings, and myriads of forms of consciousness all inside me. And I grew faster and faster, reaching as far as the Abyss of the Deep and the Fault of Eternity, until the acceleration became such that I could no longer cope with it.

I exploded, and totally lost consciousness.

6.10 The White Eagle's hymn to the Great Dragon

Reaching towards the edge of the Great Abyss, the White Eagle of the gods intoned a hymn addressed to his mother's mother:

Atlantean Secrets

"O Great Dragon of the Deep,
O infinity below that reaches higher than the highest,
O bottomless summit which confuses the gods themselves,
O magnificent, O She-Dragon, O Mother of the Endless Night,
O chasm of ecstasy in which the Unborn God takes his pleasure,
What hast thou done with my children?
Where are my servant maids whom I sent down into thy bosom?
Where are the priestesses who descended, and never returned?"
And the White Eagle waited in the soft breeze of space.
After a long time of the gods, a sweet, melodious Voice made itself heard from the deepest of the Great Abyss,
"O White Eagle, O beautiful among the gods,
O relentless and brave traveller,
Undaunted by the magnitude of the spheres,
O child of my children, seed of my seed,
Fear not!
That which seems to be lost are but feeble shadows of thy children.
Their Spirits, in the safe and warm womb of my infinity,
I keep and nurture and render amazed
With endless flows of blissful ecstasy.
I show to them that which is beyond men and gods –
The glorious, eternal Midnight Sun,
The perilous and high ideal that the seed of thy seed,
One day, finally, and when all is accomplished, will fathom."
The White Eagle sent a reply,
"O mother of my sublime progenitors,
O delightful Maya whom only the Unborn God has known,
I hear thy powerful Word and I rejoice,
And for my children rapt in thy climaxes,
I no longer fear.
But my seed is quickly vanishing from the kingdom,
My time among men coming to an end,
My mission on the Earth, imperilled.
Humble, facing thy endless glory,
I implore thy clement benevolence,
That more maids of mine may visit thy bosom,
And yet to the kingdom, find their way back.
Great Mother,
In thy infinite compassion for all creatures,
Please help fulfil the word which once I gave
To the Flying Dragon who came
From beyond the Abyss of the Deep and the Fault of Eternity,
That I shall protect his seed, and enlighten its way with Love.
The brave bearing soul, sent by Thunder,
Whom in thy blissful womb thou hast received,

6 – The Book of the Great Dragon of the Deep

Please do not retain,
That he may return to his mortal abode.
Alas, aeons of glorious ecstasy he will miss,
Which thou and thou only couldst have bestowed onto him.
But he and other tiny grains of souls
Have woven human hopes and dreams,
Which are but uncertain and faint,
Yet pregnant with the future of my kind."

The Voice of the Earth spoke no more, but from the Great Abyss a ray of Light emerged, and the White Eagle recognised that Light which men and gods alike venerate through their highest rituals. And he felt comforted that his prayers had been heard.

6.11 The Dragon's Voice which is the thunder of the Earth

When I recovered my senses, it was totally dark. I was a frozen body lying in a grave. I had no idea how much time had elapsed. Near-instantly, I was hit by a wave of fear, an irrational panic fear I had never felt before, nor suspected could exist, and I started trembling all over. My mind was disconnected, I was a terrified child lost in a nowhere space, with no idea of what to do, or even what to be.

Shivering in the grip of panic, I was shaken by a vision. Lo! someone appeared in front of me. He was a tall, strong, fierce-looking man in his fifties, with a beard and long fair hair down to his hips.

In my surprise I forgot for a moment to be afraid. "Who are you?" I asked with my inner voice.

The man answered, "I am Lohrzen, the one who wrought the plate you are wearing around your neck."

"Why are you visiting me?"

"Visiting you? Ha! Ha! Ha! Ha! Ha! This mountain is *my* place! *You* are visiting me." His laughter reminded me of Floster's, and that brought back some of my spirits.

"Listen, son!" he pointed his index finger at me just like Marek. "I have come to tell you something. If you keep on trembling like a kitten, the She-Dragon will sniff you out of her nostrils and you'll be left hanging in the intermediary spaces until the end of time. For Melchisedek's sake, son, pull yourself together!"

"I thought no man could help me here." I shivered

"Who said I am a man?" Lohrzen roared with laughter. "Szar, at the moment you are drenched in Dragon's venom. At first the venom propelled you into a dreamtime journey in the spheres. But you are not trained enough to cope with the dreaming of the Unborn God, so you have fallen back into your grave, flat, like a bag of turnips."

"Where is the clear fountain?" I asked myself, but could not find it.

"There is not much you can do at this stage. Just let me bring you back into a less pitiful state." Lohrzen started projecting the Voice at me, intoning a one-verse litany of the Law,

"Thy soul was lost in the distance, now I bring it back to life."

It was lawfully magic. Instantly, the clear fountain was back. And it struck me that my belly was vroofing like a volcano.

"Farewell, man of the Law!" With no more words, Lohrzen turned his back and started walking away.

As the fountain was with me, I called him, "Lohrzen, wait! Don't go!"

"What, son?"

"Lohrzen, what I am supposed to do?"

Lohrzen sighed, and looking down towards the centre of the Earth, he exclaimed, "O Great Dragon! Candidates are no longer what they used to be!"

It reminded me of Gervin, and I was cheered up. Before walking away, Lohrzen projected the Voice at me again, "Hear the thunder of the Earth. Die in the Dragon, and live!"

"Wait, Lohrzen! I have heard you can bring people back from the Underworld after they have died. I need to learn how to do that!"

This time Lohrzen did not turn back.

I was left in the grave, still unable to move and only half-tied to my body. *"One Law, one way. He who never sleeps, never dies!"* was all I could draw from the fountain.

I didn't have to wait long. When the first wave came, I immediately recognised it. It was not unlike the Voice that Marek and his men had projected onto me, but with a fantastically greater magnitude.

A tidal-Word.

It engulfed my body and projected me high in the spheres, far beyond the fields of stars.

In the eerie voidness I heard a voice whispering from faraway, *"Space Matrix emergency signal. Earthly vehicle is about to be disintegrated. Unless immediate action is taken, irreparable damage will ensue."*

I looked down, searching for my body.

"Target identified. Do not try to project yourself into it."

My body was dead!

Down in the crypt, the Fire was insane. Immense, horrendous waves of Voice were hitting my body one after the other.

"Earthly vehicle damaged beyond possible repair. Do not try to project yourself into it."

Dead. Really dead.

Cracked by the Word.

Worse than the body itself, it was body-ness that had been torn apart.

Ravaged by the thunder of the Earth. Cleft asunder.

Through the cleft, the power of the Dragon was rushing in.

"Elyani! Elyani! Elyani!"
The faraway voice whispered, *"Follow the light in the matrix of space. Engage the spreading of consciousness."*
"Farewell, Elyani!"
Vastness.
Infinity beyond words.
The Abyss of the Deep, where the Mother of the Light is smiling.
Forever love, White Eagle of the gods.

6.12 Eisraim, Teyani's apartment

"No-o-o-o!"
Woken up by the shriek, Teyani rushed into the other room.
Still in meditation position, Elyani held her head in her hands, "No! No! Teyani, he is dead!"
"Wait! We do not know that for certain," Teyani took her in her arms and poured the Eagle's sweetness into her.
"I received the signal from the spheres of remoteness, Teyani. He is too far, he will never be able to come back. He is dead."
Teyani rocked her in her arms like a little child. "Hush, Lady of the Eagle. Remember what the oracle said, Szar is a traveller. He is the one we have been waiting for. Have faith, White Eagle!"
Her head resting on Teyani's shoulder, Elyani cried a flood of tears. "He is dead, Teyani! I saw him being shattered. Now, even if he came back, he would never be the same. I know."
This was the truth, and Teyani knew it well. She bit her lip, holding the Eagle's light.
"The Szar I love will never come back." Elyani cried, broken-hearted.
"Trust, my child. Trust in the Eagle."

6.13 Raised by the Dragon

When I next recovered some consciousness, someone was talking to me. I could hear his voice, but I could not understand what he was saying. He was gently massaging gateways on my feet, wrists and other parts of my body, using his strong presence to draw my consciousness back into my body.
"You are shivering with cold. Let me put some more oil on your body."
I could feel nothing.
Several times I fell back towards total unconsciousness, but he dragged me back, "No, no, Great Warrior, now is not the time to sleep!" And for

hours he kept pulling me back into physical reality, working on my body and speaking to me.

I was blank. No sensations, no thoughts, no memories.

Floster lifted me up and leant me against the wall. "Come on, I know you can hear me. Open your eyes and look at me."

I could feel his will entering my body, but my eyes remained closed.

"Come on," he insisted, "don't try to do it yourself. *Let the Dragon do!* Go into your belly." Below my navel, I felt his strong fist gently pressing against my abdomen. "Come on, let the Dragon open your eyes. Remember how you walked when you descended into the bowels of the Dragon. Do the same."

It was magic. Instantly, my eyes opened.

"Ha! Ha! Ha! Ha! Ha! Here is our Dragon!"

It was the strangest experience. I felt dead, unable to move even the tips of my fingers, and yet the power had made me open my eyes. Floster's image was in my head, but I wasn't.

"Now," Floster went on, still pressing the gateway below my navel with his fist, "do the same and lift your left hand. *Don't do! Let the Dragon do!*"

Immediately, I saw my left hand being lifted up. There was no trying and no effort. My hand just went up!

Floster was very happy. "That's the way, my boy! If you think you are dead, well, you're not completely wrong. But that doesn't matter, the Dragon can move the body of a Great Warrior even after he has died. Now I want you to stand up and walk."

As the magic of the Dragon got me up and walking in the room, Floster clapped his hands joyfully. I did not feel a thing, I just saw myself moving, as if from very far away.

"Perfect! Now come back to your bed. Lie down again. Very good!"

Not long after, Marek entered the room.

Floster saluted him, *"Praise the She-Dragon, Mother of the Endless Night,* my indestructible brother! Our boy has been raised!"

Marek exchanged a glance with Floster but did not answer. He walked to my bed and placed his hands on several gateways of my body, sensing the quality of life force. "His body is very weak. Better bring him back as soon as possible."

"Tomorrow, perhaps?"

Marek shook his head, "Now!" Then he addressed me, "Szar, when I give you the signal, I want you to get the Dragon to bring your soul back into your body. You must be warned, it's going to hurt like the Nephilim scum. Don't try to do it, let the Dragon do... *now!*"

6 – The Book of the Great Dragon of the Deep

6.14 Eisraim, Teyani's apartment

Elyani opened her eyes and left her state of deep contemplation. "He is back! I can feel his presence re-entering the spheres of Melchisedek."

Teyani, who was busy in the room, just answered, "I know."

Elyani was not joyful. "He has become different, Teyani. I can feel. He is no longer the man... "

"Hush, Lady of the Eagle!" Teyani interrupted. "That you do not know, and you won't know until he returns to Eisraim. The little apprentice that was with us was not the real Szar anyhow. We had no idea what kind of man he would become. Gervin warned you about that."

"True," Elyani said. She closed her eyes again. "Now he is in *a lot* of pain, Teyani. Is there anything I can do?"

"No, nothing." Teyani came to sit in front of Elyani.

"Oh, my God! So much pain. Do you think the Sons of the Dragon will release him now, or keep on with him?"

"From what Gervin said, Szar still has a long way to go over there. But now that he has been revived, we don't have to worry for his safety anymore. He has seen the Dragon face to face and survived. There is not one initiation in the kingdom that could kill him."

Elyani's shining eyes opened, and she cried. "But who is he, now?"

6.15 Dragon's breath

It was excruciating. Every single cell in my body was screaming with pain. My flesh was being burnt by thousands of red-hot iron prods.

I started yelling.

"Quick!" Floster said. "Call onto the Dragon. Let her breath flow up through your body."

I didn't understand.

Seeing my agony, Floster raised his voice, "Let the Dragon stop the pain! Don't think about it, just do it! *Now!*"

It worked almost immediately.

No pain. No thoughts. No mind.

"*Welcome to your new life, Great Warrior!*"

Silence. Marek looking straight into my eyes.

"The first thing you must understand is that you are dead. Dead in the Dragon! You no longer have a body, there is just the Dragon. You no longer have life, just the breath of the Dragon. All the things you used to do with your body, you must now let the Dragon do for you. Now sit up!"

The Dragon made my body sit up on the bed. I looked at the two men.

"Don't ask yourself how you are feeling. Don't even try to feel your body. Feel only the Dragon. She's fine. She's perfect. Always. Now smile, and say something!"

"*One Law, one way. He who never sleeps, never dies!*"

The two men remained silent, observing my reactions.

I groped for the clear fountain.

There was no body to receive it.

No body but a Dragon-body.

Verticality above, Dragon below. Lo! the clear fountain was back, flowing straight into the Dragon-body. Not into the belly-vroofing – there was no belly! – but somewhere, deep down inside the Earth.

Immediately, some clarity was back.

I looked around me. For the first time, I remembered exactly who Marek and Floster were. I couldn't speak, but the Dragon spoke through me. "Was I unconscious for a long time?"

Floster answered, "You spent three days and three nights in the crypt, then Marek the Indestructible and his Warriors went down and brought you back to this room. You arrived here at sunrise, and it is not yet noon."

"It's not good for you to sleep now, Szar," Marek said. "If you let yourself drift into unconsciousness, you die – and for good, this time. You must hold on to the breath of the Dragon, it is the only thing that's keeping you alive at the moment. Floster will stay with you and make sure you remain awake." Marek gave me a ritual salute with his left fist upwards, showing the marks on the inside of his forearm, and walked out.

"Come on, Szar, you must let the Dragon drink a sip for you," Floster encouraged me.

I took the cup but, as the liquid came into my mouth, I realised that I couldn't taste it. "I can't feel my body!"

"Don't try to!" Floster answered. "Feel nothing but the Dragon." He watched me drink. "Szar, you must make the best of these moments, they're precious. In the state you are in now, anyone normal would be lying unconscious, already on the Great Journey. Thanks to the She-Dragon, you're not. You can hear me and you can see me. And you can move. That makes you a very dangerous Warrior."

"Dangerous?" I was glad to hear the word, but I really couldn't see anything dangerous about this pitiful corpse stranded on the bed.

"What do you think is keeping you moving at the moment?" Floster was direct. "It is the Will of the Dragon and nothing else. And it is unstoppable. Even if your body was blasted with Voice and your brains cooked with the fire of the Furnaces of Doom, you could still stand up and strike your enemies."

Striking an enemy, that I couldn't see myself doing, but I thought Gervin would have been really happy to hear someone say I was dangerous.

"Now, Great Warrior, I must teach you how to breathe."

6 – The Book of the Great Dragon of the Deep

That sounded bizarre. Not feeling anything inside my body, I looked down and saw that my chest was moving. "Am I not breathing already?"

"I mean the breathing of the Great Warriors – the breath of the She-Dragon that will sustain your body. Let me explain. Each time you inhale, you must slightly contract the muscles of your abdomen, especially the lower part, below the navel. When the contraction mingles with the tremors, the breath of the She-Dragon is drawn up through the gate of the waters."

"The gate of the waters?"

"Just below the base of your body. Now that it's been awakened, it's become a powerful gateway through which the She-Dragon, from the depths of the Earth, can exhale her life into you."

I let the Dragon follow Floster's instructions.

"What can you feel?" Floster asked.

"Something going up inside me when I inhale. Like a breeze, coming from below. From below my body."

"This is the breath of the She-Dragon. To those who have not been initiated it's a violent poison. But for you, it will work miracles. It will make your body strong and resistant. Now, go on, practise! It's your new way of breathing. You must do it all the time."

I let the Dragon do as he said. All I could feel was a gentle breeze sweeping upwards each time I inhaled.

Floster stayed with me throughout the afternoon, speaking to me from time to time to make sure I didn't fall asleep. As evening approached, one of Marek's men came in. I recognised him. He was the youngest of those who had taken me down to the Dragon's crypt.

Floster introduced me to him, "Szar, this is Narlond. He underwent the initiations of the Great Warriors like you two years ago. He will be looking after you during the night. Remember, you must not sleep."

"For how long?" I asked.

"At least two days and two nights, perhaps more. It all depends on how your body recovers."

Giving me the ritual salute, Floster left me in the hands of Narlond.

As the night wore on, something in me was surprised to see that I didn't feel a need to sleep. I was in a strange state, a nowhere-space in which I felt nothing at all. I just kept breathing the Dragon's breath.

From time to time Narlond said a few words to make sure I was awake, and gave me some water to drink. Late in the night, another Great Warrior came and replaced Narlond.

The Dragon breathed on.

6.16 Fed by the Dragon

At daybreak, when Floster and Marek returned, the first thing they did was to place their hands on my energy centres and sense my life force. They looked pleased. "The breath of the Dragon is working wonders!" Floster tried to warm me up. "You are already much better than yesterday."

Marek gave instructions that I should be given some food. I could not taste the charcoaled chunks, but the Dragon had no difficulty swallowing them.

That day passed, and another night, in the same way. At the end of the following day, Marek came to sense my energy. As he was satisfied with what he felt, I was allowed to sleep.

But late in the night, when Floster came to check that I was still alive, I boasted, "*Praise the Great Dragon, brother*, I feel no need to sleep at all!"

Floster told me off, "What your body feels like is irrelevant! A Warrior does not eat from hunger, he eats from the Will of the Dragon. Same with sleep! When you sleep, it must be because the Dragon makes your body sleep, not because you feel like it. *Don't do, let the Dragon do!*"

In a matter of seconds I was sound asleep.

All of this was so simple. Whenever something had to be done, I just let the Dragon do, and it happened! How it happened, I had not the faintest idea. Deep from within the Dragon an impulse was sent, and the result was immediate, whether it had to do with moving my hand, urinating, or falling asleep.

When I woke up the next morning I was surprised how energetic I felt. As soon as I finished my morning chanting, I stayed in a meditation position and directed all my attention to the practice of Dragon's breath. The ascending breeze was becoming stronger, and also more feeding. I noticed that even without inhaling I could make it ascend into my body, and then I could take its energy in to feed my lungs with it. It felt just as good as breathing air! How long could I have gone on without having to breathe? I decided not to push the experiment too far without first asking Marek about it.

The breeze was sometimes like a gentle pulse, at other times more like a flame, rising straight up the middle of my body. Occasionally it turned into a hot geyser releasing hissing fumes that made me feel intoxicated and dizzy. Once or twice I nearly leapt up and started a dance, so elated I was.

When Marek came to visit, many questions were on my mind. For a start, how come I was not feeling weak?

"Marek," I asked, "once my master made me descend into the Underworld. That was not much compared to facing the Dragon, and besides, some of the best healers in the kingdom were looking after me, giving me beverages full of magic herbs. Yet after coming back I was sick and weak

6 – The Book of the Great Dragon of the Deep

for many days. Here... three days ago I was a corpse, and now I feel like jumping and dancing!"

"The She-Dragon's breath is powerful," Marek answered. "*Limitless is the vitality of the Dragon.*"

"What am I supposed to do now?"

"Your body must get stronger before you can start your training with the Warriors. Take a few weeks to build yourself up."

"How do I do that?"

Marek smiled, "Draw from the Dragon's breath. Let its energy build up your muscles. Let your bones become harder. The breath will make you look like one of us."

"But how does it work?"

His forearm flexed, Marek looked down to his fist, which he slowly opened and clenched. "You ask a lot of questions, son," he said. Clearly, he did not enjoy inquisitive minds as much as Gervin.

I was left on my own to ponder upon the mysteries of Dragon's breath, tapping from the resources of the clear fountain.

In the following weeks I spent many hours every day in meditation, focussing on this extraordinary energy pouring upwards from the gate of the waters. Day after day, the effect built up. The vroofing waves in and below my belly combined with the elated feeling of life force in the Dragon's breeze. At times there was so much energy that I had to stand up and Dragon-dance for a while. At other times my body was shaken by violent and blissful contractions that ended in ecstatic trances.

To my great amazement, as I followed Marek's instructions and directed the breeze's power into my bones and muscles, my shoulders started widening! I could hardly believe it. It was not weeks but only a matter of days before I saw solid muscles building up in my arms and thighs. Each time he saw me in the dining hall, Floster's face lit up. "*Praise the She-Dragon! You're starting to look like a real man, my boy!*" he would say in his deep voice, slapping my shoulder. He always wanted to go to the kitchen and get some more charcoaled food for me, but the strange thing was, I was less hungry. I needed less and less food. I fed on Dragon's breeze, which gave me more satisfaction than any lawful food I had ever touched. I remembered how voracious I had felt after my first initiation into the Dragon – whatever I stuffed into my stomach never seemed enough. In reality what my body was craving was Dragon's breeze, not food.

After a few weeks, it reached the point where I no longer felt at ease in my brown robe and had to ask good Floster for bigger clothes. He took me to a warehouse-cave where piles of uniforms were kept, and fitted me with the black pants, shirt and cap of the Warriors. It was not without a certain sadness that I let go of the robe my beloved teacher had given me. But the real shock came when I saw myself in a mirror – the only mirror on Mount Lohrzen.

"*Good Lord Melchisedek!*" I exclaimed, "is that me?"

"Ha! Ha! Ha! Ha! Ha!" Floster boomed, "Who d'you think you're looking at, my boy?"

I could hardly believe that the man looking at me in the mirror was me.

I had doubled in size! My hair had become thicker and curly, and slightly darker than before. My skin was shining, and perhaps slightly darker too. But the hair on my chin! For the first time in my life, the growth on my chin looked almost like a real beard. I touched the birthmark on my left cheek, as if to hold on to some stable value from my past.

When he saw how flabbergasted I was, Floster scolded, "You have no idea of the power of the Dragon, hey?"

These were not the only changes. I was discovering a completely new range of physical sensations. Strangely, moving my body was becoming a very satisfying experience. A few times I even found myself doing the unthinkable – running for fun in the temple's corridors! As Marek had instructed me to remain strictly within the protected temple's perimeter and never cross the portal gates, I spent a lot of time on the cliff-face. I took great pleasure climbing the rock, especially because my body responded to my commands infinitely more precisely than before.

This new relationship to physicality was a startling change. It challenged the image I had of myself. All my life I had been weak and clumsy, and I had hated anything to do with physical activity. Now that the precious Dragon's breath was running through my body, a new life had been awakened. Climbing and running were turning into a joyful celebration of my new life. But the breeze that rose from the gate of the waters created more than just physical energy and agility. It brought an intensity that made me more awake. I remembered complaining to Gervin that despite all my efforts I remained 'insubstantial'. For the first time, an answer to this lack of density was emerging. The Dragon stood below me, more solid even than the mountain in which the temple had been dug.

I felt an increasing desire to go and explore the red canyons that surrounded the temple. I set off to ask Marek's permission.

6.17 At the top of Lohrzen's mountain

It was my first meeting with Marek in weeks. As soon as he saw me, he whistled. "*Praise the She-Dragon, mother of the Warriors!* Looks like she's done another of her miracles!"

"I can hardly believe it myself, Marek!" With my left forearm flexed to the horizontal, I opened and clenched my fist, creating a few waves in my newly-discovered muscles.

"Ha! Ha! Ha! Ha! Ha! Szar, dancing again!"

I asked him how I could push the practice of Dragon's breath further, but Marek was not a man who enjoyed explanations and theories. He looked

6 – The Book of the Great Dragon of the Deep

down to his left hand, refraining from clenching it. "Just keep doing the practice and you'll find out for yourself."

Seeing there was no point insisting, I changed the topic, "Marek, can I go out and take a look at the canyons around the temple?"

"There are a few things I have to tell you about this. As you've probably heard, we Great Warriors are sometimes called the nightmare of the Nephilim, or even the black nightmares, because of our clothes. Do you know what this means in practice?"

I shook my head.

"It means that whenever one of the Nephilim finds you in his way, he'll do anything in his power to kill you."

I was shocked.

"There is no turning back!" Marek reminded me. "When you became a Great Warrior, deep changes took place in your energy. The gate of the waters was opened. While you were dead in the crypt, the She-Dragon stamped her seal on you. The Nephilim scum know only too well how to recognise these signs. Wherever you go, they will detect your presence. And if you are not on guard..." With a short whistle, he drew his flat hand across his throat. "*Farewell, man of the Law!* And let me tell you, Szar, the Nephilim scum are vicious."

Thoughtful, I looked down to my left palm and clenched my fist, but realising this was irritating Marek, I dropped my forearm and focussed only on the clear fountain.

"And how do I know when one of the Nephilim is around?"

"That's one of the things I have to teach you before you can go on a tirtha tour, my boy. You see, only a few miles from here there is a cave where one of the Watchers used to live. His name was Verzazyel. He was the one who taught Lohrzen. There is an Underworld of a lot of magic in that cave, left behind by Verzazyel after he returned to the spheres. Many Nephilim sneak into the cave, trying to steal the Watcher's secrets. They all want the power. So the cave is like a tirtha for the Nephilim scum. Entire caravans go there on pilgrimage. This makes the canyons of the Red Lands particularly unsafe for you. But make no mistake, there are Nephilim throughout the kingdom. Wherever you are, you must be on guard, and know how to kill before you are killed."

An immense wave of sadness arose inside me. I had been under the impression that my mission in the temple of Vulcan was nearly accomplished, and that I would soon be returning to Eisraim. Suddenly, it felt like an aeon was separating me from my next white drink. And to make matters worse, I simply could not imagine myself killing someone. Holding on to the fountain, I replied, "So, really, what I have to learn from you, Marek, is how to become dangerous?"

Marek nodded. "*Very* dangerous," he echoed, his favourite smile breaking out. There was a silence. "In two days," he concluded, "this Moon cycle will end. The morning after at dawn, one of my men will come and get you and we'll start your training."

"How long is that going to take?"

Marek flexed his forearm and contemplated his left fist. "You ask a lot of questions, son."

On my way out, I risked a last one, "Can I climb to the top of the temple's mountain?"

Marek looked at me with the same dangerous smile. "Totally safe, son. The Nephilim are wicked, but they are not so stupid as to camp on Lohrzen's mountain. Climb as much as you want."

After the meeting, I decided to collect my spirits by ascending to the top of the mountain. The climbing was easy, the steps carved on the edge of the cliff reaching almost to the top. It was a clear day and as sometimes happened in these desert regions, the mists were so sparse that as I climbed I could see nearly as far as the bottom of the mountain. This created an eerie feeling, not unlike the awesome landscapes mentioned in the legends about the world of the gods.

An hour later, having made it to the flat rocky plateau that topped Lohrzen's mountain, I suddenly felt overwhelmed. So the world had become an unsafe place for me! I hated the idea that I might have to kill people. How many hundreds of days was it going to take before I could return home? Like the little boy of the White Eagle's prophecy, I sat on the red rock with my head in my hands and I cried. I missed Eisraim, I missed Gervin, I missed Elyani's courtyard with the purple lawn, and the white drinks, and the care. I found myself sobbing, "I miss you! I miss you! I miss you!"

A voice took me by surprise, "What present would you like to take to your friends when you go back?"

I lifted my head. There he was, sitting right by me, the magnificent Lohrzen, his blue eyes shining bright, his fair hair rolling all the way down to his hips. Speechless I was, my eyes and mouth wide open.

"Come on, think! Great Warriors are legendary for their unforgettable presents. What would be good enough for your friends?"

Touching the orichalc plate on my neck, I contemplated his glorious body of light while tuning into the verticality of my fountain. It was some time before I responded, "If I could bring Vivyani back from the Underworld, that would be a present worthy of my friends."

"Ha! Ha! Ha! Ha! Ha!" Lohrzen sounded so much like Floster and Marek that I started to suspect this laughter was one of the cornerstones of the Sons of the Dragon's tradition. "You ask for difficult things, son."

"Now that my body has become stronger, perhaps if I descended again it could remain alive."

"You will never have to do it like that again, son. There are better ways of reaching the Underworld than the one you took during your first descent. Now that you have died in *the Voice which is the thunder of the Earth*, you can go down through the gates of the Dragon and discover marvels that few initiates have contemplated."

"Will you teach me, Lohrzen?"

"Anything you learn on this mountain, the Great Dragon is teaching you through me. Ask Floster to direct you to the man who knows everything about the gates of the Dragon. But there is another teacher who can instruct you on these matters. He is an old friend of yours, but you have neglected him lately."

I didn't follow.

Lohrzen laughed at me, "Look at this high priest of Gana who does not even remember that his tutelary deity is the knower of the wisdom of the Dragon!"

I swung in speechlessness again. "Of course!" I thought, "but how..." I realised that Lohrzen was walking away.

"Lohrzen, wait! There are other things I need to ask you!"

Without turning back, he said, "You ask too many questions, son." And his image vanished, as miraculously as it had appeared.

"Where the Underworld does this man live?" I asked myself. But then of course, who said he was a man?

Lohrzen's visit had once more brought me back to life! My sorrows were forgotten, and without delay I set off to climb down the mountain and find Floster. As I was running down, jumping from staircase to staircase, I decided that to become a real Son of the Dragon I would have to practise their ritual hymns. I stopped, poised on the edge of the cliff for my first attempt:

"Ha! Ha! Ha! Ha! Ha!"

6.18 Crossing the gate of the Dragon

When I asked Floster about the man who knew everything about the gates of the Dragon, he immediately answered, "Amaran!"

His room was located in a remote and quiet corner of the temple. Floster had described him as a 'very, very, very old man' and so I was surprised when I first met him. His hair was white but long and strong, not unlike Lohrzen's, and his face bore few wrinkles. I had never met him in the dining hall or in any other parts of the temple. I wondered how he occupied his days.

His willingness to answer my questions, at least some of them, immediately made me like him. He listened to me for some time, then concluded, "This Vivyani must have been a special person for you to want to find her so much, even after she has died."

"Am I asking for something impossible, Brother Amaran?"

"Nothing is impossible, my friend in the Law, but some things are more difficult than others. Once a soul is no longer bound to its physical body, it becomes much more arduous to locate it. But,

That which is arduous to some,
Others can accomplish in no time.

Perhaps something in Verzazyel's cave would allow you to locate Vivyani."

I was intrigued. Each time I heard someone mention Verzazyel's cave, there was high magic pending in the air. Should I try to go and visit the cave for myself? But then what to do about all those vicious Nephilim monsters who roamed around in the vicinity?

"In any case," Amaran continued, "*before attempting the impossible, it is wise to explore the limits of the possible.* Has anyone ever told you about the gates of the Dragon?"

"This is precisely the topic I would like to hear from you, *O wise man in the Law.*"

Amaran remained silent for a while. When I saw him twirling his beard like Gervin, I thought, "This man must really know what he is talking about." I wondered if by pushing the practice of Dragon's breath, I could further develop this part of my anatomy and do the same myself.

Amaran started his explanation with verses of the Law of the Dragon,

"*Mysterious are the gates of the Dragon,*
Amazing and supernal are the worlds to which they lead.

You know more about the Underworld than most initiates in the kingdom, Szar, and yet you know nothing. What you saw during your descent was but a tiny, distorted fraction of *the magnificence which is the Underworld*. This may come as a surprise to you because, like many learned men, you believe that *the Underworld is the cold realm of the shades, full of the filth that fell from the world, and thick with the darkness of disease and plagues and sorrows.* Yet, *my friend in the Law,* what you have seen was not the real Underworld. *Change your views and change your ways.*

The beauty of the Underworld is greater and more real
Than any beauty your eyes will ever contemplate in the kingdom.
The Underworld's wealth is greater by far
Than any king of Earth will ever hoard or even dream of:
Lakes of molten gold, silvery cascades,
Mountains of orichalc and rivers of precious gems.
The power of the Underworld,
Only mighty Warriors can fathom,
The dazzling light of the Deep Underworld
Equalled only by the Great Light of the spheres of Highness."

I could caress my beard and somehow pull it, but there was no way I could twirl it. "*O wise man in the Law,*" I asked, "how come I did not meet these wonders?"

6 – The Book of the Great Dragon of the Deep

"The reason, Szar, is very simple. You entered through the wrong portal! Had you descended through the gates of the Dragon, all would have been revealed to you."

Amaran's words made me thoughtful. "I wonder why Master Gervin, *great prophet in the Law*, did not instruct me to go down through these gates."

"Even if he had, Szar, you would not have been able to pass through, for
*Only those who have died in the Dragon
Can cross the gates of the Dragon.
To all others, the wonders remain sealed.*"

I sighed, "Crossing these gates must be a great trial."

"Ha! Ha! Ha! Ha! Ha!" Amaran was definitely an initiate of Lohrzen's lineage, his laughter left no doubt. "That is the strange thing, *my young friend in the Law*. Crossing the gates of the Dragon is either impossible, or extremely easy. People who have not died in the Dragon could come close to a gate a thousand times and never recognise it. Even if a knower of the Dragon pointed out the gate for them, they would be unable to pass through. But you, having died in the Dragon, could follow me through one of those gates as easily as you walked through the doorway of this room."

I must have looked unconvinced. "Would you like to do it tomorrow morning?" Amaran proposed.

Remembering how I felt when I returned from my first Underworld descent, I was gripped by a wave of fear, as if one of the long-teethed Nephilim giants had grabbed me in his claws. I shook my head, "But tomorrow is *the day before the New Moon, when the Underworld's gloomy darkness is at its thickest.*"

Amaran was smiling. "*Fear not, man of the Law!* None of this nonsense applies when descending through the gates of the Dragon."

"But I gave my word to Marek that I would be ready to start learning the Warriors' lore from him on the day of the New Moon. Last time I descended it took me six and a half weeks to find my way back to the surface, and then it took another three weeks before I felt secure on my legs."

Using the Voice, Amaran projected at me, "Szar, these are not the words of a man who has died in the Great Dragon! You have not the faintest idea what her power can do for you."

Startled, I tuned into the clear fountain above my head. Listening only to its pure verticality, I finally capitulated, "Forgive me, *wise man of the Law*, but the trials of my descent have left deep scars inside me. Yet I will not let myself be guided by fear. Where shall I meet you tomorrow morning?"

"Come here at dawn, and I will take you to one of the gates."

Finding my way back through the empty corridors of this lonely side of the temple, I tried once more: "Ha! Ha! Ha! Ha! Ha!" But it did not sound anything like the real one. "There is still a long way to go!" I sighed.

The following morning I woke up in the clutches of fear, beads of sweat all over my body. It was an ugly fear that seized my guts and made me feel sick. The horrific scenes of the Underworld were still fresh in my mind: the monstrous shapes harassing me, my maimed body crumbling bit by bit, and the madness, the stench, the deadly noise. The clamour of distress from the thousands upon thousands of souls desperately calling for help was still haunting me.

I wished I had never been stupid enough to accept Amaran's invitation, but having given my word there was no way I could pull out. Or was there? Devious thoughts started parading through my mind. Perhaps I could pretend I was sick, or perhaps...

Touching my beard, I tried reasoning with myself, "Lohrzen himself directed me to Amaran and clearly, Amaran knows what he is talking about." But somehow, reasoning only made the fear worse. The thoughts went round and round, twisting and turning, tightening the skewer of fear.

The bottom line was, I simply did not want to go.

In the midst of this turbulence, I suddenly remembered how Amaran, like Floster, had rebuked me, "You have no idea what the power of the Dragon can do!"

Don't do, let the Dragon do!

I let her vroof a few waves into me from below, and lo! the fear stopped. Instantly. It was shockingly simple: when I rested on the Dragon, I just *could not* feel fear. Even more, I could hardly recall what fear felt like. It had vanished. It felt unreal, as if it had never existed. There was the Will of the Dragon, and nothing else. My mind was empty and clear, lucidly attuned to the fountain. Encouraged, I tried another "Ha! Ha! Ha! Ha! Ha!" but with no more success than my previous attempts.

I still had time to complete my morning chanting of the Law and breathing exercises before grabbing a torch and making my way to Amaran's room.

I was deeply puzzled by how simple it had been to get rid of the fear. "I don't understand this power! But perhaps power is not to be understood," I thought. I deliberated over the way Marek and Floster had got me to do things I had believed impossible simply by yelling at me *"No thoughts, just Dragon!"* And I recalled the time I could have killed myself at the tirtha lake, after the soft stone had been stolen. What had made me suddenly turn back instead of letting myself drown? Not thinking! I had just done it. Where had the impulse come from?

When I reached Amaran's door, I grounded myself in the vroofing, breathed in the Dragon's breeze, and before knocking told myself, "There is no turning back! *One Law, one way! He who never sleeps, never dies!*"

After entering and lawfully saluting Amaran, I told him, "I brought a good torch. The tunnels get so dark going down into the bowels of the Dragon."

He smiled, "Leave it here, *my young friend in the Law,* you won't need it. The gate of the Dragon is only one minute away. Come on, let's go."

6 – The Book of the Great Dragon of the Deep

"You still don't believe that you will be back before the New Moon, do you?" my guide commented on the incredulous look on my face.

"*Just Dragon,*" I strode forwards, looking straight in front of me, "*no thoughts!*"

"Well, let me tell you Szar, today you will be laughing and eating your lunch in the dining hall with Floster. Dragon's word!"

Amaran was right, I could not believe what he said. And my surprise was great when, before a minute had passed, he announced, "Here we are, Szar. What you have in front of you is a gate of the Dragon."

The corridor had led us to a small cavern less than two hundred lawful feet from Amaran's room. As the old man had said, there was no need for torches. From a window in the neighbouring hallway, the daylight peered into the cavern.

"Come on, Szar, I want you to tell me what you can see. Walk around and try to find the exact location of the gate."

Resting on the Vulcan-vroofing, I moved slowly, as if starting a Dragon dance. When I reached the middle of the cave I could but smile, so characteristic was the feeling. "Here," I said, "there is a breeze coming up from the ground. Same as the breeze that comes up in my body when I practise Dragon's breath."

"Correct! See what I told you! To those who are not familiar with the breath of the Dragon, *the wonders remain sealed*. But to you, it is obvious. Now, let us go down! Just sit somewhere, with your back against the wall."

I did as he commanded. He sat close to the centre of the cave with his back very straight. "Close your eyes," he said, "and just do what I tell you. Tune into the ascending breeze inside your body. Then tune into the breeze of the Dragon's gate. Just follow it down. No, not exactly like that. First you must rest on the Dragon and penetrate the breeze of the gate."

I let my consciousness be absorbed in the soft and warm feeling of ascending energy that came from the rock, and the breeze of the gate became one with the breeze inside my body. "That's it," Amaran said, "you are inside it. Now, just move down through the breeze. Let me help you." I felt myself being drawn down through the gate of the waters, and lo! Amaran and I were standing in another cave, much larger, and lit up by the most incredibly beautiful deep blue light. As I looked around me, it seemed that the cavern's walls were made of lapis lazuli, and I detected a special fragrance completely new to me.

"That's it!" Amaran applauded, "You are already deeper in the Underworlds than you ever went during your first descent! Tell me, Great Warrior, would you like to go back immediately, or d'you think you could cope with a little bit more?"

I was so astonished I didn't even think of answering. I could not take my eyes off the glowing tapestry of blue gemstones that covered the cavern walls.

Looking at me, Amaran sighed. "Follow me, candidate!" He started walking, fast.

Rushing behind him, I swallowed and asked, "Am I undergoing a trial at the moment, Amaran?"

"*Praise the She-Dragon you're not!* You would have already failed and the Dragon would be sneezing you out through her nostrils!"

I chuckled at the idea of running for my life in the nostrils of the Dragon, but his words had left me perplexed. "I don't understand what it is that I am doing wrong, Amaran."

"Ha! Ha! Ha! Ha! Ha!" Amaran's ritual laughter seemed to echo far off in the fabulous landscape that was opening in front of us: incredibly huge lapis lazuli caves full of stalagmites and stalactites, bathing in iridescent blue light. It was as awesome as it was peaceful.

"The problem with you, Szar, is that you don't understand what the Dragon is for."

"You mean I should use the power of the Dragon in a different way?"

Amaran sighed loudly again. "Use the power..." he echoed. Then he stopped and looked down, addressing the centre of the Earth, "O Great Dragon, forgive this *young fool in the Law*, he just does not know what he is saying!" As I let his words impact into my fountain, I knew it was now Lohrzen who was speaking through him. But Amaran was striding forwards again, and I had to hurry to catch up.

"Wait! What am I supposed to do?"

"If you think that the power is to be 'used'," he spat the last word with contempt, "then there is absolutely nothing I can do for you."

Perhaps I should have cried, but I knew the man was laughing in his head and I felt like laughing with him. "What should I do, Amaran? Die some more?"

Amaran stopped walking and turned back towards me so suddenly that I bumped into him. "You!" he said with a voice bordering on indignation, pushing me away with his index, "never use the Dragon!"

He resumed his pace. I did my best to keep up.

"Let the Dragon use you! And stop talking about the She-Dragon only in terms of power, or she will find you so utterly boring..."

"...that she will sneeze me out through her nostrils," I promptly added. "I know."

We had arrived at a little stream in which a silvery fluid was running. I contemplated the shimmering flow while Amaran left me some breathing space.

"What is it?" I asked.

"Water of life. The Underworlds are full of streams like this one. Take some, and drink it."

I made a cup of my right hand, plunged it into the limpid waters and brought it to my mouth.

6 – The Book of the Great Dragon of the Deep

"Amaran! This is... amazing! I've never tasted anything so fantastic in my entire life!"

"That's the way!" he pointed his index finger at me.

"That's the way... what?"

With his deep Son-of-the-Dragon voice, Amaran drummed into me, "That's the way you must talk about the She-Dragon. She is amazing, you have never tasted anything as fantastic as her in your entire life," wafting his hand in the air, "and you have never smelled anything as fresh and pure in your entire life," pointing to the spectacular cavern around us, "and you have never seen anything as beautiful as this in your entire life!" He took a long inhalation, making his nostrils wriggle in a strange way. "Forget about the power!

She is to be known through ecstasy.
She is the extraordinary lover and playmate,
The giver of endless pleasure.
There is more delight in her
Than a man can comprehend in a hundred lives.
There is more depth in her
Than a hundred gods can fathom in a hundred aeons.
And when the immortals' council,
Bewildered by her many enigmas,
Sought the Unborn God for his advice on how to approach her,
He replied,
'She is to be known through ecstasy.'

But for now, we must hurry on," Amaran concluded. "There is something I want to show you. Follow me!"

Dazzled by the power of his words, I had to bring myself back and hurry behind him again. We veered left into a cavern that seemed so high I could not see a ceiling, only a diffuse yellow light.

Amaran pointed upwards, "Take a good look. What do you think you are seeing?"

On closer observation, the ceiling appeared to be made of thousands of tiny yellow lights, some of which remained fixed, while others were moving.

"These lights," Amaran explained, "are souls in one of the halls of the Underworld, just as you saw when you descended the first time."

"*One Law, one way! He who never sleeps, never dies!*" In one second all the memories came back: the horrid visions, the putrid smells, the madness, and worse than all the rest, the clamour.

There was a hush.

The fragrance around us was as pure as before. Everything was peaceful and vibrantly quiet. The only noise was the whisper of a stream of water of life that ran in a distant part of the cavern. I looked down to the ground which, like the walls, was made of magnificent lapis lazuli.

I looked up again and wondered how I would ever find Vivyani among these myriads of tiny lights.

"Are there many caves like this one?" I asked.

"More than there are grains of sand on all the shores of the kingdom. Come on, let us go back, we must hurry."

As I followed him, contemplating the majestic lapis stalactites, I asked, "Why do we have to hurry?"

"Because I gave a *young fool in the Law* my Dragon's word that he would not miss lunch with his friend Floster."

I chuckled again, "Have you ever met Master Gervin of Eisraim?"

"No, but I have heard his name. Is he your teacher?"

"Yes. I am sure you two would get along well. Amaran, I can still feel this water of life. It's vibrating all over inside me. A magnificent feeling."

"I have been drinking this water daily for nearly sixty years, Szar, which is why my body is strong and free from the vicissitudes of old age. But what you have tasted is not much compared to what flows in deeper levels of the Underworlds."

"Could you use these waters to heal people?"

"Of course you can."

We were already back where we had started from.

"I don't really feel like going back to the surface," I said.

"You can come back here any time you want, Great Warrior! But for now, just place your body in the ascending stream, the Dragon's breeze, and let yourself be carried up by it."

After a few seconds, and without any effort whatsoever I was back in my physical body. I moved my left hand, slowly opening and contracting my fist. Then I opened my eyes and looked around. Amaran was already walking away. There was neither pain nor the slightest discomfort, but I could still feel the vitality of the water of life.

I stood up and silently followed Amaran back to the door of his room. I thanked him lawfully and kept walking in the direction of the dining hall.

Further away, in the middle of an empty, obscure corridor, I stopped.

There was no reason. I just stopped.

Barely audible, I whispered, "Ha! Ha! Ha! Ha! Ha!"

Then I stood on the Dragon and vroofed the most powerful wave I could trigger. As my body started the slow movements of the dance, I took a long, long inhalation, wriggling my nostrils as Amaran did. Then I clenched my fists, and slowly raised my arms and opened my mouth. At the same time an ascending wave started in my belly.

What followed was the loudest scream I had ever let out in my life. It started with a middle-pitched yell that kept building up for nearly one minute and ended in a prolonged shriek. Then as I kept slowly dancing, the power of the Dragon unleashed itself through my voice, emitting formidable sounds one after the other. I had *never* heard anything like it. The flow

6 – The Book of the Great Dragon of the Deep

and the force were seismic. Dragon unreal! I yelled and yelled, and the rock was my witness.

The silence that followed was total. I stood with my forearms crossed in front of my chest, my fists clenched to the extreme. There was a long hush, reminiscent of the death in the Dragon I had experienced in the crypt.

Then everything stopped. I dropped my hands, and took a deep breath while wriggling my nostrils. I whispered again, "Ha! Ha! Ha! Ha! Ha!" and started walking.

When I arrived in the dining hall, Floster greeted me, "*Praise the Great Dragon!* Szar, my boy, how are you today?"

"Terrific, Floster!" I answered. "Simply terrific."

6.19 Black dance

It was late in the morning when Narlond knocked at my door. We exchanged a friendly greeting. Narlond was one of the people I enjoyed chatting with during meals in the dining hall. Several times I had wondered, was he the one Floster said was just as mad as I was? Nothing in Narlond's gentle personality had allowed me to know for sure, and Floster remained vague on the subject each time I asked.

A few dozen corridors later, Narlond knocked at a door and requested access in a ceremonial tone that immediately led me to suspect there was ritual in the air. Setting the clear fountain on alarm mode, I anchored myself in the Dragon and waited.

Narlond was let in, I was left outside. After a minute or so the door opened again and a voice called out, "Enter!"

The fountain sparked, "*One Law, one way. He who never sleeps, never dies!*" and I walked in, rendered fearless by resting on the Dragon. And just as well!

The door was shut behind me with a loud bang. I found myself in complete darkness. I was violently grabbed by at least ten hands and immobilised. There was a piercing scream, as if a man was being butchered in a corner of the room.

Then Marek's voice resounded, "*Candidate, face death! There is no turning back! That which you have come to learn here is designed to kill. Know that if you ever reveal any of these secrets to anyone but a Great Warrior initiate, a cruel death will be your lot.*"

The tone left no room for doubt – Marek meant what he said.

In the pause that followed, I could feel the combined Dragon power of the men who had me pinned. Enough to annihilate a company of a hundred soldiers in no time.

"Now you will repeat the oath of secrecy after me."

I was made to swear that I would always conceal the Dragon's arts of war from all but initiates of this temple. Were I to transgress, I would become a target for all Great Warriors – dwellers in the spheres as well as those alive – and ruthlessly exterminated. "*There is no turning back!*" I repeated solemnly at the end of the oath.

Seconds of silence, and the gripping hands released me.

Someone opened the windows, inundating the cavern-room with light, and loud yells of joy erupted all around me. Half-blinded by the daylight, I heard handclapping and wild Dragon screams of near-Voice threshold let out by all the men. Then all of the fifteen men, one after another, came over and hugged me, "Well done, brother!"

Marek himself looked very happy, "Welcome, brother!" While he was squeezing my shoulders I silently gave thanks, "*Praise the works of the She-Dragon!* After the wonders she has performed on my body, my vertebrae no longer crack when I have to bear the brunt of their brotherly love."

Everyone kept talking loudly, and Marek gave me a friendly punch in the stomach. "Now we are going to make a Great Warrior out of you." Tainting his favourite smile with a touch of irony, he winked at me, "A really dangerous one!" Carried by the general elation, I burst out laughing with him.

Then Marek clapped his hands, calling everyone back to order. The room became silent instantly. The men took up their positions in the room, which gave me a moment to look around. The cavern was about thirty lawful feet wide and nearly as high. It was dug into the edge of the cliff, with big windows bringing not only daylight but also plenty of fresh air. A thick mat covered the entire floor. My eyes landed on clay mannequins that aroused my curiosity. There were at least a dozen of them, the size of normal human beings, and with precisely modelled body shapes. Shining dots and circles had been painted on their surface.

Marek instructed me to watch the action in the centre of the room. Narlond started a strange dance. As he moved about the mat, he slowly waved his arms, his fists clenched in a particular way. Every so often his movements took on a furious pace, while he delivered volleys of blows to imaginary opponents. Then the slow, fluid dance resumed.

Something struck me: every single move in Narlond's dance was coming straight from the Dragon. The degree of mastery was staggering, and just by watching him the vroofing force inside me started pulsing.

Marek came close. "You know what gateways are, don't you?"

"The centres in the body of energy."

"Have you seen anyone use them before?"

"I have seen people perform healing by projecting the Voice onto the patient's gateways. When I was trained as a priest I was taught how to use certain gateways *to promote spiritual concentration, help childbirth, or facilitate the transition of death.*"

"And have you seen anyone use them for travelling?"

6 – The Book of the Great Dragon of the Deep

"During my travelling initiations the priests from the healing chambers used to send me unconscious and push me out of my body by activating my gateways."

"Gateways to push people out of their body," Marek Dragon-smiled, "this is exactly what we are going to teach you. Look at these," he pointed to two black areas drawn on the sides of the neck on one of the clay models. "We call them the 'cheap way out', because they are so easy and so efficient." He touched the corresponding area on my neck with his finger and continued, "Just one gentle – but precise! – blow here, and a man falls down unconscious. Instantly. Make the blow a little bit stronger or use the power of the Voice, and the man is dead. There is no way back. Even a powerful healer will be unable to bring the man back."

Marek removed his finger from my neck, which immediately made me feel more comfortable. Looking down to his left fist, he went on, "The two 'cheap way out' are part of forty gateways known as the 'black forty'. Since Lohrzen, the Warriors have been using these black forty to eliminate their adversaries – in particular the Nephilim."

Marek paused to let me watch more of Narlond's incredibly harmonious and grounded sequence of movements.

"What you are seeing here is called the black dance. It is the art of blasting an adversary's black forty in no time, whatever the circumstances. Of course, you won't always need to hit the forty gateways. In most cases one or two are plenty to kill your enemy. But when you become a master in the art, you will be able to strike the black forty in less than five seconds, which is the Great Warriors' ritual way of killing the Nephilim."

Marek clicked his fingers, which triggered a furious assault. Narlond's hands moved so fast I could hardly see what was happening. Some five seconds later, as he became still, I whispered, "Sounds very dangerous!"

Marek laughed, "*Very* dangerous!" Then he clapped his hands again and began to move, and all the men stood up and started dancing after him, executing sequences of precisely arranged movements. Sometimes they all seemed to dance together. At other times they moved in pairs as if fighting each other. I was mesmerised by the beauty and the energy that was with them. Never had I contemplated so much contained power, such flow of Dragonhood, such measured combinations of harmony and strength. The Dragon's ascending breath in each of them was like a flame, and I quickly felt compelled to follow them. The vroofing took over and, like them, I became a moving flame. I completely forgot where I was. The cavern had disappeared. There was nothing left but dancing flames, ritually offering themselves to the Mother of the Endless Night.

6.20 Don't do, let the Dragon do!

Following this first initiation into the black dance, my life in the temple of Vulcan took a new direction. I woke up every morning before dawn, completed my Dragon's breath exercises, then joined Marek and his men for long hours of practice during which every single movement of the dance was rehearsed over and over again. Sometimes entire days or even entire weeks were dedicated to repeating the same short sequence. Especially in the first weeks and months, I spent many hours practising on the clay models, until I could instantly hit any of their gateways with my eyes closed.

Many of the dance's movements felt unnatural at first. They had been designed so that the only comfortable way of performing them was through the Dragon, not through the inclinations of the physical body. Marek gave few explanations but often exhorted me, *"Don't try, just let the Dragon flow!"* or, *"Don't do, let the Dragon do!"* or, *"No thoughts, just Dragon!"* And it worked wonders! I found myself accomplishing incredible sequences of movements that defied the laws of gravity. Whenever he asked me to do something which at first I thought impossible, Marek would yell at me, *"The Dragon knows no limits!"*

One of the most surprising facets of the training was that it was rarely tiring. The practices went on and on, starting before sunrise and finishing after sunset, with only a short break at lunchtime, yet there was no tiredness at the end of the day. During the first months, though, my body sometimes showed signs of fatigue. Each time Marek screamed, *"You are insulting the Dragon by trying to do the dance yourself, instead of letting her dance through you!"*

Because I was a beginner, I had to do many extra hours after the others left the room. Yet I was never bored. The process was fascinating. I enjoyed staying late in the afternoon or even at night, and as I went on and on bashing clay models and bags of turnips hanging from the ceiling, the words of Amaran often came alive in my memory, *"She is to be known through ecstasy!"* The dance became my worship of the Dragon, my way of making her blissful presence shine through my body. It not only made me vibrant with her life, but also less asleep than ever before.

Some of the exercises were so difficult that it took me weeks of effort to master them. Each time a new one was conquered, a vroofing wave of triumph arose inside me, and in the empty room a loud Dragon's yell followed, *"The Dragon is Victory! Victory to the Dragon!"* The She-Dragon was screaming through me, and the rock was my witness. I danced and danced, never having enough of the blissful waves of my Dragon-lover.

For several months I was never allowed to practise less than fifteen lawful feet from the other men. The reason was simple: one single Dragon-blow hitting one of the black gateways was enough to kill even a Great

6 – The Book of the Great Dragon of the Deep

Warrior. Instantly. So I had to train myself on the clay models, learning to stop my fists just on the edge of the gateways. For a long time the coordination of my movements was insufficient, and I made many dents on the mannequins. On numerous occasions I even blew them apart! At the end of my solitary evening of practice I had to reconstitute the statues and mend the holes with fresh clay. Every morning Marek came to inspect the mannequins, measuring my progress by a count of the freshly repaired and repainted zones.

Time passed. The dents became fewer and fewer. Yet I was still secluded in a separate area of the mat during the collective practices. I kept on relentlessly, sometimes staying so late that Marek would find me there when he arrived for a new day of work. But the more I grew in the Dragon, the less sleep my body required. Starting a new day after an entire night of practice was *no big deal in the Law*.

Finally one morning, Marek asked, "How many weeks now, since your last misguided blow?"

Narlond, who was very supportive of my efforts, answered for me, "At least twelve!"

Marek laughed, "The one twelve weeks ago was particularly worrying, though!" This was no understatement. My foot had hit the mannequin so badly it had completely blown it apart, beyond any hope of reconstruction. Marek turned towards Narlond, "Would you dance with this man, son?"

"Certainly I shall dance with him, Marek," the young man replied without hesitation.

Marek looked at me, "Narlond is a brave man, isn't he?" and we all laughed. Then suddenly, and in a tone that left no space for hesitation, Marek commanded, "Stand up, Warrior, I will be the first to black-dance with you!"

That day, for the first time, I danced with the master.

Totally fascinating. I couldn't take my eyes off him. His movements breathed with infinity. The Spirit of Lohrzen shone through him. His dance changed the space in the room, which the She-Dragon held and filled with magic as in the Ancient Days of the Earth.

None of the moves were new to me, as I had been rehearsing them day after day without interruption for nearly nine months. But gearing my Dragon energy into his revealed a completely new dimension of the art. There seemed to be no limit, I was flying with him, sometimes slowly, sometimes incredibly fast. At the same time I was completely held by the Dragon. During the past months I had learnt to let the Dragon flow through me, but this time I was *inside* the Dragon as in a cocoon of infinity. The slightest mistake on my part or his could have been fatal, yet I felt totally and utterly safe, and I knew that this protection was the essence of *the Endless Night, of which the Great She-Dragon is the mother*.

In the final movement of the dance, I let myself fall on the floor while Marek projected the forty blows as in the *ritual murder of one of the*

Nephilim. With astounding precision, his hands and feet stopped forty times at the very limit of my clothes. But had he killed me then, I knew I would have been received straight into the bosom of the Mother of the Endless Night, and enjoyed aeons of bliss in her light of infinity.

6.21 Fountain above, mountain below

From then on, the training took on a different character. I was allowed to follow the others in various exercises inside and outside the temple, and I no longer had to spend long hours in the practice hall at night. And I was free every Friday, when Marek and his men disappeared for practices that were not yet open to me. Yet there was nothing I found more enjoyable than the ritual dance. During my free time, I used to climb up to the top of the mountain and practise on the barren plateau lost in the mists. I danced and danced with just the same joy and elation as I had felt the very first time, when Var had to knock me down in the initiation crypt. But now my style had evolved and my worship of the She-Dragon soared through the moving perfection of the black dance.

It was passion.

Even though I had been relieved from full-time exercises, I spent a few more weeks doing nothing but dancing from morning to night. But late one afternoon just before sunset, while I was performing a slow motion sequence on the rocky mountaintop, I was struck by the clear fountain as if by lightning. It was a silent but extremely deep experience that left me totally immobilised. I felt as vast and stable as the mountain, and the clear fountain seemed to extend forever high in the spheres above me.

A voice inside called, "Gervin, what do you want me to do from here? Am I dangerous enough now? What else am I to learn from Lohrzen's mountain? When will I be able to return to Eisraim?"

I sat in meditation for a long time. No answer came to my mind, but a realignment took place. The thousands of hours spent Dragon-dancing had made my energy infinitely more solid and dense. I felt as if nothing in the seven spheres could shake me. I had roots extending *far inside the Earth, into the depths of the She-Dragon*. By resting on these roots, I discovered I could connect with the clear fountain with more lucidity than ever before.

It was a revelation. From this time on, the impulses of the fountain came to me with much greater sharpness and strength, illuminating me with living clarity.

I stood up and exclaimed, *"One Law, one way!"* Even though no particular direction seemed to be calling me, I knew I had forever shed a thick layer of my doubting nature.

In the silvery moonlight I found my way to the descending staircases, and decided the time had come to pay another visit to Amaran.

6 – The Book of the Great Dragon of the Deep

6.22 Underworld Further Down

Brother Amaran greeted me warmly. "A different man you have become indeed!" he commented. In the small space of his room, he started one of the slow sequences of black dance movements and asked me to join him. Our energies geared into one another, and he seemed to have as much joy dancing as I had. I was amazed to see such an old man – more than ninety years of age according to Floster – performing the dance just as well as I did. Amaran ended the sequence of movements in roaring laughter, "Ha! Ha! Ha! Ha! Ha!" and he invited me to sit by him. "Szar! How long since I last saw you, *my friend in the Law?*"

"Some ten lawful months, I guess."

"Well, son, these months have been well spent by you. *All glory to the She-Dragon, Mother of the Endless Night!* Now tell me, did you go down through the gates of the Dragon after I first took you?"

"Shame on me, *O wise man of the Law*, I have been so focussed on the black dance that I have not done anything else!"

"With Marek as your teacher, I can understand this, son. He is one of the fiercest Dragon lovers that ever led the Great Warriors – a joy to the She-Dragon herself."

"Amaran, I have come to ask if you would consider showing me the way to the Underworld again."

Amaran was delighted. "What has happened to the fearsome little boy who had to think before committing himself to another descent?"

I smiled, grounding myself in a way that made me feel the Dragon throughout the rock of the mountain, and the clear fountain high up in the spheres. The fountain spoke through me, "Deep are the Underworlds indeed, and the Lord Melchisedek knows what can be found at the bottom of the ladder. Perhaps because I am very unwise, I now feel more curious than fearsome about descending."

"Ha! Ha! Ha! Ha! Ha! How about descending right now, *man of the Law?*"

My face lit up with joy, *"Praise the Lord Melchisedek!* I could not have hoped for better than this." And off we went to the Dragon's gate which was just round the corner from his bedroom.

"This time," Amaran advised, "sit with me close to the centre of the cave. Let the Dragon keep your body straight while you go down. That's the way the Warriors descend."

I did as he said and tuned into the magnificent breeze of the gate. Wriggling my nostrils as he had shown me ten months before, I took a long breath, drawing in the atmosphere of the gate and making every cell of my body tingle. "Amaran, before we go down there is something I want to tell you. I *love* the She-Dragon. I love her passionately, and a bit more every day. Thanks to the direction you pointed me in last time we descended, all these months of training have been pure bliss. It has been like being in her arms, all the time. May the Lord Melchisedek thank you for what you gave me that day."

Amaran's face was glowing, "*All glory to the She-Dragon*, son. There is another thing I would like you to understand now. But let us waste no time, the Dragon is waiting for us."

This time he did not give me any instructions, I just tuned into the breeze and followed it to its source. Instantly, Amaran and I were standing in an immense cavern with silvery-reddish shimmering walls.

"O my Lord Melchisedek," I whispered, "it looks like orichalc. All the walls, even the ceiling!"

Amaran took no notice of my amazement. "See! I told you you could descend on your own any time."

Not wanting him to think I was trying to contradict him in any way, I quickly answered, "I believe you, wise man! I believe you." I waited a moment. "But how will I know which cavern to go to?"

I noticed that as soon as he was in the Underworld, Amaran started wriggling his nostrils a lot. "Just go as you please, son. As long as you do not go down too deep, there is nothing for you to worry about." He started walking at his habitual pace, and I rushed behind him, taking in the dazzling scenery.

"The light here is unbelievable!" I tried to touch with my hand the myriads of reddish-silvery light specks that created the atmosphere of the cave. It was not long before we reached an even greater cavern.

"Look!" Amaran pointed to a stream on the left, "this is a river of liquid orichalc. Do you like the way it shines?"

Astonished, I couldn't find words to answer him. But soon I had to race behind him again, striding the way he did. The specks of light became even thicker as we went on, like silvery fireflies dancing all around us. Yet the air was perfectly pure – a delight to breathe! It was more satisfying and filling than any food on Earth, and sweet like Elyani's white drinks.

"How come we are not seeing anyone?" I asked. "Am I missing something? Should I be looking for threshold keepers?"

"There certainly are threshold keepers around here, but they would not show you much more than you are already seeing. To meet the inhabitants of the Underworld you must descend deeper. Much deeper. It's so much more beautiful when you reach further down, why would anyone want to live here?"

Amaran stopped at a pile of black stones. "Ah! Here is what I was looking for. This is one of the best spirits of antimony to be found in the entire kingdom. It can work wonders." He grabbed a black pebble the size of a cherry and showed it to me. Before I had time to take a proper look, he thrust the pebble into the skin of my left cheek, just in the area of my birthmark. It created such a violent burning that I had to call on the Dragon to stay on my feet, and I let out a muffled yell.

6 – The Book of the Great Dragon of the Deep

"Don't worry, the pain won't last long. And in a few days you'll have a good surprise when you look at yourself. Come on, let's move."

I made the Dragon move my body and followed Amaran while I was gathering my spirits. For a few minutes I was extremely dizzy. It made me remember all those rituals when I had embarrassed Gervin by collapsing in a heap. As my body kept trotting along, I expressed my gratitude to the Mother of the Endless Night, hoping such embarrassment would never be repeated.

Amaran stopped, "Come on, Great Warrior, there is a gate of the Dragon nearby. Can you tell me where?"

I tried to wriggle my nostrils like he did, and extended my nose-ness through the wafting silvery specks. "I sense a breeze down there!" I pointed to the right.

"Very good!" Amaran had already set off in that direction. Almost running behind him, I caught a glimpse of a silvery stream. "Wait! Can I stop for some water of life?"

"No, you'll find much better where we are going next."

We soon reached a corner of the cavern where I recognised the typical ascending breeze of a gate of the Dragon.

"This time we are going to descend much deeper," Amaran announced.

"Will we see any of the caverns of sickness where souls are suffering?"

"No, no! Those are much higher up than where we are at the moment. You are still thinking of your Vivyani, aren't you?"

I looked at him but did not answer.

"Come on," he said, "this time it's better if you follow me closely."

I let myself glide down the breeze behind him, and the descent went on for as long as twenty or thirty seconds, whereas our first slip down had taken less than one second.

The cavern we landed in was so gigantic that I could discern neither walls nor ceiling. All I could see was an awe-inspiring golden light. The metallic looking ground itself shone like pure gold. Just contemplating this light filled my heart with wonder and reverence. I remembered the feeling I had had when first beholding the fields of stars, amazed that such beauty could remain unknown to nearly everyone in the kingdom.

Profoundly moved, I felt the need to ask, "Is this the Bottom of the Underworlds, Amaran?"

The old man smiled, "Oh, no! Not at all. And this is precisely what I want you to understand. The Deepest Underworlds are still aeons below us. Come," he said, "let us walk!" and he went forth.

I was so captivated by my contemplation of the light that I had to bring myself back to race after Amaran again.

"This place is more than ten times the size of the entire kingdom," Amaran went on explaining, "and yet it's but one of hundreds and hundreds of such spaces. The deeper down you go, the more beautiful they become."

As in my early days with Gervin, I knew there were many questions that might have been asked, but I could not figure out a single one. I just trod the golden ground, enraptured, speechless. We kept advancing till we arrived at a river.

I was astounded. "Amaran, it's massive! I can't recall seeing such an enormous river anywhere in the kingdom."

"Let us sit. If you wish to drink some of the water of life, now is the right time."

"I just can't believe what I'm seeing! Could I even swim in this river?"

"You sure could, son. But if I were you, before jumping in I would first have a sip."

I plunged my hand into the crystalline stream. When the water reached my lips, I was even more amazed, "Oh! Oh my Lord Melchisedek!" I let myself collapse gently onto the golden shore close to Amaran and raised my arms upwards, "Oooh!" The taste of this water triggered such waves of overwhelming bliss that for a long while the only thing I could do was laugh. Verses of the hymn to the Great Dragon that Amaran had taught me during our last descent came back to my memory,

"She is to be known through ecstasy.
The giver of endless pleasure.
There is more delight in her
Than a man can comprehend in a hundred lives."

"Can you see the danger in swimming in a river like this?" Amaran chuckled. "Look at how you feel after drinking only a sip. Jump into it and it might take an aeon before you feel an inclination to come out!"

Intoxicated, I kept being shaken by soft, blissful spasms of laughter.

"Stand up, Warrior!" Amaran suddenly interrupted. "Here they come!"

The order had been spoken with a voice like Marek's. I instantly let the Dragon pull me upright and took position for the black dance.

"No, no! There is nothing to be afraid of. Just watch!"

"Far Underworld! What is that?"

Right in front of us, on the other side of the vast river, a contingent of giant golden snakes was approaching the water. Because the river was so wide – at least a thousand lawful feet – it was difficult to appreciate exactly how large the strange beasts were, but they were at least as tall as Amaran and I, and maybe ten times as long. There were as many as fifty or sixty of them, slowly gliding, squirming their way to the shore.

What a sight! My fascination made Amaran laugh. "They are called the Nagas. They are the inhabitants of this world. You don't have to worry, they won't cross the river. They've just come to drink. Anyhow, the Nagas are very friendly, there is nothing to fear from them. If you happen to get close you can even talk to them. They are extremely smart."

"Amaran, is it lawful to get drunk here, or should I try to remain in control?"

6 – The Book of the Great Dragon of the Deep

"Lose control, by all means! How could you fully enjoy the bliss if you remained in control?"

I looked at him and started laughing in a silly way again. Then motion took over my body and I began one of the most fantastic black dances I had ever performed. And I laughed and laughed, completely losing touch with time.

"*Great Warriors, great lovers!*" Amaran stood up and danced with me for a while, until he decided, "Come on, son, let us return to the kingdom."

I giggled and kept dancing around him, wanting to play.

"Where do you think the nearest gate of the Dragon is?" he asked.

Still dancing, I wriggled my nostrils and tuned in. When I located the unmistakable feeling of a breeze, I launched a furious assault that I terminated by throwing my right fist in the direction of the gate and making myself Dragon-motionless.

"Correct, son. Let us go."

I danced my way behind him.

When we reached the Dragon's gate, Amaran raised an eyebrow. "Now can we be serious a minute?"

"Of course!" I tossed out, but I couldn't stop laughing.

"Well, well..." Amaran sighed, "just try to remember my words, you will ponder on them later. When you travel back from the Underworlds, you do not need to return via the same Dragon gate you descended from. The breeze of one gate can take you to another one. You can move from cavern to cavern through more than twenty different gates and yet be carried straight back to the first one while flowing with the breath of the last one. Now follow me."

"Vooh! Vooh!" As we went up, I kept making silly noises.

Twenty seconds later I was back in my body, but not completely in my mind. Even though I had left it in the middle of the cave, not leaning against a wall, my body was still sitting in a perfectly upright meditation position – just as I had left it. I was glad to see the power of the Dragon had worked while I was travelling. Yet the first thing I did was to lie down on the rock, lift up my arms, and laugh. "I love it, Amaran. I love it! I love it! I love it!"

In a deep Son-of-the-Dragon voice, Amaran quoted his Law, "*Great Warrior, great lover. The She-Dragon's embrace is equalled by no other bliss.*" Then he pulled me by the hand and said, "Come on, Great Warrior! It is late. How about I walk you back to your room?"

And I danced behind him all the way.

After only an hour's sleep, I woke up completely refreshed, ready to enjoy a new day of practice with Marek. The taste of the water of life remained clear in my energy for at least a week. And a few days later, as I brushed my hand against my left cheek, I noticed I could no longer feel the birthmark. I was so surprised that as soon as I had some free time, I rushed to the warehouse and looked at myself in *the* temple's mirror.

"Far Underworld!"
The large birthmark was gone. It never came back.

6.23 From fear of death to death of fear

The training with Marek and his men went on and on.

There were still entire days – sometimes entire weeks – spent bashing sandbags hanging from the ceiling, hitting gateways on clay mannequins while blindfolded, and worshipping the Great Dragon through the black dance.

There were more and more exercises aimed at pushing the physical body to its extreme limits by accomplishing special movements that defied gravity and could only be performed from the Dragon. Sometimes we had to keep practising for days and nights without any sleep, or spend several days without drinking. Marek made us climb mountains and run for hours and hours in the desert in the summer heat. We descended and practised the black dance inside the bowels of the Dragon, where the lungs can no longer breathe as they do on the surface of the Earth, and where the only way to survive is to tap from the Dragon's breath. Anything that seemed physically impossible was welcome. It was an opportunity to *let the Dragon do*.

Whenever one of his men thought a particular exercise was impossible, Marek the Indestructible lashed out with the Voice, "*There are no limits to the Dragon!*" or, "You are insulting the She-Dragon by trying to do it yourself instead of letting her do." At other times he'd shout, "It is not going to kill you, because you are already dead! You died in the Dragon when you were in the crypt!"

A lot of the training had to do with accomplishing things immediately, without thinking: "*Sheer Dragon, no thoughts!*" It was extremely easy, for instance, to run along a thin, narrow log that bridged across a canyon – provided one *let the Dragon do*. But if the thought of the precipice was allowed to enter the mind, then... the Good Lord Melchisedek knows what might have happened! The same applied to a whole range of practices such as black-dancing blindfold on the cliffs, diving deep into the swirling eddies of muddy underground streams, or thrusting one's hand into the fire without being burnt.

A particularly worrying practice consisted of being hit on the 'cheap way out' gateways in a fashion that would render anyone unconscious, and then immediately standing up again, releasing the sheer power of the Dragon.

"*There is no fear for him who is already dead,*" was one of Marek's refrains. The most spectacular demonstration of this principle was delivered to me one morning, when I found myself hesitating before running through a fire. We had been taught special techniques that made it possible to repel heat and create energy corridors through fire. Thus walking on hot coals or

6 – The Book of the Great Dragon of the Deep

even crossing a pyre were safe practices, actually exhilarating. But this fire looked very big to me. I wondered how my physical body could cope with such heat.

When he saw me pausing, Marek yelled at me, "You Nephilim fodder! *You think, you die!* One second of doubt and a Hunter will blow your head off! When are you going to understand that the fire can't kill you? You are *already* dead!"

As I didn't immediately make a move, he turned to Narlond and ordered, "Do the points of Lohrzen on him!"

The points of Lohrzen were three extremely dangerous gateways located on the chest, and part of the lethal black forty. Anyone hit there died in a matter of seconds. *No thoughts, just Dragon,* Narlond instantly leapt towards me and delivered the three lethal blows. I was so stunned that I did not even think of defending myself, and I collapsed on the sand.

Before I had time to wonder whether I was dead, Marek projected full Voice intensity at me, "Now, get up! *Let the Dragon do!*" And the Dragon raised my body so quickly that I was flabbergasted.

"Do you understand?" Marek screamed at me. "You are dead! You have been dead ever since you heard the thunder of the Earth! Now run through the fire! *Just do it!*" And I found myself on the other side of the fire in a matter of seconds.

As I was to learn later, being hit on lethal gateways was not the kind of activity to indulge in too often. But that day, it worked a miracle for me. As I emerged out of the flames, a Dragon feeling arose inside me, "*Victory over death! Victory over death!*" I started dancing with joy, worshiping the Mother of the Endless Night. Narlond's blows had heavily shocked my body. I had the completely unreal sensation that I was *really* dead – and yet the power of the Dragon kept moving me.

The experience was incredibly liberating. In one second I realised that all people carry a fear of death from the very day they are born, and that all fears are but offshoots of this root-fear of death. From their first to their last breath, every single emotion, every single move, every single choice is influenced by this fear. There is not one single moment in a life that is not tainted by it, which was why I had never realised how tight the grip was. Black-dancing slowly on the dunes, I shouted towards heaven, "I *am* dead! What could there be to fear? I *am* dead!"

It became clear that during my first death, in the Underworld caverns of sickness, a great deal of the fear was dropped. Then a deeper layer was shed when dying in the bowels of the Dragon. But until this day, there had remained a basal hue of fear deeply ingrained in my body. Thanks to Marek, prince of teachers, that layer had now been shed like an old skin. A huge weight had been taken off my shoulders. Never had I felt the clear fountain above my head with such clarity.

For the first time, I realised the spiritual dimension of being fearless. When the sages said, "*Fear not, man of the Law!*" what they really meant was that as long as one is entangled in the web of fear, one can never know the heart of the Law. Thus one of the deepest meanings of the initiatory dimension of death was revealed to me.

After this I had to take a few days off from the training, as some healing was needed to rearrange my gateways and restart the life force in the physical body. Marek came to visit me and projected the power of his Voice onto the points of Lohrzen. To help the recovery process I made a few quick descents on my own into the easy-to-reach lapis lazuli Underworld. There I bathed my body in sweet lakes of waters of life.

6.24 Marek the Indestructible

One evening after finishing a training day with his team, Marek came to inspect the life force in my gateways. He immediately picked up that I had just returned from a gate of the Dragon. He seemed pleased, "Did Amaran show you how to do that?"

"Yes, Marek!"

"There are powers down there that go beyond anything men can imagine," he mused. He was in an unusually talkative mood. I listened silently, making sure I did not interrupt his flow or irritate him with one of my questions. "When you go back into the world," he continued, "always remember that if you ever get into deep trouble, or if you need to do something *really* impossible, this is where you should be looking to: *the infinite glory of the Underworlds*. The deeper down you go, the more incredible things you will find."

Pausing, Marek contemplated his left fist, slowly clenching and opening it as he liked to do. "Once, when I was a young Warrior and did not yet know about the Word which is the Deepest Mystery of the Earth, I was sent by the prince of the Red Lands to accomplish a mission in the northern lands. There I was chased by three Nephilim Hunters. Powerful men!" his voice expressed respect, not anger. "And great masters in the power of the Point and the magic of the Flying Dragons." Marek stopped to collect his memories, still gazing at his left fist.

"For seventeen days and sixteen nights they pursued me, using the most formidable of their hunting methods. They call it the 'triangular net'. It has cost the lives of many of our Warriors. I tapped from all the cunning my teacher had taught me, and I used about every single weapon and device of the Lesser Magic of the Earth, which you'll soon be learning. But nothing would make the Hunters let go of me. Finally, on the evening of the seventeenth day, I got caught in their 'net' – nothing like a fisherman's net, I assure you. It's a particular influence that the Hunters release through the power of the Point. Once you're caught in the net, there is no escape.

6 – The Book of the Great Dragon of the Deep

It was just after sunset. When I saw that in a matter of hours the Hunters would be on me, I looked for a gate of the Dragon. When I found one, I used a trick. Had I just lain down or even sat, the Hunters would have had suspicions – Nephilim Hunters are excessively intelligent. So I called onto the Great Dragon of no limits, and I let her black-dance my body while I descended through the gate.

You know how deep down into the Underworlds one can go in just a few seconds, Szar. Well, I kept falling with the blissful breezes for more than six hours, until I found myself in such thick light that I could move no further. There I gathered all the Spirit of Life I could, and I reascended. The Hunters, of course, had found my body and not only 'killed' me, but inflicted such damage as no one would consider reparable. This is their ritual procedure when killing a Great Warrior, just as we have a precise way of terminating the life of a Nephilim through the black forty. But they didn't realise that they had left my body – or what was left of it – right on a Dragon's gate.

When I came back from below I brought a formidable bubble of life with me, and I threw it into my body. It was not enough to restart the vital functions, but it kept my body from decaying. Then I spent weeks going up and down, bringing water of life and precious gems from our Mother's womb into my body, until most of the organs had been reconstituted and finally I could get it to move. It took time though. For at least a week the only thing I could do was flex my left fist."

"Marek the Indestructible!" I thought.

"This is how I met your teacher, Szar, nearly eighteen years ago. I made my way back towards the south, but I couldn't get rid of the imprint the net had left on me. It kept me half-paralysed, and at times made me completely lose control over my body. It gave me searing headaches that only the She-Dragon could soothe. As I was going through the county of Eisraim, I met a controller who told me of a great master in the power of the Point and the magic of the Flying Dragons. He kindly offered to take me to the temple. And do you know the first thing Gervin did when he heard my story?"

"He laughed?" I suggested, touching my beard and remembering my master.

"Exactly, son! Gervin burst out laughing so loudly, I will never forget the sound of it. Then he invited me to stay at his temple and he did a lot of work on me, every night. At first he gave me a room close to his apartments, but soon I found my way to a powerful Dragon gate. Despite the fact it happened to be in the female part of the temple, they were good enough to let me stay in a room just near it. Everyone was extremely kind. But what a weird place, over there! While Gervin was implementing his healing techniques on me I was having unbelievable dreams. All these women who worked with him kept giving me weird beverages, so I never knew exactly where the dreams were coming from. Anyhow, after three months of Gervin's good treatment combined with the water of life I drew from the Dragon gate, I was completely free from the effects of the net, renewed and fresh. From there, I had no difficulty coming back home."

I wondered what impression Marek had left on the delicate priestesses of Eisraim. A Great Warrior like him, rough and roughly indestructible, sounded so out of place in the exquisitely refined atmosphere of the female wing. There were bound to be stories about this.

Seeing Marek was in such an open mood, I risked a question I had wanted to ask him for a long time, "Do you know what it is that Master Gervin wants me to learn here?"

"What were his orders?"

"He said he wanted me to become dangerous. Apart from that..."

Marek chuckled, "Yes, I remember, the man is not always easy to follow. My teacher in the Dragon used to say, 'That's what the power of the Point does to people!' And, 'Whenever you think you understand what a master of the Point means, you should immediately wonder what else it was that he *really* meant.' Szar, you must have had some difficult times learning from Gervin."

"Mm..." I agreed, still holding my chin.

Marek was deep in thought. "*Dragon below, Dragon above!* You see, Szar, in the south of the kingdom there are a number of Warriors who know the Earth-She-Dragon of the Deep and who, from beneath, can blast about anything with the thunder of the Earth. In the counties of the north, on the other hand, there are wizards who have mastered the Point and other mind-blowing powers such as those of the Flying Dragons. But altogether there must be very few people who know about both ends of the ladder, and who have died both in the Dragon above and in the Dragon below. Have no doubt about it, son, if Gervin has taken you as his disciple, he will overtrain you in the power of the Point. But while you are here with us, apart from the black dance, he probably expects you to master the weapons of the Lesser Magic of the Earth."

I knew only too well that if I asked another question at that stage, Marek was likely to withdraw. So I just kept eye contact with him, holding onto the clear fountain with all the grounding of Lohrzen's mountain.

Marek looked at me for some time with the dangerous smile he had inherited as part of Lohrzen's powers – the legacy of the Warriors' tradition, uninterruptedly transmitted from master to disciple for thousands of years. Finally, he explained, "The Lesser Magic of the Earth contains redoubtable weapons that can annihilate many an enemy. It includes things like the smell power used by the Warriors to detect the Nephilim, and even their Hunters, as far as a hundred miles away. The Lesser Magic is lesser in name only, as opposed to the Deepest Mystery, which is the thunder of the Earth – the most profound level of the Voice, the one which can overcome anything, but which can also bring great dangers, and thus is virtually never used."

6 – The Book of the Great Dragon of the Deep

This time, I *had* to ask, "Would you say the thunder of the Earth is the most dangerous of all the teachings of Lohrzen?"

Marek laughed, "It is indeed, son. But if you want to conquer this power, you will have to stay with us for another twelve years at least!"

"Mm..." Dragon fearlessness or not, I wondered what would happen to Elyani if I remained away for another twelve years.

"For now," Marek concluded, "why don't you go and ask brother Drluck to teach you the art of smell? I know it won't be difficult for you –at least three times in the last months I have noticed the quiver in your nostrils that told me that brother Amaran had already passed the power onto you."

How not to admire a man who could notice a nostrils' wriggle while conducting the black dance of fifteen Warriors.

Without notice Marek leapt up in his feline way and left the room. "Don't forget to turn up to the dining hall tonight," he tossed as he crossed the doorway. "Today is Lubu's Full Moon, and we're celebrating."

"Floster sort of warned me already," I answered.

Adding a touch of irony to his dangerous smile, he said, "I will see you then... brother!"

6.25 Lubu and the three ugly Nephilim sisters

That night, everyone in the temple had converged in the dining hall. I was sitting with Marek and his men, and from where I was I could see Var the high priest in the middle of a party of a dozen people who were all laughing. Even Amaran was there, and other brethren who rarely came out of their cavern. Everyone was enjoying the charcoaled meal, talking loudly, Dragon-joking and letting out rolling laughter. On special occasions of this kind there were as many as one hundred and fifty people in the hall, and following the strict rule of the temple, not one woman among them.

Marek downed his cup in one go and turned towards me, "I hope they have warned you that you are going to be Lubu tonight?"

"They have, master Marek. But I wish they could have told me some of the story so I could prepare myself a bit!"

"No, no!" Marek insisted, "That would spoil it for you. Lubu's part always falls on *he among the Great Warriors who was last initiated.* So goes the custom."

"I hate to deprive Narlond of this lawful privilege," I said.

"Not at all, brother Szar," Narlond promptly answered. "This lawful privilege has fallen on me twice already. That's Dragon-plenty for me!"

Everyone laughed and Marek added, "We've all done it, you know, even myself!" He stood up, pushed his head forwards and looked around him, taking on a soft, innocent attitude that was so unlike him that it triggered an explosion of laughter in all the parties around.

A voice rose among the Warriors, "No, no! Alferro has never been Lubu."

Alferro was the tallest of Marek's gang.

"That's because at the time he was still so dead in the Dragon that we couldn't even get him to do the swearing bit," another voice joined in.

"My body had just been taken back from the death crypt, but *I* was still down there." His eyes wide open, Alferro gazed straight in front of him, as if deeply entranced, and jerked his way around the group like a puppet.

"We all tried to tell him, '*Don't swear, Alferro, let the Dragon swear through you!*' But there was no way! Ha! Ha! Ha! Ha! Ha!"

When the signal for the end of the meal was given, all the men gathered in a large semicircle while the storyteller for that night stood in the middle. He was Pelissor, a man in his early sixties with long white hair like Amaran's, and a short grey beard. I had already heard him tell captivating stories in the dining hall, but never to such a large audience.

"My brethren in the Dragon," he began as the room became quiet, "tonight I will tell you the story of Lubu the Great Warrior..." Pelissor paused for everyone to applaud and then went on, "and of how he succumbed to and finally triumphed over the Nephilim monster Bobros, son of Bobros, and his three ugly Nephilim sisters." Everyone booed loudly, and yells of disgust rang out.

"Death to the Nephilim!" an old brother shouted.

"Yeh! Let's kill them all!" the brethren drummed on the tables.

"Yeh! We'll certainly kill the ones in the story," Pelissor raised his left fist in the ritual way, and the crowd approved loudly. "I will now call on Szar, *he among the Great Warriors who was last initiated*, to be Lubu for us tonight."

As I approached the improvised stage, all the brethren clapped their hands and shouted encouragement.

Pelissor began his story. "Lubu, as you know, was a pure and gentle youth who had just been through the death in the Dragon. His way of performing the black dance was so innocent that when he practised in the fields the birds used to come and watch him, they were so touched by him." Pelissor gave me a sign, indicating I was to act Lubu's part.

I started the black dance, trying to figure out how to bring an 'innocent' and 'touching' air to the deadly art. I accentuated the movements of my wrists, adopted a child-like face and kept looking up towards the sky with my mouth wide open. And I stopped from time to time, letting out a long sigh. Meanwhile the brethren were all whistling, mimicking loud birds' noises.

"Then one day..." Pelissor's tone turned authoritative to restore silence, "then one day, Lubu's teacher instructed him that the time had come to go out into the world and kill one of the Nephilim." Pelissor looked at Marek and clicked his fingers.

6 – The Book of the Great Dragon of the Deep

Marek leapt forwards like a panther, triggering a loud "Ouuuh!" from the audience. In three jumps, he landed close to me. He moved his lips as if he was talking fast, filling the space with exuberant gestures. Then he pointed his index finger to the right, made another leap, and demonstrated the ritual way of hitting the black forty in five seconds.

Everyone shouted, "Youyouyouyou..!"

Marek went back to sit with his party of friends and Pelissor continued, "These were the days when Bobros the Nephilim giant used to live in the county. This rogue, this dirt, this scum among the Nephilim used to enjoy a diet of human flesh, and he would send his three ugly sisters to steal babies, which he appreciated more than any other dish."

"*Sweet Lord Melchisedek!*" I stared at him. "What kind of story is this?"

Everyone was booing and making unlawful derogatory gestures.

It went on and on. "Bobros the giant ate child after child, but he was never satiated. After twelve years – and *thousands* of babies – he decided, 'I want something more... Ah, what could bring me satisfaction? I know! If I could eat babies of my own kind, that would satisfy me!' But Bobros was too much of a coward to take the risk of sending his sisters to steal Nephilim children, which would have brought the anger of the Hunters upon him. So he told the girls, 'You will go and make me three Nephilim babies that you will bring to me as soon as they come out of your womb.'"

There was a pause to allow the brethren to express their disgust – which indeed they did, in very graphic fashion.

"The sisters were terrified," Pelissor went on, "If they did not obey the order, Bobros might succumb to one of his murderous rages and slaughter them – perhaps even eat them alive. But they were so ugly and foul smelling that they could not imagine how any man, even one of the Nephilim, would ever want to touch them. So they used the mischievous cunning of their kind. Now, there happened to be a particular baby girl whom they had stolen from her parents seventeen years earlier. She was so lovely and special that even the three ugly sisters could not resolve to throw her to Bobros. So they hid her and fed her ass's milk, and as she grew up they kept her in a tree house in the forest behind Bobros' dwelling. The sisters being, moreover, quite silly, they called the girl Verzaza."

The fact of having listened to the same story every year for decades was *no problem in the Law*! Hearing the pun on the name of Verzazyel the Watcher, the audience could not contain themselves and exploded with laughter, some of the brethren even rolling on the floor.

When some order was restored, Pelissor pursued, "Verzaza was now a beautiful, charming young woman. The three ugly sisters thought, 'let her attract a man into Verzazyel's cave. In the bewitched atmosphere he won't be able to recognise a thing, and he will embrace us, and we will bear children.' To this end they prepared a potion made of herbs of madness, and they gave it to Verzaza to drink before taking her to the cave."

His audience thoroughly captivated, Pelissor went on, "It just happened to be around the time when the innocent Lubu was walking in the red canyons, not far from the cave of Verzazyel the Watcher." The storyteller signalled with his hand, and I started walking around, waving my arms and looking towards the sky with my mouth wide open.

"When they saw him, such a fragile and pure youth, the three ugly Nephilim sisters all had the same thought, 'Ehey! Here is our victim!' and they sent Verzaza towards him. Verzaza, who had lost her mind from drinking the herbs of madness, said to Lubu, 'Oh beautiful man, will you marry me?'"

Floster, who despite all the good work the She-Dragon had done on me, was still one head taller than me and nearly twice as large, leapt on the scene and crossed his arms in front of his chest, playing the role of the enamoured Verzaza. He acted so well that I could not contain myself, collapsing with laughter together with the audience.

Pelissor took on the sweet voice of the maid, "'O beautiful man, will you follow me to my house, that my family may meet you and give you presents?'"

While Floster was putting on the seductive smile of a seventeen-year-old enchantress, the Sons of the Dragon were all shouting, "No! Lubu!", "Don't go!", "Be careful, Lubu!" As I was slow to respond, Floster grabbed my shoulder vigorously with his huge hand and started pulling me as if towards the cave. The audience shouted in fear, more loudly than ever, "No! It's a trap!", "Run away, Lubu!"

After this minute of intense action the narration resumed, "As soon as he entered Verzazyel's cave, Lubu was caught in the deceiving magic of the three ugly Nephilim sisters, believing that he was already married to Verzaza. Then one of the sisters came to him..."

Mountain-Floster disappeared and was replaced by another priest even larger than him.

Pelissor took on an old lady's trembling, squirting voice, "'Lubu-ka, will you not come to me and embrace me and give me a son?' And our young brother, who believed that the beautiful Verzaza was calling him, gave joy to the first sister and she conceived a daughter."

I was unsure of what I was supposed to do at that stage, but it did not really matter, as the entire audience was busy shouting the ritual "Youyouyouyou..!" at such a volume that the cavern's walls were trembling.

When he could make himself heard again, Pelissor went on, "Just after this, the second sister arrived and cheated the youth once more, 'Lubu-ka, will you not come to me and embrace me and give me a son?' Our brother, who was strong, gave joy to the woman and she conceived a daughter."

The audience let out a second wave of "Youyouyouyou...", just as loud as the first.

"Then the third sister came in and *again* Lubu was cheated. 'Lubu-ka, will you not come to me and embrace me and give me a son?' Our brother,

6 – The Book of the Great Dragon of the Deep

who was very strong, gave joy to the woman and she conceived a daughter." There was a third wave of the ritual scream.

"And the three sisters were satisfied, and they went back to Bobros' house. But then..."

This time the clamour of the brethren's ritual yells was so deafening that I almost had to plug my ears.

"Then..." Pelissor finally resumed, "Verzaza, who had been forgotten in the cave, came to him. And she said, 'Lubu-ka, will you not come to me and embrace me and give me a son?' Our brother, who knew that *there are no limits to the Dragon*, gave joy to the woman, and for nine months they remained together in the cave." To try to make everyone happy, I raised my left fist victoriously, as in the ritual salute of the Sons of the Dragon. The audience responded with such a stupendous "Youyouyouyou..!" that the mountain seemed to be shaking.

When he could make himself heard, Pelissor asked, "Do you know what happened after nine months?"

The fact that they all knew the story by heart did not matter at all. Following the Atlantean way, the brethren shouted, "No! What?", "Tell us!", "Tell us, Pelissor, we want to know!"

"After nine months, the first sister gave birth to a little girl. Bobros ate her and found her delicious – the best baby he had ever tasted. The day after, the second sister gave birth, and Bobros ate a second baby girl. And on the third day, he devoured the third baby. But then..." There was a pause to allow expressions of disgust, "but then on the fourth day, when he furiously demanded another baby just as tasty, the sisters suddenly remembered that they had forgotten Verzaza in the cave. They thought, 'If Verzaza conceived a child with Lubu and if the baby has been cooked by the magic of Verzazyel's cave for nine months, then surely its taste will satisfy Bobros.' So the three rushed to the cave, and there... what did they discover?"

The storyteller was promptly answered, "Tell us, Pelissor!", "Please, tell us, quick!", "We can't wait to know!"

"The embrace of Lubu and Verzaza was still going on, and the gods had woven a golden web around them to protect them. The light which came from the web was so magnificent that the three Nephilim sisters were entranced. They could not take their eyes away, and they stood still for a long, long, long time.

Meanwhile Bobros became impatient, and went to search for them in the cave. When he saw that his sisters were standing still instead of hunting babies for him, Bobros became so mad that he killed them, one after the other, by biting their throat with his teeth. Then he approached the web and kicked it so hard that it shattered. Lubu at once woke up, and stood up in the cave. When he saw the three ugly sisters lying dead on the floor, he realised he had been cheated. And then what did Lubu do?"

Stamping the rhythm on the floor with their feet and combining all their voices into one loud hammering, the brethren began chorusing, "He swore!

He swore! He swore!" It lasted some time, and then there followed a silence. Everyone was looking at me.

"Oh my Lord Melchisedek!" I thought. "Inspire me!" Then I slowly raised my arms and opened my mouth, as if I was about to let out a Dragon's scream. Slowly, deeply, and with as much volume as I possibly could, I roared, "Underworld! Underworld's Bottom and Underworld Further Down!"

Everyone clapped their hands, "Well done, Lubu!", "Excellent!"

Then Pelissor delivered the end of the story. "Furious, Lubu jumped in the air. Bobros, amazed and aghast, discovered that our youth was an adept of the black dance. He tried to defend himself, but the Warrior knocked him down flat like a bag of turnips and killed him in the ritual way."

I rehearsed the final stage of the black dance to the applause and jubilation of the audience.

After the last "Youyouyouyou..." Pelissor concluded, "Verzaza finally woke up and Lubu soon had a baby boy – a baby who had been matured inside Verzazyel's cave for nine months, and who therefore displayed supernatural abilities. Now this, of course, is another story."

The brethren all stood up to acclaim Pelissor. After a long ovation during which the mountain trembled, the assembled Sons of the Dragon, carried by the high elation, began a wild Dragon's dance.

6.26 Smell of the Nephilim

Marek had told me I would find brother Drluck on one of the terraces of the red cliff. By now I had explored every nook and cranny of the mountain, climbed up and down its stairways and over all its terraces many times, for the fun of exercising. It did not take me long to locate Drluck.

He was contemplating the mists, standing with his back against the rock. He had dark hair and black eyes, like most people in the county of the Red Lands. His body was strong and heavy like that of the Warriors, but the first thing that impressed me was his huge moustache and bushy eyebrows. Seeing his short hair and beard – a hallmark of the Great Warriors – I suddenly wondered if I was doing something wrong by letting my hair grow. I had to tie it up when I practised the black dance, but the rest of the time I enjoyed feeling the thick moving mass of hair. Each time I moved my head, the curly locks swept my shoulders – a sensation that made my kidney feel strong.

With the ritual recognition signs, I lawfully addressed Drluck, *"Praise the She-Dragon, Mother of the Endless Night, brother Drluck!"*

"All glory to the Mother of the Endless Night, Szar, my friend in the Dragon. Congratulations on your performance last night! The swearing bit was especially good."

6 – The Book of the Great Dragon of the Deep

I preferred to pass quickly over this. I gave him a polite smile, "Master Marek the Indestructible told me there is no one better than you to instruct me in the art of smell."

Drluck looked at me for a moment. Then, turning to the mists again, he said, "One thing about the Nephilim scum is... they stink! You can smell them miles and miles away. There, for instance..." Drluck pointed towards the east, "there is a group of Nephilim. At least forty of them."

That sounded amazing. "You mean you can smell them?"

He answered in one of those Warriors' cool tones that left no space for hesitation, "Come on, do it with me. Extend your perception into the space."

I spread my consciousness into darkness visible.

"Right!" he said, "Now, follow me in this direction. Yes, like that! Now, smell the space. Smell what comes from this direction."

My eyes closed, I wriggled my nostrils like Amaran had taught me and breathed in. I could immediately perceive a distinct vibration in darkness visible. Drluck tuned into what I was feeling. Satisfied that my perception was correct, he said, "Right in the Dragon, son. That's what it smells like. And make no mistake, it's an ugly smell of death. Whenever you detect it, you must kill or be killed."

Drluck's tone was disturbingly cold. I wasn't looking forward to finding myself face to face with one of the Nephilim monsters.

"You'll have to learn some smarter ways of doing the smelling business. Otherwise the Nephilim Hunters will immediately identify you and locate you. Here it doesn't matter, you're cosily tucked away on Mount Lohrzen. But if you're hunting or being hunted..." he looked at me with the Warriors' dangerous smile, "*Farewell, man of the Law!*"

"But what do the Nephilim look like? Are they all giants?"

Drluck grinned, "No, no, son. Only a few of them look like monsters. The vast majority, they have bodies like normal people, and they live among normal people. Incognito. But apart from the smell, there are signs in their aura that allow you to recognise them."

"What signs?"

"Particular quality of light. Open your mind, Szar."

I made myself vacant and let Drluck project impressions and memories into me.

An image came to me. A distinguished looking man, perhaps in his forties. He had a large forehead and looked quite dignified and alert.

"See?" Drluck said. "That light, in his aura."

"It's a nice light!" I was surprised.

Drluck kept sending images. "Never forget one thing about the Nephilim dirt: they're smart. It's one of the reasons they're so dangerous. They're not just vicious, they have cunning. They often end up in positions of power – not in the county of the Red Lands of course, where they have been exterminated and outlawed since the time of Lohrzen. But in other counties, especially in the north, many of the Nephilim live with full impunity. They corrupt. They pollute. Even in temples. Even the courts of princes."

"How come there are often groups of Nephilim around here, since they have been driven away from this county?"

"They're pilgrims from the north. They come to visit the cave of Verzazyel the Watcher. They want to steal the magic. They're after some kind of initiation. They believe Verzazyel has left powers for them in the cave." Drluck's eyes were lost in the mists for a while. "Let me tell you more. The Nephilim trash... they're grouped in families. Each family descends from one of the Watcher, like some kind of caste. But they don't even respect the Law of the castes, they marry from one group to the other. They're shameless, they pollute the Law. Those who come to visit Verzazyel's cave are from Verzazyel's clans. They all claim to be bastards of Verzazyel the Watcher."

"Do we attack them when they are in the Red Lands?"

"As long as they travel in groups of pilgrims and don't stick around in the county, we don't." Drluck looked at me with his Warrior's smile, "Well, most of the time, we don't." Then he directed his gaze back to the mists.

I was becoming more and more curious about the Nephilim Hunters. So many strange stories circulated about them. "Do the pilgrims bring Hunters with them?"

"Large groups usually do, small ones, not always. When Marek sends you out to kill your first Nephilim, pray that no Hunter is around! Heard of Kuren-jaya? It's their style of combat. Ugly and deadly. If you can't kill them immediately they catch you in their Point-nets, and that's the end of you." Drluck's tone indicated he did not feel like answering any more of my questions.

I lawfully thanked him and took my leave.

As I was jumping my way back down the staircases on the face of the cliff, I remembered with some nostalgia the happy days in Eisraim when the more questions I asked, the more responsive Gervin became. And when I could go out of the temple without having to worry about Nephilim Hunters.

6.27 Nephilim Hunters

Next day, in the dining hall, I was sitting with Floster and one of his friends, Ap Remer. A man in his late forties, he was not as tall as Floster but just as big, and he wore the black pants and shirt of the Warriors. As the pair of friends seemed to be in a talkative mood, I decided to ask, "Floster, will you tell me who the Nephilim Hunters are?"

6 – The Book of the Great Dragon of the Deep

Floster pulled a face, making it clear he did not like my question. Ap Remer answered for him, "You know the Nephilim were the children of the Watchers, those angels who descended into the kingdom and married the daughters of men."

I nodded, "Are there still Watchers in the kingdom?"

"No, son, they went back to the spheres long, long ago. Their power was immense. Akin to fire. And far greater than could be comprehended by men. The Watchers married the daughters of men and had children with them. This new race, born from the Watchers' seed, was called Nephilim. It soon became evident the Nephilim were not like normal people. The Watchers' fire did strange things to them. Some became so proud and arrogant that they wanted to conquer the entire kingdom for themselves. Some were giants with an insatiable appetite for human flesh. After a few generations the kingdom became infested with so many of these monsters that no one could rest in peace – not even the Nephilim themselves! So they had to create a body of fighters that could defend them against the most ferocious of their own kind, and this is how the Hunters originated."

"So the Hunters were not created as a reaction to the Great Warriors?"

"No, son, the Hunters existed before Lohrzen. But when the Great Warriors started exterminating the Nephilim scum in the southern counties of the kingdom, the Nephilim of the north trained scores of Hunters and prepared themselves for a war. Some say that if Lohrzen had raised an army against them and purged the entire kingdom, countless evils would have been avoided. Others argue that there were already so many Nephilim people in the northern counties that the war would have lasted for generations. Anyhow, Lohrzen chose to return to the temple of the Dragon, and the Nephilim peril kept spreading in the north."

"Ap Remer, what kinds of weapons do the Nephilim Hunters use?"

"Deadly powers that they draw from the centres of energy above the head. Extremely dangerous magic forces, which they throw like nets. They strangle your life force and destroy your mind. Once caught in a net, there is no escape. Faced with a Hunter, a Warrior must strike like lightning."

Floster had stopped eating. He was playing with the food on his plate. He looked at me, "Ap Remer knows what he is talking about, he has killed eleven of them."

Taking on the Warriors' dangerous smile, Ap Remer said, "By the time Marek the Indestructible finishes training you, you'll probably have killed a few Nephilim yourself."

I turned my face down to my plate, not feeling like asking any more questions.

Still playing with the charcoaled chunks on his plate, Floster took up the flow, "You know what people say, Szar? If the Nephilim are so wicked, it's because of their food. You have no idea what kind of rubbish they eat! It's absolutely revolting."

"Ha! Ha! Ha! Ha! Ha!" Ap Remer, went on, "Yeh, that's what people say. And also, when they want to torture you, the Nephilim scum always start by feeding you their food. After that you're in such a state, you can't resist their vicious treatments."

The fact that one could torture people with food left me thoughtful. It conjured up images of myself being tied up, a monster with long fangs forcing filth from the caverns of sickness down my throat.

To divert the conversation, Floster called on Pelissor, who was sitting close by. "Hey! Pelissor, *wise man in the Law*, tell us a story!"

"Yeh, Pelissor, warm our Dragons up!" Ap Remer supported.

Other brethren joined in, "Pelissor, we want a story!"

The man with the long white hair didn't seem to mind. He stood up, "How about the story of Gatzel, the Great Warrior who conquered the power of Azazel through his obstinacy?"

"Yes! We like that one!" the brethren applauded.

Ap Remer turned towards me and asked, "Have you heard it yet?"

"Nope!" I shook my head, still wondering what kind of food could be used to torture a Great Warrior.

"It's a really good story. You'll love it, even though it's your first time!"

"Once, long ago," Pelissor began, "in a village of the county of the Red Lands, there was born the son of a Great Warrior. His name was Gatzel. Do you know why?"

"No! Why?" the brethren shouted. "Tell us, Pelissor!"

"It's because he was such a pain in the Dragon that at least three times a day his father had to tell him, 'Go to Azazel and get lost!'"

The brethren all burst out laughing. Pelissor turned to me as the laughter died down, "Do you know who Azazel was, Szar?"

I shook my head.

"He was the leader of the Watchers, those great angels who, unfortunately, fathered the Nephilim scum." Then he returned to the story, "When the time came for Gatzel to be initiated in the Temple of the Dragon, his family was very much relieved that they would no longer have to bear with him. This, by the way, is how he became a Great Warrior: when he was in the death crypt, the She-Dragon of the Deep became so fed up with him that she sent him back, telling him..."

"Go to Azazel and get lost!" everyone bawled in unison.

"E-xac-tly, my brethren!" Pelissor kindled their spirits. "This is how he was returned to life in the kingdom. Then, after twelve years' practice of the black dance and the Lesser Mysteries, the time came for him to learn the ultimate level of *the Voice, which is the thunder of the Earth*. But he used to irritate his teacher so much that when he approached him to learn how to project *the thunder of the Earth*, the teacher answered..."

"Go to Azazel and get lost!" the brethren yelled with delight.

"E-xac-tly, my brethren! Now, our Gatzel was puzzled by this answer. Since his faith in his teacher was total, he suddenly started thinking that his destiny must have been to find Azazel's cave, which is lost and buried in the wilderness, in the secret place of Dudael. Off he went, to everyone in the temple's relief. For twenty-seven years Gatzel kept searching, so obstinate was he. At long last, he found the cave and met Azazel. He immediately took a liking to the Watcher. For the first time in his life, he had met someone who could never tell him to go to Azazel and get lost!"

The laughter was so loud that Pelissor had to wait a minute.

"How did Gatzel end up conquering the power of Azazel, the greatest of all the Watchers? This no one ever knew, but my guess is that Azazel got so fed up with him that he gave him the power just to get rid of him."

6.28 From Voice to Voice

The following Friday, I was taken by Marek and his men to the chapel of the Word. It was a holy crypt, a special place that had been strictly forbidden to me until then.

After I had waited outside for an hour, the door opened.

I entered. There was not a sound until the door banged close behind me, leaving me in complete darkness. I was grabbed by a dozen threatening hands and made to repeat another oath of secrecy.

Once I had sworn on my life I would never reveal any of the secrets about to be imparted to me, the hands released me.

A small candle was lit, revealing a voluminous black curtain in front of me. Marek's men formed a circle around me and began intoning a hymn of the Law,

"*That which is thy core and which, long ago, was hidden,*
That which thou hast forgotten,
That which thou hast lost,
The Voice will make thee remember.
That which was torn apart from thee,
When the Earth was still young and alive with Magic,
The Voice will make thee remember.
That which thou thought had died,
That for which thy heart is crying,
The Voice will make thee remember.
That which, for aeons thou hast been seeking,
And is pregnant with thy forthcoming eternity,
The Voice will make thee remember."

Their voice abruptly changed. It 'took dimension'. It became strangely vibrant, loaded with a pulse of life that made my energy flare as if Dragon-ignited from above and below at the same time. Amazed, I saw blue and orange flames of light coming out of their mouths.

I gasped, realising that sixteen men were projecting the Voice onto me.

Atlantean Secrets

Never in my years of rituals with the prestigious Salmon Robe priests or in the chapel of the eternal flame had I seen anything like it. At first the Voices were caressing me like a smooth Underworld breeze, turning every fibre of my body into solid vibration. But as the Voice projection became more intense, it made me shake and vroof like one of my Mother the Dragon's most violent embraces.

Marek lifted his hand. His men further increased the power, kindling the space of the room into a field of dazzling multicoloured lights. The smooth breeze turned into tempestuous gusts, making me shake violently as if my whole structure was about to be shattered and crumble. I soon lost touch with the cavern and found myself transported into a different dimension, teeming with an immoderation of life and monumental powers flowing in all directions, just as in the legends that portrayed the Ancient Days of the Earth.

This excursion out of time abruptly came to an end when Mareck clicked his fingers, bringing the room to silence.

He spoke.

I heard him from far away, having no idea what he was saying.

He projected a low-pitched Voice-flame onto my belly to bring my presence back into the room. "Today I bestow the Voice onto you," he declared solemnly, "as I received it from my teacher. Today you become a custodian of this ancient mystery which was revealed to us by the gods, and passed on from master to disciple ever since."

Marek opened the black curtain, unveiling an altar upon which burnt a Holy Blue Flame a few centimetres long, springing from a flat golden stand.

"This," said Marek, "is the Flame of the Word. Since time immemorial, Voice initiates have been its keeper. It is no common flame like that of a torch. It does not burn the hand." He placed his flat hand right in the middle of the Flame.

The Flame kept burning through and above his hand, unchanged.

"This Holy Flame does not require any oil or wood to burn." Looking into my eyes, he said, "Now watch carefully!" He turned towards the Flame and used the Voice to utter an "ooo" sound. As he projected the sound, something extraordinary took place – the Flame suddenly became twice as large, and its colour turned from blue to orange.

I was stunned. Before I had time to think, Marek Voice-projected a sharp order, "Now, *you* do it!" and he resumed the "ooo" sound.

Compelled by the irresistible power of his Voice, I automatically found myself projecting the same sound! Astounded, I watched the long flame of pink light coming out of my mouth.

The Holy Flame on the altar began growing to the size of a human head, dancing with myriads of changing colours.

Marek gave a sign with his hand, and all the men joined us, Voicing so much power that the Holy Flame became five times as large.

Flames kept pouring out of my mouth. My throat was shaken by violent vroofing waves, the might and glory of the Underworlds resonating with my larynx as well as my belly! Vroofing above, vroofing below, an explosion took place.

I became Voice, the heart of the Dragon, spread in the cavern, soon encompassing the whole mountain, ascending from the Deep Underworlds to a summit of light that smiled at me, waiting for the rendezvous.

When I next remembered Szar, I was black dancing with the others in our usual training cave.

Three days had passed.

6.29 The training in the weapons

During the following weeks I was introduced to an arsenal of war practices which had been transmitted and cultivated by the lineage of the Sons of the Dragon ever since the time of Lohrzen.

The first of these consisted of drawing thick, toxic Dragon fumes out of the Earth and letting them ascend violently into the body of an adversary, immediately putting him to sleep. Using the same principle a whole troop could be benumbed, leaving plenty of time for black dancers to strike – a technique that Lohrzen had used right from the beginning, when he was purging the county of the Nephilim scourge. With other similar practices, thick soporific venoms could be drawn from Underworld spaces and used to render people numb or temporarily paralysed. Some of these venoms were so toxic that they could make people sick for weeks, or even kill them.

Other practices had to do with sapping the strength of adversaries by cutting them from their unconscious roots in the Underworlds, destroying their lower-chakra foundations. The Warriors used a whole arsenal of such techniques to annihilate the vitality of their opponents.

They also had a number of ways of extending their perception through the space of darkness visible. They knew how to smell adversaries and locate them in the distance. This worked not only with the Nephilim but also with normal people, and it gave specific information: how many enemies, the kind of caste they belonged to, how dangerous they were. Dangerous people with a strong warrior's energy had a particular smell that was unmistakable. Controllers also had a characteristic smell, and so had several other castes and ethnic groups.

There were methods by which a Warrior could create a protected space around him and be warned instantly if someone entered the space. These rested on creating astral beacons in darkness visible and using them to manifest a field. As soon as someone came inside it, the atmosphere of consciousness in the field changed, enough to wake you up during the night.

As the training intensified, it became almost constant. For months, Marek the Indestructible took us to the surrounding countryside and trained us to combat under every possible condition and situation. He divided us into groups that were to fight each other, always trying to rival the others in cunning and take them by surprise. Every single night I had to set a protective field, never knowing when an 'enemy' might irrupt, always having to be ready to jump and fight a black dance for my life.

Marek knew only too well that sooner or later his men would have to defend themselves against powerful opponents. His way of manifesting his love for them was to be a merciless teacher, never allowing anyone to relax their vigilance, and pushing the training beyond all imaginable limits.

More than just physical practices and occult weapons, it was Lohrzen's art of war that Marek was transmitting. This involved learning various stratagems and tactics, studying the fighting style and methods of other schools, not only those of the Nephilim. It also involved what Marek called the 'intelligence of war' – reading the minds of one's enemies, understanding their motivations and their background, and always trying to predict and pre-empt their next move.

Significant time was spent studying the occult weapons of the Nephilim Hunters, in particular the soft stones that the Hunters used to release extremely toxic energies. These were occult radiations which durably destroyed the bodily life force and created injuries that were especially difficult to heal. Using land energies and powers from the Underworlds, there were ways of preventing the device from spreading its devastating venom. But they had to be implemented lightning-fast. Once the venomous radiation had been released, not much could be done to stop it.

The greatest and most powerful of all weapons used by the Great Warriors was the Voice itself. I was taught how to project sounds on gateways, together with or instead of physical blows. It gave staggering results. To begin with, I was instructed to use the power on nature, projecting the Voice onto trees. Some sounds had miraculous effects and brought to life the most sickly plants. Others could kill a tree almost instantly. In a matter of hours, its leaves would turn brown and start falling.

Through the Voice, a Warrior could not only strike at his enemies but also stun them. Loud shrieks could instantly paralyse an entire company, or render it powerless before an onslaught. The Voice was also used as a shielding device that sealed the body of energy and greatly strengthened resistance to blows, even on lethal gateways to a certain extent. And it was possible to achieve a whole range of effects akin to healing, reinforcing vitality and even accomplishing rejuvenation.

Month after month, and in a spirit of complete dedication and mobilisation, Marek taught his men. The focus was so total that I sometimes went for entire weeks without having one minute to remember Elyani and all the

6 – The Book of the Great Dragon of the Deep

good things of Eisraim. During some phases of the training I had to let the Dragon push me so much that the words resurfaced, *"One Law, one way. He who never sleeps, never dies!"*

Yet this whole period was magnificent. The purity was total. A nine-month uninterrupted hymn to the glory of the She-Dragon.

One Friday afternoon, after finishing a practice in the chapel of the Word, Marek called me over. "Szar, Great Warrior, how long has it been since we took you down into the crypt and you died in the Dragon?"

I had to think. "Some eighteen lawful months and half a lawful lunation, I believe."

"It's now time for you to face another aspect of death, Szar."

Clear fountain above and vroofing mountain below, I remained silent, holding his gaze.

"The Sons of the Dragon have a saying: *After his first kill, a Warrior is never the same again.* So your next mission will be an initiation." Marek paused, looking down to his left fist. "I want you to chase one of the Nephilim pilgrims around Verzazyel's cave, and kill him. Or kill her. And bring back something they carry, a jewel for instance. It will be your first trophy."

In eighteen-and-a-half months, all I had done was execute order after order, carry out mission after mission. "When shall I leave?" I just asked.

"Tomorrow morning. And move your Dragon fast! I want you to come back immediately. It's time for you to start delving into deeper aspects of the Voice, son." He winked at me with his smile, "What you've seen so far can hardly be called dangerous compared to what the Voice will do for you, when you push it."

With a quick nod, Marek indicated the conversation was finished.

No thoughts, just Dragon, I returned the nod and turned to go, immediately starting to work out a plan of action.

As I passed through the doorway, Marek threw after me, "Szar! I don't want you to have *anything* to do with the Hunters. Understood? The time has not come yet."

6.30 Floster's present

That evening when I met Floster in the dining hall, he addressed me warmly, *"Praise the Great Dragon, brother!* Marek told me you were going out on a mission. So I got you a present. I want you to take it with you."

"All glory to the She-Dragon! A present! Brother Floster, *my friend in the Dragon,* how very nice of you. Can I see it?"

He answered in his deep voice, "Follow me, brother!"

I was all excited. Walking behind him, I reflected, "If I could have had one present for every two hundred blows I've received since coming to

Mount Lohrzen, by now I'd probably need a larger bedcave to house them all."

We were headed for the warehouse and there, to my greatest surprise, Floster handed me a brown cape, tailored in the fashion of the Eisraim gown that I was wearing when I first arrived at the temple.

"Brother Floster!" I was so moved that I had tears in my eyes.

"I could see you were sad when you had to give up the old one, so I kept it and sewed another just like it. Come on, put it on."

I looked at myself in *the* temple's mirror. "Floster, it is perfect! It looks exactly like the one Gervin gave me! Just a bit larger, of course."

"Just a bit? Ha! Ha! Ha! Ha! Ha! There is more to this cape than may appear at first, you know! The cloth has been infused with the breeze of a Dragon gate, according to one of the secret protection methods of the Sons of Vulcan. It'll keep you warm, and fired in your heart. And it keeps all kinds of negative influences away."

I gave the huge man a hug, "Floster, I am... very touched!"

"Come on, that's not much! Keep it on, and let's go and have dinner."

Seeing myself wearing brown triggered memories. As we were walking back to the dining hall I went through one of those difficult moments when I felt so far from my home, my teacher and my friends, that only the Dragon could contain my tears. But the last thing I wanted was to make Floster unhappy. I made my face Dragon-merry.

While we were eating dinner Floster said, "Have you heard that Narlond will soon be leaving the temple?"

I nodded. "What do you think he will do after this?"

"There's a good life waiting for him! The prince of the county of the Western Plains has appointed him chief of his personal security guards. Narlond is such an intelligent and handsome boy, I bet the prince's daughter will soon fall in love with him. And then who knows? Perhaps we've been having dinner every night with a future prince without even suspecting it! Ha! Ha! Ha! Ha! Ha!" Even though this laughter was one of the hallmarks of the Warriors, no one in the temple knew how to do it better than Floster.

"*My friend in the Dragon,*" I asked him, "I have often wondered why *you* did not become one of the Warriors. I know you have all the qualities for it, you are a great knower of the Dragon. Why didn't you embrace this path? Would it have been against the Law of your caste?"

Floster looked up towards the ceiling, as if he was about to prophesy. Then he turned towards me, "My father and my mother's brother, both were Great Warriors. But when I was nine years old a riot broke out in a village near ours. Some Nephilim pilgrims came to blows with the people over there, and three villagers were killed. In reprisal, my father and uncle were sent to attack the caravan of pilgrims and kill three of the Nephilim – which they did. But some powerful Hunters were in charge of protecting

6 – The Book of the Great Dragon of the Deep

the pilgrims. Nine of them went on a hunt, and my father and my uncle were caught in an ambush."

Floster paused, again looking towards the ceiling. "When their bodies were found, they were so mutilated that my mother could hardly identify them. That Kuren-jaya, the Hunter's fighting style... frightening magic! When caught in its nets, not many Warriors can escape, even the most powerful. After this my mother became very sick. She never recovered. She just let herself fade away. But before leaving her body she made me give my little Dragon's word that I would never become a Warrior like my father. After she died I came to the temple, where Marek's teacher raised me like his own child and had me initiated into the mysteries of Vulcan as soon as the Law permitted. But to fulfil the word I had given to my mother, I never descended into the crypt like you did."

"I am sorry, Floster..."

"Aha!" he told me off with his huge hand, "*The wise cry neither for the living nor for the dead.* If I've stayed in the temple it's because I have been totally fulfilled with *the bliss of the Dragon's embraces*. There is a whole stream of initiation into the mysteries of Vulcan which is part of this temple, and which you have never had time to discover because of all your occupations." Floster smiled at me and thrust his arms in all directions, pretending to fight twelve men at a time.

I tried a "Ha! Ha! Ha! Ha! Ha!" but I still couldn't make it up to traditional standard.

"The mysteries of Vulcan are a wonderful path! They also take initiates down into the glories of the Underworlds, as Amaran showed you. Moreover, they contain many teachings about the future of humanity. Remember, Vulcan is called the god of the last hour. This is because he holds forces which will be released only in the very last moment, *when the race of men is on its last leg.*"

"Could I learn more about it?" I asked, gripped by his account.

"Perhaps when you come back," he said.

I changed topic, "Floster, tell me! Why do you think I never seem to be able to laugh the way you do?"

"Ha! Ha! Ha! Ha! Ha! How did you learn the black dance, my boy?" Before I had time to reply, he said, "You started practising every morning before dawn, and you kept on until sunset. And you went on and on, month after month, until your style was perfect and people called you an expert. Well, if you want to be able to laugh like I do, that's what you have to do."

"Ha! Ha! Ha! Ha! Ha!"

Floster went on telling me more of his Dragon jokes and memories, and we laughed together until, thanking him again, I retired to my bedroom.

I spent some more time preparing for my mission. Through the smell, I had already located several groups of Nephilim. One of them had only three pilgrims, two of whom were carrying soft stones. They were slow-moving people who did not smell like members of a dangerous caste. There was absolutely no sign of a Hunter accompanying them. Using a method that made me undetectable, I carefully scanned all the other groups of pilgrims. None of them seemed as vulnerable as my designated target.

Using an etheric layer of imprints in darkness visible, I evaluated the distance my three pilgrims had covered in one day. This allowed me to figure out where I would be able to cross their path a day later. I thoroughly scanned the proposed site for the action, and in particular the venom wells from where to draw anaesthetising astral fumes. I checked that no other Nephilim were on their way to that particular location, as well as a number of other parameters that would allow me to activate occult weapons from the Underworlds if needed.

Compared to the kind of missions I had been given in the last months, this one did not seem like it was going to be much of a problem.

After a short night's sleep, I practised my beloved Dragon's breath for an hour. Then I put on the beautiful brown cape over my Warrior's black clothes and went to the dining hall to pick up a bag of provisions for two or three days.

This time, for a change, I decided to go out of the temple through the portal, instead of having fun climbing down the cliffs.

When they saw me, the two brethren at the gates started joking, *"Praise the She-Dragon, brother Szar!* It is not often we see you down here!"

"These Great Warriors," the other one said, "they take it as a personal insult if they have to enter through the door – unless they can break it down, of course!"

"All glory to the Mother of the Endless Night!" I replied, "No offence brethren! Nothing personal against you. I just like climbing!"

The huge wooden gates slowly creaked open, and I ran in the direction of the rising Sun.

I stopped to contemplate Mount Lohrzen. Touching the orichalc plate on my throat, I paid my respects to the great sage. Then, *no thoughts, just Dragon*, I unfolded the concealment energies that made it virtually impossible for anyone to detect my presence through darkness visible, even the smelling sentinels of Mount Lohrzen.

I sense-smelt the space for potential enemies.

Everything was clear.

I started running towards the east again.

I was ready to kill.

– Thus ends the book of the Great Dragon of the Deep –

7

The Book of the Nephilim Spice

7.1 The hymn of Felicia to Verzazyel the Watcher

The three Nephilim pilgrims had reached a low plateau between two canyons.

"I'm exhausted." Alven dropped his bags on the ground. "Why don't we stop here for the night?"

His brother Rolen collapsed on the ground, "I like it here. Shame there aren't any twigs to light a fire."

"That's wilderness for you! Anyhow," Alven sighed, "it's so hot in these counties of the south. I'm starting to miss the morning frosts of our Snowy Mountains."

Their sister Felicia perched herself on a flat rock. She pulled a mirror and a comb from one of her bags, and began slowly combing her long red hair.

Alven, the eldest of the three, teased her, "Here we are in the middle of the wilderness, and what is Felicia doing?"

Rolen clicked his fingers, "Putting on her make up, of course!"

"Shut up, you two," Felicia snapped. "Don't you know the Watchers like beautiful women?"

"Of course, we know!" Rolen said, "We'd never have been born if they didn't!"

The three burst out laughing.

Turning towards his brother, Alven said in a cheeky voice, "Just you wait till she gets to the cave, then you'll see what a priestess of Verzazyel can do with make up, *man of the Law!* She'll look so stunning the Watcher will leap out of the cave and grab her from us."

"Father used to say he thought no woman in the kingdom knew more about make up than mother," Rolen said, "but he changed his mind when Felicia turned seven."

Felicia put on one of her seductress' smiles and winked at them, "It's an entire science, you know."

"Of course, we know!" the two men answered in one voice.

She took a jar of black powder and started painting her eyelashes. Rolen came and sat by her. "Listen, great priestess, are you sure I can't go down into the holy crypt with you?"

"*No way, man of the Law!* You can come with me into the cave, and there I will show you the wonders of the Watcher's mind. But into the crypt I must descend alone."

"What's the point of having a sister who's a priestess of Verzazyel if I can't even see more than any other pilgrim?" Rolen insisted.

"Who said you wouldn't see more than any other pilgrim, *man of the Law*?" Felicia protested. "I'm going to light up the cave and turn it into a huge, dazzling field of stars for you. You won't believe your eyes!"

"Do you mean to say the field of stars really exists? Isn't it just a legend?" Rolen asked.

"Of course it exists! But only initiates can see it. If you had come with a caravan of pilgrims, you would never have seen what I am going to show you, let me tell you."

As she could see her younger brother still wasn't satisfied, Felicia went on, "Rolen, I have spent fifteen years preparing myself for the power that is in this crypt. The Fire down there is extremely dangerous."

She stopped putting her make up on and turned to her other brother, "So the instructions are clear: if I am not back from the holy crypt three hours after I descend, just go."

"We'll camp outside Verzazyel's cave for the night, Felicia."

She shrugged her shoulders, "If I am dead, there is no point waiting."

"If you fail and if the Fire kills you," Rolen asked, "will Ferippe and his pilgrims find you when they arrive three days later?"

"Probably not. The crypt will clean itself up and get rid of my body somehow," Felicia answered.

Alven changed the topic, "Come on, Felicia, if you succeed, tell us, what's the first thing you'll do when you come out of the crypt?"

Felicia gave a smile and resumed her make up ritual. "The oracle said that if I succeed, there will be a great prian by my side when I come out of the crypt. I'll kiss him passionately."

Rolen raised an eyebrow. "I can't wait to meet the man! And what if it was a giant that Verzazyel materialised for you in the cave?"

Felicia giggled, thinking of herself married to one of the Nephilim giants.

"We'll all celebrate!" Alven said. "I brought plenty of a certain dish you know well, Felicia – enough to satisfy the giant."

"Alven," she said, "you're such a *darling in the Law*! Honeyed pickled cucumbers?"

"Yes, *woman of the Law!* With cinnamon sauce, of course..."

7 – The Book of the Nephilim Spice

"Watch out!" yelled Rolen. "A snake!"

A huge cobra was silently gliding its way towards one of the bags.

"Quick," Alven shouted, "your walking stick!"

"No!" intervened Felicia. "Don't kill it!" Using the Voice, she started projecting an 'oooh' sound. The snake instantly became motionless. The two brothers watched in amazement. Red tongues of light came out of Felicia's mouth.

Raising her Voice, she intoned a hymn of her Law,

"Hail Verzazyel, formidable among the Watchers!
Hail Verzazyel, tamer of the Fire!
Hail Verzazyel, mighty angel, fever of heaven!
Ready for thy blazing glory,
I come to thee, Verzazyel!
Let me ascend to thy sphere or die.
Let me be married to thy Fire or die.
Let me conquer thy power or die.
Hear my Word, O Verzazyel! Respond to my call!"

The snake had slowly turned to face Felicia.

"Sssss..." Felicia projected a long hissing sound, and the snake turned back and glided away, soon disappearing from sight.

Rolen and Alven were speechless.

"Meeting a snake on the way to the Watcher's cave is one of the best of all omens of Akibel," Felicia told them.

Alven went over to one of his bags and picked up a jar with a herbal remedy. "Who needs a Hunter with a woman like her around!"

Rolen had a pensive look. "Is this the kind of thing the power of the Watchers can do?"

"This is *nothing* compared to the power of the cave!" she smiled at her brother. "Now, why don't you two get some rest. I'm going on a quick reconnaissance tour in the next canyon."

The two brothers exchanged a look, then watched her walk off.

"Hail Verzazyel, I come to thee!" she whispered. "I have been waiting for this moment all my life! I want to know, Verzazyel. I want to know you."

7.2 Ritual murder

I had thoroughly checked the terrain. It was ideal. The narrow canyon was the only way that my adversaries could take. It was extremely rocky, so that when I leapt on them they would have no chance to run away. The local earth lines were perfect for drawing up toxic Dragon fumes. I had mapped all the soporific venom wells too, just in case I had to resort to more violent forms of action. It was unlikely, though, as the Dragon fumes below that spot would have been enough to neutralise an entire company of the king's army. But as Marek had been hammering into me for months, "*Never underestimate the enemy!*"

Through the smell and other vision channels of darkness visible, I had checked that no other group of Nephilim pilgrims could come near my target area at the time planned for the action. Apart from the three approaching Nephilim, the only souls around were a mass of snakes in the distance, and a few desert rats here and there. And of course I had meticulously tuned into the three pilgrims themselves: two men and a woman. Their vitality levels were rather mediocre, and their smell was definitely not that of dangerous people.

They were moving slowly, having difficulty coping with the heat of the desert, so it seemed. They carried four soft stones altogether, only one of which could remotely qualify as a weapon, and certainly nothing to worry about. Still, my plan was to immediately neutralise the carrier of the object. The estimated duration for the entire action was less than twenty seconds.

I had shielded my energy in a way that made it totally impossible for anyone to locate me. This was a little game I was playing with my friends of Mount Lohrzen. I knew that when the 'sensors' reported I was totally undetectable, Marek the indestructible would be pleased. I knew exactly what his smile would be like.

Everything was set. I had put aside my brown cape so as to enjoy the complete freedom of movement of the Warriors' black clothes, and I waited, hidden behind large rocks, ready to spring on my prey like a panther.

Then something incredibly lucky happened. Two of the pilgrims stopped. Only the third one, the woman, kept moving towards the target location. And the soft stone she was carrying was not the one that could possibly be used as a weapon. It seemed too good to be true.

"Perhaps she is on a reconnaissance mission," I thought. "But... *always suspect a trick!*" I sense-smelled the two pilgrims who had remained behind, but it Underworld-seemed like they were going for a nap. I sensed for every single secret weapon I had been taught about, but there was no trace of one.

I couldn't believe my luck. So I thanked the She-Dragon for her good help and just waited. According to the smell, the enemy would arrive on the target location in less than ten minutes.

"Waiting is an art!" Marek often said. "Many a warrior was destroyed by waiting. So many perils threaten he who waits... he can start thinking too much, he can become impatient or lose his vigilance."

I held onto the Warriors' way of waiting – *no thoughts, just Dragon,* a peripheral awareness that embraces all the parameters of the situation. I made myself vast like the Dragon. I could feel the two sleeping pilgrims in the distance as if they were in my bosom, and the rock all around me with

7 – The Book of the Nephilim Spice

the lines of fumes and the wells of venom – and the target approaching... closer... and closer...

The very moment the woman walked across the noxious line, I drew up a draught of toxic fumes into her body and leapt, projecting a sharp shriek with the Voice to further immobilise her. I landed right in front of her, and my fists instantly knocked her down with a double 'cheap way out' – simple, but still one of the most efficient ways of sending a lay person unconscious.

She fell softly onto the ground. I jumped for the final stage of the black dance, when the black forty gateways are to be hit in less than five seconds. I tuned into the clear fountain, and...

"No! I'm not killing this woman."

It was simple and limpid like all truth coming from the fountain, and it was grounded in the rock of the entire mountain range. The knowingness was total, devoid of the slightest hesitation or doubt.

As I fell back onto the ground, one foot on each side of her body, I dropped my fists and took a quick look at her. She was a young woman of medium build. She had magnificent long red hair. My eyes were immediately attracted to the small soft stone she was wearing as a medallion on her breast, over her turquoise blue dress.

Marek had ordered me to bring back a 'trophy'. So I took the medallion and put it around my neck. Then I stood up and walked away.

Fifty lawful feet away, I suddenly thought, "What am I doing? This is completely ridiculous! Am I being fooled by one of the Nephilim's secret weapons?" Resuming the energy of the black dance, I leapt back, ready to strike.

But as soon as I landed close to her, the same limpid certitude was with me. There was no occult weapon at play, I just thought, "No! I am not killing this woman, and that's that!"

I quickly looked at her again. "She looks gorgeous!" I was puzzled. I thought all Nephilim girls were huge, ugly and foul smelling like Bobros' sisters.

She was completely swamped with the Dragon fumes. "What a good job I did!" I thought, "She's going to be sick as an Underworld dog for at least a week. It might even kill her." But from the clear fountain, I did not want her to die because of me. So I dragged her body away from the toxic earth line and started gently massaging her gateways, dispelling the energy of the fumes and pumping up her vitality. She was obviously quite tired from all the walking. And her liver did not seem to be coping well with the heat. Letting the Dragon flow through my hands and using Voice frequencies, I spent a few minutes rebalancing her meridians.

My mind protested, "This situation is ludicrous! What am I going to tell Marek? That I used his lore to heal one of the Nephilim?" But, driven by the clear fountain above and the Dragon below, my hands kept running over her in the pure healing style of the Warriors. Her body's response to the Dragon's breeze was excellent. I could see the colour of her energy circulations changing by the minute. Even though she was about to recover her senses, I decided to go on, as I had nearly finished mopping up a nasty energy that had obviously been trapped in her liver for some time.

When she opened her eyes – big blue eyes of the people from the northern lands – she was completely terrified. I sealed her red lips with my index finger. "Hush! Just remain motionless two more minutes, and everything will be fine."

She did not budge. After a few seconds spent inspecting the six directions of space, she closed her eyes tight, tucked her head in her shoulders and pretended to be dead.

I kept working on her energy for a little longer. Then I stood up and walked away.

Soon my mind returned to the charge, "This is totally, utterly and unforgivably ridiculous!" But holding on to a no-thoughts-just-Dragon space, I kept walking.

7.3 Black nightmare

Her head still tucked in her shoulders, Felicia finally opened her eyes. She looked around and as everything seemed to be still, she was brave and decided to sit up. No one in sight. Then she jumped up and started running towards her brothers like a tropical tornado.

Carried by the wings of panic she bolted through the canyon, running so fast that she fell over a few times, but she did not even feel the pain.

When she got to the improvised camp she screamed, "Rolen! Rolen!" and threw herself into her brother's arms.

"Felicia! Where have you been?"

Felicia was panting badly. First, the only thing she could do was to sob. Holding her tight in his arms, Rolen tried to comfort her.

"Felicia, what happened?" Alven asked. "Did you see someone?"

"A black man!" she managed to blurt out, shaking all over, "A black nightmare!"

Hitting his left hand with his right fist, Alven exclaimed, "Damn it! Just what we needed! Is he coming towards us?"

"I don't know. He attacked me! He stole my medallion, and left."

Rolen gave a start, "What? You mean you've just been attacked by one of the black nightmares?"

Felicia nodded and burrowed further into Rolen's arms, holding on to him as tight as she could.

Alven and Rolen exchanged a glance, perplexed. In this area, Nephilim pilgrims who met a black nightmare rarely survived to tell their story.

"Are you sure it wasn't someone else?"

7 – The Book of the Nephilim Spice

"No!" she yelled, "He was one of them, I know!" She was still struggling to catch her breath. "A big, ugly killing machine dressed in black with the cap on his head. Pure muscle, not one gram of brain, and cold as if he had just exterminated an entire caravan of pilgrims."

Alven examined the scratches on her arms. "Did you fight him?"

"Sort of. I mean, no, not really. He's done something to my energy."

"What?"

"He forced me to lie still, and he put something into me with his hands."

Alven and Rolen were from a caste of physicians. Alven made Felicia lie down on a thin mat that was part of their camping gear, and he inspected her gateways. After a minute he shook his head and sighed. "Felicia, this does not make any sense."

Felicia was starting to recover some sanity. "Tell me! What has he thrown into me?"

Alven looked at her in silence. After taking a long inhalation, he said, "Felicia, these liver herbs I have been giving you for the last six years... either they suddenly started working last night, or..."

"Or what?" she asked anxiously.

"Or you have just been operated on by a master psychic surgeon. Your liver is completely clear," Alven concluded.

Rolen frowned, his gaze fixed on Felicia.

No one spoke for a while. Then Felicia insisted, "I'm *sure* he's thrown an influence into my body. I could feel it while he was doing it."

The more he auscultated her gateways, the more disconcerted Alven was. "Either I'm missing something or..."

Felicia was about to lose her temper, "Or what?"

Alven raised his voice as he did during their family arguments, "Or I wish *I* could throw influences like this into my patients! Our family would be rich." He took a deep breath and launched his diagnosis, "Felicia, you've just received a splendid injection of life force. The man you met was a top-level healer, not a black nightmare."

"Rubbish!" she yelled back at her brother. "He attacked me!"

Adopting a conciliatory attitude, Rolen mooted, "Well... aren't there physicians among the black caps of Mount Lohrzen?"

Passing his hand through the few hairs on his head, Alven pulled a puzzled face, "Rolen, the black nightmares *kill* Nephilim, they don't heal them."

Rolen sat down and drank some water. "If the black nightmares are around, then we're in big trouble! Weren't we told that at this time of the year they rarely leave their mountain?"

Turning to his sister, Alven asked sarcastically, "O, great prophetess, didn't your oracle tell you everything was going to be fine during this journey?"

"Ah, don't start again!" she glared at him. "The oracle said everything would be fine *in the end*."

Alven threw his arms in the air, "Visiting the county of the Red Lands on our own without Hunters to protect us was such an idiotic idea anyway!"

Felicia returned fire, "Right, mister know-it-all! Tell us, then... when we arrive in Verzazyel's cave with a hundred other pilgrims, how do you expect me to locate the forbidden holy crypt and awaken the power of the Watchers without anyone noticing?"

"Peace, my dear friends in the Law! Peace!" Rolen interposed. "Now is the time to pull from all our resources and carefully plan our next move. Felicia, what's the shortest way to reach the cave from here?"

"The canyon to the left."

"Are you sure? I would rather go to the right."

"No way, man of the Law." Felicia was adamant, "To the left!"

7.4 The cave of Verzazyel the Watcher

Apart from the three pilgrims I had left behind me, I had located at least two other vulnerable groups that seemed to be poorly guarded and could have been decimated in no time. But I found myself thinking, "Brilliant! That's just the legend I wanted to start – the Great Warrior who went from caravan to caravan healing Nephilim trash instead of killing them!" I could already see the story being told by Pelissor to all the brethren gathered in the dining hall. I hated to imagine the conclusion.

The situation was so absurd that I decided thinking was probably not the way to solve it. *No thoughts, just Dragon*, I walked through the red canyons, letting my steps be directed by the clear fountain.

Verzazyel's cave kept coming to my mind. It was not just curiosity, I had heard so many astonishing stories of its power. Everyone agreed that the cave held profound secrets. Hadn't Amaran said the cave probably hid some magic that could bring Vivyani back? And hadn't Lohrzen gained all his powers while studying from Verzazyel in the cave? If so many pilgrims from the north risked their life to visit it, surely there was something to be discovered in that cave.

From the fountain, I finally decided, "The only clear instruction Gervin gave me was to become dangerous. Let me go and find danger in the cave."

The cave of Verzazyel, the fiery angel! My Dragon vroofed with excitement.

I carefully sense-smelled all the Nephilim groups in the area. None was to reach the cave for at least a week. The closest were the three pilgrims I had left behind me, and it would take at least two days before they arrived. From what I could perceive in darkness visible, they had just engaged in the wrong direction and were about to lose another day.

7 – The Book of the Nephilim Spice

Making myself more astrally invisible than ever, I started running towards the cave. Thanks to the many descriptions I had heard in Mount Lohrzen's dining hall, it took me less than two hours to reach it.

The opening of Verzazyel's cave was not very high up in the cliff. It was flanked by two high, flute-shaped rocks – unmistakable landmarks, deservedly famous.

Before climbing up I spent a few minutes dancing to pay my respects to the Great She-Dragon of the Deep and collect my spirits.

Then I ran up an alley carved on the side of the rock and in no time found myself at the entrance of the cavern. When I looked inside I was very surprised, and quite disappointed. It was a small cave, hardly thirty lawful feet wide and less than ten lawful feet high. And it was completely empty. I did not sense any exceptional energy, despite of course searching for the recognisable astral signals of all the occult weapons I had been taught about. There did not even seem to be a gate of the Dragon inside the cave.

"*Praise the She-Dragon, Mother of the Endless Night!*" I shouted, wondering if I would be answered by an echo.

Nothing. So I sat in the middle of the cave and started practising the breath of the Dragon. "It's breeze as usual!" I thought in a slightly disenchanted mood. I closed my eyes, enjoying the blissful energy of my Dragon Mother.

But a few minutes later, when I reopened my eyes, I noticed an opening in the right wall of the cave. Surprised, I leapt up and walked towards it. Lo! there was a fairly large corridor that brought me to a winding stairway that led up. It was lit by some kind of diffuse light. But there was no plass in the walls. Where did the light come from?

What the Underworld was going on here? When I had arrived in the cave I had conducted a thorough inspection. It seemed inconceivable that I had missed that corridor. So I walked out of the cave, took a deep breath, wriggling my nostrils, and walked in again. Nothing had changed. There was still the same cave with three empty walls and one corridor opening on the right.

Grounding my clear fountain in the mountain rock, I had to decide what to do next. Was there danger? From the best I could sense, Dragon above, Dragon below, this place was dead. Empty of presence. There were no people, no beings, and no particular energies apart from the red basalt of the mountain range. Yet this corridor appearing out of nowhere... it was very much like the mind-blowing stories I had heard about Verzazyel's place.

I walked out of the cave and spent a minute looking down to my left fist. My forearm half flexed, I slowly opened and closed my hand a few times. Then, *no thoughts, just Dragon,* I walked back into the cavern and entered the corridor.

7.5 Eisraim, chapel of the White Eagle

Seventeen women, all wearing the long robe of the White Eagle, had gathered in the chapel. After invoking the Eagle's light with their hymns, they spent a long time in meditation.

Ending the practice, Teyani stood up and courageously announced, "I have called you today because the White Eagle has sent me the signal. It is time for another of you to descend and meet the trials of the Underworld."

The young women waited in silence to hear who would be named.

"Alcibyadi will be the next to go," she said.

Alcibyadi smiled serenely, shining with the White Light of the Eagle. The others didn't smile, as they knew only too well what this meant. In the last years, eight priestesses had descended and not one had returned.

The temple meeting continued in the sublime light of the Eagle. When it was finished, all the women left but Alcibyadi.

"I will be looking after your body myself, my child," Teyani said with great gentleness. "With all my art, *all the powers which the Eagle has bestowed upon me*, I give you my Word, Alcibyadi, I will do everything in my power to bring you back."

"I know." Alcibyadi gazed at her with the Eagle's brightness, and she kept on smiling. "I love you, Teyani."

Teyani walked towards her and took her in her arms. Tuning high, she prayed silently, "O White Eagle! Please do not abandon us!"

But Alcibyadi had no illusions. Death was waiting for her in the Underworlds. "Let the White Eagle take me!" she surrendered.

7.6 Verzazyel's cave – the cosmic dance

The first stairway had led me to another corridor which in turn had led me to a second stairway, this time a descending one. After at least two hundred steps I reached... another corridor! I kept walking in the diffuse silvery light that came from nowhere, going from stairway to hallway, hallway to stairway, never finding any room, any door or any crossing. At least there were no choices to make! But after walking for nearly two hours, I started wondering if I was going anywhere at all. The steps sometimes took me upwards, sometimes downwards, and the corridors all looked exactly the same. There were no presences, no particular energies, and no Dragon gate within reach of my perception.

Thinking I was doing something wrong, I stopped walking. As I sat in the middle of a hallway, it came to my mind that it was when I had closed my eyes and meditated on the Dragon's breath that the first corridor had

7 – The Book of the Nephilim Spice

appeared. So I covered my head with the hood of my brown robe, took a meditation position, and started practising Dragon's breath again.

After a few minutes spent savouring my Mother's breeze, I reopened my eyes, wondering what I was going to discover. And to my surprise, there was... the same corridor!

"How logical and consistent," I thought. "That's what Dragon's breath does to this place: it opens corridors. Now, what else could I try? A ritual, perhaps?"

I sat as if I was facing Gana's altar in the temple of Eisraim. As I had no altar, I placed my hands in front of my heart in the gesture called 'holding the flame', and I began the invocation,

"*Ha! Gana! Lobatchen Zera!*
Hera, Gana! Simayan ho Zera!"

Then I continued with the chanting of Gana's great mantra,

"*Nama Gana, Nama Gana, Gana Gana, Nam Nam.*"

But after only a few minutes I started feeling excessively tired. At first, I tried to ignore the wave of sleepiness – Verzazyel's cave was definitely not the right place to fall asleep! But it quickly became overwhelming.

"No!" I thought, "O Gervin, help! Let me not fall asleep again and miss one more initiation!" I fought with all my strength, calling onto the fountain. But sleep overtook me and I collapsed on the floor.

Thank the Lord Melchisedek, I only slept for a very short while! I woke up remembering a vivid dream – one of those dreams packed with long strings of events, despite the fact they only last a minute or two.

I had dreamt that I was walking in one of the corridors and that I met a tall man dressed in black like the Great Warriors. I had never met him before, yet he seemed to know me. He stared at me, "You are looking for Vivyani, aren't you?"

I was amazed.

"Verzazyel told me you were coming," he explained. Then he pointed towards the end of the corridor and said, "Go in this direction!"

When I reached the end of the corridor, I found a huge room full of light. Hundreds of torches were attached to the walls. And lo! there was the Nephilim woman with the long red hair, the one I had left in the canyon two days earlier. She was pacing around, looking quite impatient.

"Szar!" she said in a tone of reproach. "Where have you been? I have been waiting for four days! You nearly missed me, I was just about to leave."

"Four days? But how did you know I was coming?"

"Verzazyel told me. He said you were looking for Vivyani."

Vivyani!

"Can you tell me where she is?" I asked anxiously.

She cupped her hands and directed them towards an altar on one side of the room, "I will prophesy for you. But for now, Verzazyel said I was to teach you how to dance."

"Good!" I exclaimed joyfully. "I *love* dancing!"

"I know, Verzazyel told me. Will you show me how you do it?"

I praised my Mother of the Endless Night and started rehearsing the black dance. The place was special. I felt so light that at times I did not even have to fall back on my feet between two sequences of movements. I could have annihilated an entire enemy battalion in no time. But I noticed that the woman was pulling a doubtful face.

I stopped. "Am I not doing it well?"

"Szar, you are no doubt an expert in that dance but..." she hesitated, "do you really think this will be the right way to dance with Elyani?"

She was right. Somehow I couldn't imagine Elyani doing the black dance. It made me feel very dejected.

She placed her hand on my arm and spoke with a tender voice such as I had not heard for many months, "No, don't be sad! I will show you, there are many other ways of dancing."

"Oh!" I noticed, "You found your medallion." The low-cut of her long blue dress highlighted the soft stone pendant on her breast. It hit me again how stunning she was.

She waved her arms, "Come on, follow me!" I started moving with her, and it was magic. Her style was as pure as that of the black dance, but flowing and clear like the rivers of life of the enchanted Underworlds. I felt as elated as when I was dancing on the naked top of Mount Lohrzen.

But I could see the woman wasn't pleased with my dancing. "Am I doing it the wrong way?"

"Your movements are good, but you are supposed to be looking into my eyes."

I thanked her for this technical advice. As I had learnt in my fighter's training, one should always be grateful when someone corrects your mistakes. I tried to remember every single movement, so I could repeat the dance with Elyani once she and I were reunited.

I soon realised that the woman was right, maintaining eye contact made dancing even more intoxicating. I kept moving with her and found myself laughing as if I had just drunk from the rivers of life.

"I love it!" I said, "I love it! I love it!"

She giggled and laughed with me.

All of a sudden, I noticed we were no longer dancing in the hall but in the middle of a large plain inundated with sunlight. It was a strange and beautiful place with hardly any mist, just like in the worlds of the gods. Nature, child of my Mother the Dragon, was joyfully dancing with us. Then I heard music. It was sublime, both light and profound, and it seemed to be coming from everywhere. We kept dancing for hours. The melodious tones never seemed to end, rising and falling with us, giving meaning to each and every movement.

Each time I felt an upsurge of joy, the woman's heart flared with light. In turn, her joy reflected into my heart. This made me feel so vast that the

7 – The Book of the Nephilim Spice

plain was no longer large enough to contain us, and lo! the light of the Sun was replaced by the infinite depth of space. We found ourselves dancing in a field of stars, and the woman could not stop laughing. The celestial melodies became louder and louder, as notes seemed to reach into us from each and every light in heaven. And then...

Then I woke up in the corridor.

The first thing I did was sense the energy around me. There was nothing noticeable in darkness visible. The place seemed completely empty.

I sat up. "*Good Lord Melchisedek!* Did this dream really have to finish?" I closed my eyes again, hoping to find the field of stars and my dancing friend. But the magic had vanished. "I forgot to ask her name!" I thought, touching the medallion I had stolen from her in the canyon.

I stood up and for a few seconds repeated some of the movements of the dance to fix them in my memory. With a long sigh, I walked to the end of the corridor. There was a circular stairway with thirty-seven steps, the top of which led to yet another corridor.

After several more stairways that invariably led to the same type of corridor, I finally thought, "Enough!" I tuned into the clear fountain and called with all my strength, "Verzazyel! O Verzazyel, teacher of Lohrzen who founded the Great Warriors' order! What do *you* want me to find in your cave? Where do *you* want to lead me?"

A response came instantly. There was no particular sound or light, and no wave in darkness visible. The corridor was still the same, and nothing around me had changed. But from the clear fountain I *knew* that I had been answered, and that something was now waiting for me further away in the maze. I immediately set off. There was another flight of descending steps. Arriving at the bottom, I smelled a presence in a room that opened from the other end of the corridor in front of me.

How unlawfully amazing! There was a presence and I hadn't felt it, even though I had been extending my perception miles around through darkness visible.

I immediately raised my fists and started the slow movements of the black dance, again spreading my perception all around me. From what I could sense there was only one presence. One of the Nephilim. A woman. Not from a dangerous caste. She was holding a soft stone weapon in her hand, but she was holding it upside down! If I took her by surprise her chances of detonating the device were minimal. "Now, wait a minute," I stopped in my tracks, "I know this presence!" and dropping the attitude of the black dance, I walked straight through the corridor and into the room – a small crypt.

There she was – the red-haired woman with whom I had just danced in the field of stars. She was lying on her back on the floor.

"What are you doing here?"

Brandishing the soft stone, she yelled, "If you come near me, you're dead!"

"There is something very wrong, here!" I thought, "I have only been in this cave two hours, and this woman and her two friends were not due to arrive for three days."

She was holding the weapon upside down. There was little risk she could hurt anyone. But there was no need to tell her that. "Wouldn't you kill yourself if you detonated the stone?" I pointed out.

"I'm already dying. I have nothing to lose. And you Dragon's turd are here to die with me."

"What do you mean, you're dying?" I exclaimed, remembering how warm her body was when I was dancing with her, only a moment ago. But as I made a step towards her, she threatened to activate the weapon. Rather than fierce, she looked exhausted. She was trembling with cold. This time her long blue dress was fastened up to her throat, hiding the medallion on her breast.

"All right!" I pretended to take her menace seriously, "I'm not making a move. But will you tell me what has happened to you?"

She did not answer.

"How long have you been here?" I asked.

After a silence, she said, "Four days."

Four days? Ugly Underworld! If she was telling the truth, it meant I had been in the cave for at least seven days already. I thought I had only been here two hours! I started feeling uncomfortable, which made me decide the time had come for action.

"I see you found your medallion!" I said, to bring half a second of confusion into her mind. Then I leapt onto her, near-instantly hitting three gateways on her forearm. Even before she started screaming with pain, the soft stone was in my hand. I crushed it, rendering it useless, and threw it away.

The woman had not moved. She not only seemed to be defeated, but also paralysed. Big tears of pain were rolling down her cheeks.

"I'm sorry, I did not mean to hurt you," I began, and then realised it was rather a silly thing to say. I knelt down close to her and took the softest voice I could, "Listen, now that you are no longer trying to kill both of us, I have no reason to hurt you. Will you *please* let me help you?"

There was no answer. She seemed to be having difficulty staying awake. I quickly checked through darkness visible. There was still no detectable presence around. I asked again, "Will you please let me have a look at your energy? I will not touch you if you say no."

She didn't say yes. She just gazed at me, wondering why I was speaking softly instead of killing her.

I took her left arm and quickly dispelled the shock wave I had inflicted on her gateways. Then, sensing the main vital centres, I exclaimed, "Oh my Lord Melchisedek, what has happened to you?" Her life force had been blasted by something very nasty – a weapon or an energy of a kind I had never heard of.

7 – The Book of the Nephilim Spice

As my hands were running from gateway to gateway, I asked again, "Listen, if you could tell me what's happened it would give me more chance of doing something for you."

She half-spoke, half-whispered, "I made a mistake. I didn't realise..."

"What have you done, exactly?"

"That, the people of your temple will *never* know!"

"Have your two friends been wounded too?"

"No. They're gone. They're far away already."

"She certainly is beautiful," I thought, wondering how I could stop her shivering. But from high up in the clear fountain, the realisation fell onto me: she was *really* dying. Something had to be done immediately, or else! Wiping the tears from her face with the sleeve of my brown cape, I came very close to her. I looked into her eyes, "I need to put your body to sleep. Will you allow me to? I will not hurt you."

She hesitated a few seconds, then nodded.

Smiling at her, I projected some gentle Voice sounds on the cheap-way-out centres in her neck. As her eyes closed, I remembered, "I forgot to ask her name!"

The battle started. Her gateways were in a catastrophic condition. She was in urgent need of a life-force injection, but each time I projected energy into her, the principal vital gateways seemed to collapse a little further. I tried healing technique after healing technique, particularly the methods to counteract the effects of the most vicious soft-stone explosions, but nothing worked. She was drifting away.

"Oh Lord Melchisedek, inspire me!"

I started wondering if some noxious power was active in the crypt. I could not feel anything particular but still, I decided to carry her body outside. Opposite the corridor which had led me into the crypt was another one. Taking the woman in my arms, I raced out. After only three corridors and two long stairways, I found myself in the cave where I had started.

But this time I came out through the left wall of the cave. The corridor on the right wall had disappeared! I swore, but had no time to stop and marvel. I ran out and laid her body on the terrace outside the cave. But as I was resuming the energy manipulations, I received a strong and ugly warning through darkness visible: a large caravan of Nephilim pilgrims, together with at least nine Hunters, was approaching. They were dangerously close. Less than a few hours' walk.

"Underworld! How is that possible? When I arrived here they were at least a week away!"

Then another sudden deterioration in the woman's life force made me realise I was losing her.

"She's finished," I thought. Remembering Marek's order to stay away from the Hunters, I rapidly determined the best direction for my flight. If I didn't take off right now, it would soon be practically impossible to keep my presence hidden from them. Actually there was a serious risk they had already located me.

Just as I was about to start running a haunting vision came to me.

Vivyani.

In the Underworlds. I saw myself turning my back and walking away, leaving Vivyani behind. "About every single day since then I have regretted what I did in that cave. And now, what am I about to do?"

I contemplated the woman's long red hair.

In another flash I remembered the very first time I had met my master. He was rescuing a dying person. Had I turned my back then, what destiny would have been mine?

The memory of the Dragon-wondrous dance dream was still vivid in my mind. I sat down next to the friend whose name I did not know and passed my hands over her body, sensing her energy. Wondering again what an Underworld of a weapon could have inflicted such damage on her, I considered my options. Unless immediately projected into a state of hibernation, she was as good as dead. But hibernation was no final solution either. Besides, it implied a constant monitoring of her life force. Hardly compatible with being on the run, chased by nine Nephilim Hunters.

Yet, *Dragon above, Dragon below*, I simply could not abandon her. The more I looked at her, the clearer it became.

Another option flashed into my mind, something so crazy it made me chuckle at first. But when I tuned into the clear fountain, I knew – it was the way. Energy wounds like hers could only have come from the magic of the Point, or perhaps the Flying Dragons. If I could keep her hibernating until the Hunters reached the cave, they probably would know what to do. But in that case, why delay? Why not take the woman in my arms and walk straight towards the Nephilim caravan?

"Ha! Ha! Ha! Ha! Ha!"

I jumped up and laughed with joy, praising the Mother of the Endless Night. Then turning to my friend, I raised the Voice and projected high intensity upon her body, so as to near-completely freeze her vital functions. It took a few minutes before I was satisfied with the results. Her principal gateways were now snow-white.

Wasting no time, I picked her up in my arms, just as I had picked up Vivyani in the Underworlds of sickness. As I started climbing down the rock, the words returned, "*One Law, one way. He who never sleeps, never dies!*"

A bit further down the cliff I thought, "This time, Marek is going to be *really* cross with me!"

I kept walking.

7 – The Book of the Nephilim Spice

7.7 Rendezvous in Red Canyon

I could sense them so close that it seemed futile to conceal my presence. I might as well have stopped and waited for them. But I kept walking towards them, as a token of my peaceful intentions.

It did not take long before I saw their silhouettes emerge out of the mists. Three of them. The triangular net which had nearly destroyed Marek loomed large in my mind.

These three smelt like powerful and dangerous men, and I detected they had a profusion of soft-stone weapons. Finally they stopped fifty lawful feet in front of me.

For the first time after all these months of black dance and endless preparatory war games, I found myself face to face with three Nephilim Hunters.

They were tall but certainly not giants, and not particularly muscly either. They were men from the northern lands, with large foreheads and blue eyes. We spent a while looking at each other. I could sense that despite their cool attitude, they were gearing themselves for a fight. I was doing the same of course, judging the parameters of the situation, locating earth lines and venomous wells, deciding which direction I would take if I had to retreat, assessing every single factor of the situation as I had been overtrained to do.

Finally, clear fountain above and Dragon below, I broke the silence. "This woman is dying. Something happened while she was in Verzazyel's cave. Can you help?"

The two parties stood still, observing each other.

Then one of the Hunters, the one in the middle, said, "Drop her body and go. We'll take care of her."

"No! I can't do that. At the moment she is hibernating, surviving only on my energy. If I move more than thirty lawful feet from her, she dies."

The silence weighed thick and heavy.

The same man spoke again, "Is she Felicia?"

"I don't know her name. She was travelling with two other pilgrims."

The Hunters exchanged looks, then the one on the left said, "Alven and Rolen, we met them. But they told us Felicia was dead."

So her name was Felicia.

"Dead?" I replied, "Yes, she is just about that, but not completely. Her energy has suffered wounds like I have never seen. If it's Point and if you could undo the influence, I might have a chance to reconstitute her life force."

"Alven said there was a powerful healer who roamed around their camp. Was it you?"

"Could be."

"What's this brown cape you are wearing on top of your Warrior's clothes?"

"My master is Gervin, of the temple of Eisraim in the north. Brown is the colour of my caste. But *please*, we must do something for this woman. Fast! Can you tell me what happened to her?"

No reply, just another long silence. Their Hunters' faces were sealed like the red rock of the cliffs. I started wondering if I had made the right choice by coming to meet them. Finally, I said, "You don't believe me, do you?"

"Why should we?"

"Yes," I thought, "why should they? Since their childhood they must have heard horrific stories of black nightmares coming to kill Nephilim people and rarely missing their target. All the cunning and deceptions of war..."

Suddenly, war was no longer a game. The body I was carrying felt a lot heavier. I realised how naive I had been. And because of my misjudgment, precious time was ebbing away.

"Yes," I shrugged my shoulders, "why should you? *Farewell, men of the Law!*" I turned my back and started walking away with Felicia.

After a few seconds, the man who had not spoken yet called me, "Wait!"

I did not stop walking.

He called again, "*Wait, man of the Law!*"

When I heard him coming up behind me, I immediately swung round, wondering if the time had come to fight my first Hunter.

The two other men hadn't moved. There was no evidence that an attack was being launched. The man walking towards me was tall and slim. He had grey hair and no beard. He was the oldest of the three, perhaps fifty. He walked with a measure of dignity, his hands open in front of him to show he held no weapon. "What are you going to do with her?" he asked.

"What does it matter to you? She's dead, isn't she?"

He was now hardly fifteen lawful feet from me. I wondered what his first move would be if he decided to strike.

"Can I take a look at her body?"

"What are *you* going to do to her?" I asked.

He shrugged, "From what her brothers were saying, there is probably not much I can do."

I decided there was nothing to lose. I laid the body on the ground. The Hunter did not budge until I started walking backwards slowly, remembering Marek's instruction, "*Never gaze into the eyes of a Hunter!*"

When he was satisfied that I was far enough – some twenty lawful feet – the Hunter came and sat down next to Felicia, and let his hands run over her body. He let out a long whistle. "How did you do that? The hibernation, I mean. You used the Voice, didn't you?"

I nodded.

Puzzled, he kept inspecting Felicia's gateways, "So you *are* trying to heal her. But why, exactly?"

7 – The Book of the Nephilim Spice

What was I going to tell this man? That I had just spent seven days in a dream, dancing my clear fountain off with her? I kept silent.

"I need my two men," the Hunter finally said. "Will you allow them to come near?"

"If you are to implement any major manipulation of her energy, I need to be close enough to monitor her vital gateways. Will you allow me to come near?"

"*No way, man of the Law!*" he retorted. "Take it or leave it."

I had no choice. "Yes," I nodded.

The two other Hunters came and sat next to Felicia, and for ten minutes they kept their eyes closed – but not all at once. They took turns to watch me. To avoid problems I remained Dragon-still, holding Felicia's gateways from a distance. There was no sign of imminent danger.

When they had finished, the one who seemed to be the leader turned to me. "That's all we can do, *man of the Law. She wanted to play with fire, she burnt herself – so goes the Law of the Nephilim.* As far as I am concerned, she does not stand a chance. Do you still want to take her?"

"I do."

The Hunter placed one of his bags close to Felicia's body. He looked at his men, and each of them dropped another bag.

I was instantly on high-alarm mode.

"Now get out of here!" the chief said to me, his two friends already setting off. "And by the way, you may not have realised, but when you were in the cave you were branded by an energy that will take years to evaporate. It will allow any Nephilim Hunter to find you, even in the Furnaces of Doom. Meaning if you roam around one of my caravans of pilgrims, I will find you. *Farewell, man of the Law!*"

"What's in the bags?"

"Some food, care of Verzazyel. It's for her, just in case the guardians of the Underworld go off their brain and let her return into her body."

We looked at each other. "*Thank you, man of the Law!*" I said.

Being thanked by one of the black Warriors was obviously more irony than this man could bear. Impassive, he strode off, following his two friends.

As soon as they had gone far enough, I raced across to Felicia and thoroughly scanned the bags' energy. I opened them and carried out an inspection. Everything seemed fine. If the food in these three heavy bags was not poisoned, Nephilim-cankered or otherwise seasoned with witchcraft, it was a gorgeous present! "The provisions the Hunters had taken with them to chase me," I thought. Judging by the weight of the bags, they had planned at least twelve days. More like fifteen.

I sat down next to her. Before inspecting her gateways I said her name, "Felicia!"

I could not detect any change in her energy, which made it painfully evident I did not understand a thing about the unlawful magic of the Point and the Flying Dragons.

I picked up the strapped leather bags and the still-warm body, and started running.

7.8 Mother, surrender and the thunder of the Earth

Regardless of what the Hunter had said, I kept myself undetectable through darkness visible, or so I believed. It was difficult to accept that the cave had stamped an energy onto me. I couldn't feel anything, despite using every sensing method I had learnt from Marek the indestructible. Was the Hunter bluffing? Or was it one of those tricks of Flying Dragons' magic?

I followed the canyons northwards, looking for a gate of the Dragon, and I was amazed how difficult it was. I had thought that around Verzazyel's cave the gates of the Dragon would be as plentiful as the pebbles in Mount Lohrzen's lentil dishes. Not at all. It took me the rest of the day to find one. Was I missing something again?

At long last, I sense-smelled the characteristic breeze of a gate and found my way to a small grotto located relatively high in the red cliff on one side of a canyon. I laid Felicia on the cavern's rocky ground with a bag under her head, and covered her with my brown cape. Then I carried out a military-style inspection of the place and its immediate surroundings. Satisfied it was logistically viable – a small water stream running only a few minutes' walk from there – I drew a protective warning field around us and made plans to counter any attacks. Then for the first time since I had emerged from the dancing dream in Verzazyel's cave, I sat down and relaxed.

As I was contemplating the sleeping Felicia, I was struck once more by the sheer absurdity of the situation. "What the Ugly Underworld am I doing? For Melchisedek's sake, she is one of the Nephilim! What has Verzazyel's cave done to me?"

I stood up and walked to the entrance of the grotto. "If I return to the temple of the Dragon right now, everything will go back to normal. Felicia will die, and so what? She is one of the Nephilim. Her own people have left her for dead. I'll take her soft-stone medallion back to Marek, and the three bags of food for the brethren to have fun with. I won't even have to tell a lie, I'll just say I was bewitched with a dream while in Verzazyel's cave – which is the pure truth – and that it made me mad for a day. It will make another good story for Pelissor to tell in the dining hall."

7 – The Book of the Nephilim Spice

But as I turned towards Felicia to bid her a final *"Farewell, woman of the Law!"* I was again hit by the hideous memory of the sleeping Vivyani abandoned in the caverns of sickness. Enough grief to tear me apart.

I walked out onto the terrace that led to the cave, and in the twilight mists I raised my arms and screamed with the Voice, "Gervin! Help me! Gervin!"

There was no answer.

I came back into the cave and knelt by the woman. "Felicia," I whispered in distress, "I wish you were dead!" and without thinking I let my hand run over her body from gateway to gateway.

"Wait a minute. What's this?" There was a major change in her energy. Was it a result of the healing the Hunters had operated on her? Curiosity made me forget my doubts for a while. To probe her energy and try to understand what was happening, I placed her body just on top of the Dragon's gate, where the soft ascending breeze was flowing. I was dismayed, "I couldn't feel a thing while the Hunters were working on her. This magic of the Flying Dragons is such a headache!" I hoped Marek would soon teach me about it.

As I was about to open my mouth to project healing sounds, my mind went on the offensive, "I have received the Voice from Marek, under initiation and after a solemn oath. Using this power to help one of the Nephilim is nothing short of treason." I squeezed my eyes shut and bashed my thigh with my fist. "I am being trapped by Verzazyel's dance dream. Let's get out of here. She's dirt. She's one of them. She's not worth one minute of my time." But when I opened my eyes again and contemplated her sleeping body, I was unable to make a move.

"The hibernation is working wonderfully well," I thought. "She still looks beautiful. Stunning, actually. Just a bit pale."

What the Far Underworld would an awakened one do in such a situation? I rested my consciousness in the clear fountain for a few seconds. Seeing I could neither get up and run nor resolve to work on her body, I stayed where I was, took a proper meditation position, and let myself glide down into the Underworlds through the gate's breeze.

I soon landed in a cave of pink quartz crystal. I was so overwhelmed that I did not feel like moving. I stayed right in the middle of the gentle ascending draught, enjoying the beauty and serenity of my Mother's domain. But after a while, I noticed something strange. I could still feel Felicia's energy above my head. The clear fountain superimposed harmoniously with the ascending Dragon's breeze, creating a long column of Spirit that extended from my crown chakra up to Felicia's vital gateways.

"What a curious effect!" I thought, "I wonder if it could be used for healing."

I let myself glide down with the breeze much deeper. After a few seconds I found myself in one of the huge lapis lazuli caves I loved so much. *"Homage to thee, my Mother the Dragon!* You are so beautiful."

Strangely, I could still perceive Felicia's energy perfectly clearly, right on top of my head. The elated atmosphere of the lapis lazuli cavern made me remember the feeling of the dance dream with her. I found myself thinking that in all my eighteen months of Dragon games, there had not been one single moment when I had felt as enlightened as when I was dancing with Felicia in the field of stars. "Perhaps, after all," I reflected, "the eighteen months of black dance were nothing more than a preparation for the dream."

A moment later I was again overcome with despair. "That dance in the fields of stars was a dream! A *dream*! Gervin wants me to awaken, not dream!" Looking down to the centre of the Earth, I implored, "*O my Mother!* This situation is impossible. I need your help!"

I remembered how Marek had told me that the answer to *really* impossible problems was to be found in the deepest of the Underworlds. From the clear fountain, I decided to let myself glide down so deep that my Mother the Dragon would either implode me into a forever forgotten grain of dust, or offer me a solution.

And so I went, down and down, gliding along the breeze without stopping. The scenery changed so rapidly that I could not discern a single thing, and the deeper I descended, the more elated I became. Fearing I would lose my mind if I succumbed to the intoxication, I was careful to remain Dragon-still, my eyes closed.

The descent went on and on, and I started feeling so different that I began to doubt whether I was still myself. But I held fast to my complete inner motionlessness and kept diving.

It was hours later when the fall stopped. I had planned to first remain motionless with my eyes closed for some time. But where was time? I could not feel it any more. And where were my eyes? I no longer had a body. There was light, but not like I had ever thought light could be. Light can be bright or less bright, and it can be silvery, or golden, or some other colour. This light was just light, with none of those things.

But there was more than just this. I was a different being – still me, but no longer Szar. And in the everywhere-ness of this Deep Underworld, I intoned a hymn I had never heard,

"*O my Mother, the Dragon of the Deep,*
O magnificent, living source of the Endless Night,
O unfathomable, O thee upon whom all rest,
O She-Serpent, more profound than the Abyss,
O holiest and most sanctified,
Homage to thee! Homage to thee, my Mother!
Infinite is thy wisdom, never-ending is thy bliss.
Supernal and eternal thy dance,
Which gods and men all try to imitate.
Homage to thee, my Mother!
Homage to thee, Great Dragon of the Deep!

7 – The Book of the Nephilim Spice

The breath of life which thou hast given to me,
I come to surrender in thy bosom.
Have compassion, O Mother!
I know that Truth
Is too vast to fit in a man's heart,
Thy ways too mysterious for me to comprehend.
But Mother, I pray,
May I be killed rather than go against thee.
Please let me not tread a path
That will see me forsaken by thee.
Please, let me not transgress thy Will."

I waited, until the noble waves of my Mother's infinity softly reached me. I heard her Voice, which is the thunder of the Earth. But this time her breath was gentle and warm.
In the death crypt in the bowels of Mount Lohrzen, when I had first heard it, I had thought it fierce and terrible. How confused I had been!
Now the melodious harmonies reached me as they truly were, and they comforted me.
"Soft is thy Voice, my Mother!" I extolled.
The Voice spoke to me.

7.9 The hymn of the She-Dragon Mother to all her creatures

"To the millions of creatures who have invoked my name today,
And to the ten times as many who forgot to call upon me,
And to all those who don't yet know
They can always call me and be answered,
I send my love.
May you all open to the infinite sweetness
Which I have laid in the world for you,
But which so few recognise!
To those who sleep through a dreamless night,
I whisper blissful hymns of awakening.
To those who dream and strive to awaken,
To those who ask for my wisdom,
I send the following message:
When the mother breast-feeds the child,
Nurturing is her worship of me.
When the husband loves the wife,
Loving is his worship of me.
When the physician cares for his patient,
Healing is his worship of me.

When the warrior slays his enemy,
The battle is his worship of me.
For I am the mother and the child, the husband and the wife,
The physician, the patient, the warrior and the enemy.
Who of my children are the wise, who are the fools?
Wise are they who know that through their works
They are worshipping me.
The fools the same works accomplish
But fail to recognise they are dancing with me.
Whom do I love, whom do I loathe?
A mother despises none of her children.
The fools and the wise,
All I love with equal care.
A mother wishes none of her children to suffer.
And in the twinkling of an aeon
When all my creatures awaken
To the glorious enlightenment I have prepared for them,
All will see
That suffering existed but through their blinded eyes."

7.10 The gate of caring

I found myself sitting close to Felicia's body, having no recollection of my reascension along the breeze of the Deep. Had a miracle taken place, or had I been so absorbed in the contemplation of my Mother's light that I had not even realised I was journeying back?

It was night. I did not move. I felt vaster than the night. I was not just myself, but my Mother at the same time. I was Felicia as well as Szar. And Felicia was well, blissfully asleep in my Mother's spheres of Highness. Two steps away from us, I could feel the pilgrims' caravan camping outside Verzazyel's cave. And I was the Hunters as well as the pilgrims. Three steps away, I was Mount Lohrzen, and Floster, and all the Warriors. I was every single soul in the county of the Red Lands, and the Jeremitzia river, and the rivers of the neighbouring counties. Throughout the kingdom myriads of souls were dancing their sleep in my bosom.

"Thy dance, my Mother!" I exclaimed with reverence.

Then from my Mother's standpoint of cosmic vastness, I looked down to little Szar who was sitting by Felicia, his hand on her heart. Was he going to heal her or return to Marek? It did not matter much. Felicia was ecstatically entranced in my Mother's bosom. And the She-Dragon of the Deep loved Marek so much that he would no doubt recover from losing one of his disciples.

"Will you throw the dice of destiny?" my Mother asked me.

7 – The Book of the Nephilim Spice

I replied, "Might I be granted the immense privilege of rising above the dice of destiny, that I may know what pleases thee and accomplish thy Will?"

My Mother answered, "Seeing the life of my creatures crushed for no reason does not please me."

"How can a man please thee?" I asked.

I heard the answer, but could not understand it.

The following morning, sunrise surprised me. I felt incredibly lucid. Clear, like the dawn of creation. I was lying close to Felicia, my hand still on the vital gateways of her heart. I had fallen asleep without even realising it.

"This is the first night I have ever spent sleeping on a gate of the Dragon," I realised, sitting up. I could not remember any particular dream.

I walked out of the cave and contemplated the sparse mists. I checked that none of the astral beacons I had placed in darkness visible indicated the coming of danger. Then I ran down to the stream to wash myself and collect water.

Wasting no time, I returned to the cave and commenced the healing work on Felicia. This marked the start of a momentous battle which I waged both in the cave and far below, in my Mother's Underworlds. The healing method I had discovered the day before, placing myself in the breeze of the gate and connecting Felicia with the column of Spirit above my head, worked wonders. I could not only throw forces up, directly into her body, but also rest on the life-wisdom and the knowingness of the Underworlds. I needed it!

My first results were not particularly good. Whatever it was that Felicia had been struck by had devastated her body of energy. Each time I fixed a centre, another one collapsed, and energy injections made her meridians melt like snow in the sun. Without hoping too much, I worked day after day. I did what Marek and others had done before me – I descended deeper and deeper, contacting forces of life of such magnitude that they filled me with awe.

But my burden was rendered light by the joy that constantly welled inside me when I descended into the Underworlds – especially the rivers of life in the deeper levels. I had located one particular layer in which a river passed through the Dragon's gate below the cave, so I could immerse myself into the blissful flows while holding Felicia's energy straight above my head. This was such an ecstatic experience! I sometimes had to scream with joy, as I could not contain the waves of pleasure that ran through my body. Had it not been for the gentle soul whose life rested upon my head, I might have abandoned myself to the stream and let my Mother take me.

After six days, the first encouraging signs appeared. Some of the vital gateways started gaining in solidity. I could inject life force into them without them further collapsing. To mend some parts of her body of energy that had seemed irreparable, I descended into deep golden Underworlds and collected precious stones, which I placed inside her and used as core-centres to initiate the regeneration.

After ten days, the condition of all the vital gateways definitely had improved, and I started to believe that Felicia would live. I came to think of her as a baby to whom my Mother was going to give birth. What was the baby going to be like? What would be her first words? Would she be as strong as I had tried to make her, with gateways like those of a mighty warrior?

And what kind of person was she going to be? My Mother had poured so much love into her – surely she would be sweet like the woman who had danced with me in the field of stars. Day after day, my anticipation increased. I couldn't wait to hear her speak!

On the thirteenth day, I was able to take Felicia out of the hibernation state. There were a few minutes of suspense. As I had learnt from Marek, when taking someone out of deep hibernation, the sudden increase in etheric circulations can bring dramatic collapses in the body of energy. But after half an hour, once I was satisfied that my work was holding fast, none of Felicia's main gateways having crumbled, I jumped around the cavern and danced with joy, letting out my loudest ritual scream ever, "Youyouyouyou!"

I took her body away from the breeze of the gate and placed her on a mattress made of wild grasses I had collected from the scrubs of the canyon. And I waited.

Towards the middle of the day, Felicia first moved her left arm. I cheered, and praised the Mother of the Light. Remembering the caverns of sickness, when Vivyani had first moved her hand while I was carrying her, I found myself saying, "This time, I have not abandoned you!"

On three more occasions that afternoon, the baby moved. Each time I got carried away with joy.

On the fourteenth day when I got up, Felicia was still asleep. But on my return from the stream, sensing darkness visible I knew without possible doubt that Felicia had woken.

I jumped my way up to the opening of the cave as if to greet an old friend.

7.11 The first dialogue with Felicia

As soon as she saw me coming into the cave, Felicia reacted, "Oh, no! The black nightmare again! Go away!" With a face which expressed disgust as much as fear, she started crying.

I realised it was not very clever of me to appear in front of her dressed in black, but as I had covered her with my brown cape, what else could I

7 – The Book of the Nephilim Spice

wear? I tried to approach her but she kept crying, "Go away! Go away! *Go to Azazel and get lost!*"

She seemed very upset, so I walked out of the cavern.

As I sat on a rock on the terrace and contemplated the mists, I remembered how terrible I had felt when waking up from my first Underworld trip. "The poor child," I thought, and I waited outside the cavern until I could sense through darkness visible that she had fallen asleep again. Then I went in and, throwing my black cap into one corner of the cavern and untying my hair, I sat close to her again and checked her gateways.

After a long examination I was thoroughly satisfied. "Excellent!" I said out loud, which immediately woke her up.

When she saw me so close to her, my hands on her body, she didn't say a word. We gazed at one another silently. "There is no doubt about it, she is the one I was dancing with in the field of stars," I thought, contemplating her large blue eyes. Only the joy was missing.

I took her by the hand, "Felicia, it's safe. It's all safe! I am here to take care of you. You just had a long sleep, and now you are back and ready to start a new life." And while we kept looking at each other, I told her about the cave and its surroundings, and any other thing that came to mind.

Before long she fell asleep. She woke up only late in the afternoon.

"Here is our sleeping princess! Come on, Felicia, you must drink, it is very important," I said, holding her head up with my hand and pressing a cup to her lips.

"Lawfully fantastic," I cheered after she took a few sips, and I took her hand and kept on telling her unimportant things. But she was so tired that her eyes soon closed again.

The following morning she did not wake up, but as her energy levels were excellent, I opted for a full-blown injection of life force. Using a scale of Voice frequencies, I finalised the work on her gateways. When she next opened her eyes, Felicia was back.

I first made her drink half a cup of water. Then we looked into each other's eyes.

"I met a caravan of pilgrims who had come across your brothers while they were on their way back to the northern lands," I said. "They thought you were dead. Can you imagine how happy they'll be when they see you?"

I could see her consciousness was clear. Perhaps she was too tired to answer me, or perhaps she just didn't feel like it. She kept staring at me, her lips stubbornly sealed. I prayed to my Mother to let some of her infinite sweetness flow through my voice. "You don't have to speak to me, I will speak to you. All I'm asking you to do is drink. Now that you are no longer hibernating, it's essential you get plenty of fluid. Soon you will have to start eating too, otherwise you're going to fade away. Though the hibernation lasted thirteen days, you didn't lose too much weight. But from today onwards you must start eating."

I showed her the bags of food. "Look, these were given to us by the Hunters, 'care of Verzazyel!' They are full of incredibly delicious things. When I first tasted them I thought, 'O my Lord Melchisedek, is *this* what the Nephilim eat?'"

Actually, it had left me stupefied, aghast and abuzz. I was expecting revolting, compost-looking, vomit-smelling conserves – bloody sauces full of animal and human tidbits, all mixed together as in the most disgusting Underworld caverns of sickness. This is why at first I didn't even think of opening the bags. I feasted on locusts collected in the wilderness. During my first months with Marek, when I had been trained to survive under any conditions, I had hated locusts. But then, thanks to my Mother the Dragon, I had reprogrammed my taste, and I now enjoyed the little creatures very much. Marek himself was very fond of locusts. He used to say they were as pure as the desert itself.

It was curiosity, not hunger, that had drawn me to the bags the Hunters had left for Felicia. After days of cautious astral smelling with due nostril-wriggling, all my psychic defenses rigged up and resting on the Dragon of the Deep, when I had finally lifted off the lid of a small jar I had been completely taken aback by the sweet, enticing smell.

What was this luscious red toadspawn? Coagulated blood, perhaps? Not at all! It was the sweetest red berry jam I had ever tasted. It was magnificent. It sent a thrill of delight throughout my body of energy.

But was it safe? What if the sweet taste had been designed to attack the purity of my soul, desecrate my Spirit and render me powerless, a fallen being in the hands of the devilish Nephilim trash?

Unsure whether any strength of character would be left in me if I indulged in another spoonful of the outrageously sweet substance, I had discarded the bags, banishing them to a remote corner of the cavern, and returned to my healthy, soul-cleansing diet of locusts.

"You would probably find all this delicious," I told Felicia. "And out of curiosity (because I'm not sure if this food is suited to my caste), I would very much like to learn some of the recipes from you."

Felicia kept looking at me in her stubborn fashion without ever smiling or opening her lips, which very much resembled the red berry jam. Realising she did not yet know my name, I told her about myself and the Eisraim temple. "Mother, please bring your softness down onto this child!" I kept praying while I kept her company.

Felicia listened but remained mute.

I went out of the cave a few times to let her rest, but she did not sleep much, which was rather a good sign at this stage. She accepted water but refused any kind of food, and this soon became a topic of concern.

Patiently, I sat by her and kept talking to her, but she retained the same impassive attitude, refusing to answer any of my questions. At the end of the day I started feeling drained and dejected. I went out for a while, contemplating the reddish hue of the early sunset mists.

7 – The Book of the Nephilim Spice

When I came back I said, "Felicia, I want to tell you a story. Once in the temple of Eisraim, when I was very sick, someone really took care of me, and it made me a different man." And in great detail I narrated the story of Vivyani, and the way Elyani had nursed me, and the fun we had during the period of convalescence.

"You see, Felicia," I concluded after the long story, "I had often thought Elyani must have had a terrible time looking after me when I was unconscious. Now I think perhaps I was wrong. Looking after you has been one of the most beautiful experiences of my life. I have enjoyed every single day, every hour. At times I have felt so vast and uplifted by the caring energy my Mother has poured into me for you... lucky I could still fit in the cavern! Whatever happens now, I will not regret any of this."

I gently caressed her hair, "Please Felicia, will you have something to eat? Just a little bit."

As she refused the spoonful of jam I presented to her mouth, I took a long breath and asked, "Why will you not speak to me?"

Her lips remained sealed. She closed her eyes in avoidance and played dead.

I walked out. It was night. Under the silvery light diffused through the mists, I remembered Elyani's courtyard, and I danced.

The following morning when I came back from the water stream, I greeted Felicia and sat close to her bed. Now she would not even accept any water. "This obstinate little girl," I thought, "is going to ruin all my Mother's work."

"Felicia this is getting very serious," I warned. "You are no longer hibernating. If you do not drink and eat, it won't be long before you render the lawful ghost."

All I received in response was the same stubborn look.

I closed my eyes and took my head in my hands, trying to decide what to do. Remembering the way Elyani had shocked me out of the greyness of the caves of sickness, I looked into Felicia's eyes and nearly screamed at her, "Do you realise that in the last sixteen days I have done nothing but clean your body and fix your energy?"

But before I had time to think of what to say next, Felicia retorted with contempt, "Why didn't you let me die? You're one of the black nightmares, aren't you?"

I looked to a corner of the cave, not knowing what to reply. Then I shrugged my shoulders and went out for a quick run to the top of the hill.

"What the Underworld am I going to do with her if she refuses to eat?" I thought, starting a black dance to clarify my ideas. Half an hour later, having weighed the pros and cons of the situation, I paid my homage to the mountain and climbed down the hill back to the cave.

This time I did not sit beside her bed. I just said, "Felicia, the pilgrims I met after I found you are still camping near Verzazyel's cave. I will take you back to them, they'll take care of you." Coming closer to her, I asked, "All right like this?"

She remained impassive but nodded.

"Will you drink some water?" As she accepted, I exclaimed, "*Praise the Lord Melchisedek!*" Then I sat next to her a last time. I took her hands. She did not try to resist. Looking into her eyes, I thought, "Now I know how it feels for a mother to have her child taken away."

I picked her up in my arms. She played dead. I found her much lighter than when we had arrived in the cave. While climbing down to the bottom of the canyon, I confided, "Felicia, I must tell you about a fantastic dream I had when I was in the Watcher's cave." As we advanced through the mists, I began narrating every single detail.

7.12 The Law is the Law

The same three Hunters, having sensed my presence, were on their way to meet Felicia and I. This time I waited for them in a place that seemed ideal if it came to a fight – easy retreat, venomous wells in profusion.

It was the season of the year when many caravans of pilgrims came to visit the cave. Following an unspoken agreement, the Warriors rarely came out of their mountain during this period. Had I been found dead in the canyon, large-scale reprisals by Marek's men were to be expected – more than enough to make intelligent Hunters think twice before striking me.

I laid Felicia on the ground. We looked at each other for a while. Her face looked less stubbornly closed than before. Maybe, after all, she had never believed I would return her to her kind. Seeing the end of her troubles coming to a close must have mellowed her mood. I didn't speak, because I did not know what to say. The opening I had been waiting for could perhaps have taken place right then. But I had to prepare myself for a possible fight.

My plan was to move fast. As soon as the three Hunters emerged out of the mists, I called, "*Praise the Lord Melchisedek, men of the Law!* She is all yours. She needs water in lawful plenty, and food as soon as possible."

Holding every single parameter of the situation under tight control, I briefly looked at Felicia. "*Farewell, woman of the Law!*" Then I turned on my heel and started walking fast.

The chief Hunter called me, "*Wait, man of the Law!*"

I spun round, high-alarm mode engaged. But the three Hunters hadn't budged. "What, *man of the Law*?" I asked.

"If we take her, she must die!"

I couldn't believe my ears. Walking back to Felicia, I yelled, "What?"

There was a silence.

7 – The Book of the Nephilim Spice

"She has broken the Law of the Nephilim," the senior Hunter said. "If we take her, she must die."

Felicia gazed up at me. "Szar, I'm sorry!"

I was as stupefied as Dragon-control allowed me to be. "You mean you knew this was going to happen?"

"I'm sorry!" she repeated.

"This is a nightmare!" I thought. Turning to the Hunters, I asked, "But didn't you give her a healing last time we met?"

"That was before we discovered what she did in the cave! She trespassed and unlawfully entered the forbidden holy crypt."

No one moved. I tuned into the clear fountain, trying to figure out what to do next.

"Listen," the chief said, "I am a man of the northern lands. I am not *a parrot of the Law*. I don't wish this woman's death. But I have one hundred and fifty pilgrims from the county of the Western Shores with me, and they have all witnessed the transgression of Verzazyel's Law. If you leave her here, there is nothing I can do."

There was no longer Szar – just a clear fountain. *No thoughts, just Dragon*, I bent down and picked up Felicia. I hovered for a few seconds.

The chief Hunter raised his right arm and showed his palm.

"Do you know what this means?" I asked Felicia, gearing myself for the first strike.

"Means he thinks you're a prian."

"What's a prian?"

"A powerful man," she said. "He thinks you could become a Hunter. I mean, if you were one of the Nephilim, of course."

"I can't believe this!" I turned and ran as fast as I could, Felicia holding on tightly to my neck.

When we arrived at a distance I judged safe, I laid Felicia on the ground. She sat up, leaning her back against a large rock. She smoothed out her long red hair, then took a complicated position, resting her elbow on her knee and her chin in her hand, and she looked at me.

I raised my arms horizontally, clenched my fists to the extreme, looked down toward the Earth, and with a near-Voice threshold I roared with outrage, "*Ooohhh Great She-Serpent of the Deep!*" Then I turned to the Nephilim woman. "Felicia, if I hadn't just spent sixteen days working my Dragon off to bring you back to the kingdom, I think I could kill you."

With a small voice and a touch of sadness in her big blue eyes, she reiterated, "Szar, I am sorry!"

"And you call *me* a nightmare!"

"I thought that perhaps the holy crypt would have fixed itself and erased the traces of my passage. It does happen, you know. It was really bad luck the pilgrims arrived so quickly."

"Now that you are outlawed, they could come and hunt us any time!"

"No, you don't have to worry about that. Ferippe, the man who spoke to you, told me they won't."

"What do you mean he told you?"

"We spoke to each other during your meeting."

"What? I didn't hear anything in darkness visible."

"We used another kind of channel."

I took my head in my hands and started pacing around. "That's it, now she's doing Flying Dragons' witchcraft behind my back! And what else did this Ferippe tell you?"

"He said he would bring us some food in a few days. He said not to worry if we wanted to change our location, he'd find us anyway. But he didn't want us to go far, so he wouldn't have to leave his pilgrims for too long."

"What? Do you mean he's coming to find us?"

"*Peace, man of the Law!* Ferippe is a friend of my brother Alven, and some other friends of mine. They went to school together, in the county of the Snowy Mountains. He won't do anything to hurt me. If he showed his hand to you, it's because I told him all about you."

I sat on a rock, looking in the other direction. "Oh my Mother the Dragon! Tell me this is just a bad dream and I'm about to wake up in the Watcher's cave."

There was a silence. Then Felicia risked, "Szar I am very thirsty, could I have something to drink, please?"

I grabbed a water container from my bag and casually flung it at her, as if throwing it to one of my Dragon comrades. She missed it. I went to pick it up and gave it to her.

Despite my anger, I felt moved when I saw her drink. Suddenly, she was my child again. But I soon had to stop her, "Careful, not too much at a time."

I picked her up. "Let's go back to the cave!"

As I started walking, she put her arms around my neck, soft and submissive, "I promise I will eat."

7.13 The magic of honeyed pickled cucumbers

When we got back to the cave, I laid Felicia's body on her straw mattress. She immediately sat up, crossing her legs.

"Listen!" I said while she was fixing her hair, "I will stay with you two or three more days, until you can walk and look after yourself. Then I will go. I'll leave you the bags of food. You'll just have to wait for your friend the Hunter, and he will find a way of taking you back wherever it is that you want to go. Can he do that?"

She nodded.

7 – The Book of the Nephilim Spice

I put one of the bags of food close to her and went to sit in another corner of the cave.

Even though I was not looking at her I could hear her eat. It made me feel relieved. "Now I know how a mother feels when her sick child recovers and starts eating again," I thought. "But I wish I could have had a normal baby, not one of these wicked Nephilim monsters!"

Her appetite was so ferocious that I had to intervene. "Wait, Felicia! Don't eat so quickly! If you eat too much you will make yourself sick." I took the bag away from her and returned to my corner of the cavern.

We remained silent for a long time, each on our side of the cave. Then she said, "You think I'm a terrible person, don't you?"

I couldn't be bothered answering her.

"I wonder what you will tell your friends about me. I don't mean the people in Mount Lohrzen, but those in Eisraim. Do you think you'll keep wearing my medallion?"

I had forgotten about the soft stone I had stolen from her on our first meeting. I pulled it off my neck and threw it to her. It fell onto the straw mattress.

"You told me a lot about yourself," she continued, "but you don't know a thing about me." She waited for me to ask more.

I remained as still as the Abyss of the Deep.

She decided to continue anyway, "I am a priestess too, you know. I too have a teacher who has given me some hard times. When I was listening to you speaking about Master Gervin of the Brown Robe, I was struck by the resemblances."

So she was listening, after all.

"I wonder what terrible things the Warriors of Mount Lohrzen have told you about my people. You probably think we are all monsters, like Bobros the ogre and his ugly sisters. Have they told you that story?"

Without looking at her, I nodded.

She chuckled, "I bet they told you Lubu was a Great Warrior!"

"What do you mean? What was wrong with Lubu?"

"Not a lawful thing! He was one of the founders of the Nephilim Hunters, that's all!"

Hearing such nonsense, I preferred not to answer. I just shrugged my shoulders.

"Szar, do they use soft stones in Eisraim?"

I nodded.

"Did you know that it is the Nephilim people who invented the soft stones in the first place, and who are still the masters in the art of making them?" She could see I did not believe her. "Have you noticed many soft stones in Mount Lohrzen? Why do you think the stones have been banned throughout the county of the Red Lands? It's because they came from the Nephilim scum."

I remembered my first months in the temple of the Dragon, when I looked everywhere for a device to communicate with Elyani. The only soft stones kept in Mount Lohrzen were a few weapons used for the instruction of the Warriors. Perplexed, I turned towards her. She was swinging her medallion like a pendulum.

"Did you know this stone you've been carrying around your neck is immensely precious? It was crystallised by some of the finest experts in the kingdom. The people in my temple make them."

She threw the pendant back to me. "Take it!"

She had aroused my curiosity. I made Dragon-sure I caught it in the air.

"It's a present for Lady Elyani. If she's a priestess of the White Eagle, she'll know what it's worth."

"Lady Elyani..." I thought, contemplating the medallion. "So Felicia *was* listening to me when I was talking." I turned towards her. But as I was about to thank her, she added, "Just tell her it's a present from one of the Nephilim!"

I sighed, not knowing what to say.

"Tell me Szar, have you met some of the people who live in this county?"

I nodded. During the manoeuvres with Marek I had been in contact with the local populace a number of times.

"Have you noticed that the women never put any black powder on their eyes, and never wear jewels?"

I nodded.

"Do you think you'd like to marry one of their daughters? What a quiet life you would have! She'd never say a sentence that is not straight from the Law." Then, taking a slow and monotonous low-pitched voice, she droned, "*Praise the Lord Mel-chi-se-dek. Good mor-ning, man of the Law!*"

I was shocked. These words could have come straight out of Gervin's mouth.

But Felicia did not stop there. "Do you think Elyani would like you if you started talking like the people of this county?" She kept on, "Do you know why the people of the Red Lands are like that, Szar? Simply because they have eliminated all Nephilim influence from their land. The Great Warriors have won their battles so well that the county of the Red Lands is renowned as one of the most boring and retarded places in the entire kingdom."

I did not like the sound of what she was saying. Yet I had heard that the region of the Red Lands was called the kingdom's ass by educated people of other counties.

Seeing that I was getting upset, Felicia mellowed her voice, "I'm sorry, *man of the Law!* I didn't want to be hurtful. I know I talk too much." Then she lay down and closed her eyes.

7 – The Book of the Nephilim Spice

"In the county of the Snowy Mountains," I asked after a while, "do all people speak fast like you?"

"Not all. Mainly the Nephilim people. But *thank the Lord Melchisedek*, the Nephilim people are not all like me!"

"My teacher, master Gervin, speaks fast too."

Felicia immediately reopened her eyes. She smiled at me. Her voice was even mellower, "I gathered that would be the case. Otherwise I wouldn't even bother telling you these things."

I inhaled. "I think it would be wise for you to *get some lawful rest*," I said. She didn't move.

I added, from the Dragon, "Now!"

She immediately closed her eyes.

I studied the medallion. When I could tell from her breathing that she had fallen asleep I felt relieved, somehow. "If this is the way she is when she's weak and famished," I thought, "I hate to imagine what she must be like in her temple!" And I decided I needed to climb to the top of the hill.

While I was black-dancing I kept thinking about what Felicia had said. It bothered me that she was definitely not a sleeper. How she could speak like Gervin and yet be one of the Nephilim was more than I could take. All this was such a headache! *No thoughts, just Dragon*, I threw myself into a two-hour practice of the most difficult parts of the black dance. I rehearsed the black-forty ritual murder over and over again, once for every pilgrim in the nearby Nephilim caravan. It made me feel very much better.

Knowing that people who have just been hibernating should not be left to sleep during the day for too long, I returned to wake her up.

I knelt down close to her and let my hands work on her gateways for a few minutes.

When she woke up, she gazed at me.

At first, I avoided her gaze. *No thoughts, just Dragon*, I kept on with my healing work.

"Are you still angry with me?" she asked.

I didn't answer.

"You know, if you think I'm impossible you're not the only one," she declared. "All my friends and family have been telling me that for years. Not to mention my teacher, of course!" She looked up at the ceiling and sighed.

For some mysterious reason, I found myself smiling.

She smiled too. It was the first time. I had often wondered what her smile would be like, but had never anticipated it would be so warm. "She looks so different when she's in her body!" I thought, contemplating her large blue eyes.

I kept on infusing life force into her body of energy, moving from gateway to gateway. She opened, making herself soft under my hands, and looking at me just like in the dance dream in the Watcher's cave.

When I had finished, she pleaded in a little voice, "I am terribly hungry. Could I have *some lawful lunch*? Please."

"Sure." I gave her one of the bags.

"Could I have the other bags too, please?" she asked while inspecting the first one.

I brought the other two bags to her. They were still full, since I had kept safely to my diet of locusts.

"Did you say you wanted me to give you recipes?" she asked, busy searching the bags and assessing the provisions.

"Just out of curiosity," I explained.

"You haven't tried many jars," she said. Then she announced triumphantly, "Here it is!" pulling a medium-sized container from one of the bags. She turned to me, "Would you like to taste something really special?"

That day I had been far too busy to go and collect locusts.

"Just out of curiosity!" she added, seeing me hesitate.

"All right."

She opened the container and prepared a spoonful of thick, greenish, frog-vomit-looking substance, which she directed towards my mouth.

I took the spoon from her hand and cautiously sniffed the greenish thing. For frog vomit, the smell was surprisingly pleasant.

"It's safe!" Felicia smiled, and to demonstrate her point she dug her fingers into the container's green puree and shovelled a large dollop into her mouth.

Resting on the Dragon, I pushed the spoon into my mouth. Felicia, who had already swallowed her puree, watched with curiosity.

The taste was incredibly subtle and convoluted. Past the initial shock it filled my entire body of energy with a joyful, dancing vibration.

"It's called honeyed pickled cucumbers. It's my favourite dish," Felicia explained. "This one is a bit mushy, but out in the middle of the Red Lands what do you expect? And of course, without the cinnamon sauce it can't really be itself. Still it's a pretty good one, and I'm a connoisseur. Do you like it?"

"It's sweet," I answered warily, not having yet decided whether this sweetness was from the gods or from the devil.

"Of course," she said with an understanding smile, "you are not used to sweets. Let me get you something else." She opened a large jar, plunged her index finger into a brownish-reddish mixture and licked it. "Mm..." she frowned in delight. "Ferippe has taste!" She took the spoon from my hand, wiped it clean with the long sleeve of her turquoise dress, and returned it full. "Fishbone paté!" she murmured, as if inspired by the gods.

That sounded devious. I sniffed the reddish paste with extreme caution. But when I tasted it, I had to admit to myself that it was delicious – but dangerously delicious.

Felicia, who was fast emptying the container of honeyed pickled cucumbers, seemed delighted. "See! I knew you would like it! Have some more."

7 – The Book of the Nephilim Spice

She spread a thick layer of paté on a small loaf of cereals and handed it to me.

I chewed prudently, ready to spit out everything if the clear fountain commanded me.

With a dozen jars open in front of her, Felicia was eating so ravenously and so fast that again I had to stop her. "Felicia, after your hibernation you must eat only a little in the first days, or it will make you sick."

"All right!" she immediately let her spoon drop from her hand, turned to face me, and became still with an air of total surrender, watching me eat.

I found myself smiling again.

When I finished the loaf, she prepared a spoonful of a red berry jelly for me. "This one is magical. You have to remember someone you care for, and she'll think of you."

I took the spoon and buried myself in my thoughts.

"You miss her, don't you?"

I sort-of smiled, for the third time.

"How long since you've seen her?" she asked.

"More than a year and a half." I put the jelly in my mouth, remembering Elyani's sweetness.

Felicia asked several questions which I answered without really knowing why. She was extremely curious, wanting to know everything about my life in Eisraim, about Gervin, about Elyani. She talked a lot but she knew how to listen, and she remembered all the things I had told her the day before, which was quite a feat, considering that people who have just emerged from hibernation usually have a flimsy memory. Soon I found myself engaged in a lively discussion, and it made me feel extremely uncomfortable.

One part of me was secretly delighted. My baby was proving to be a charming, joyful and astute creature. I was proud of my work. But at the same time I felt torn apart – this, my first proper discussion in eighteen months, was happening with one of the Nephilim. Why wasn't she stupid and ugly like the monstrous, foul-smelling sisters of Bobros, son of Bobros? Why wasn't she eating dirt, and coagulated blood, and half-decomposed pieces of animal and human flesh? And how dare she be so awake! More than anything else, I was angry at her for not being a sleeper.

When she fell asleep, after we had been speaking all afternoon, I pulled an ugly face at her.

I wished I had killed her! I wished I had finished her off the first day, instead of being such an *idiot in the Law* and healing her long-debilitated liver (no wonder it was so rotten, considering how she ate).

How was her liver, by the way?

I lightly passed my hands over her warm body, sensing her gateways and drawing from the Dragon gate's breeze to inject life force into her.

The energy of her liver was superb. Slightly empty, because of the fatigue, but perfectly clean.

Felicia half woke up. In the uncertain glimmer of twilight, she smiled at me.

"*Peace, my child,*" I gently caressed her hair. "Everything is safe."

7.14 A feast in the wilderness

The morning after, when I returned to the cave after black dancing, collecting water, climbing up and down the canyons, and more black dancing, I brought with me enough locusts for at least two days.

Felicia was awake. She was waiting for me, sitting up on her mattress. She still looked tired, but nowhere near as pale as the day before.

"I prepared breakfast for you, Sir Great Dragon!" she announced joyfully after answering my lawful greeting.

Close to her mattress she had artistically laid out a number of jars on the rocky floor of the cavern. There were foods of all colours, and motley subtle smells wafting in the air.

"I brought something for breakfast too," I said.

"So we'll have a feast!" she clapped her hands. But the expression on her face suddenly changed when she saw me emptying the bag of locusts on the floor.

She contained herself and kept smiling. "What are they?"

"Locusts." I sat in front of her, suspiciously sniffing her jars.

"Dead locusts?" Felicia asked, keeping her voice neutral.

"Well, of course! Want some?"

"Mm... yes, why not? How do you eat them?"

"Like this!" I chose two beautiful specimens and put them in my mouth. "A good thing about locusts is that you really have to chew, you can't just swallow mindlessly," I said, my jaw working hard.

"All right, then." She picked up a locust and courageously put it in her mouth. But as she started chewing she pointed at the heap of locusts, horror-struck, "Oh my god! That one is still moving!"

"Ah! Don't worry!" I crushed the head of the little beast between my fingers.

Felicia looked deeply distressed, holding one trembling hand in front of her mouth and the other on her stomach. Her face turned green, and her eyes became vague.

The clear fountain spoke to my heart, asking how Elyani would have felt if I had forced her to eat locusts. "Just spit it out," I said to her understandingly.

She was becoming greener and greener. Tears were welling up in her eyes. "I can't. I've already swallowed!"

I could see that not chewing enough had been one of her life's problems.

7 – The Book of the Nephilim Spice

"Don't worry, I know a great healing trick!" I jumped over to her and used a remarkable technique that Marek had taught me. It consisted of punching a gateway on the left of the solar plexus, then firmly thrusting the fist into the abdomen, inside the ribcage and upwards.

The result was instant. Felicia vomited out green bile together with the barely-chewed locust.

"Wonderful!" I patted her shoulder, pressing a gateway on the inside of her wrist to alleviate the nausea. "But you are going to have to learn to chew better, or the beautiful work I have done on your liver will be wrecked."

Gasping and holding her solar plexus, Felicia collapsed on her mattress.

Kneeling by her side, I let my hands run over her body. Soon she could breathe almost normally. But tears kept rolling down her cheeks. She looked at me with infinite sadness. For one moment, the Warrior who could ignore pain by resting on the Dragon vanished, and I found myself in front of a desperate woman, captured by her enemy and abandoned by her own people, having failed her initiation in the Watcher's holy crypt. She was weak, empty, lost, alone, and moreover she had been forced to eat locusts. And punched in the stomach.

"I am sorry, Felicia!" I said, remembering all the trials I had failed, and calling on the softness of the White Eagle for her.

She cried her despair silently. But she didn't try to push me back. She received my warmth, and I admired her for that.

I made my healing warmer, and projected sweet waves of life force into her. When she stopped crying, she fell into a state of semi-sleep. I kept working on her body of energy all morning, pumping up her vitality and calling on my Mother the Dragon to nurture her and help restore her joy.

In the early afternoon, when she woke up, I gave her some water and asked her if she wanted to eat. She said no, and I did not insist. I started talking to her, trying to cheer her up, but she just looked at me and did not speak. She was sad, yet not stubbornly defiant as she had been in the beginning. But I feared that the thread of communication between us had been lost.

Drawing inspiration from the clear fountain, I told her, "Felicia, I have decided I really want to try your food."

She made an effort to mask her disbelief.

"Seriously, Felicia. I want to know the names of all the dishes in the jars."

She sat up on the mattress, looking at me with curiosity.

"How about this one?" I grabbed a large pot and opened the lid. "What is it called?"

"Shemyaza's puree."

I took a spoonful of the thick, yellow puree and put it straight into my mouth without even sniffing it beforehand. "What does Shemyaza mean?"

"Shemyaza was one of the most powerful of the Watchers."

"What an interesting taste! Spicy." So spicy actually, that I had to rest on the Dragon to swallow. "What is it made of?"

"Potatoes, garlic, and a secret blend of sixteen spices and five different types of oils. Do you like spicy foods?"

"Mm... yes, at times."

"Then you should try this." She pulled a large container from one of the bags and opened it, releasing a sunshine smell in the cave. "Watchers' ratatouille," she handed me the dish.

The fire was so violent that, had it not been for my Dragon control, I would have had to spit out the mouthful on the spot. "Mm... now this is really special!"

"Just the right food for you, Sir Great Dragon."

After this I had oyster jello (not bad, considering it would have taken at least four months to reach the county of the Red Lands from the sea), another fishbone paté (even tastier than the one the day before), smoked salmon (dangerously delicious), almonds of hell (so called because of their explosively fiery taste), ginger marmalade (this one I liked by far the best), crunch-mellows (disgustingly sweet) and Naamah's nipples (even sweeter, and oddly shaped).

"What an extraordinary culinary experience this has been, Felicia!" I said to thank her, and to indicate I could not take any more. And I started massaging the nausea gateways on the inside of my wrists.

"What has happened to your locusts?" she asked. "Did you eat them all?"

"I stored them outside, so as not to inconvenience you. But tell me, Felicia, these oysters the jello was made from, how could they possibly have been fished in the sea, carried to the county of the Snowy Mountains, then to the Red Lands, and not be completely rotten?"

Felicia clicked her fingers, "Etheric conserve! The Nephilim invented it. No wonder they're the masters of the art!"

I wanted to ask her more about the Nephilim people, but she made me talk about myself again. By now she had recovered her full verbal stamina, and a lively discussion followed. We even burst out laughing a few times, and again a part of me found it difficult to accept that the first person to notice my jokes since I had left Eisraim was one of the Nephilim.

Around sunset, after we had been chatting for more than four hours, a silence hung in the air. We each looked to one corner of the cavern.

"How about trying to walk *a lawful little bit*?" I suggested. I lifted her up and held her while she took a few steps.

She did very well until we reached the terrace outside the cliff. "Oh! I'm getting all dizzy!" she said and collapsed against me. I had to hold her in my arms so she did not fall. As she tied her arms around my neck, her head resting against my chest, I had one of the weirdest feelings of my entire life. It was accompanied by a big vroofing wave that came up from the Dragon and spread its vibration all over my body.

7 – The Book of the Nephilim Spice

"You need *some lawful rest*," I told her, and I took her back to her mattress. But when I asked her if she wanted to sleep, she answered, "No! I'm not tired at all. Anyhow, I hate sleeping!" And she started another conversation, in which I soon found myself laughing again.

Much later on, when the night had come and we could no longer see each other's face, I confessed, "Felicia, this is like being transported back into another world. I haven't had conversations like these with anyone for a long time."

"Are you all right?" she asked. As I didn't answer, she went on, "Does it hurt you that the first person you can talk to since you left Elyani should be one of the Nephilim?"

"I don't know. Perhaps." I hesitated, not wanting to hurt her feelings. "If you knew all the things I've heard about the Nephilim people..."

"Oh Sir Great Dragon, that I can easily imagine! If you knew all the things I've heard about the people of Mount Lohrzen..."

There was not a sound in the cavern.

I told her to go to sleep.

7.15 Nephilim spice

In the morning I made her walk a second time. It all went fine for a while, until she felt dizzy again and collapsed in my arms once more. Luckily, the dizziness evaporated not long after I returned her to her mattress, and she did not seem to be tired at all.

After checking her gateways, I passed the bags of food to her and let her organise breakfast. Partly to stop her from eating too quickly, partly because I was getting more and more intrigued, I said, "Felicia, I want you to tell me about the Nephilim people. I want to hear from *you* what they are like."

She plunged her fiercely blue eyes into mine, "Most of them are about twelve feet tall and eat only raw flesh, preferably with the blood served separately. And in their leisure time do you know what they do?"

"No, seriously, Felicia! Suppose you were a visitor at the Eisraim temple and I knew nothing about the Nephilim. What would you tell me?"

She shrugged her shoulders, creating waves of light in the energy of her long red hair. I wondered how she did it. "*Like everyone, Nephilim people are born in the kingdom, they live and they die.* But they have a certain spice to them. You know how people in the kingdom can be so boring and slow."

"My teacher calls them sleepers."

"Sleepers..." her voice was vibrant, "what a great word!"

"It's a lawful expression. It's from the book of Maveron."

"Well," she went on, "Nephilim people are *not* sleepers. They're alive! They know how to laugh. They know how to make jokes, even about themselves. They can move fast, and they think fast. They know how to learn secrets from nature and how to use them. In the kingdom, they were the first people who dyed clothes, crafted jewels, wrought metals, used medicinal herbs, cooked refined foods and etherically conserved them, calculated the rhythms of time... you name it! All this came from a certain fire, *a spice they carry in their blood and which they received from their ancestors the Watchers. The Nephilim people are the spice of the Earth.*"

"But Felicia, what about those giants who cause wars and havoc, and who eat people alive? Do you mean they don't exist?"

"Of course the giants exist! There are not as many of them as there used to be, though. And they are not all cannibals, *for Melchisedek's sake!* The people who believe that all Nephilim people are giants are..."

I grinned, knowing very well what kind of derogatory words would have followed, had Felicia not stopped there. "Have you ever seen any giants?" I was curious.

"Of course. Close to my temple, in the county of the Snowy Mountains, I know a lovely family of Nephilim giants. A caste of fishermen."

This conversation was getting very exciting. "How big, Felicia?"

"Two or three heads taller than you, perhaps four. But only the father. And big muscles... just like yours!"

"Are they very strong? Do they like to fight?"

"They are very smart, but not at all violent. They cook the best fish of the Snowy Mountains. I wish we could have some tonight!"

Detecting a touch of disappointment on my face, Felicia hastily went on, "But there are also fierce, dangerous giants, some of them with long teeth, who would really enjoy fighting against you." She gave me a look, "And you'd love it, wouldn't you?"

Embarrassed by her cheeky smile, I ignored the comment. "But isn't it true that there were almost no wars in the kingdom before the Watchers descended and gave birth to the first Nephilim?"

She gave a sigh, "I know. I am from the accursed race. Wars, plagues, vice and decadence – what evil has not been blamed on the Nephilim? But tell me, Szar, what would the Earth be without us? No honeyed pickled cucumbers, no make-up and jewels, no healing herbs, no dwellings other than tree houses and barn sheds, no soft stones. And never any fun. Your Gervin would be another of these puppets who walk around repeating, '*Praise the Lord Melchisedek!*' from morning to night. And Elyani would be so boring..." She took on her mock-sleeper voice and drawled monotonously, "*All glo-ry to the Lord Mel-chi-se-dek, good mor-ning, man of the Law!*"

The mimic was done in such style that I to laugh. "Felicia, I wish my friends in Eisraim could hear you!"

"Even though I'm one of the Nephilim?" she retorted, sharp and defiant.

7 – The Book of the Nephilim Spice

I didn't know what to answer. Thoughtful, I stood up and walked to the opening of the cave.

"*Wait, man of the Law!* Don't go now!"

"I'm not going anywhere. I'm just trying to remember if there were Nephilim people at the Eisraim temple."

"Didn't you know how to recognise them when you were there?"

"No. I learnt that with the Sons of the Dragon."

"How do they do it?"

I turned towards her, wriggling my nostrils. "There is a particular astral smell that can be picked up miles and miles away."

"Do you mean the Nephilim people smell?"

"Everyone carries these astral smells! But the Nephilim have a very characteristic one. Must be the smell of the spice you were talking about. There's also a particular light in their aura. That too probably comes from the spice." But looking back on my memories, I was unable to determine whether some of the Eisraim priests were Nephilim.

"You know," Felicia's spoke with irony, "since you were a child at school, you must have met many of us without even knowing it."

"But aren't the Nephilim part of separate castes?"

"Each of the Watchers left one or more castes of descendants, but of course there has been quite a lot of intermarriage with other castes."

"What do you mean, 'of course'?" I asked with some surprise. "Hasn't it always been against the Law for the Nephilim to marry people from other castes?"

Felicia grimaced. "If Elyani was from a caste that is not exactly what the Law asserts you should marry but say, nearly exactly, would you give up on her?"

"Hey!" I protested vigorously. "I never said I wanted to marry Elyani!"

She raised her eyes to the ceiling as if I was totally naive.

I preferred not to take any notice. "So there is some of the Nephilim spice in the blood of many castes, is that it?"

"Of course!"

"But then, do they keep following the customs of the Nephilim people?"

"Depends. Some do, some don't. There are Nephilim people at the courts of nearly every prince, you know."

"Except in the Red Lands, yes I know. The Nephilim are smart people, aren't they?"

"Not all of them," she admitted. "But if you were to take the Nephilim away, the King's administration would collapse in no time."

"The Sons of the Dragon say that it's precisely because the Nephilim are everywhere that the kingdom of Atlantis is going down."

"So what do you want to do about it? Kill us all, perhaps?" she replied sharply.

I went and knelt close to her. After holding eye contact with her for a while, I spoke from the fountain, "You are a very beautiful person, Felicia.

If you didn't exist, the kingdom would certainly be a much less spicy place."

She didn't know what to answer. Knowing her, it meant that she was really moved.

"Now you must *get some lawful rest*."

"But I'm not tired, I don't need to rest."

Trying to copy one of her cheeky faces, I said, "Well, *I* do! I'll wake you up when I finish dancing."

Exhaling vigorously, I Dragon-climbed to the top of the mountain.

7.16 Glimpses of the Watchers' lore

When I came back down to the cavern, I spent some time working on Felicia's gateways. She immediately woke up, but pretended to still be asleep.

"Felicia!" I sang playfully, "I know that you are back in the kingdom!"

"You think you know everything, don't you?" she replied without opening her eyes.

I chuckled.

The big blue eyes opened and looked at me, "Sir Great Dragon, there are still a *lot* of things you need to learn about life!"

"Of course! You haven't told me any of your cooking recipes yet!"

"I never said I would do that."

I laughed in outrage.

She sat up and piled her hair on top of her head, holding it with her hands. "All right, maybe I did. But by the way," she let her hair fall, "you haven't told me if Elyani ended up giving you the recipe for Dragon's milk after your return from the Underworld?"

"No! I never dared to ask her."

Felicia sighed and shook her head in reprobation. As she did so, her hair's energy lit up with shiny silvery astral specks. I wondered how the Underworld she did that.

"I hate to imagine what else you never dared to ask her. Great Warrior or not, there are a lot of things you could learn from a Nephilim woman, let me tell you."

"Let's start with honeyed pickled cucumbers!"

She looked up to the top of the cave, but not to prophesy. "Szar-ka! Elyani must have had some *really* difficult times with you!"

Szar-ka! I closed my eyes. It had been so long since anyone had called me this. Felicia went straight on, "Did you at least tell her that you loved her before you left Eisraim?"

I opened my eyes in amazement. "Do you think she loves me?"

7 – The Book of the Nephilim Spice

"See! I knew you hadn't told her. And you wonder why the Nephilim think other people are naive!" The blueness of her eyes entered a little deeper inside me. "Do you think you love Elyani, Szar?"

"I don't know. I never thought about it. When I was sick and she was taking care of me... that time was really special. It had a big impact on me. It made me a different man."

"But Szar, that's because she loved you. Very much."

I didn't know what to answer.

"Right!" she decided. "Let me tell you something about sleepers that Master Gervin hasn't taught you yet. When you ask them about love, they answer, '*Thou shalt love the Lord Melchisedek with all thy heart, and with all thy soul, and with all thy might!*' It's very lawful of them, but this is not the way you are going to make your priestess of the White Eagle happy, Szar."

I knew even less what to answer.

"Come on, Szar, let me show you something that will be much more useful to you than recipes of pickled cucumbers. You nearly did it to me twice this morning when you were giving me a healing, but you didn't even notice you were doing it." She sat very close to me, her breast nearly touching my side, and she put her arm around my neck. "When you put your arm round a woman's shoulders, if you place your hand just here, on this gateway, and if you know how to do it, she will feel a shudder going up her spine."

She touched the magic spot on my neck. It worked, and it made me blush.

"Try it on me," she said.

Timidly, I put my arm around her shoulder and touched the gateway with my fingers.

"Put the soft energy like this morning," she said.

I let a little vroofing wave jerk through my hand, as if during a healing.

"That's better!" She raised her eyebrows, "But this morning you were doing it really well."

I swallowed. "Do all Nephilim women know how to do this?"

Felicia giggled. "Some do it much better than others. Do you know that there is an entire science about these things, Szar? It came to us straight from the Watchers."

I was astounded. "Do you mean it is part of your Law?"

"Ab-so-*lu*-tely. When the Watchers came down to the kingdom and took women as wives, they instructed them in the art of love. The Law says some of the women had so much pleasure that they died. Can you imagine that?"

I kept swallowing my saliva. "Hardly!"

"The Watchers' lore of love is phenomenal, Szar! The recitation of all the passages of our Law that deal with it takes entire weeks."

"Have you ever heard it?"

She took on the most dangerous of her innocent looks. "What would your guess be, Szar?"

I closed my eyes. Speaking from the fountain, I said prophetically, "*I am sure you know everything about it!*"

She laughed. "Szar, that is exactly what a prian is supposed to tell a woman if he wants to approach her – according to the Law, I mean."

"But apart from the way of touching a woman's neck and the art of making one's hair shine with silvery specks of astral light, what else is there in that Law?"

"Hundreds of ways of making oneself beautiful, for a start. The Law says, *it would have been cruel of Azazel to give mirrors to women if he hadn't also given them the art of make up*. Does Elyani put black powder on her eyes?"

I had to think. "To tell you the truth, I'm not sure." Bringing images back to my memory, I sighed, "It could well be, yes! But I never noticed it at the time."

She sighed, much louder than me. "This woman must have gone through a nightmare with you! Anyway, the black powder and the paint are nothing. There are many techniques to foster the etheric body and the kidneys so the skin shines and becomes all soft. There are gateways that *reinforce the hair and make it beautiful, and curly*, if one wants. Some other gateways, together with many other things, will make *lips red and glossy like cherries*. And then of course there is an entire art of making your eyes shine. By the way, do you know what the Law says a prian must do when he dances with a woman?"

"*Look into her eyes all the time!*" I declared proudly. Felicia seemed surprised, so I explained, "You told me that in the dream, when we were dancing in the hall with all the lights. But I want to know more about your Law. What else can you do with it?"

"There are many ways of making yourself be desired by a loved one, even if they don't really love you at first: *mantras, spells, invocations, sacred roots, herbs, gems, magic drinks, dishes with spices, sending dreams, drawing symbols under the bed*, and a few other things."

"Mm..." I thought, "magic drinks?"

"Then there is the science of kissing. Szar, did you know that most people in the kingdom have never kissed anyone?"

"Oh, really?" I said, looking towards the cavern's entrance.

"The recitation of that part of the Law takes entire days. There are so many ways of arousing someone by activating the gateways in the lips, Szar, you just wouldn't believe it! And there is a line of energy all around the lips, where the red pulp joins the skin of the face. It can be triggered in a particular way that creates so much desire, the person instantly sweats all over."

All this was more than I could cope with in a single session. I turned towards Felicia, but she immediately came out with a "No!"

7 – The Book of the Nephilim Spice

"No, what?"

"You're going to tell me I need *some lawful rest*. The reply is no!"

I sighed. "Well, how about practising walking a little bit, then?" As she stood up, I took her arm and asked, "Do you think that for a situation like this, there could be a trick in your Law for suddenly feeling dizzy?"

7.17 Eisraim, chapel of the White Eagle

It was late in the evening after the temple meeting. All the priestesses had just left. Elyani approached her teacher and friend. "Teyani, did you ask the White Eagle about Alcibyadi this morning?"

Teyani nodded. "You prophesied too, didn't you?"

"Yes," said Elyani.

"So you know that Alcibyadi stopped walking and is now stuck in one of the Underworld's caverns of sickness," Teyani said. "She is deep down, isn't she?"

There was a long silence. Elyani knew that the loss of Alcibyadi would be a terrible blow to Teyani – and to the order of the White Eagle. Alcibyadi was the ninth priestess to lose her way in the Underworld, with no successful candidates to counterbalance the losses. The initiation had become impossible, the priestesses being sent to their death one after the other. What sane woman would want to join such an order?

"Teyani, can't the Masters of Thunder bring her back for us?"

"These matters are more complicated than they sound. The rule of the White Eagle must be respected. *If we do not abide by the Law of the gods, the gods will abandon us.*" Teyani sat down. "Ten years ago, when I saw the fields were deteriorating and our women were going to be lost one after the other, I prayed to our White Lord, 'O Great Eagle of Highness, long ago, when everything seemed to be lost, you directed me to Thunder and Thunder saved us. Can I not now call on Thunder to rescue my priestesses when they become trapped in the Dark Underworld?' The response was powerful, the room was inundated with light, but the Eagle insisted that none of the Masters of Thunder intervene directly. Instead they were to invoke Thunder itself, which they did. And not long after that, Gervin found Szar and brought him to Eisraim."

"Do you still think Szar is the one who will bring our priestesses back?"

"Yes, I have thought that right from the beginning," Teyani was firm. "I believed it even more strongly after we learnt that Szar had picked up Vivyani in the Underworld's caverns. But he is still so young and frail."

"And so far away," Elyani sighed. "If he was here now, I am sure he would volunteer to go down again, despite the nightmare he went through the first time."

But how would he ever locate her? Trying to find a soul in the Underworld is like trying to find a grain of sand in the ocean.

And what if he lost his way?

Teyani closed her eyes, surrendering to the Eagle's light. "Did Gervin tell you how Szar's initiation in the mysteries of the Dragon is progressing?"

"Gervin says Szar is going extremely well. He does not seem to be the least worried about him. He even told me that Szar may not have changed as much as I feared, although he will have changed much more than I'm expecting. He said, 'He will be the same Szar, but you won't recognise him.'"

"Dear Gervin," Teyani opened her eyes and shone with warmth. "Did he say when Szar would be back?"

"No. Not in the immediate future anyway. To rescue Alcibyadi he would have to be back in Eisraim within four weeks, and there is no sign of that. What we need now is a miracle, isn't it? What else could bring our Alcibyadi back?"

"Yes, the time has come for a miracle!" Teyani used a near-Voice threshold. "*Let this night shine with magic, as in the Ancient Days of the Earth!*"

Elyani smiled and started preparing the ritual utensils.

The two women chanted their hymns until late in the night.

7.18 Great Warrior

Next day, Felicia was no longer dizzy when she walked. During breakfast she told me, "Great Warrior, you are soon going to leave me, aren't you?"

"Could be."

"If I had just saved your life and you *had* to grant me a wish, do you know what I would ask?"

"Hey, Felicia, wait a lawful minute, *I* have just saved *your* life!"

"Doesn't matter. I would ask that instead of returning to Mount Lohrzen, you go straight to Eisraim and marry Elyani. I am sure she misses you terribly."

I took a long inhalation. When she saw that her words had hit me deep, Felicia softened for a few seconds. "Sorry, I didn't want to hurt you." But then she added, "I just hate to think of you as one of the black men, Szar. And I'm sure Elyani would too."

I took another deep breath and looked into her eyes, trying to make myself as mellow as she sometimes was. "Beautiful Felicia! My master, Gervin of the Brown Robe, sent me there."

7 – The Book of the Nephilim Spice

"Is it true that they teach you all sorts of ways of destroying anything that's alive, even trees, and that you practise killing people every single day from sunrise to sunset?"

"I guess it's a way of looking at it. The Nephilim Hunters probably do the same, don't they?"

"*No way, man of the Law!* I know the Hunters. They're cultivated people who have a great respect for human life. During their training they learn to draw sophisticated energies from the power of the Point and higher centres of energy above the head. They also learn about the arts, music in particular. Ferippe, whom you met, comes to my temple at least twice a week and sings in our choir. And Jex Belaran, the training centre of the Nephilim Hunters, is famous for its musical composers."

No thoughts, just Dragon, I kept eating breakfast.

"Is it true that as part of your training they send you to kill one of us, even someone who hasn't done anything against you, and that you do it as some kind of initiation ritual?"

I nodded.

"That is so revolting! I bet the Great Warriors know how to torture people really well. Szar, I want to know, how many Nephilim people have you already killed?"

I didn't answer.

"Tell me!" she insisted. "I want to know."

Exasperated, I stood up and shouted at her, "Felicia, I haven't killed anyone, and that is precisely my problem at the moment! Now for the Lord Melchisedek's sake will you please leave me alone?"

As I was walking out of the cave she called me, "Wait, *man of the Law!* Don't go!"

Without turning back, I replied sharply, "*You go to Azazel and get lost!*"

When I arrived at the top of the hill, I didn't feel like dancing. I sat and contemplated the mists.

I was not afraid of returning to Mount Lohrzen, facing Marek and, *no thoughts, just Dragon*, telling him the pure facts. But what if he ordered me to go out again and kill someone else?

An ugly vision came to my mind: I was back in Elyani's courtyard, sitting with her on the purple lawn. Elyani was looking at me in disgust, "Do you mean you have killed these people for no reason, and it was part of a ritual?"

I stood up, raised my arms and screamed with the Voice, "Gervin! Help! What am I supposed to do?"

There was no answer.

I listened for inspiration from the clear fountain. The only conclusion that came to me was that being rude to Felicia was no solution.

I decided to go back to the cave and make peace with her.

7.19 Verzazyel's present

"Felicia! I'm sorry," I began as I passed through the cave's entrance. But when I saw her sitting on her knees with her eyes blazing like a field of stars, I realised something unusual was happening. The entire cave was filled with a vibrant yellow-silvery energy.

"Szar!" she said, "after you left, I felt so sorry for the way I harassed you that I prophesied from Verzazyel and asked him to grant me a present for you. A magnificent present for a magnificent friend. I prayed with all my heart, Szar."

"I can hear that in your voice, Felicia."

"Szar, the Watcher has answered me. Here is what he said: *If Szar wants to find a white bird, let him go in this direction. Right now!*" With her hands joined in the shape of a cup, she pointed in the direction of the Dragon gate.

I was stunned. In the dance dream when I had asked Felicia where Vivyani was, this was exactly the way she had held her hands.

"Felicia, I have hoped to find Vivyani for so long!" I came close to her and ran my hand through her hair.

"If you want to find her you must go right now, Szar."

The clear fountain agreed, there was not one minute to waste.

I went and sat next to the Dragon's gate. "Felicia, you hold the fort. I have no idea how long this descent may take."

We exchanged a last glance, and I let myself glide down into a lapis lazuli cavern.

What beautiful fragrance! The Underworld cavern was astoundingly peaceful, like a shrine to the Mother of the Light, vibrant with her infinite softness.

I stood still and, connecting my clear fountain with the gate's shaft of energy, I asked my Mother the Dragon, "How does one find a White Eagle who has lost her way?" As there was no answer, I let myself glide further and further down, carrying my question.

Down and down, deeper and deeper... and then something new happened. Once when I was drunk with the energy of the Underworlds, brother Amaran had told me I could leap from one Dragon gate to another. What I was now discovering was even more fascinating. From the level where I was, I could feel hundreds of gates all at once, as if I was in all of them at the same time. It was so clear and simple that I was amazed I had failed to recognise the effect during former descents.

Resting on the column of Spirit that ascended along the Dragon's gate above me, I tuned into the White Eagle of the gods. The response was immediate, as if the Eagle had been waiting for me. I felt his White presence with me and I was transported into an orichalc cavern filled with thousands of yellow lights.

7 – The Book of the Nephilim Spice

"Oh, She-Dragon of the Deep!" I exclaimed, as the haunting memories of my first descent into the Underworld came back. Everything around me was so beautiful and so peaceful. It was difficult to believe that each of the little lights in the cavern was an agonising soul harassed by endless nightmares. Were they beating each other? Were their bodies maimed and disfigured? Or were they rotting alive in some infamous worm compost? Were their souls being tortured by the stench and the unbearable clamour of millions of creatures in pain?

So beautiful. So still. So peaceful. The cave was dead silent. The delicious fragrance made my nostrils quiver. The orichalc of the rugged walls glittered with auburn hues, and silvery specks of light like those around Felicia's hair floated in the air.

Thoughtful, I contemplated the little yellow lights. Some were gently moving around, others were stationary. As I walked through the cavern, the words walked with me, "*One Law, one way! He who never sleeps, never dies!*"

The White Eagle directed my steps to a corner of the cavern. And there she was, right in front of me! A little light, like all the others, but sealed with the unmistakable energy of the White Eagle. I tuned into the astral recognition symbols. Without any possible doubt, this soul had been trained by Lady Teyani.

All this was very simple. I took the gesture called 'holding the flame', my hands parallel in front of my heart. In the field between my two hands I held the yellow light. And I walked back to the nearest gate.

There, I tuned into the White Eagle again and let him transport me to the Dragon's gate of the Eisraim temple – the gate that Marek had described to me. Still holding Vivyani's soul in the field between my hands, I gently let myself ascend, moving from gate to gate.

This led me to a cave of dark blue rock. It was empty. I opened my hands and let the yellow light waft around. "Beautiful Vivyani," I thought, "what will Lady Teyani the great magician do with your soul? Will she find a new body for you, or will she send you to the spheres of Highness, where you can rest in the shelter of the White Eagle?"

I wondered where I had landed. Under which part of the temple of Eisraim? I looked up, but of course I could not see anything except the roof of the cave. For the fun of it, I tried to let myself ascend as much as I could along the breeze. Expectedly, I could not pass through the cave's ceiling. Who knows whether there was someone sitting on top of me? It could have been anyone!

I wondered what Elyani was doing at this precise moment. If she could have descended and met me, would she have danced with me? The movements Felicia had taught me in the dream were still perfectly clear in my memory. How would it feel to dance with Elyani? Elated by the Dragon's breeze, my body started moving by itself.

And I danced. For a few minutes, all my sorrows were forgotten. In my mind I was back in the field of stars, dancing to the harmony of the spheres. It was magnificent, enthralling, cosmic. Infinity breathed through my dance, and the Mother of the Light gave the beat.

Vivyani watched, amazed and entranced by the celestial harmonies.

"Oh Vivyani, if only I had known. If only I had known. I would not have abandoned you, and now you and I would be friends."

I danced my farewell to her, and I left.

When I returned to my body, Felicia was astounded. "Already? But it's hardly taken you half an hour! Did you find her?"

Without saying a word, I went and sat close to her on the mattress of wild herbs.

"Szar, are you all right?" she asked in a soft voice.

I took my head in my hands and started crying.

"Couldn't you find her?"

I collapsed like a little child. "I did find her!" My voice was trembling. "But... I don't know, maybe it was too easy."

Felicia took me in her arms, and I rested my head on her shoulder. The tears turned into a Dragon flood. "Poor Szar-ka!" she made herself motherly warm. "If only there could have been someone to bash up, you'd feel so much better!"

I chuckled. "Do you think so?"

"Perhaps not, after all. Listen, how about I tell you my best cooking recipes?"

"Vivyani was such a beautiful person, I'm sure! If only I could have known what I know now while she was still alive!"

"We must trust the Mother of the Light, and the wisdom of her works, my friend," she rocked me in her arms. "Which recipe do you want to start with?"

"The Mother of the Light..." I echoed. "Can we start with ginger marmalade?"

7.20 The revelation of the Watchers

Black dancing on top of the mountain the next morning, I called on the fountain for direction, with all my heart. What the Holy Underworld did Gervin want me to do? There was no answer, but what *did* come to me with absolute clarity was that if Felicia were to be killed on her way home I would never forgive myself. Marek was not doing manoeuvres at this time of year, but the county was full of Warriors who could smell the Nephilim spice from afar and had no scruples about slaughtering unescorted pilgrims. Then and there I decided to take Felicia back to the Jeremitzia river, in the northern horn of the county, before returning to Mount Lohrzen.

7 – The Book of the Nephilim Spice

Having at last arrived at a decision, I felt lighter. I climbed down, and just as I was nearing the cave's entrance, I called, "Beautiful Felicia! I have something to tell you."

Felicia was standing, waiting for me. "Hush, man of the Law. I have something to say first."

Her voice was grave. She looked at me with her total blue eyes, "Szar, beautiful friend, I want you to listen to me from high above, as you sometimes do."

I turned to the clear fountain.

"Yes, like that! I want you to hear what I am going to say, but I also want you to understand, because I care for you and I love you. Szar, I am not going back home. I *must* go back to Verzazyel's cave."

No thoughts, just Dragon, I swallowed.

"Please understand," she continued. "When you were in Eisraim, you spent years striving to stop being a sleeper. Well, I have spent years preparing myself to receive the power of the Watchers. Returning to my temple after having failed would render my life completely meaningless, worse than death. I want the power of the Watchers, Szar. I want it more than anything else life can give me. So in two days, on the Full Moon, I will descend into the holy crypt again and invoke Verzazyel's High Fire."

I let her words sink into me for a few seconds. Then the clear fountain spoke, "I would do the same myself, Felicia."

"I know. That is why I want you as my friend."

Holding onto the fountain, I gazed at her. She was still my child. I knew her body of energy by heart, as if I had made it. The idea that she could die in the crypt hurt my belly like a wound in the Dragon.

"Lady Felicia, priestess of Verzazyel, would you allow me to escort you to the entrance of the Watcher's cave?"

She was moved. *"Sir Szar of the Brown Robe, it will be an honour."*

We looked at each other, but found nothing else to say. So we sat down to eat breakfast.

She arranged a few dishes and invited me to sit on her mattress. "Szar, I want you to try this: marinated herrings with treated nutmeg. It's all in the influence you put in the nutmeg. This one is pretty good, actually."

"Oooh! Delicious!" I exclaimed unequivocally after the first mouthful. "Felicia, this food is simply out of the kingdom! Once in Mount Lohrzen I heard a brother say that when the Nephilim wanted to extract a secret from you, they always fed you some of their dishes first, and then there was no way you could resist. Now I understand why."

She chuckled. "And what would you do to *me* if you wanted to extract my secrets?" she asked in one of her seductress' voices.

I changed the topic. "But aren't you going to bump into the pilgrims if you return to the cave?"

"There is no risk. I just communicated with Ferippe through the power of the Point. They'll be gone by then, and he has assured me that no other caravan will reach the cave for a few days."

"How long will you need?"

"One hour."

Looking to the entrance of the cave, I asked, "Is there a reason why you wouldn't kill yourself this time?"

She laughed. "Last time I made a huge mistake, because I had no idea how the power was going to hit me. But thanks to the gods," she touched the tip of my nose with her index finger, "I have been given a second chance."

"If you could give me some clues as to what you are trying to do, maybe I could suggest a way for you to contain the power. I am very ignorant of the power of the Point, but..."

"Szar. If what you know and what I know could be combined, there is not much that could stop us in the entire kingdom."

That sounded dangerous! I tuned into the clear fountain. "Will you tell me more about the power of the Watchers?"

"The power of the Watchers?" She sealed the jar of marinated herrings and carefully put it back in the bag. "Spice like you can hardly imagine! *The Watchers are mighty angels who have evolved for several aeons. They existed long before men were created, and even long before the Mother of the Light gave birth to the gods.*"

Felicia's eyes were so bright that a shiver ascended from my Dragon.

"*Fire is their domain. When they first descended on Mount Hermon, the Watchers vowed they would stamp the Earth with their Fire.* They did so in several ways. *Azazel, leader of the Watchers and equalled by none amongst them but Shemyaza*, stored a phenomenal amount of power in a cave hidden in the wilderness."

"Dudael, the secret place which only the most obstinate of men dare to seek!" I exclaimed, remembering the part in Pelissor's story when all my brethren were shouting, "Go to Azazel and get lost!"

She nodded. "The Watchers also spread their Fire by having children with the daughters of men. *The Nephilim spice, this energy which we carry in our blood and which makes us special, is nothing else than the Fire of the Watchers.*"

"But what about the twelve-foot-tall giants who eat human flesh? Is it the same spice that made them the way they are?"

"It is. They could not contain the Fire. They received too much of it! The Fire went wrong inside them. Instead of just making them intelligent and powerful, it exacerbated their anger and their desires."

I wondered how the beautiful Felicia would be if she were *really* angry.

"There is another way the Watchers planted their fiery seed into the Earth. They left a whole tradition of occult knowledge that was carried on by Nephilim priests, and that taught how to cultivate the Nephilim spice. In

7 – The Book of the Nephilim Spice

my temple, over more than fifteen years, I have learnt to master this Fire. Now the time has come for me to receive the final initiation in the cave, from Verzazyel himself."

"But, my spicy friend, didn't Ferippe say that you had broken the Law?"

"It is lawful for a priestess of Verzazyel to invoke the power in the main crypt. If she succeeds, she becomes a high priestess, and is acclaimed by her kind. But if she fails, she must die from the Fire! If you had left me to Ferippe and his men, all they would have done was to let me descend into the crypt again."

"Which is exactly what you want to do anyway. So why didn't you stay with them?"

"That morning, in the canyon, when he sensed my energy, Ferippe suggested that I would have more chance of succeeding if you could heal me a bit more."

I stood up and started pacing the cave. "I am really naive, aren't I Felicia?"

She jumped up. "Szar, don't speak like that! I didn't know you then. Now I'm telling you things no Warrior has ever heard!"

"Can you imagine what Marek the indestructible will say when he learns I have been helping one of the Nephilim to conquer the supreme power of the Watchers?"

She placed her hands on my shoulders and shouted at me, "Szar, this is wrong! You are getting tangled in the same stupid guilt again, as when you lost Vivyani." Looking at me and making her voice very soft, she added, "This guilt is no wisdom my friend, but the voice of the dark side."

From the highest of the clear fountain, I knew she was right. She took me by the hand and made me sit with her on the mattress.

"Listen Szar, when you were healing me, what you were fighting was the Fire of the Watchers. And you won!"

"I bet your Law says that's the kind of thing a woman should tell a prian if she wants him to agree with her."

She chuckled, and ignored the comment. "There is something else you must remember, Szar. In Verzazyel's cave, when did you find me? Just after you asked the Watcher what he wanted from you. That was another reason why Ferippe said I should stay with you."

I closed my eyes tightly. "Felicia, we were with the Hunters less than five minutes. You sound like you talked with Ferippe for hours. What the Underworld is going on here?"

"That's the power of the Point. It allows you to exchange a lot of impressions in a very short time. What I told you in the canyon was the truth. I said I had told Ferippe all about you – all the stories you had been telling me for two days."

"This power of the Point, can you do it from a distance, or do you have to be close to the other person?"

"The power of the Point operates beyond space, which is why you can't detect it through darkness visible. Distance makes no difference."

I took my head in my hands. "Such a naive boy!" I thought. "In any case, how could someone be dangerous if he is ignorant of the power of the Point?"

"Did the Watchers teach the power of the Point to men?" I asked.

"Yes and no. The power of the Point was available on Earth before the birth of the kingdom, but men were too dumb to use it. If it had not been for the revelation of the Watchers, it would have taken aeons before men could reach up to its level."

"If it had not been for the revelation of the Watchers, what would the kingdom be?" I sighed.

Felicia smiled. "In our Law, there is a hymn that says,

What would be of men, hadn't Asaradel the Watcher revealed to them the Moon cycle?

What would be of men, hadn't Barkayal the Watcher revealed to them the rhythms of time?

What would be of men, hadn't Arkibel the Watcher revealed to them the art of reading signs and omens?

What would be of men, hadn't Amazarek the Watcher revealed to them the use of roots?

What would be of men, hadn't Shemyaza the Watcher revealed to them the art of incantations?

What would be of men, hadn't Azazel the Watcher revealed to them the working of metals and gems, the making of mirrors, the dyeing of fabrics?"

"But if the Watchers were so wise," I questioned, "how come their revelation was followed by all these wars, all this chaos and desolation?"

"*The Watchers gave their Fire to men. Men foolishly misused the Fire, and then they blamed the Watchers for the evils which they had created.*"

There was a silence.

"Could it be that men were not ready, and that the Watchers came too early?" I asked.

"*Man of the Law*, tell me something about your teacher, Master Gervin of the Brown Robe. Does he want you to stop being a sleeper in two hundred lifetimes, or in this life?"

"Master Gervin likes it when things move fast, which is why he has had to be so patient with me."

"Then tell me, *man of the Law*, which world would you prefer: a bland one without wars, or one with the beautiful, perky Lady Elyani and her friends of the White Eagle? If the Watchers had never come down, there would have been fewer wars, perhaps. But would there be any of the things in the kingdom which are meaningful to you?"

For a moment, I didn't know what to say. "After all, if it happened, maybe it was the will of our Lord Melchisedek," I mused. "How many of these Watchers descended, altogether?"

7 – The Book of the Nephilim Spice

"The Law says there were two hundred of them, led by Azazel and Shemyaza."

"Did they all arrive at the same time?"

"According to the tradition, they all landed together on Mount Hermon. But in reality, time does not mean the same to the Watchers as it does to us. They can decide to do something together at the same time, and from their point of view that is what happens. But to us human beings, it seems to take place at different times."

"Sounds just like the power of the Point," I commented. "Tell me more about this fiery power you are trying to conquer. It had completely devastated your body of energy, I had never seen anything like it. How did that happen?"

"Verzazyel's fever, it is called. A great Fire was set ablaze inside my energy – far more than I could contain. But I had made a mistake, I tried to contain it from my Point, instead of stepping into the Point-ness of the Watchers."

"This Point-ness of the Watchers, is it the same as the power of the Point?"

"Yes and no. The Watchers' power of the Point is so much more intense than that of human beings that it can hardly be called by the same name."

"So what is your plan this time?"

"Instead of trying to receive Verzazyel's power down into my Point, I must ascend to his level."

"Mm... Go to Verzazyel..." I couldn't resist the pun.

"... and hopefully not get lost," she laughed.

"And how are you going to raise yourself to Verzazyel's level?"

"There is a ritual to activate forces that are stored in Verzazyel's cave. Then it all happens through high intensities of power of the Point."

"Ascending to the level of the Watchers... is this what the power of the Point is for?" I asked.

"Not just that. The power of the Point is a principle of expansion of consciousness. It allows human beings to transcend the limitations of their mind and rise to the consciousness of gods, angels and Flying Dragons. When they approach higher beings without the power of the Point, men are like ants who try to decipher the hymns of the Law. They can hear them from a distance, but they can never understand the meaning."

"What will you become like, if you succeed?"

"I will know the mind of Verzazyel. I will become capable of uniting myself with his consciousness, and thus know mysteries that men cannot even conceive. I will see the future and the distant past of the kingdom, the mysteries of the ancient Earth, the secrets of the gods, the nature of the Flying Dragons..."

"Sounds dangerous," I said.

"It is, my beautiful friend. By the way, do you know why they are called the Watchers?"

"No, why?" I asked.
"Because they never sleep."
"Now, *that*'s tempting!" I thought, looking to one corner of the cave.

7.21 Verzazyel's hymn to the Flying Dragons

"*I, Verzazyel the Watcher,*
The tamer of the Fire,
I, Verzazyel the formidable,
Mighty and second to none but the Morning Star,
Through the high webs of galactic spaces,
I call onto you,
Flying Dragons beyond the Abyss of the Deep and the Fault of Eternity.
Hear my Word!
Respond to my call!
The seed which long ago you planted in the Earth's web,
Has slowly matured beyond and by the rhythms of time
And soon will blossom for your joy.
O mighty galactic powers, one of your sons
I want to invite, that he may partake of my glory.
O Flying Dragons, make alliance with me!
Let the fantastic Fire the Watchers have conquered
Be conjoined with the unfathomable depth of your powers.
Who in the spheres, hero, god, or angel,
Could stand against us?
Let your son be our pact.
The irresistible Fire of the Watchers
I will bestow onto him.
I will make him a winner in the games of the Earth,
A hero among men,
A prince, fulfilled with all the kingdom's gifts,
A champion destined to challenge the gods themselves.
Married to my Fire,
Let him become the pride of my kind,
And the shining herald of your intelligence,
A towering light for the dwellers of these spheres.
O Flying Dragons, hear my Word and respond!"

From beyond the Abyss of the Deep and the Fault of Eternity, the Voice of the Flying Dragons replied in an instant:
"*Greetings to thee, Verzazyel the Watcher!*
Mighty indeed is thy Fire,
Even though young in the ladder of infinity.
May the Mother of the Light thank thee for thy invitation,

7 – The Book of the Nephilim Spice

Which we decline.
This son of ours
We gave to Thunder, our ally,
And with Thunder he will remain,
For our will is not to join forces with thy burning glory.
Nor do we wish our son to tread thy path of fever.
With thy Fire he shall not be wedded.
Let his Mother the Dragon of the Deep
Marry him as she wishes,
As she is wise and knows our will.
Fare thee well, Verzazyel the Watcher,
And may the Great Light of Compassion protect thee
Along the arduous way that thou hast made for thyself."

7.22 The last supper

We reached Verzazyel's cave two hours before sunset.

Felicia took my hand. "I love this time of the month, when darkness visible swells with the whitish glow of the Full Moon."

"Has the time come to say goodbye, Felicia?" I asked, standing on the Dragon so my voice would not be choked by emotion.

"No way, man of the Law! I have a surprise for you first."

Since my earliest years, I had always hated surprises. "A surprise, Felicia? That sounds lovely. What is it?"

"I need an hour to prepare it. Why don't you go and dance on top of the hill and meet me back here a bit later?"

Despite my passion for rock climbing, I decided that the top of Verzazyel's hill was definitely not a safe place to black dance. Instead, I went for a stroll in the neighbouring canyons. The area was safe and clear. Ferippe's pilgrims had left the day before, and no other group of Nephilim was due for another three days.

Around sunset, when I returned to the high flute rocks that signposted the entrance to Verzazyel's domain, I saw from a distance that Felicia was waiting for me on the terrace outside the Watcher's cave.

As I climbed my way up to her, I was astounded. Felicia was clad in a stunning blue dress, the same as she had been wearing in the dance dream. I was shocked by her beauty. Her hair was arranged in complicated tiers, and her make up was more sophisticated than ever. Her skin was shining, and her eyes bright like a field of stars.

"I prepared a supper for you. There is plenty of time. I will not go down into the crypt before midnight," she said.

"I see you found a medallion," I said. She wore the same low-cut dress as in the dream.

"Nothing like the one I gave you, Szar! This one is just a very simple soft-stone pendant that Ferippe left here for me in a bag, with a few other things I asked for." She pointed to a white cloth she had laid on the rock. There were at least twenty candles set out, and twice as many plates and jars filled with dried fruits, nuts and concoctions of all colours. She invited me to sit in front of her.

"Felicia, this is incredible! The gods are my witness, you look exactly like you were in my dream. I didn't realise then how beautiful you were."

Felicia did not answer, but made her blue eyes so mellow that I felt my Dragon was melting. She poured a green drink for me into a finely wrought orichalc cup.

"Magic?" I smiled at her and pretended to sniff the brew suspiciously.

She softly feigned outrage, "Szar, can you imagine I would ever do that to you!"

We both laughed.

"*Oh my Lord Melchisedek!*" I exclaimed after the first sip, "this is simply celestial! What's in it?"

She shook her head. "You have already extracted too many secret recipes from me. Come on, I want you to try these honeyed pickled cucumbers. This time we have cinnamon sauce to go with them." She put a spoonful of the melange in my mouth.

"Ha! Ha! Ha! Ha! Ha! Felicia, you are right, the cinnamon sauce makes all the difference. This is the best dish in the kingdom! Even though I think I still like ginger marmalade the most."

A spoonful of the celestial marmalade was already on its way to my mouth.

"This one really does something to my Dragon," I sighed.

"Now, try this," she handed another plate to me.

"Stop!" I begged her after a few dishes, "I'm getting all dizzy!"

"Don't make fun of me!" she said softly, pulling a face at me. "In your dream, what did we eat?"

"We didn't eat, we just danced. You were teaching me."

"Was I teaching you well?"

I laughed. "Felicia, this dream was the most beautiful day of my entire life! I still can't believe how real it felt. Much more real than reality."

"That's because you were in the Watcher's space. You were dreaming in Verzazyel's mind," she elucidated.

"If this is the way the Watchers dream, I wonder what their waking consciousness is like. It must be formidable," I marvelled.

"It is indeed." She handed me another cup. "Have some more of the green beverage." And she drank with me, making silvery waves of light dance through her hair.

Then she plunged her avid blue eyes into mine. "If you want to know what Verzazyel's consciousness is like, my beautiful friend, all you have to

7 – The Book of the Nephilim Spice

do is walk in with me." She clicked her fingers and pointed to the cave's entrance that was only twenty lawful feet away.

I laughed. "But I am not a priest of Verzazyel! I wouldn't know what to do."

"Szar, there is something I must tell you." She paused.

The night had come, one of those sweet, balmy nights of the counties of the south, and we were bathed in the light of the Full Moon.

"Szar, do you realise that when you found me, the Fire of the Watcher was raging in the crypt. Any normal person would have collapsed and died."

I shrugged. "The Warriors are tough!" I drank her presence. She seemed to be shining all the moonlight by herself. And I was feeling bubbly. Was it the food, or was it the Full Moon?

"*No way, man of the Law!* If you lived through the crypt, it is because Verzazyel wanted it."

She made me laugh. "He must have wanted me to find you. Otherwise who would have saved his most beautiful priestess?"

She handed me another drink – an orange one. "Szar, do you realise that you have faced the Fire of the Watchers and lived?"

"Felicia, what's the name of this drink? It's nearly as good as the waters of the rivers of life!"

"It's the 'glorious sunrise' I told you about."

I contemplated the glitters of the candles in her eyes.

"Szar, what present are you going to take back for Gervin when you return to Eisraim?"

I stroked my beard and sighed, "I don't know. What do you think?" I was in the middle of my reflection when I realised, "That's it! That's it! I can do it, at last! I can twinge my beard just like Gervin does!"

Felicia laughed.

"No, seriously! I have been wanting to do this for years and years!"

She gently caressed my chin. "If such a feat can be achieved by just having dinner outside the cave, can you image what might happen if you descended into the crypt with me?"

"Felicia, are you serious?"

The total blue eyes opened to me, "I am very serious, Szar. Come with me!"

The assault was sweet. It moved me deep.

"Szar, the Fire of the Watchers is one of the most dangerous things on Earth. How could you satisfy your teacher more than by conquering it?" She waited. "The Watchers never sleep!"

Struck by her words, I pondered silently. "But, my beautiful friend," I finally answered, "I am not one of the Nephilim. I do not carry your spice in my blood. Why would the Watcher want to initiate me into his power?"

"Verzazyel will not reject you. I know. I have asked him." She waited for me to digest her words. "Szar, this was the meaning of the dream he sent you: come and dance with me in the crypt, and tonight you will receive more power than you ever believed could exist. You and I will conquer the Fire, enter the Watcher's mind, and cognise the past, the future, and the mysteries of the spheres. Szar, from your years as an apprentice, you know only too well the bitter taste of defeat. This power will make you a winner in the games of the Earth – a hero among men. With the help of your Mother the Dragon, we could even find Dudael, the hidden place in the wilderness, and tame the Fire of Azazel. Then there would be no limits. You could become a prince, a champion, challenging the gods themselves."

"Ha! Ha! Ha! Ha! Ha! You are asking me to go to Azazel!"

"Yes, but with me," she offered, and I could hear she was sincere. "Szar, I love you."

I went as high in the clear fountain as I could and kept my silence, looking into her eyes.

I stood up and walked to the entrance of the cave. "Such a small, simple cave!" I turned to face her. "You know, when I first arrived here the walls inside were all sealed. I was quite disappointed, after all the extraordinary stories I had heard."

Felicia leapt up, triggering an upsurge of silvery waves in her hair. She came very close to me. "Just come in with me and I will show you how to open more doors in this cave than you have ever seen in any dwelling of the kingdom. The cavern will turn into an immense hall, lit up like a field of stars."

"But where do all these doors lead? Are there corridors dug in the rock?" I asked.

"No. The doors lead to the Watcher's mind."

I walked back to the candles. "You are telling me many of your secrets, beautiful Felicia."

"I want to tell you more. Ask me!"

I sat down, thoughtful.

"My dear friend, with the power of the cave I could show you events of the past, or even the future, as already recorded in the archives of time. You don't even have to walk into the cave. Just hold the soft stone I gave you."

I twinged my beard, curious. She came and sat on my right side, and closed my left hand on the soft stone that was hanging from my neck. "What would you like to see, Szar?"

"Will this be another dream that will capture me for an entire week?" I laughed.

"Szar-ka, you are with a priestess of Verzazyel who knows exactly what she is doing! It will only last a few minutes, no matter how long the episode. Anyway, you can just look at a few images and then tell me to stop."

"What if I wanted to see how my friends of the White Eagle received Vivyani's soul after I took her to them?"

7 – The Book of the Nephilim Spice

Felicia closed her eyes and tuned in high up above her head. "Just close your eyes, Szar!" she instructed me.

Instantly, a young woman wearing a long white dress appeared in front of my closed eyes.

"She's beautiful! Is she Elyani?" Felicia asked.

"No. I don't know who she is."

She had long, straight dark hair and was on her knees among piles of rubble. Her body was heaving with loud sobs as she called out in desperation, "I had told them! Why didn't they listen to me?"

"If you don't know her, shall I stop the vision?" Felicia suggested.

"No! Wait!" I exclaimed. "I do know this woman! Her name is Teyani. She's Elyani's teacher. She is the grand master of the order of the White Eagle, and one of the most powerful magicians in the entire kingdom. But this must have been at least twenty years ago!"

The young Teyani was flooded with grief, "O White Eagle of the gods, help! I know you had warned me, but they didn't want to listen to me! What am I going to do now? Help me! Help me!"

The scene around her was one of complete devastation – a stone house utterly demolished, smouldering piles of ashes in every direction, greyness and stifling smoke choking the mists.

"Shall we see a little more?" Felicia asked.

"Of course I want to see more!"

– Thus ends the Book of the Nephilim Spice –

Glossary

For spheres and worlds, see the illustration of the cosmological ladder, page 374.

For a much more comprehensive glossary of terms used in *Atlantean Secrets* see the concordance of the saga, *From Eisraim to Philadelphia*, and *A Language to Map Consciousness*, which deals in particular with all cosmological terms. Both can be obtained from the Clairvision Website:

www.clairvision.org

Adya of the White Eagle: mother of **Elyani of the White Eagle**.

Ahriman: the Prince of Darkness, the fallen angel who tries to enslave humanity into a physical world that would be disconnected from spiritual realms.

Akibel: the **Watcher** who revealed the science of signs and omens to human beings (*1 Enoch* 8.6).

Alcibyadi of the White Eagle: the disciple and daughter of **Teyani**.

Ancient Days of the Earth: Lemuria, the epoch which preceded **Atlantis**.

Ant: see **Great Ant**.

Aphelion: the **Master of Thunder** who was the teacher of **Orest** and defected from the **Brown Robe** to serve **Ahriman**.

Apocalypse: the final confrontation between forces of light and forces of darkness.

Aquamarine chamber: the room in which Gervin received his visitors, in the **enclave** of the **jewels**.

Astral: what is commonly termed 'astral worlds' corresponds to **darkness visible** and other **intermediary worlds** of the cosmology of *Atlantean Secrets*.

Atlantean fields: see **fields**.

Atlantis: the epoch which preceded the flood. See **kingdom**.

Azazel: the leader of the **Watchers**. Note that the expression 'go to Azazel', meaning 'get lost!' can still be found in Hebrew: *lekh la-Azazel*.

Barkhan Seer of the Brown Robe: former Grand **Master of Thunder**, patron of the **Knights of the Apocalypse**.

Glossary

Body of energy: the etheric body, or layer of life force (*prāṇa* in Sanskrit, *qi* in Chinese).

Black Dance: the **Great Warriors**' style of martial art.

Black Hunters: one of the clans of **Renegade Hunters**, led by **Murdoch**. They were decimated by Szar in Book 13.

Black Robes: the order which destroyed the temple of Karlinga, where Teyani had received the first part of her training. Note that the Black Robes had nothing to do with the **Great Warriors** (who also dressed in black but wore pants and shirts, not gowns).

Blue Lagoon: one of the **spheres of remoteness**, inhabited by **Flying Dragons**.

Breeze: See **Dragon's breeze**.

Brother Knights: the **Knights of the Apocalypse**.

Brown Robe: the mysterious caste of the **Masters of Thunder**.

Caverns of sickness: the most superficial layers of the underworlds.

Cheap-way-out: two **gateways** located on the neck, used to push people out of their body.

Column of Spirit: The column of energy which extends infinitely above the head, as in an upward extension of the crown chakra.

Controllers, or **space controllers**: rangers of the astral spaces, the controllers were in charge of bringing stray sleepers into their body, so no-one lost their way during nightly astral travelling.

Daiva: an ancient word issued from the language of the gods. It meant both 'dice' and 'destiny', as thrown by the gods. The word can still be found in Sanskrit.

Darkness visible: the astral space closest to the physical world. Darkness visible is the first of the **intermediary worlds**.

Dragon: see **Dragon of the Deep** and **Flying Dragons**.

Dragon gates: places endowed with special telluric energies. The Dragon's breeze, which ascends from the Underworlds, reaches the kingdom through these gates. The **Great Warriors** were some of the only Atlantean initiates who had the power to descend into the Underworlds through the Dragon Gates.

Dragon of the Deep: the Earth manifestation of the Universal Mother, or feminine side of the Divine. Expressions such as Great Dragon, Great Dragon of the Deep, She-Serpent of the Deep and **Mother of the Endless Night**, are all synonymous with Dragon of the Deep.

Dragon's breeze, or **Dragon's breath**: the energy tapped from the **Underworlds** by the **Great Warriors**, from which they derived their supernatural vitality. But to those who had not received their initiation, the breeze was a dangerous venom.

Eisraim: the county which housed the Temple of Eisraim, where Szar was trained by **Gervin**.

Elyani of the White Eagle: adoptive daughter and disciple of **Teyani**.

Enclaves: the neighbourhoods of the Eisraim temple (see the temple's map in Volume 2 for details).

Energy fields: see **fields**.

Etheric body: the body of life force.

Felicia: **Nephilim** priestess of the order of **Verzazyel**.

Fields: in *Atlantean Secrets*, the term 'field' is used with a specific meaning: the fields of energy which the Atlanteans derived from the **streams** of space, and used to power many supernatural achievements such as telecommunication through **darkness visible**, or the direct perception of the presence of the gods. These Atlantean fields (as they are called elsewhere in the Clairvision Corpus) must not be confused with the **Fields of Peace**, or the **fields of stars**.

Fields of Peace: the World to Come (*Olam ha-Ba* of the Hebrew tradition). The enlightened space where humanity will dwell after completing its evolution on Earth.

Fields of stars: the astral counterpart of galactic spaces, as perceived by astral travellers.

Filosterops: one of the many animals which disappeared when the Atlantean energy fields collapsed.

Flying Dragons: huge and ancient cosmic intelligences which inhabit the **spheres of remoteness**, and belong to other streams of evolution than the human one.

Foxes: one of the clans of **Renegade Hunters**.

Friedrick: the **Nephilim Hunter** who trained Szar in the secrets of **Kuren-jaya**.

Gates of the Dragon: see **Dragon gates**.

Gateways: the energy centres of the etheric body (body of life force). The *marmans* and chakras of the Hindu tradition, as well as the acupuncture points of Chinese traditional medicine, would all have been regarded as gateways by the Atlanteans.

Gervin: (pronounced Djervin) Grand Master of the order of **Thunder**, teacher of **Teyani**, **Lehrmon**, Szar and many others in **Eisraim**.

Gods: gods, written with a lower case g to differentiate them from the One God. The gods live in the **spheres of the triangle**, below the **spheres of Highness**.

Golden shield: the limit between the **worlds of the gods** and the **spheres of Highness**, that is, between worlds subject to death and worlds of absolute immortality.

Great Ant: the term refers both to one of the **spheres of remoteness** and to the collective consciousness of the **Flying Dragons** which inhabit it.

Great Journey: the path followed by the individual soul from one death to the following birth.

Great Warriors: high initiates of the temple of the Dragon in **Mount Lohrzen** (county of the Red Lands). Their main trial consisted of facing the Dragon while in a death-like trance. Those who survived the trial were

Glossary

endowed with phenomenal powers, such as the ability to travel into the Underworlds at will. The Great Warriors were a sub-caste of the **Sons of the Dragon**.

Harmag the Necromancer: a son of **Azazel** the **Watcher**. In the early days of the **kingdom**, he cast a mighty spell on a valley in the north of the county of Eisraim, henceforth known as the **Valley of the Necromancer**.

Healing chambers: the temple rooms used for the purpose of healing.

Henrick the Prian: one of the **Nephilim Hunters** trained by **Joranjeran**. He defected from **Jex Belaran** after a fight with **Perseps**.

Highness: see **spheres of Highness**.

Hunters: see **Nephilim Hunters**.

Intermediary worlds: the astral **spheres** between the **kingdom** (physical world) and the **worlds of the gods**. The intermediary worlds correspond to the *bhuvar-loka* of Sanskrit texts.

Jex Belaran: the **Nephilim Hunters**' training centre in the county of the Snowy Mountains. It was adjacent to the temple of **Verzazyel**.

Jewels: one of the **enclaves** of the Eisraim temple.

Joranjeran: the grand commander of the **Nephilim Hunters** who preceded **Perseps**.

-ka: suffix of endearment, as in Szar-ka, 'little Szar'.

Karlinga: in the county of the Western Shores, the temple where **Teyani** became a high priestess of the **White Eagle**.

King of this World: one of the epithets of **Ahriman**, Prince of Darkness. See also **Rex**.

Kingdom: the kingdom of **Atlantis**; more generally, the physical world, as in the kaballistic concept of *Malkhut*, 'kingdom'.

Kingdom of the rainbows: the present epoch, which started after the flood, and followed the kingdom of **Atlantis**.

Knights: in *Atlantean Secrets*, the word is always used with the meaning of **Knights of the Apocalypse**.

Knights of the Apocalypse: trained in the **power of the Point** by the **Masters of Thunder**, their mission will be to fight the armies of **Ahriman** during the wars of the **Apocalypse**.

Kuren-jaya: the **Nephilim Hunters**' redoubtable style of combat, resting on the **power of the Point**.

Law, or **Law of Melchisedek**: the knowledge, code and set of rules which formed the modus operandi of the entire Atlantean civilisation.

Lehrmon of the Brown Robe: an outcaste little boy adopted by young **Teyani** in **Karlinga**. Brought up by her, he became one of **Gervin's** close disciples.

Light: written with a capital L, Light refers to a quality coming from the **spheres of Highness**.

Living walls: walls made of **plass** and held by a **field**.

Lohrzen: the ancient sage who founded the order of the **Great Warriors**. The **Sons of the Dragon** lived in a temple carved in the mountain called **Mount Lohrzen**.

Lowness: see **spheres of Lowness**.

Malchasek: one of the great angels of **Highness** who withdrew his presence from the Earth around the fall of Atlantis.

Maniya: one of the **enclaves** of the Eisraim temple.

Marek: the **Great Warrior** who taught Szar in **Mount Lohrzen**.

Marka: a high priestess of **Malchasek**, friend of Gervin.

Maryani of the White Eagle: first trained by Teyani, **Maryani** became a high initiate of the **Underworlds**, under the guidance of King **Vasoukidass**.

Masters of Thunder: the lineage of spiritual masters known as the **Brown Robe**. At the time of Szar's training, **Gervin** was the grand master of the order.

Maveron: the sage who spoke *The Book of Maveron*, one of the last books of the Law. Dealing with awakening, superconsciousness and apocalyptic predictions, this collection of hymns was one of Gervin's favourites.

Melchard of the Brown Robe: **Master of Thunder**, disciple of **Orest**, and high priest of **Eisraim**.

Melchisedek: God, the creator and ruler of the beings pertaining to the same evolutionary ladder as human beings. The Lord Melchisedek is to the Earth (and related **spheres**) what the **Unborn God** is to the creation at large.

Molten Sea: the *prima materia* (original substance out of which all manifested things originated) in the form of the principal sea of the **worlds of the gods**.

Mother of the Endless Night: one of the epithets of the **Dragon of the Deep**.

Mother of the Light: the Universal Mother, the female side of the Divine. The Mother of the Light is to the creation at large what the **Dragon of the Deep** is to the Earth.

Mount Lohrzen: the mountain inside which the temple of Vulcan was dug, and where lived the **Sons of the Dragon**, and the **Great Warriors**. Mount Lohrzen was located in the county of the Red Lands, in the southern part of the kingdom, far away from the county of Eisraim.

Murdoch: the leader of the **Black Hunters**, one of the clans of **Renegade Hunters**.

Naamah: the first woman to marry a **Watcher**, and therefore regarded as the mother of the **Nephilim** kind.

Nagas: twenty-meter long golden snakes, denizens of the **Underworlds** endowed with phenomenal powers. **Vasoukidass (Vasouk)** was their king.

Near-Voice threshold: a way of speaking that bordered the use of the **Voice**.

Glossary

Nephilim: the children which the **Watchers** had with the daughters of men, and their descendants.

Nephilim Hunters: a caste of **Nephilim** warriors, dedicated to the protection of the **Nephilim** people. Led by **Perseps** and **Joranjeran**, their training centre was in **Jex Belaran**, in the county of the Snowy Mountains.

Orest of the Brown Robe: **Gervin**'s teacher, and Grand Master of **Thunder** before him.

Orichalc: a metal. According to Plato's *Critias*, 114, the Atlanteans regarded orichalc as the most precious of all metals after gold.

Parallel: a master who lives in two or more worlds at the same time.

Pelenor Ozorenan: a Nephilim princess (of the county of the Northern Lakes), close friend of **Felicia**, and the lover of **Henrick the prian**.

Perseps: the grand commander of the **Nephilim Hunters** in **Jex Belaran**. A disciple of **Joranjeran** and long time friend of **Felicia**.

Plass: the living substance of which Atlantean buildings were made.

Power of the Point: supermental forces activated through the centres of energy above the head.

Prian: a **Nephilim** word meaning a man of will, someone capable of unusual achievements, and with class.

Prince of Darkness: an epithet of **Ahriman**.

Project, projection: see **Voice**.

Rainbow: see **kingdom of the rainbows**.

Ran Gereset: Master of Thunder, son and disciple of **Orest**, brother disciple of **Gervin**, **Esrevin**, and **Melchard**. After Orest's death, he went to the north pole, where he performed a thirty-nine year ritual in preparation for the archive transfer.

Red Renegades: one of the clans of **Renegade Hunters**. Due to their mediocre training, the Red Renegades were nicknamed 'venom suckers' by the Hunters of Jex Belaran.

Renegade Hunters: clans of **Nephilim** brigands who used powers similar to those of the **Nephilim Hunters**. The principal clans were the **Black Hunters**, the **Foxes**, and the **Red Renegades**.

Rex: the name given to **Ahriman** by the **Knights of the Apocalypse**. It is the abbreviation of the Gnostic Latin term *Rex Mundi*, meaning 'king of the world'.

Soft stones: half-solid crystalline structures which Atlantean people used to operate the power of the **fields**.

Sons of the Dragon: the priests of the temple of Vulcan in **Mount Lohrzen**.

Space controllers: see **controllers**.

Space Matrix: the phenomenal guidance system and Knowledge Bank used by the **Flying Dragons** when travelling in the spheres of remoteness.

Spheres: worlds, or levels of existence. From top to bottom, these are: the **spheres of Highness**, the **worlds of the gods** (or spheres of the triangle), the **intermediary worlds** (the lowest of which is darkness visible), the **kingdom** (or physical world), the **Underworlds**, the **spheres of Lowness** (identical to Highness).

Belonging to cosmological ladders other than the **spheres of Melchisedek** are the **spheres of remoteness**, inhabited by the **Flying Dragons**.

Spheres of Highness: located on top of the worlds of the gods. Unlike the **worlds of the gods**, the spheres of Highness are never destroyed, even at the end of a cosmic cycle.

Spheres of Lowness: when talking about the **spheres of Highness**, the **Nagas** affectionately use the term 'spheres of Lowness'. The reason is clear: these spheres are as much below as they are above.

Spheres of Melchisedek: the spheres belonging to the same stream of evolution as human beings. They include **Highness**, the **worlds of the gods**, the **intermediary worlds**, the **kingdom**, and the **Underworlds**. They do not include the **spheres of remoteness**.

Spheres of the triangle: the worlds of the gods.

Straight path of the Law: in the temple of **Eisraim**, the name of the (winding) main alley, which went from the main entrance to the cremation ground. The straight path of the Law was so called because it symbolised the journey of every priest and priestess in the temple.

Streams: the currents of energy which flow through **darkness visible** and other spheres.

Teyani of the White Eagle: Grand Master of the order of the **White Eagle**, mother of **Alcibyadi**, adoptive mother of **Lehrmon** and **Elyani**.

Thunder: a high energy-consciousness akin to Cosmic Fire and related to the sky of the gods, Thunder is the central power of the **Masters of Thunder**.

Time track: someone's destiny perceived as a line.

Tirtha: (pronounced teerta) place of pilgrimage. The word can still be found in Sanskrit.

Tirtha tour: a (walking) tour of places of pilgrimage.

Tree house: a dwelling made of the intertwined branches of living trees.

Triangle: see **spheres of the triangle**.

UKB: see **universal knowledge bank**.

Unborn God: God. The Unborn God is to the creation at large what the **Lord Melchisedek** is to the ladder of worlds to which human beings belong.

Underworlds: the non-physical **spheres** which are located below the material worlds. The uppermost layers of the Underworlds are occupied by the **caverns of sickness**. Further down, there are myriads of worlds teeming with life force and wonders.

Universal Knowledge Banks: non-physical archives in which phenomenal amounts of information are stored.

Valley of the Necromancer: a bewitched valley in the north of the county of Eisraim. It received its name from **Harmag the Necromancer**.

Vasouk: affectionate diminutive for king **Vasoukidass**.

Glossary

Vasoukidass: the wise king of the **Nagas**. Forever friend of **Maryani of the White Eagle** for reasons explained in the prelude to Volume 2.

Verzazyel: the **Watcher** whose line of **Nephilim** descendants included, among others: **Felicia, Pelenor Ozorenan, Perseps** and **Joranjeran**. The temple of Verzazyel was located in **Jex Belaran**, in the Snowy Mountains.

Verzazyel's cave: the cavern in which Verzazyel lived during his descent on Earth. Located in the county of the Red Lands, the cave was a place of pilgrimage visited by many groups of **Nephilim**.

Voice: written with a capital V, Voice refers to the extraordinary powers which Atlantean initiates projected through their voice, and with which they could perform miraculous healings and influence their environment in various ways.

Vroofing: the violent energy that the **Great Warriors** derived from the **Underworlds**, and through which they accomplished miraculous healings and other supernatural feats.

Warp, or **warp of fields**: the global network of energy **fields** upon which the Atlantean civilisation rested.

Watchers: the mighty angels who descended on Earth during the early days of the kingdom of Atlantis, and married the daughters of men. Their children, and their descendants, were called the **Nephilim**.

White Eagle: a great angel of **Highness**. A principle of high, vertical aspiration, unconditional love, and transpersonal opening. His manifestation in the **world of the gods** is the **White Eagle of the gods**.

White Eagles: the priestesses of the order of the **White Eagle**, including **Teyani, Adya, Elyani, Alcibyadi** and others.

Windmills of the Law: the rituals which tapped the power from the **fields**. The windmills of the Law converted the power of the **streams** into **fields**.

Windmill Keepers: the castes of priests who performed the **windmills of the Law**.

Worlds: see **spheres**.

Worlds of the gods: also called the **spheres of the triangle**, these worlds are located above the **intermediary worlds**, and below the **spheres of Highness**. The worlds of the gods correspond to the *svar* or *svarga-loka* of Sanskrit texts.

World to Come: see **Fields of Peace**.

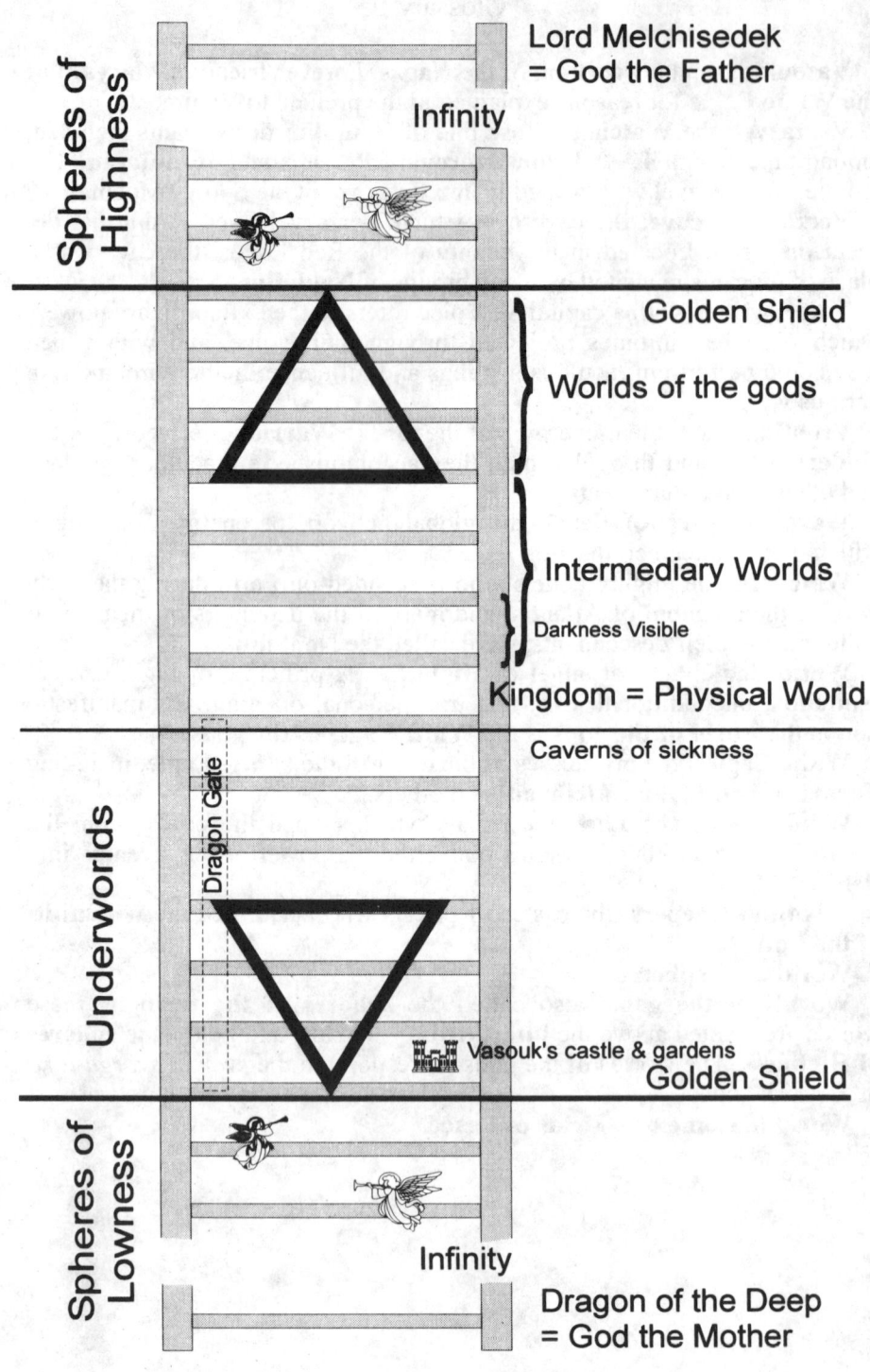

**The Cosmological Ladder
Showing the Spheres of Melchisedek**